Ope
Jack

Open Your Eyes, Jackson Ryder

Rudy Castañeda Lopez

escalator press

First published in 2015 by Escalator Press

Escalator Press
Whitireia New Zealand
SX 33471
Wellington
www.escalatorpress.co.nz

ISBN 978-0-473-29569-1
Cataloguing-in-publication data for this book is available from the National Library of New Zealand

Editing and production: Whitireia Publishing
Cover design: Spencer Levine
Printed by Printing.Com

This book was taken from manuscript to bookshelf by students of the Whitireia NZ publishing programme, who worked on editing, production, design, publicity and marketing. For more information about our editing and publishing training, visit www.whitireiapublishing.co.nz

Dedicated to Isaac Ramón López
Luftmensch

1

VAN GOGH HAS A LOT TO ANSWER FOR. He really screwed us over big-time. If it weren't for him, people's ideas of how an artist is supposed to be would be totally different.

Because of Vincent Van Gogh everybody expects artists to be poor – and more than a bit wacky. They expect them to be assholes to women, or men, in the cases of Francis Bacon and Caravaggio. They expect them to overindulge in all manner of substances: absinthe for the Impressionists and alcohol for everybody else, including my namesake, the incomparable Jackson Pollock.

I've looked at the faded print on my hospital wall for days now. In and out of consciousness, twisted blue and black trees reach desperately for the last rays of life. Branches, thin and bare as the fingers of starving children, beg for light. The distant sun reaches to them too – heavy, sprawling – like a father's blind bear hug, like an *abrazo*.

I know the original painting well. It's bright and intense and strange in its joyful sadness. This one is bruised and paper pallid but it still packs a punch.

It's *Pollard Willows at Sunset*, from 1888, and I knew it long before I was stuck between these four beige walls. I'm looking at it now and my head is clearing.

If Van Gogh hadn't cut off his ear, would he really be the name he is today? I'm not trying to take anything from the guy – I admire his work immensely. But you have to admit, it's a pretty impressive PR stunt.

Everyone seems to want a big, dramatic story – some passion play to wrap around the work, like it isn't valuable enough by itself. The reality is most artists trudge along, doing their day jobs, paying bills and simply working. You wouldn't recognise the majority of artists if you passed them on the street. They're just like you. The one thing they have in common is a flame that caught light in them sometime in the past, maybe even in the womb. For most, it dies or is blown out. All kinds of crap can get in the way. It's a fragile, tenuous thing ... and you never know which way it's going to go.

I was raised in New York City, in Greenwich Village, not long after the war. We lived near where realist painter Edward Hopper lived. My mother – Mutti to me – pointed him out one spring morning as we were feeding pigeons in Washington Square. He looked like any other old man with his gaunt frame, praying mantis-like gait – and when he took off his brown fedora – that polished dome, like the Capitol building in Washington DC.

Mutti was crazy about art and artists. Soon after we saw Hopper she took me to the Museum of Modern Art and pointed out his paintings. The one that stood out for me was a painting called *New York Movie.* I loved movies – everything about them – the stories and actors, sure, but even just going to the theatre: popcorn, the smell of rancid butter and cigarette smoke, being in the dark with a bunch of strangers, all seeing the same thing at the same time. At the end you shared something. It was comforting and exciting.

'What do you think, *liebchen*?' she asked me, like she always did, before saying anything about the artwork itself.

I shrugged my shoulders.

'What does it make you feel?'

The painting was set in a movie theatre but you could only see part of the screen. To the right there was an usherette in a blue uniform leaning against the wall. Her hand was on her cheek. She wasn't even looking at the screen. Basically everything I knew and loved about going to the movies was missing from this painting. 'She looks sad, lonely.'

'*Ja*, that is true. It is not a pleasant painting. But that is part of living too, is it not?'

'I guess, but I'd rather see happy things – you know, like cartoons.'

'*Ja, ja*, cartoons are good – fun – but would you want to eat ice cream and nothing else all day?' I grinned at the idea. 'Perhaps that was not such a good example.' She came down low and put her forehead to mine. I laughed, she giggled. She said, 'Hopper shows us things about being human we wish to keep hidden, secret. It isn't fashionable, but he will always open people's eyes.'

I looked closer. What was so important that the usherette was ignoring the movie? What was going on with her? Why the hell did Hopper paint it? I thought about that painting a lot. I still do.

The walls of our brownstone were covered in paintings, drawings and prints. New stuff popped up all the time. Tate – it rhymes with satay – is what I called my father. It's Yiddish. Tate and Mutti would drag me to galleries, artists' studios and neighbourhood markets on the weekends. They argued and laughed. I looked and ate doughnuts. One muggy summer morning I was playing in the lounge with my Lincoln Logs. My parents were in their bedroom, across the hallway, talking. Tate was in his undershirt and Mutti was in her slip.

'But *Meine Liebe*, how in the hell are we going to pay for this?' Tate said in a strained voice. He was holding a small painting of an American flag.

Mutti drew lightly on her cigarette and tilted her head back. 'It is an important change for Jasper Johns. I think we must have it.'

'But, darling, I'm already driving double shifts as it is,' he pleaded. Then he noticed me. He stopped talking, got off the bed, came over to the doorway, smiled and closed the door softly. I heard their voices, muffled behind the heavy door, rise and fall over and over. I kept building my log cabin but a piece was missing from the roof and I couldn't finish it. I was going back to my room to look for the piece when the bedroom door was flung open. Tate stomped out, the buttons on his shirt undone. He didn't see me. He rushed for the front door and slammed it behind him. Mutti was still sitting on the bed in her slip, looking for all the world like a woman in an Edward Hopper painting; holding her cigarette between her thumb and forefinger the way I'd seen Conrad Veidt do in an old 1930s movie. She turned to me dreamily and raised one eyebrow. Her mouth turned down at the corners. 'I think we need some apple strudel and ice cream, *nein*?'

That winter I helped her to fill an album with photos from a shoebox under her bed. It started with a black-and-white shot of her and Tate – so young – in front of some church with onion domes. Tate was in his uniform and looked a lot like Tyrone Power – all dark eyelashes and a pencil-thin moustache. Her hair was lighter – almost white – and she was holding a bunch of flowers. 'Was this when you got married, Mutti?'

She glanced at the photo. '*Nein*, we had a wedding in front of a judge. That was at the Frauenkirche in Munich; the city where I was born.' She puffed on her cigarette and ran her finger down the side of the photo. 'If we had married in a church, that is the one I would have liked it to have been in.'

There was a photo of some guy and Tate sitting in a jeep pulling goofy faces. There was a picture of Mutti pregnant in a loose smock at a potter's wheel and one of me, with a face like a withered plum, in Tate's arms. One photo – my favourite – was a very small shot of Mutti in front of Niagara Falls. When I was a kid I saw the movie *Niagara* and I thought Marilyn Monroe was Mutti. She put a few photos – mostly landscapes of wooded mountains – back in the box. I picked up one of the discarded shots. It was of a teenage girl, obviously Mutti, with a white-haired man and a plump woman. The woman was in a flowered dress and he was in a German officer's uniform.

'Mutti?'

She took the photo from me and put it back in the box. 'That is from a long time ago, a different life. It is not going in the album. Do you understand?'

I didn't, but I didn't say anything.

*

Mutti used to bring home meat from the butcher wrapped in brown paper. I would steal the wrinkled waste paper, with its rusty brown and pink stains of blood, and draw things from the shapes of the stains: werewolves, Victorian gentlemen, pirates, Bugs Bunny. Mutti saw my butcher paper drawings and sat down next to me. She fingered the surface and said, 'You know, Jacksonlein, this is like something Leonardo da Vinci said. He told artists to look at certain walls stained with damp, or at stones of uneven colour. He said if you add some little lines you will be able to see in these the likeness of divine things.'

The next day she brought home a whole roll of new, clean butcher's paper. She was so excited, but I didn't know what the hell to do with it. The paper had no personality, nothing to stir my imagination. The roll of paper sat in the dark of my closet for many years.

Mutti also bought me art books, mostly used but sometimes new ones. She insisted I treat every book like it was the Bible. I wasn't allowed to put them on the ground, write in them or fold the corners of the pages. I had to have clean hands before I touched them – almost impossible at the best of times – but I tried. She gave me books on the Renaissance, the Impressionists, classical Greek and Roman art, African tribal art, medieval German church art and the Fauves. I liked Matisse instantly. I could see that he really liked to play. In his painting of dancers the figures moved lightly and free from care. It didn't matter that the colours were unnatural and the anatomy was all off. It was totally about the feeling. I dug Miró and Dubuffet for the same reason. I copied from art books but also from comics. Batman, Captain America, and Thor were my favourites. I copied from magazine photos and things I saw around me, like my dad watching *The Honeymooners* on TV.

In my last year in New York I had more than a bit of interest in a girl named Desiree Rêveuse. She had the unnerving habit of staring with the most liquid, bright, amber-brown eyes. I got the impression that somehow she could see more; she could see into my soul and judge me wanting. She didn't smile, didn't say, 'Boo'. She just stood there and looked at me. I was captured by her eyes. I hardly saw the rest of her. Later, I noticed that her skin was tanned a wonderful, creamy copper and her black hair was curly – not Larry Fine of the Three Stooges crinkly – but a fine tight curl that bunched up on her head like foam on a wave.

On the first day of class, in the cloakroom, she had a tin lunchbox with Elvis Presley embossed on the front. I looked down at the box and saw an opportunity to talk to her. 'So, you like Elvis?' I asked her through a trembling larynx. She didn't answer. When I finally dared to look into the face of that ethereal being she was smiling, but it wasn't a friendly smile. How could I have been so stupid? Of course she liked Elvis. Why else would she have his smirking, pudgy mug plastered on her lunchbox?

I got up that Sunday, found a photo of Elvis in one of Mutti's *LIFE* Magazines, and decided to copy it. My plan was to give the drawing to Desiree and dazzle her with my skill and artistic power. I worked on it for hours and finally when it felt done I took a good look.

Well, I could tell it was human, but that was about all.

I got another piece of paper and tried again. This time it went faster and at the end it sort of looked like Dick Nixon puckering his lips, with one of my mother's strudels placed firmly on his head. I was ready to give up, but I didn't. The next one actually looked like the bastard – granted he looked worried or constipated – but it was him. When Tate saw it that evening he sang, 'You ain't nothin' but a hound dog.' and punched me lightly on the shoulder. I grinned but none of it meant anything compared to what I hoped would be sweet Desiree's reaction.

But that was when everything in my body was rebelling. I'd look in the mirror every morning and all the changes just got worse. My nose and Adam's apple started to swell, small volcanoes erupted all over my face and the downy hairs above my lip – and in front of my ears – started to show up in photographs. My brass-coloured hair, which had been straight all my life, started to spiral out in tight coils. My hands and feet looked like they had been stung by a dozen bees. I stunk, and my voice refused to obey my commands. I couldn't walk without tripping or reach out for a glass without dropping it. I was locked in someone else's joke.

I hesitated to give Desiree the sketch and in the end it never happened. Her father pulled her out of school in early fall and spirited her off to Martinique, his home island in the Caribbean, with no explanation and little warning. I never heard from her again.

I had never lost anyone before. I didn't think I could be in such agony. So, with leaves falling all around and the biting wind coming out of Canada, what kept me awake at night were sad fantasies of what it could have been like to be married to Desiree, what our kids might have looked like and what it might have felt like to hug her and rub my hands all over her body. I whispered her name over and over in the dark, 'Desiree, Desiree, Desiree, Desiree.' I was in rigid, torturous ecstasy like a pubescent version of Bernini's *Ecstasy of St. Teresa*.

But lost love, pubes, wet dreams and raging anger all took a back seat when it was just me, the pencil and the paper. All of the awkward, painful things were soothed by my ability to make a world where I was completely in control.

I drew a lot that year. I drew so much that the second finger on my left hand grew a callus next to the fingernail, where the pencil pressed against the skin. Time stopped, the noise of the city disappeared, and I wasn't hungry, thirsty, sad or alone. It always felt like I was floating in a painting by Chagall.

By the second year of middle school, my folks let me take the subway by myself. One Saturday, in the Fall, the movie *El Cid* was playing at Radio City Music Hall starring my favourite actor, Charlton Heston.

'Please Mutti, I need fifty cents.' I pleaded, 'I'll do extra chores. I promise I won't be late.'

'What am I going to do with you, Jacksonlein? Your father never sees you anymore.' Her eyes got big. 'I hardly see you.'

'I can't help it if he's never around. Most of the time he doesn't seem to be here, even when he is.'

'Don't be like that. You know how hard he works.'

'Well, answer me this: is he going to be here today?'

'He is at work until midday and then he is going to the jazz festival at the Bluetone Club.'

'See? That figures.' I held out my hand, palm up.

She stared at me without moving. 'I was hoping you would come look at some drawings at the Allan Stone Gallery with me.'

I breathed out audibly and rolled my eyes. 'Who is it?'

'A young German woman, named Eva Hesse.'

'But I've been looking forward to this movie all week!'

'She is Jewish too. German and Jewish, like you.'

'I'm an American.'

She appraised me calmly. Finally, the corners of her mouth curled up slightly.

'*Ja, ja,* of course you are.' She looked at her purse then turned back to me. 'Come with me today and I will take you to the movies tomorrow. Maybe your father will come too.'

'Mutti,' my voice was a tone higher now, 'I'm going to meet some guys from school. It's really important. I'm going to die if I don't go. Just give me the money, *pleeease,*' I squeezed out.

She went to the kitchen counter and picked up her purse, 'Maybe we see Eva Hesse next week. Be home half an hour before dinnertime, *ja*?' As I raced out the door, she called out, 'Enjoy yourself but eyes open, *liebchen.*'

I waved without looking back.

The movie was spectacular – lots of sword fighting and Sophia Loren looking impossibly anguished with her big, pouty lips. It was more than three hours long and the last scene of the movie really got me. Poor old El Cid is stone dead, but they strap him into his saddle so he can lead his troops to victory. After they win, the horse tears along the seashore. The Spaniards are so damn happy that nobody bothers to catch the horse. Imagine – it's the year 1099 and you're sitting there on the Costa del Sol, making a sand castle or some shit, not even aware that there's a battle going on up the coast, and along comes this dead guy on a prancing Andalusian stallion.

I got home later than I'd promised and I was worried, but I had my story all worked out to a tee. Mutti's best friend, Helen, answered the door. She was wearing her usual beret, black sweater and a tight skirt. She liked to pepper her language with things like 'in the groove', 'dig', 'hip' and 'solid' – terms borrowed from the jazz musicians of the '20s and '30s. I guess she was a beatnik. I didn't give it much thought because it was the Village and everybody talked like that.

'Hi, Helen.' I could see people in the living room and kitchen. 'Is there a party?'

This was getting better by the second. Then I noticed her eyes were bloodshot and her mascara was smeared.

'Honey, come upstairs.'

'What's going on?'

She took me to my room and closed the door. She sat in my desk chair and faced me, hunching forward with her hands clasped in front of her, 'I have some …' She started to cry.

'What?'

'Oh, honey.' She came over and hugged me. 'Your mother, baby, she's gone.'

2

'WHAT DO YOU MEAN?' I tried to pull away from Helen but she wouldn't let me go. 'Mutti,' I called. 'Where is she? *Muttchen*?' I knew what Helen meant, but I wouldn't believe it. 'Mutti!'

'It happened so fast, without warning. We were sitting in the garden having a cup of joe, like normal. Your mother said she had a headache and then she … the doctor said it was an aneurysm. A blood vessel burst in her brain.'

'I gotta see her. Where is she?'

'She's at the funeral home, honey. We can't see her until tomorrow.'

Somehow I ended up downstairs, where I found my dad in his TV chair surrounded by some of his jazz friends and other taxi drivers from work. They parted like the Red Sea when they saw me. He was slumped in the overstuffed chair like a sack of flour, staring at the Persian rug.

'Tate?' I managed.

He looked up and started to rise from his seat. I ran into his arms, sending him back into his chair. He held me tighter than he had ever done before. He was shaking.

'*Sha, sha, benyokhed*,' he whispered as I started to sob. '*Nisht veynen, nisht veynen.*'

It was the most Yiddish I had ever heard him speak. I didn't know what the hell he was on about, but it didn't matter. I wanted to stay there forever.

Everyone kept telling me they were sorry, which struck me as weird. It still does. Why in the hell do people say that, as if they've done something wrong?

The women hugged me and the men put a hand on my head like I was a kid. The rest was a blur. It was like clips from a film noir classic; deep shadows and hard lights, tons of people milling around our living room, kitchen and even the damn bathroom. Everything smelled of cigarette smoke and coffee.

Tate and I saw Mutti's body the next day at the Bleecker Street Mortuary. I had passed its white facade a hundred times – Mutti and I had bought tea from the Puerto Rico Importing Company next door – but I had never noticed the mortuary. The inside was all stained glass, cherry wood and polished brass. It was quiet, warm and unbelievably tidy, in a kind of public way. I smelled the flowers and candles before we even entered the room. The stink almost made me puke. I've had no time for flowers since.

Tate held me and we approached the black coffin slowly. Her nose came into view first, like the peak of a snow-capped mountain, and then the rest of her face. There was the wispy hair at her delicate temples, the wide cheekbones, the strawberry lipstick she had started using that year. It was all there, but it wasn't her. I couldn't feel her presence. Even in sleep she was active – tossing one way or another, eyes flicking under eyelids, sighs from deep inside. She simply wasn't there, she was gone. She had left me without so much as '*Auf Wiedersehen*'.

Tate had his fist to his lips but he didn't make a sound or

drop a tear. He grasped her hand, but I couldn't do it. My eyes were open wide, but they were dry. I kept saying to myself, 'It isn't her, it's not her,' but inside I knew it was her, all right, and someday it would be me. That freaked me out.

Tate and I didn't talk. By the time people got there to pay their respects, he had pulled himself together enough to appear composed.

The only relative to come to the funeral parlour was my dad's uncle, Leo. I had only met him a couple of times before that.

'*Badoyeren, mayn yingl, badoyeren,*' he whispered as he patted my hand. We were the same height, but his hand covered mine completely, like a catcher's mitt. 'No one should lose a mother's love so young. No one.'

I could see liver spots peeking out from under his black velvet yarmulke. He was bald and stocky – everything my dad wasn't – but I could see the family resemblance in his heavy cleft chin, his gentle voice and his lively eyes. He caressed my cheek.

'Look at you. You're getting to be such a *mensch* already. You remind me of your grandfather, when he was your age.'

'Really?'

'Do I sound like I'm joking? What kind of joke would that be?'

Someone else who came to the funeral parlour was Charlie Salmond, all the way from California. I recognised him from the photo of him and Tate goofing off in the jeep during the war. He was about ten pounds heavier and his thin hair was darker but the mischievous angle of his eyebrows were still the same. As we left the funeral parlour, Charlie walked next to me.

'Damn, it's cold.' He clutched his thin cotton trench coat around him as we walked towards the waiting taxi. 'I forgot how cold it could get here. How are you holding up, sport?'

He spoke like we had known each other all our lives.

'I know, I know, it's a tough one, buddy. No matter how old you get, it's shitty.' Before we got in the cab Charlie stopped me and looked over his shoulder. 'Say, is your mother's friend, Helen, married? Does she have a boyfriend?'

'Huh?'

'No. You're right. Never mind.'

The funeral was three days later. My parents knew a lot of people. There were tons of musicians and artists there. Bob Dylan sent flowers. Afterwards there was a reception at the house. A few people stayed on, including Uncle Leo.

The day before he left, Tate, Charlie, Fetter Leo and I were sitting quietly together in the lounge. Over a cup of Russian Caravan tea Leo asked me, 'How are you doing in your studies, *yingl*?'

'Mostly okay, I guess.' I liked Uncle Leo but I was exhausted by then. I just wanted to sleep. I wanted to be away from the whole thing. I thought about Mutti lying in that box. It pissed me off that nobody was actually talking about her. Tate had a cup of tea but he didn't touch it. I had to force myself to listen to Fetter Leo.

'When my brother, your grandfather, was your age back in the old country, he could read and write; which was a rare thing, let me tell you. He helped our parents by working as a scribe in our *shtetl*. For a few *kopiyky* he lent a hand to the local peasants so they could write to their relatives who had fled the *pogroms* and the bleak life of the Ukraine for the promises of the New World.' Leo topped up his strong brew with boiling water from the silver samovar that was always in the corner of our dining room. He added a dab of jam and a squeeze of lemon juice to his teacup.

'He saw money being sent back and read the wonderful tales of hope and success. It put a fire in him and he fixed hard on going to America, making it big and saving all of us from our misery.'

'Really, Fetter? I didn't know,' I said. It was true; I couldn't imagine how bad it had to be for him to leave his home, everyone he knew. There were no telephones then and mail took weeks. Mutti had done the same thing too, come to think of it. As Uncle Leo talked I could see the grey and brown tones of the old country. I felt Grandpa's toil and his determination. I wondered how I would manage if I had to leave everything important to me and start a new life. I wanted to know more. 'When did he change his name?'

'Doesn't the boy know this story, Hymie?' Uncle Leo chuckled. Tate kept sitting there, saying nothing. Leo shook his head and turned back to me. 'He knew a word or two of English and when he got to Ellis Island he kept repeating, "I am writer, I am writer." The immigration officers decided that Asa Ryjowscovitz was too difficult to write, so he became the only thing he could say – Ian Ryder.' Leo laughed from his stomach, put a sugar cube between his teeth and sipped from the steaming cup. I waited patiently. Eventually he continued, 'Your grandfather was a generous man, bless his soul. He sent money back to us for years and even paid my way over to this country. He was a great man, a saint. May he rest in peace.'

'Did any of our other relatives come to the US?' I asked.

Leo looked up. 'What do you mean? Don't you know, *yingl*?' He turned to Tate and said a long string of words quickly in Yiddish.

I shook my head. 'Tate never talks about the family.'

'*A brokh iz mir. Oy gevalt,*' he sighed. 'My family – our family – they are *shkhite,* dead, all of them. My mamele, my tate, everyone. The ones Stalin did not starve to death in the '30s were murdered by the Nazis at Babi Yar, they and one hundred and fifty thousand innocents souls, just like that.' He pointed his forefinger at his yarmulke, flicked it into the air while tossing his head, 'like it was nothing.' I sucked in air, realising I hadn't breathed for too long. He gravely shook his head and whispered, '*Oy vey,*' then turned to Tate and raised the palm of his hand. 'This, you should have told him, *Plimenik. Shod* – shame on you.' Tate searched every corner of the Persian rug but didn't answer.

'Hurry, drink your tea, Hymie, or it'll get cold,' Charlie said. Tate picked up his cup slowly.

Fetter Leo sighed. 'Know these things, *yingl.* Remember, please – someone has to remember.' He glared at Tate.

I held my teacup halfway between my mouth and the saucer. 'I'm so sorry,'

'I am sorry too, but what can I do?'

'What about Grandpa? What happened to him?'

Leo paused and glanced at Tate, who flinched. 'He died, *yingl.* While your father was in Germany, before you were born, he died.' He tapped his chest. 'He had the heart of a lion, but, he suffered too deeply. He could only take so much. May he rest in peace. I am the last of the family Ryjowscovitz.'

'What about Tate? What about me?'

'True, true – a rose by another name, *ye*?' He gently laughed to himself.

We finished our tea in silence.

That night, as I lay between my extinguished lamp and uneasy sleep, I thought about Mutti and how I hadn't hugged her or kissed her goodbye. I thought about my grandfather too and how if it wasn't for him, it could have been me kneeling in front of a mass grave with a Lugar pointed at my skull, a relative of my mother fingering the trigger. My head was spinning and it didn't stop, not even in my sleep.

Before Leo left the next day, he embraced Tate and held him close for a long while. They looked into each other's eyes for a long time. Fetter Leo's were smiling. Tate's eyes shone like glass. Leo patted Tate on his forearms. 'Don't worry, *Plimenik. Lebn leizung forois* – you have lived enough to know this.' Holding up his forefinger he said, 'Tell *dayn zun* what he should know, *ye*?' and Tate nodded. When it was my turn, I buried my face in the fur collar of my great uncle's overcoat. He took my hand.

'*Benyokhed*, your heart is empty now, a void as black as night. Forgive your mother for leaving you and go forward for your tate's sake, as well as your own. Everything changes, everything, but life goes on. Remember that – don't ever forget, learn to open your arms to what comes.' He gently smiled. 'It will get better, I promise you.'

He loosened his tie and undid the top two buttons of his shirt. 'Wait, I want you to have this.' From beneath his shirt, he pulled out a chain with an intricate gold cylinder, about the size of my thumb, attached to it. 'My tate gave this mezuzah to me when I left our *shtetl* for America more than forty years ago, now. I know you are half *goy*, and you don't eat kosher, but this is not about religion. It is about family.'

'I couldn't, Uncle Leo.'

'Don't be a *schmo*, of course you can. I want you to have it.' He put it around my neck.

'Thank you, Fetter.'

'Don't mention it.'

He kissed me on both cheeks, waved to Tate and Charlie and got into the taxi cab.

Charlie stayed with us for weeks. He and Tate played cards a lot – almost every hour of the day. Tate played easily, even mechanically, but he was pretty quiet most of the time. Charlie didn't seem to mind and he didn't have a problem with being the only one talking. As he dealt a Gin hand he said to Tate, 'Remember that time Birgit, you and I took that jeep and a couple of bocksbeutel of Silvaner up to Neuschwanstein?' He chuckled and turned to me. 'Walt Disney used that chateau as the model for Sleeping Beauty's castle, sport. I'll tell you, we had a hell of a time.' This raised a brief, but far away, grin from Tate. Charlie kept up the stories until Tate's eyes went blank and he stood up and staggered off to bed.

Charlie and I stayed up a bit longer. He stretched and said, 'I might take a walk. I'm still on LA time and it's only after dinner there. Where's the nearest bar, kid?'

'Mutti and Helen sometimes go to Gertie's … I stopped cold, 'used to go,' I whispered.

Charlie got up slowly, came over and put his arm around my shoulder. 'It's okay, sport, that's going to happen.' He patted my shoulder and I couldn't hold back. Everything inside me that was tight, jagged and sweaty-hot gushed out uncontrollably – my own Niagara. He stayed with me until I was spent and sleepy and happy to go to my room. 'You say Helen goes to Gertie's?'

Minutes later I heard the front door close.

The next night Charlie came home with a couple of six

packs of Spaten Doppelbock – where he got it from, I'll never know – and he and Tate sat up into the night, playing cards again and sipping Munich's best. I fell asleep on the couch but before I lost all consciousness I actually heard Tate talking, rejoining Charlie's constant chatter, with short, abrupt sentences.

After a week Charlie insisted that Tate go back to work, and he and I hung out together during the day. He didn't stop talking and I didn't mind. I liked listening to his stories. They kept me from thinking too much. As he was making spaghetti one evening he told me he joined the army as soon as he turned eighteen.

'So, how did you meet my dad?'

Charlie lit the gas stove and grinned. 'Your dad was an easy spot. He looked like a classic Sephardic Jew, you know – dark, intense, handsome in an "Ahab the Arab" sort of way.' He put my mother's large pot on to boil. 'But, when I found out his last name was Ryder I knew he wasn't Sephardim and he must eat treif, not kosher. I mean, Ryder – what kind of lame-ass WASP-sounding name is that, anyway? No offence.'

'That's okay.'

'We met at Monte Cassino in the field hospital. I took shrapnel in the tuchus; he took a bullet to his torso; between the ribcage and the hip bone. "Sweetheart wounds", we called them. Both could have got us out of action, but we didn't want to leave. We spent a few weeks recuperating in the ward playing Gin, Speed or Aces Up and shootin' the breeze. He was *haimisher mensch*, you know. I felt comfortable with him right away.' Charlie sipped on a Tuscan Chianti Classico while he stirred the fettuccine noodles into the pot.

'We bonded over music and belonging to the lost tribe.

Hymie introduced me to basic mechanics and we took up light duty in the motor pool.'

Charlie took me to Papaya King on 86th and Third Avenue and we ate hot dogs. He offered to take me to the Eva Hesse exhibition too, but I said no.

We went to the Central Park Zoo for the day instead. He wore a wool overcoat. He dug his hands into the pockets. 'You know, I was the one that introduced your mother to your dad.'

'No kidding?'

'Yeah. It was in the Marienplatz in Munich in '45. I was assigned to drive this Monuments colonel at what we called the CCP, the Munich Central Collecting Point, where all the Nazi stolen art was processed. This colonel had a hot civilian colleague. She was a looker, you know what I mean? No offence.'

I nodded.

We walked quietly past the elephants.

'I wanted her to go out with me so I gave her stuff. You know, chocolate, nylons, that kind of thing. But she wasn't interested. She knew what she wanted and it wasn't me. All this time I was going back to the barracks, see, and telling my best buddy about her. I wanted him to meet her so he could see that she was everything I said she was. Then the bastard stole her.' He laughed. 'No offence.'

'No offence taken.'

'You know, your dad's like a brother to me. I was happy to stand up for him, to be his best man, when they got hitched. He's a great guy and she was one classy dame.'

'I'm glad you're here, Mr Salmond. I'm really glad.'

'Call me Charlie, sport … or Uncle Charlie, like in *My Three*

Sons. Mr Salmond sounds like I'm some old, bald-headed fart.'

We laughed as we passed the hyenas, then Charlie sobered and put his arm around my shoulders. 'Don't you worry, sport. Uncle Charlie's going to look after you and your old man. It's all going to be okay. Trust me.'

I smiled. I wanted to believe him. I had to believe him.

You might think my mother's death would have made me retreat into my drawings, to make me work frantically and with intense focus, that somehow the act of creation would be cathartic, a way to salvation. Yeah, that's what Vincent might have done. I wish I could tell you that that was the case. Instead the opposite happened – I stopped drawing completely.

I picked up a pencil and all I could see was Mutti's face, smiling sadly at me. The paper was perfect – white, like her skin. Flawless. Empty. Dead. My hand felt like a claw. I dropped the pencil. I tried again, but, it wouldn't move. I couldn't even make a mark. I couldn't save her with art, I couldn't bring her back. The one thing that had got me through my life was gone – song over, lights out. It felt like shit.

Something shifted in Tate too. The week after Mutti died he boxed up all of her stuff and put it in storage. Her art books disappeared from the bookshelves, too. The next Saturday I went past their bedroom and saw him taking down their paintings. His face was dull and his eyes raw. The *Savarin Coffee Can* and *American Flag* paintings by Jasper Johns, the watercolour townscape by Fredrich Wasser, even the small oil study for *The She-Wolf* by Pollock disappeared. My drawings that Mutti had pinned to the walls next to their paintings went too. That especially hurt.

By midday the blue walls were empty and he didn't put anything back in their place. Over the next week everything came down from all the walls of the apartment. Like so many things at that time, I saw, but it didn't register in any way that mattered. I couldn't say anything to him and he didn't say anything to me. I got the message pretty clear, though. After that I stopped carrying the pencil I always had in my pocket.

I had more time, and I didn't want to see anybody. I looked over and over again at the photo album Mutti and I put together the winter before she died. I couldn't look at those photos for too long without feeling wretched, so I would pick up a book. I read *The Catcher in the Rye* and *A Separate Peace*. I wasn't ready for *Catcher*. All I could think was, 'Stop your whining, Holden, and get on with it.' On the other hand, *A Separate Peace* said something to me. I can't remember what it was about, except there was an intense love/hate thing between two boys that ended in a tragedy or a drowning. I didn't really care about the boys but I cried in the dark of my bedroom anyway.

I watched a lot of TV too – *The Beverly Hillbillies*, *McHale's Navy* – crap like that. I suppose they were funny. I don't remember much about them. Tate didn't care so I dozed off in front of the box all the time. Charlie would usually wake me and send me to my room to sleep. Sometimes it was after midnight and there was nothing but fuzz on the TV screen.

Whenever I wasn't distracted by TV, books or Charlie, this thought that I had somehow caused Mutti's death oozed into my head. Why did I argue with her? I was convinced that if I had spent the day with her looking at art or hadn't stayed at the goddamned pictures so long I could have saved her life. I could have defied nature and science and willed her to live.

Tate started to talk more. He would answer simple, boring stuff. I waited every day for him to get home just so I could try to weed something out of him. If he wasn't home by the time I thought he should be I freaked out.

'Why isn't he home yet, Charlie?'

'Relax, sport, he's not even late yet.'

He always got home and I was relieved. He wouldn't say much – and I felt cheated – but he was there. This dragged on and on – minutes seemed like hours, days like weeks. I couldn't see it ever changing.

One Friday afternoon I came home from school and my dad met me at the door. I could smell that he had been drinking. That was weird because he never hit the bottle during working hours.

'What's up, Tate? I thought you had the eight-to-six shift today.'

'Not anymore.'

'What do you mean? Did you get a new job?'

Charlie came up behind Tate, dancing like the floor was covered in hot coals. Tate took me by the shoulder. 'We're moving to California.'

3

I DIDN'T RESPOND AT FIRST. I couldn't really understand what Tate said. I mean, I understood the words but it sounded like goo to me; disjointed and baffling. I blinked several times and felt my feet stick to the sidewalk. 'What are you talking about?' I said with a dry mouth.

'I just started a Chevy dealership out of LA, near Disneyland,' Charlie explained, 'and I need someone I can trust to help me to get it going right. I've asked your dad to come work with me, to be my partner. Believe me, you'll love it there, sport. It's warm all the time, there's the beach, surfing …

'The Beach Boys,' Tate added.

'Yeah, The Beach Boys, movie stars and the birds are hot, hot, hot.' Charlie did a swinging little Frank Sinatra move.

We were standing on the stoop. The autumn chill cut through my skin like a wire. *No, no, no. No thank you, no way, no how* – at least that's what I wanted to say.

Tate smiled. It wasn't a broad smile, or relaxed or free of misery, but it was the first time he'd smiled since Mutti died. I don't know what kind of face I made, but he quickly added, 'That is, if you're okay with it. I told Charlie already that it's got to be right for you too or it won't jive. You dig?'

I had to turn away from him. I looked back and his smile had ebbed. I could see the worn sadness underneath.

'Let's go inside,' he mumbled. Once we were within our apartment he said to Charlie, 'Give us a minute, Chaz.'

'Solid. I'll be in the kitchen.'

Tate took me upstairs, guided me into my room and closed the door. He sat on my desk chair and pointed me to the bed. He put his elbows on his knees, his hands on his face and rubbed like he was trying to push something deeper. He showed his face, blinked and raised his eyebrows. 'Look, I know this is heavy. We haven't talked since, you know, your mother. With everyone around – and now Charlie here – it hasn't been easy. I know I haven't been here for you. How are you doing, kid?'

'Why do we have to go, Tate? Everything I know is here. Everything I love. Everything you love.'

'Everything I love? Everything I love is … he rubbed his forehead. 'There's nothing for me here, now. It's all gone. You're it.'

He stared at me with his vacant, bloodshot eyes. 'I get what you're feeling, but this is a real break. I've had time to think, to reconsider everything. I've been knocking myself out driving cabs in this stinking town since before you were born. We've got nothing to show for it. I want to do more. I want to give you a home – a real home – with some stability.'

'We have a home.'

'Yeah, we did, but that's gone. I don't like it, Son, I don't want it, but there it is.' He held up his hands, fingers splayed. 'Give it time to soak in. I don't expect you to say yes on the spot. I had to think hard before I decided this was the best thing. It took me a long time.'

‘Best thing for who?’

‘It’s the best thing for both of us – a fresh start, a chance to be new people, to put everything behind us.’

‘Everything? *Everything*? I don’t want to put everything behind us.’

‘You know what I mean.’ He paused. Then he opened his mouth and I expected more bullshit to come out of it. Instead he seemed to lose air, to collapse like a tent with no poles. I couldn’t bear to look at him. He stood up. ‘Think about it.’

He left and I was alone. I felt like I was floating free – but not like a Chagall.

We didn’t talk about it again. Every time it looked like a good chance, Charlie seemed to pop up or Tate left the room or the apartment or something else came up. He and Charlie made plans in low, serious tones and boxed things up. The whole thing rolled in that direction like it was inevitable. I was too weak – and maybe too broken – to stand up to it.

I don’t know. Maybe a part of me did want to go. Maybe I wanted to run away, to forget, to pack up the paintings of my heart and hide them somewhere far away. I felt like one of the damned at the bottom of Michelangelo’s *The Last Judgement*, behind the altar in the Sistine Chapel. One way or another, I wanted the one thing I couldn’t have – my mutti, and I didn’t want to feel this torture anymore.

It should have been an exciting trip, my first time driving across the US. The truth is, my head was in a murky vacuum most of the time. It must have been that way for the lost souls in the painting, drifting across the River Styx with Charon as gondolier.

Charlie got a brand-new 1964 Chevrolet Impala hard-top to drive us out to California. They weren't for sale to the public yet. I don't know if he bought it or rented it, or if we were delivering it. Once we hit the West Coast, I never saw it again. And come to think of it, I never saw Charlie in the same car twice.

I sprawled in the back seat and didn't look out the windows much. I marked the miles between me and home reading the comics I'd brought for the trip: Captain America, Fantastic Four and Classics Illustrated.

'Don't read in the car, Jackie, it'll give you a headache,' Tate said before we even crossed the George Washington Bridge.

I couldn't hear the two of them talking in the front seat very easily, unless they made an effort to include me. Charlie turned and talked about his dreams for the car dealership through most of New Jersey. 'I tell you, your old man and I are going to do something really different, kid. There's a lot of car dealers in LA – it's a car city. There's a lot of competition but most car salesmen think everyone's a *schnook*, a sucker. They'll take them for every nickel they got and do it with a greasy smile. That's always pissed me off. We two know cars and I'm a good salesman, a damn good salesman. With a straight arrow – like your dad – to keep me in line, I know we can shake things up in California. I got this idea to use the TV to advertise too, you see? It'll reach everyone. We'll have to turn them away.'

I tried to look interested, because I liked Charlie, but I couldn't have cared less.

Tate was driving, something I had never seen him do outside of his old Checker cab. Without thinking, I traced the drawings on the comics with a finger. He tilted the rear-view mirror towards me, looked over his shoulder and bit my head off.

'Stop that drawing!'

'But I'm not drawing.'

'I can see you, Jackie. Just stop it and don't give me any lip.'

'But I …'

'I mean it, Jackson.' He held up his forefinger. That was the last warning sign. I knew that at any moment he would stop the car and wail on my butt if I carried on. I didn't dare try to explain that I was tracing with my finger, not drawing. Charlie raised his eyebrows and turned to face the front.

About the time we crossed the Kentucky state line Charlie got tired of his own voice and turned on the radio. It was mostly static. Every station we could pick up sounded like some affiliate of Radio Hayseed. If a song didn't have a fiddle and a yodel in it, they stuck them in for good measure. Charlie toyed with the dial until he picked up a news station. 'Martin Luther King has gone to Birmingham, Alabam … parents of the Negro girls … Sixteenth Street Baptist Church …'

With Mutti's death and all I wasn't following the news much, but I did know about the Birmingham church bombing. Four girls – three of them my age – died for no better reason than that they were black.

'I hope they catch the *mamzer* who did it,' Tate said.

'You think that's going to happen? It's Alabama, it's *fercockt*. They'll probably give those murdering assholes a medal and erect a statue of them right in front of George Wallace's statehouse.'

The radio signal hissed and faded every time we went into a valley, 'Secretary McNamara … Vietnam. The … tary of Defence said … finished by 1965.'

'The Secretary and the military don't have a flying clue what those people are fighting about,' Tate muttered. 'I'll lay you ten we won't be out of Vietnam by the end of '65.'

'You got it. Mac knows what he's talking about. You saw what he did with the Ford Motor Company before he became Secretary of Defence.'

Tate snorted. 'That's the problem with this country. If someone's a good businessman, we think they'll make a great statesman. What a joke.'

I had never heard of that place – didn't know where it was or who Mac was – and I couldn't understand why anybody was interested in what some secretary thought about it anyway.

We hit Memphis around breakfast time. I didn't know Memphis was on the Mississippi River, and even though I was starving, Charlie insisted that we drive along Riverside Drive so we could take a good look. 'I need a break, anyway,' Charlie muttered.

'Jeez, I hate those motherfu–'

'Chaz, easy – think of the boy,' Tate snapped.

'Oh, yeah, yeah. Sorry, kid. No offence. I just can't sit down for as long as we've been driving without my tuchus acting up. You know, the old war wound.' It was already clear that Charlie's ass was going to dictate when and where we stopped a lot of the time.

'Don't worry; I've heard worse at school.'

'I bet.'

He found an exit onto Mud Island. It was a flat, glorified sandbar, but it looked over the majestic breadth of the waterway. We parked, got out and leaned against the car. We stared out silently at the mile and a half expanse of river.

'Yeah,' Charlie said, 'that's one hell of a lot of water.' He winked at me.

'I never thought I would see the ol' Mississippi,' Tate said.

I wasn't feeling half as light or amazed as Charlie and Tate. On the other side of the bridge was the West. The river was the great divide – my River Styx.

'This river has been here for ten thousand years. It's been the same but completely different too.' Tate crossed his arms. 'Even the water that was here when we parked the car is miles away by now, heading towards the Gulf of Mexico. It's all about change.'

'Same old Hymie,' Charlie sniggered. 'You're a *luftmensch*, my friend.'

'What's that?' I asked.

'A dreamer.'

My dad stared at the water and then looked at me. His eyes softened. I looked at him too but I tried to deaden my face, make my eyes go hard like a snake's. He wiped his lips and got in the car. Charlie punched me in the arm. I grinned at him. We got back in and this time Charlie drove.

We stopped for breakfast the next day in Fate, Texas. The wiry old man behind the counter didn't say much – he didn't have to. There was a newspaper on the counter and Tate picked it up after we ordered.

'The president is going to be in San Antonio tomorrow and in Dallas the day after,' he told us.

'Can we see him?' I asked Charlie.

'Sorry, Jackson, we're on a schedule and we're behind already. I can't afford to take a day or two more. I'll tell you what, though – the president will come out to LA sooner or later and, when he does, I'll take you to see him. I promise.'

The proprietor plonked Charlie's farm breakfast on the table. 'Sumbitch,' he muttered under his breath.

'Beg your pardon?' Tate said.

'That damn sumbitch in the White House,' the old man repeated. 'He's gonna git hisself killed, he comes down here.'

Tate and Charlie stared at each other. The man chewed his cud and started to walk away, but stopped himself short. 'He's all tangled up with that no-good coon preacher and folks down here don't like it one bit.'

'*Schmuck.*' Charlie stood up and threw a couple of dollars on the counter. 'Let's get the hell out of here.'

Tate stood up and grabbed my shoulder. I pulled it away. 'Come on,' he said. I stood up, reluctantly. The breakfast steamed away as we walked out the rickety screen door.

The weather was warm enough for me to wear a T-shirt. I drank Coke after Coke. Charlie and Tate sipped on longneck bottles of Lone Star beer.

After Big Spring, it got drier and dustier. There was no doubt we were in desert country. Down the road I could see a mirage – a long, narrow lake in front of us that we never reached, no matter how fast or far we went.

We got to a junction on the interstate. 'This reminds me of the road to Tit Mellil,' Tate said in a flat tone.

'Yeah, I can imagine that,' Charlie said with a slur.

My ears pricked up. I thought Tate had said 'the tit of Lil'. Anything to do with tits was fascinating and ridiculously funny to me. This didn't seem to be either. Not only that, but we were in the middle of a goddamn desert. I couldn't figure out the connection.

'Was that after Casablanca?' Charlie reached down between his feet for another bottle.

'On the road to,' Tate said. He gripped the wheel tighter. His hands were at the ten and two o'clock positions – textbook perfect.

Of course, when I heard 'Casablanca' I thought of Bogie and that song, Ilsa's luscious lips and my favourite rogue, Louis, the corrupt French Chief of Police. I imagined my dad in a white tuxedo and black tie, slugging back Scotch and sacrificing love for duty.

'When were you in Morocco, Tate?' I asked. 'You never told me that.' He didn't answer.

Charlie popped open his beer with a church key bottle opener and threw the cap out the window. 'Operation Torch, kid. Your daddy was in the first landing in North Africa, the first American action against the Nazis during the war. That was before I joined up or I would have been there too.'

'They weren't Nazis,' Tate said, shaking his head. 'Chuck one of those over.'

Charlie handed over the beer and grabbed another for himself. 'I meant to say the goddamn Vichy French.'

Tate glanced at Charlie and took a long swig on the bottle. 'Can it, Charlie.'

'Who are the bitchy French?' I asked.

Charlie laughed. Tate didn't. Charlie's laugh died to a throaty chuckle and he turned in his seat. He had that well-oiled look that went with his slur. 'Vichy, my boy, V-i-c-h-y. When the Krauts – no offence – invaded France, some of the Frogs made a deal with the Germans. They collaborated. The Germans let them set up a government in the spa town of Vichy.' He glanced at Tate. 'They were the *mamzerim* who were running

French Morocco at the start of the war. Didn't you ever see the movie *Casablanca*?'

'My favourite film.'

'Yeah, me too. I had a thing for Ingrid Bergman for a hell of a long time.' He stuck his head halfway out the window, letting the hot wind tousle his hair. After he took another swig he looked at me, 'Tough luck about your uncle, Nathan,' he said casually. 'I would have liked to meet him.'

'I told you to can it, man!' Tate exploded.

'What uncle?'

'Hey.' Charlie put up his hands, fingers stretched wide. 'I'm sorry, man. Okay. Oh, shit. Doesn't he know?'

'Know what? What uncle, Tate?

My dad's knuckles were white on the steering wheel until he slouched in his seat and sighed, 'Jesus, Charlie.' Charlie raised his eyebrows, shrugged and looked at the passing desert. Tate shook his head and half turned it towards me. 'I had a brother, Jackson, a twin brother. I lost him on the road to Casablanca on the second day of the war. That's all.'

I wanted to know everything. Mostly I wanted to know why he had never told me, but I didn't ask. I was that close to him I could blow my warm breath on his neck but I had never felt further away.

Charlie was quiet after that.

We ambled into El Paso in the evening. Finally Charlie broke the icy silence. 'Why should we stay in some *drek* Texas stink-hole when we can have an international experience on the cheap? Have you ever been out of the country, sport?'

'Nope.'

'Well, man, you're in for a treat. What do you say?'

'I'm not in the mood, Charlie.' Tate's voice was flat and tight.

'Come on, man. It's just what we need, somethin' to distract us from the road.' Charlie downed the bottle and threw it out the window.

I heard the sound of it smash and fade in a flash.

'Let's do it, Tate,' I said to the nape of his neck. He didn't answer.

We stayed in a cheap-but-clean hotel off the main plaza in Juárez, Mexico. Every wall was a different colour, more intense than any colours I had ever seen on walls before. It was jarring and odd but amazingly festive. We had dinner at a café on Venustiano Carranza, not far from the cathedral.

After we ordered there was a long silence until Charlie said, 'Remember when we entered Rome, Hymie? The crowd, those flowers and those *bambinas* on the Via Cavour?' he gestured like he was balancing two globes. '*Abbondanza*! And what about the vino? Man, were they happy to see us. God, that was swell.' He downed the last of his third beer. 'Sometimes I think I should have stayed in Italy.' Tate grunted in response. I wanted to hear more, but Charlie didn't take it anywhere.

Tate was silent all through dinner. While we ate Charlie rambled on about the surgical bombing of Florence and how the Nazis blew up all of the bridges except the Ponte Vecchio. 'Even one that Michelangelo was supposed to have designed.'

'The Ponte Santa Trinita.'

'Yeah, sport. How did you know?'

I looked at Tate, then at my plate.

'He was born on Michelangelo's birthday. Birgit told him all about the famous artist he shares his birthdate with,' Tate said.

'Yeah. Of course. I should have remembered.' Charlie raised the last of his eighth beer. 'Well, *salud*.'

Afterwards, Charlie wanted Tate to go out on the town with him but Tate said, 'Not tonight, Chaz. Jackie's too young to go honky-tonking. You go.'

Charlie argued, 'Are you kidding, buddy? This is Mexico! A foetus can order booze here, if he's got the cash. No offence, kid,' he said to me.

Tate shook his head. 'I won't leave him in a dive, in Juárez, by himself. That's the bottom line. I don't feel like painting it red, anyway.'

I looked at Tate and smiled, but he didn't notice.

Charlie leaned forward. 'You don't know what you're missing, buddy. I've been down here before. They make 'em tender in these parts.' He looked at the waitress clearing our table and then winked at me. 'The *señoritas* are a lot like them I-talian birds we knew in Rome, but spicier.' I looked at the waitress too. She was younger than me but was dark under the eyes and had beads of perspiration on her forehead. She just looked worn out. 'Okay, suit yourself.' He wiped his mouth, patted me on the shoulder and disappeared down the road.

Tate paid the bill and came back to the table with a bottle wrapped in a brown paper bag, 'What's that for?' I asked.

'I want another drink.'

I took a deep breath and let it out slowly. I was hoping he just wanted to hang out together. The bottle suggested a different story. We went back to the room in silence. Tate went out on the balcony alone and I tried to watch TV on the cheap twelve-inch in the corner but the reception was crappy and I didn't understand the Spanish anyway. It was a distraction, but it wasn't enough to keep Mutti, and now an uncle I never knew, out of my head.

Even though it was a Thursday night, the sounds coming from the street made it feel like a weekend. There was music, laughing, the occasional shout and even firecrackers. I went out to the balcony where Tate sat with the bottle and a shot glass. He perched on the cement block railing, leaning against a heavy wooden post.

I wanted to say I was sorry about his brother, that I was sorry that the whole thing had come up and that he was feeling sad – or mad – or whatever it was he was feeling. But he had been drinking all day. I seriously doubted he would remember anything tomorrow. I gave up on the idea of spending time with him. 'Goodnight, Tate,' I muttered and turned to go inside.

'Wait, Jackie.' He downed a shot. I looked at the bottle. It was nearly empty. 'I owe you an explanation.'

'No. It's okay, Tate. Really.' I didn't want to hear a schnapps-soaked confession.

'I've got to tell you.' His eyes were red and raw but I could see he wasn't going to give up on this one. 'It's just you and me, now, just you and me.' He poured another shot but didn't drink it.

'I've carried this thing inside of me for a long time – this ache, a sorrow that I haven't been able to talk about. Try to understand. Nate was … he was as much a part of me as my hands or my eyes. We did everything together from the time we were little kids. We even signed up for the army together.' He winced. I thought he was going to cry.

'I understand, Tate. You don't have to tell me.' I turned to go inside.

'Hold on,' he said insistently. 'When I lost him … I had to put him aside, you know what I mean? I had to forget about him, I had to, to survive.'

My stomach sank. I didn't want to hear this. It didn't belong to me. I nodded and tried to head for the door. He grabbed my arm tight. 'Wait.' He downed the shot in one gulp, took a deep breath through his nose and straightened his back. 'Outside of Tit Mellil, we stopped beside a *wadi*, a dry creek bed, for a ten-minute break. We were easy-going, considering it was only the second day of our war. We hadn't run into too much trouble and we were all pretty relaxed. Nate was sitting next to me, lighting up a Lucky Strike.' Tate stopped talking. In the silence I heard fireworks – or were they gunshots? He continued, 'I heard a crack and his head just … *gvald geshrign*, his head …' Tate's face slowly pleated up like it was being pulled down into his body from the inside.

'Shit,' I said. Tate didn't react.

'I … I tried to put him back together. I tried but it was …' he sighed deeply. 'There was another crack and the guy on the other side of me slumped in the dust. Then something happened – I went on automatic. All of my training kicked in. I didn't feel anything. I had a goal and that was the only thing that mattered in the world. I tracked the sniper down myself and I …'

'You killed him?'

He didn't answer for a long time. The terrible street sounds filled the void. 'Her.'

'A woman?'

'I didn't know. She was a girl, just a girl. She couldn't have been older than seventeen. I turned her over as carefully as I could. She looked like she was alive, but she wasn't breathing.

Her eyes were green and clear. She had light freckles and auburn hair – very *zaftig*.'

'A girl? A French girl?'

He filled another glass and downed it. 'Our new allies, for God's sake.' In the dim light his eyes glistened.

I stared at him. My stomach tightened and my forehead broke into a sweat. Were these the same hands that tucked me in at night, tossed a ball with me out in the street and hugged me when my mother died? Was this the same man who cried when he listened to Billie Holliday singing 'Strange Fruit'?

I knew, vaguely, that he must have shot people in the war ...– of course he did – but I couldn't imagine him killing a girl.

'Why didn't you tell me before?'

He looked in my direction but didn't look at me. 'I lost my only brother, right in front of my eyes. I couldn't stop to say the *Shema* over him, and I couldn't afford to mourn him. I killed someone for the first time, on the same day – and it was a girl – not even a soldier. I didn't know how to deal with it, the whole damned thing. I couldn't take it in. It was the second day of the war. For the next two years ... his voice trailed off, 'by the end of it, blocking hard things out was just what you did – we all did it. Then, I couldn't change it. I just ...

Tate had never talked about the war, never. Now I knew why, and I wished I didn't. He was all shadows and flashing neon, drunk and spent. He whispered, 'I did what I had to do to go on.'

I shuddered. Somewhere inside of me something echoed – a kind of harmonic. Was I doing the same thing with Mutti? Was I blocking her out?

'Come on, Tate.' I drew him off of the top of the balustrade without trouble and walked him inside. He fell into bed. I took off his shoes and covered him. I lay on my bed, eyes wide in the darkness, and tried not to think about tonight, Mutti, my uncle, nothing. There was a bullfight poster just visible on the wall and a calendar image of a naked guy with a huge feather headdress carrying an unconscious girl with big boobs up the side of a volcano. I tried to distract myself by figuring out what that was all about. I dropped off, but I heard Charlie come in about four in the morning, tumbling, muttering and singing.

The next day I realised that reception was better in the day time if I pointed the rabbit-ear antennae on the TV towards the US. I caught the end of the morning news with Mike Wallace. At the end he talked about this new craze in England for a rock 'n' roll band. He played part of a song they did called 'I Want to Hold Your Hand'. It was light and fast and filled with the painful yearning I was feeling all the time. I liked it.

We didn't get on the road until after eleven that day. Tate didn't say a word about the night before. Maybe he didn't remember. Charlie was, for once, muted.

As the desert sped by, saguaro cacti appeared, like soldiers at attention in the midday heat. I mulled over what Tate had spilled out on the balcony of the cheap Mexican hotel. He had always been a simple notion to me – distant but steady. Now I knew things I didn't want to know any more. Didn't I have enough junk to deal with already?

Tate and Charlie both wore dark glasses and didn't say a word until we stopped for gas in Mesa, Arizona. We pulled into the

Flying A service station in a cloud of dust and waited to be served.

'Me,' Charlie whispered, pointing to the bathroom, 'going to the can.'

'I gotta go to the head, too,' Tate said, 'when the attendant comes, tell him to fill it up.' He peeled a ten from his money clip and slapped it into my palm. 'And have him check everything.'

'Yes, sir.'

He walked away, making a visor across his forehead with his hand. I looked out of the open window. Even in the shade, the heat was unbearable. I was thirsty and we had run out of drinks. In the office I could see people huddled around a portable black-and-white TV. No one was coming to pour our gas. What the heck? This was a service station. I expected to be served, not ignored because of reruns of *The Phil Silvers Show* or a Green Bay Packers game on the tube.

A bell attached to the screen door tinkled as I entered the sweltering service station. Walter Cronkite's distinct voice, like oak and honey, was talking about the capture of someone named Lee Harvey Oswald.

If you ask anybody who was alive and conscious on November 22, 1963, they can tell you exactly what they were doing and where they were at, in the same moment that I walked through that service-station door. They can tell you what they were wearing, what the weather was like and the exact words they spoke, even after all this time.

A crowd of people were looking up at the TV, which was sitting on a shelf above quart cans of Pennzoil.

'From Dallas, Texas, the flash, apparently official: President Kennedy died at one p.m. Central Standard Time.' Walter

Cronkite looked up. 'Two o'clock Eastern Standard Time, some 38 minutes ago.' He paused and put on his glasses. I noticed he was in his shirtsleeves. 'Vice President Johnson has left the hospital in Dallas, but we do not know to where he has proceeded. Presumably he will be taking the oath of office shortly to become the 36th president of the United States.'

'Oh sweet Lord,' exclaimed an old black man.

A woman in a sleeveless gold dress gasped and the Mexican guy behind the counter hung his head and muttered, '*Chingado*.'

'Excuse me, what's going on?' I asked. No one answered. Tate and Charlie came in, looking raw as fresh meat. 'What's happened?' I said loudly.

'The president,' the woman in gold pressed her hand to her lips, 'the president.'

'They killed him. The *pinché* bastards killed him,' the attendant cried. The name 'Paco' was stitched in red onto his shirt. He pulled a handkerchief out of his back pocket and blew his nose. '*Madre de Dios*.'

'What?' Charlie managed through his haze. Tate was already with it. His mouth hung open as he stared at the screen.

'What happened?' I yelled. 'I'm sorry. What happened? We've been driving all day.'

'Oh, child,' the woman lowered her hand. 'The president was in Dallas this morning.'

'He was driving through Dealey Plaza in the centre of town,' the old man said. 'Do you know Dallas?'

I shook my head.

'That fella … *como se llama*? Oswald, he …' Paco mimed holding a sniper's gun and cocked his right thumb, 'shot, right in the *cabeza*, three times.'

My father recited in Hebrew under his breath: '*Shema Yisrael* ... I didn't recognise the words.

'I bet it was that *cabrón* Castro, him and the *pinché* rednecks.'

Charlie was as pale as milk. His eyes were bulging from his head. He muttered, '*Oy gevalt.*'

On the TV, Walter recapped what had happened. Every word seemed like it was the most important news I had ever heard in my life. Little did I know I would hear it all again, over and over and over, for the next four days and far beyond.

'Poor, poor Jackie,' the lady moaned.

I flinched. I thought she was talking about me.

'An' them kids,' the old man added.

'All of us,' Tate said.

'Amen.'

We stayed in that office for more than an hour before we asked to be served. I wanted to be with people and Tate and Charlie didn't move either. The TV showed the plaza, the hospital, the casket being loaded onto Air Force One, Oswald, bound and bruised, and Vice President Johnson and the First Lady standing together as he was sworn in. She had on the dress she wore when her husband was killed right next to her. Because it was a black-and-white TV, the bloodstain on her skirt looked dark grey instead of red. I stared at the stain and thought of my mother and the uncle I had never known. I thought about the girl my dad killed in Morocco. Death was all around me, ripping everything I knew from my life. I needed something to hold onto.

Eventually we headed down the road, with the radio on. Like the TV, it repeated the same thing over and over with minor details added a bit at a time. For hours very little changed. None of us spoke. Charlie turned up the volume or tuned into another channel if the signal wavered. We stopped for a rest in Quartzite and the few people around looked like zombies.

Towards evening, I started to cave into my head. I couldn't recognise anything that was going on. This life. I was tearing across the Sonoran desert with no mother, no home, no uncle and the entire country dressed in black. Everything was moving so fast I couldn't grasp it. I had to concentrate just to breathe.

We crossed the Colorado River at Ehrenberg and had to stop at the agricultural station.

'Anything to declare?' the sleepwalker in uniform at the checkpoint booth asked. Tate shook his head.

'Anything new?' Charlie asked him, 'We aren't getting good reception on the radio.'

The officer didn't miss a beat. 'Johnson's president, the body is back in Washington and they don't know yet if this Oswald character was alone.'

'Or if he even did it,' Tate corrected.

'Right. Well, welcome to California.' He waved us on before turning back to his TV.

The landscape changed, from lifeless rock and sand in Arizona to tilled fields across the Colorado River. Minutes later we passed a whole street of motels in Blythe. We checked into one with a pool, past Commercial Street. We then walked to the Denny's down the road for dinner. Inside the air-conditioned diner, talk was mostly about Oswald. Someone said his wife was Russian and he had lived there for a couple of years. Did Khrushchev have the president assassinated?

'Could o' been Castro,' an old guy in overalls and two day stubble offered. 'He's in cahoots with them damn Commies.'

The waitress was red-eyed and distracted but we didn't care. We watched the TV mounted on the wall. I ate, tasting nothing.

Charlie and Tate were still feeling seedy. We found a liquor store easily and they got a couple of six packs of beer and a bottle of Johnny Walker Red. We got back to the room and they stayed glued to the TV.

'What's going to happen now?' I asked.

'I don't know,' Tate mumbled. 'They'll try this Oswald guy.'

'Find out if he was working alone,' Charlie added.

'No, I mean to us. What's going to happen to the country?'

Tate sighed. 'Johnson's got ideals but he's an old-style politician. It's going to be like it used to be before President Kennedy – dull and stodgy bull-shit – politics as usual.'

'God, I just want to kill that little Oswald bastard,' Charlie hissed. He handed a beer to Tate.

I wanted to see what was happening on the TV but I didn't want to sit around while Tate and Charlie got plastered again.

Even though it was nearly December, the motel pool was clean and full of water. When I asked to go swimming Tate waved me away like the agricultural officer had done to us earlier in the day. I didn't have swimming trunks so I took my oldest pair of slacks, cut the legs off with a knife from the kitchen, and left the room by myself.

The pool was an amateur job, above ground and constructed from concrete blocks. It was five-and-a-half feet deep all around. I dropped my towel onto a folding chair and dove into the water. It was almost like diving into a lukewarm bath. The Carmine Street Pool and the YMCA back home were never this warm. When I resurfaced, I was startled by a voice.

'I can tell by your particular shade of pink that you aren't from this part of the world.' Right in front of me was a girl in a white bathing cap, hanging onto the ladder.

'I didn't see you,' I stammered.

'You surprised me, too.'

'Sorry. I … it's my first swim in California.'

'It's my second – that is, my second try. I don't know how to swim.' Her teeth were chattering. 'It's colder than you would think, isn't it?'

'Yeah, but a few laps should warm you up.' She gave me a half smile. 'Let me help you.'

'How?'

'Well, first of all, you gotta get a divorce from that ladder.'

She looked down like she hadn't noticed she was gripping onto it, and then let go a surprisingly hearty laugh. I laughed too. 'We haven't been introduced,' she said. 'My name is Beth, Mary-Beth Spencer, but call me Beth.'

Her eyes were pale blue, practically drained of colour, and she had freckles sprinkled across her nose. I could see wisps of strawberry-blonde hair under the white cap. She was older than me, maybe a couple of years.

'Pleased to meet you, Beth. I'm Jackson Ryder, but you can call me Jack.'

She let go of the ladder and extended her hand towards me. Her shake was firm and sharp.

I kept her hand for as long as was appropriate. Then I said, 'Okay, now let go of the ladder with your other arm. Don't be afraid, relax. I'm going to show you how to float.'

'I don't know if I can.'

'Of course you can. We have the same gravity as water, which means we have neutral weight in water. When you fill your lungs with air you make yourself lighter than water. We're kinda like … meat balloons.'

'I know that. It's just that … look, I'm gonna get out. I'm freezing.'

'Scaredy-cat,' I said, and then regretted it. Here was a girl older than me, almost a woman, and I was calling her names like a five-year-old.

'I'm not a scaredy-cat. I nearly drowned when I was ten years old. Since then I haven't been able to get into water if I can't touch the bottom. That's what I was trying to do here when you bounded in.'

That changed things. I had been excited and intimidated – she was older, close to naked and we were alone. Now I saw her vulnerability, and she gave it freely. 'That's really brave,' I said. She stared at me for a moment, then her shoulders relaxed and she smiled. Encouraged, I went on, 'Listen. Even if you sink to the bottom I'm here. I can drag you to the edge before you take one gulp. Come on, you can do it.'

She edged away from the ladder slowly.

'That's it. Relax.' I pulled her closer and placed my left hand on the small of her back. With a firm but gentle lift, her hips and legs moved towards the surface.

'You want to lie on the water and spread your weight evenly.' She was tense, but she did start to float. 'Tilt your head back. Watch out.' Her body rose, emerging from the water like islands in the sea. Then she stiffened and her body jack-knifed. I tried to pull her back, slipping my hand further down her body to get leverage.

'Do you always grab a girl's derrière on the first date?'

I felt the blood rush to my face, 'Sorry.' I pulled my hand away, but Beth faltered and started to sink. She gave a yelp and, before I knew it, my neck was her ladder. I kicked hard, forcing my body backwards towards the side of the pool. I could touch the bottom, barely, but I couldn't keep her up too. The chalky edge of the pool was only about three yards away, but she held me so tight that I just about went under.

'It's okay,' I managed through my squashed throat, 'we're safe.' Her hand touched the side and I felt her ease into my embrace. Only then did I feel the intense sensation of my skin on hers. Her breath was as sweet as ripe strawberries and in the setting sun her face was bathed in gold. She fixed her eyes on mine.

'My hero,' she whispered.

I stared at her soft, full lips. Floating on a cloud of pleasure and delirium, I forgot that an hour earlier I had felt utterly cold, alone and abandoned. I wanted more. I needed to bathe in her tenderness, to be enveloped and rocked to sleep in it. I leaned in to kiss her.

'Hold on, cowboy.' She jerked away.

I didn't let up.

'Get away, Jack.'

She was my size but I was stronger. We struggled. Finally, she gave me a whopping big slap across the cheek. Let me tell you, in the movies it looks funny but in real life it stings like hell. My ear was ringing and my cheek was throbbing, but it had the desired effect. I stopped. She pulled away from me and scrambled towards the ladder.

'I'm sorry. I don't know what … you know, with the president killed and …'

'What?'

'It's just that I'm so upset.'

'You've gotta be kidding.'

She stood above me and pulled the bathing cap off. Her pale hair fell to her shoulders. She put her hands on her hips, 'You know what? I'm glad he's dead. He was a nigger-loving, pope-ass-kissing Paddy who was a sucker for the Jews and weak on the Commies.'

Oh, Jesus, I thought. What is this *thing* in front of me?

'You know what?' I said. 'You go to hell, you ugly, nasty … bitch.'

In the fading light I saw her eyes flash and her cheeks flush. She gave me the finger and stormed away. I fell back into the water, letting my feet float to the surface. The sky above was a shade of navy blue and I could see the evening star shining brightly, alone.

4

I WOKE AND DIDN'T KNOW WHERE I WAS AT. The clock radio said one in the morning. Tate and Charlie were snoring, in syncopated time, in the other room. Once I had my bearings I closed my eyes but they wouldn't stay shut. I tapped my fingers on the bed railing for a few minutes before I turned on the lamp. I dug out the drawing pad from the bottom of my suitcase.

When we packed up to leave home I dumped a lot of art gear. Unless it had a special memory of Mutti I didn't want it. Everything I kept was being shipped to California but I packed this one drawing pad. I didn't even know why I did it. Habit, I guess.

I got up and looked around the lounge and kitchen. I found an HB pencil along with a writing pad – compliments of the motel. It would do. I went back to my bed, propped up two pillows and turned the lamp towards me. I wasn't going to draw, not really. I just wanted to try to put down what I felt.

I thought about Odilon Redon's coal-black spider images with weird human faces and *The Nightmare* by Henry Fuseli, with its gnome-like demon sitting on a helpless woman and staring out at the audience as if to say you're next. More terrifying to me, though, was the blind horse poking its head out from behind a heavy curtain. What in the hell was that about? I drew in the semi-darkness with these two spectres on my shoulders. I worked fast and feverishly, tearing the paper a couple of times. The pencil tip went round, then almost flat, right up to the wooden casing. I didn't have a pencil sharpener, so I peeled back the wood fibres with my fingernails, but it wasn't enough to free the pencil lead. Finally I lay back, exhausted.

It was nearly three.

Tate woke me at six-thirty. Wrapped in a picnic blanket in the early morning chill, I stumbled like a wino towards the car. In the back of the Impala I slept again. We knifed through the Colorado Desert, where even cacti won't grow. The heat woke me at about ten.

Jack Ruby shot and killed Lee Harvey Oswald live on TV while we ate pancakes in The Desert Palm Café in Indio. Nothing like that had ever been on TV before. I almost choked. I couldn't believe what I was seeing was real. A part of me thought it was justice. Another part felt badly for that pinch-faced little sod. But even as an ignorant teenager, I knew something had changed in this country. This wasn't *The Adventures of Ozzie and Harriet*. There was something horrible behind all the smiles, pastel colours and mock-Mondrian wallpaper.

Tate and Charlie were quiet about the whole thing. They hadn't uttered a sound since Blythe. They both kept their shades on.

'Jeeze, Charlie, is it always this hot?' I asked.

He was driving, a Marlboro stuck to his bottom lip. He tilted his head to the side and said, 'Only when you don't want it to be, my friend.'

Near Riverside, the sky turned a rusty grey. The desert gave way to houses, then some industrial buildings came into view, then there were trees, crossroads, traffic and the feel of an urban centre, but it wasn't anything to get too excited about. Every once in a while there was a two-storey building. Past the redwood picket fences in backyards were swimming pools – unheard of in New York. In another life I might have been excited, but in this life I felt nothing. Right about then, my eyes started to sting and I was short of air. Tate coughed.

Charlie said, 'Don't worry about your eyes. That's a little thing called smog. Get used to it. Welcome to LA.'

We headed west on Interstate 10 until we reached Route 60. From there we drove south-west through a long canyon. There was scrappy grass and dense shrub that Charlie called chaparral. Dotted everywhere were low-lying oak trees. We saw the odd cow lounging in its blue shadow. Oil pump jacks with giant, metal insect-heads lazily bobbed up and down.

'This is San Sebastiano Canyon Road,' Charlie explained, 'There are still deer, rabbits, rattlesnakes and skunks up here. There might even be bears. No one knows for sure. I bet it's the last patch of wild scrub country in the LA basin.' He put out his cigarette in the ashtray instead of flicking it out the window like he usually did. 'Oil companies own most of it and aren't doing much except sucking it dry of the black stuff. The first ones to find it were Spanish soldiers back in the 1760s when they camped here.'

'Except for the Indians,' Tate said.

'Which reminds me, we have to stop for gas.'

Up ahead a small valley opened up and the road straightened out. There was a T-junction and an old-time gas station like the one in Mesa where we'd heard about President Kennedy. There was a word I hadn't heard much of until two days ago: assassination.

The faded sign said Magnolia Oil Company. It had a red flying horse as its logo. The Mobil oil logo. It's like they had missed that memo. Charlie pulled up to the pump and honked the horn.

'These people are friends of mine,' he opened the door.

'Charlie!' exclaimed a swarthy man in beige overalls with wide cheekbones and thick, black hair.

'Hollywood Joe!' They shook hands.

'Nobody calls me that any more except for you.'

'You're still a good-lookin' guy.'

'Find your own man, he's taken,' a woman called through the screen door.

'Maggie, come on out here, I want you to meet my best friend.' Charlie embraced the woman. She was as dark-skinned as Joe.

'Maggie and Joey Dos Osos, this is my buddy Hymie Ryder and his son, Jackson.'

I tried to be polite, for Charlie's sake, but I really wanted to be left alone.

'Oh Charlie, can you believe the president is gone?' Maggie asked.

Charlie took off his sunglasses, shook his head and wiped his eyes. 'We were in Mesa, Arizona, getting gas when we heard. I was as sick as a dog from the night before and had just come out of the bathroom.'

'Joe and I had just finished our lunch. I was scraping the

plates into the pig's slop bucket when the radio stopped playing Doris Day.'

'Doris Day,' Tate said to no one in particular. 'It feels like one of our family has died.'

That made me shudder. They talked on. Had Oswald been alone? Could Johnson keep the country together and would Bobby Kennedy run in '64? Maggie invited us to stay for dinner.

'Thanks, Maggie. We don't have much daylight left and I've got to get these guys settled. It's been a long trip.' Charlie kissed Maggie on the cheek and nodded at Joe. We were off again.

I paid more attention to our surroundings now. We came out of the hills and drove down a wide road lined with citrus groves. They stretched for miles. There were fruit stalls on the roadside but they were closed for the winter. We drove over railroad tracks and under a metal sign that stretched across the road. 'Welcome to San Sebastiano, home of the Citrus Archers' it said in red script lettering.

'This is home,' Charlie grinned. 'I'm going to take you through once then swing around to the apartment.'

I looked out the window and dissected everything with my eyes. The town basically went for two blocks before it started to peter out. It was dusty and dry, but apart from that there wasn't much to distinguish it from any of the other small towns we had been through in the past week. There was a bank called The Bank of America, which I had never heard of, a midsized market called the Farmer's Basket and a park on one side, a police station on the other and a municipal pool between them. Across the road was a fire station, a clinic, a music store and the Monte Vista movie theatre showing *It's a*

Mad, Mad, Mad, Mad World. There were several small stores and a car dealership. I jumped. The large sign read *Salmond Chevrolet Motors*.

'Charlie!'

'It's mine, sport – soon to be ours.'

Charlie made a hard left at the lights, cruised past the showroom window and made another sharp left at the service entrance. He parked the Impala – now sporting three thousand miles of dust, mud and grime – under an awning in front of a door that had an office sign above it.

'Charlie!' A brunette with a bouffant hairdo rushed out of the door and flung herself into his arms.

'Mandy, sweetie.'

'My name's Sandy,' she pouted and dropped her arms.

'Sandy, *Sandy*, right. Like the beach. Sandy, meet my new partner, Hymie Ryder.' As she shook my dad's hand Charlie said, 'This is our new secretary, since the day before I left for the funeral.'

A tall, lanky red-headed guy in blue overalls came out of the shadows of the service garage door, followed by an older man gone puffy around the edges.

Charlie introduced my dad and me to the mechanics, Stretch and Buzz.

'How'd the Impala perform, boss?'

'Like a top, Stretch.'

'Can the kid wash it tomorrow?' he asked Sandy.

'He quit,' Stretch answered. 'He went to work with his pa in Signal Hill.'

'Okay, no matter. I'll be back to talk shop when I've dropped these guys home.'

We said our goodbyes and Charlie drove us off the lot.

'Sandy?' Tate questioned Charlie.

Charlie grimaced. 'Well, at least this one knows how the return on the typewriter works.'

Tate shook his head.

Down the main drag, Charlie pointed down side streets towards places of interest before he turned the car around. 'Two blocks that way, sport, is San Sebastiano Memorial High School, your home for the next four years.' It sounded like a prison sentence.

'It ain't New York City, is it?' Tate said.

'Give it time, Hymie. Look, you've got Disneyland over there and the prettiest beach you could want twenty miles that way. Twenty minutes' drive on the freeway you've got Hollywood and Vine, and two hours behind us you have the best skiing west of the Rockies. And Mexico is two-and-a-half hours to the south. What more do you want, buddy?'

'No, no, you got me wrong, man. I meant that as a good thing. Fresh air, space, quiet. It's just what we need.'

Just what *you* need – I thought. I felt like I was in a Radio Hayseed top-ten song: 'The San Sebastiano Backwater Blues'.

5

CHARLIE HAD SET US UP in the apartment complex he lived in, El Caballero, on Western Avenue. He lived there in a studio apartment on the top floor. The complex was two storeys high with a flat roof and a central courtyard. It was surrounded by a high fence and the outside cladding was stucco that sparkled in the sunlight like orange sherbet. But, best of all, in the centre of the courtyard was our very own swimming pool.

The evening we arrived half-a-dozen kids splashed in the pool. An older man waved at Charlie from the second floor, where he was barbecuing on his balcony. We didn't see anyone else that first day.

Charlie led us around the pool to apartment twelve, pulled out a set of keys and opened the orange-red coloured door. The room was dark, cool and smelled of new paint. He pulled up the Venetian blinds and the room flooded with amber light.

'Welcome home, gents.'

The walls were painted off-white and the apartment was furnished with hip-but-cheap Danish Modern stuff. There were two god-awful prints on the wall – some sort of tropical art deco scene with flamingos wading in a pool, and a loose and sloppy LeRoy Neiman-type picture of a sailboat in a shining sea, a whitewashed port in the distance. I couldn't figure out which one made me want to puke more.

'There are two rooms. Sport, you take the one through that door, your dad has the one down the hall. I'm on the second floor – practically right above you – so keep the noise down, especially if you have a bird over.'

Charlie winked. That was his idea of a joke. I headed into the bedroom with my suitcase and collapsed onto the bed.

When I woke it was pitch black and I was covered in goosebumps. My eyes went everywhere; I couldn't get enough air. 'Mutti? Tate?' I called. I didn't have a clue where I was. On my belly, my mouth open over a wet spot the size of a small pizza. I heard the gentle rumble of muted voices. My eyes made out the contours of the room, but that didn't help. I could dimly see the doorway and a glow came from outside. The voices were clearly Tate and Charlie's. I got up, stumbled up without turning on the light and headed towards the screen door in the lounge. Out by the pool I could see Tate and Charlie's silhouettes. They sat on folding deckchairs beside a small, round table. They were sipping beers.

Tate was saying in a low rumble, 'Mamele called her a Nazi *shiksa Estrie*, a fascist vampire right to her face. Can you beat that?'

Charlie shook his head. 'Jesus.'

'I don't know, man,' Tate said. 'I'm not sure anymore.'

'Give it time, buddy.'

'I shouldn't have dragged Jackie out here. That was shitty. He's right to be mad at me.'

'It's gonna be tough on Jackson, but he'll get over it. He'll adapt. He's young and sharp. I'll tell you, once he gets a load of those California girls he'll forget everything.'

'That's your answer for any situation, isn't it? But you don't get it. It's me, you dig? I don't know if I can make it. I don't know … I miss her so fucking much.'

I sucked in air. My father never used 'the eff word'. Even in my groggy state it was a shock.

Charlie sipped his longneck.

'It isn't fair. I know that. But shit, Hymie, how many guys were slaughtered in front of us? How many did we kill? And what about us? Why did we make it through? Why were we special? Life isn't fair, or right, or just. It's what it is. I know it's hard to be thankful right now. But look what you got: you survived the war intact, you found true love, and you got a great kid out of it. Be thankful that it was real and that you have those memories.'

'I just don't know what to do.'

'You gotta move on, you gotta move forward one step at a time: for Birgit, for Jackson, but most of all for yourself. Someday you are going to wake up and the first thing you feel isn't going to be a gaping hole in your life. Some day you are going to get up and you're going to smile. The only question is how much life is going to pass by until that happens. Six months? Fifty years? You have to grieve, sure, but you gotta fight too. Ya hear me, soldier? Ya gotta fight.'

I couldn't see Tate's face or hear his response over the hum of the pool filter and the muffled sounds from the other apartments. Someone laughed out loud. Tate raised his bottle.

'You know, man, you call me a *luftmensch* but you're a little weird yourself,' he said.

'You *mamzer*.'

'You're the bastard.'

They chuckled.

I sighed deeply. I wished I was with them, but I didn't move.

My stomach hurt and I realised I was probably hungry. I stepped away from the door and into the kitchen. There were two large paper bags, several empty Pabst Blue Ribbon bottles and half a bag of Fritos on the counter. 'Neat.' I reached into the corn chips. As an afterthought, I opened the door of the Frigidaire. There was half a pizza in there – or what passed for pizza on the West Coast – and a bottle of fresh orange juice; my first meal in our new California home.

The next day over breakfast, Tate said, 'I've thought about it and with the Christmas break so close, I wonder if it would be better for you to start school in the new semester in January. What do you think?'

I did the math: five days left in November, thirty-one days in December and the first few days of January off for New Year's equalled forty days.

Although my heart was doing double-time I answered, 'That would be okay, I guess.'

Although the moving van left New York before us, it didn't arrive at the apartment until a couple of days after us. There wasn't much to deliver except my dad's phonograph records, a few boxes of kitchen gear, some of the art that was too valuable to store and our clothes – all of them too heavy and warm for California. Almost everything else went into storage. Tate and I were opening boxes and figuring out where to put stuff. He was unpacking things slowly, just regular stuff like plates and silverware, but the muscles in his face were squeezed tight and his eyes were far away.

At one point he sniffed, cleared his throat and said, 'Thanksgiving is coming up.'

I laughed to myself. There was so much *not* to be thankful for – Mutti, leaving New York, the president.

'It's our first holiday on the West Coast and I think we should do something like going out, you know, to someplace swank.'

'What about Charlie?'

'Yeah, I was thinking the three of us. Who else have we got?'

'Charlie's cool and all, but ...' I exhaled sluggishly, 'can't we do something, just the two of us?'

He stopped what he was doing, looked at me and nodded, a smile in his eyes. 'Yeah, I dig.'

Just then Charlie knocked on the screen door and barged in.

'Hey, Charlie.'

'What's up, sport? Have you tried that pool yet?' I shook my head. 'The sooner you get out there the faster you'll get that West Coast tan all the chicks think is hip.'

'I'll go out after this.'

'That's the spirit.' He looked around. 'The movers finally got here, huh?'

'It was hardly worth the expense, but what are you going to do? Did you remember it's Thanksgiving this Thursday?' Tate asked.

Charlie stationed himself across the table from Tate and pulled bundles out of a cardboard box. 'I forgot to tell you ...' he unwrapped a Bavarian beer mug, ' ... Joe and Maggie – you know, the Indian folks that have the gas station – they asked us over for Thanksgiving dinner.'

'You're kidding.' Tate looked over at me.

'Maggie's a great cook. She said it wasn't right for you guys to have Thanksgiving alone.'

'Thanksgiving with Indians,' I couldn't help saying. What an incredible chance. It meant Tate and I wouldn't spend it just the two of us, but, what could be cooler? I figured there was plenty of time in the next forty days to make it up. 'It sounds boss,' I said.

Tate stopped unwrapping the silver samovar. 'You sure, Jackie?'

'Thanksgiving with Indians – that's something you wouldn't get in New York.' Charlie tossed some wadded-up newspaper on the carpet.

'Unless Detroit played the Kansas City Chiefs instead of Green Bay on Thursday,' I quipped.

Charlie laughed.

'Yeah, it's okay,' I said.

I peered out the window. The swimming-pool kids had arrived as usual. I watched the sun play on their heads and bare shoulders like sparklers on the Fourth of July.

Three older kids showed up: two boys and a girl. They were probably two or three years older than me, and it was obvious that the shorter boy and the girl were brother and sister. Their shared features looked good on her, not so good on him. The other guy had the hots for the girl but she didn't seem interested. Were the two boys friends, or was the tall guy using shorty to get to the chick? I couldn't tell. I marvelled at how tanned they were. It was almost wintertime, and they had more colour than anyone on Coney Island in midsummer. I couldn't imagine that I could ever get that dark.

The brother jumped into the pool but the girl and Mr Lost Cause sat in the same chairs Tate and Charlie had used on our first night here. He tried to look nonchalant, but he was holding himself too formally and shifting with angular movements. He was clearly wound up like a rubber band on a balsa-wood airplane. She was clearly somewhere else.

He leaned towards the girl and the next thing you know, she hauled off and slapped him so hard I could hear it from inside the apartment. It was sharp and quick. I remembered the sting of Beth's hand on my cheek. Another time I would have laughed.

I noticed then that Tate and Charlie were whispering to each other. I got a little annoyed.

Suddenly Charlie said to me out loud, 'Sport, take a ride with me,' as he dropped another wadded newspaper on the floor.

I looked out the window, then at Tate. He mumbled, 'Yeah, sure. Get outta here.'

'Where we going?' I asked, as we walked past the pool. Charlie glanced at the couple on the chairs. I thought I heard a low growl. I caught the eye of the 'sister' but she only held my gaze for a moment.

'I've got a business proposition.'

We headed out the gate of the complex and a new red two-door Chevy was parked right in front. 'A Biscayne?' I asked in amazement.

'Hey, I know it's not top-of-the-line but it's got a 425 horsepower, Turbo-Fire 409 V8 under the hood, you cheeky little twerp.'

I laughed.

We ended up at the Bus Stop Café just half a block from Salmond Motors. It was an old-time looking place, lots of chrome and aquamarine vinyl, with a middle-aged waitress named Mabel who never cracked a smile. Charlie ordered a coffee and Danish for himself and a banana split for me. He lit a cigarette. 'You wouldn't know it, but she loves me.' He took a long drag and flicked the ash in the tin tray on our table. 'So how you doin', kid?'

I couldn't tell if he was just making small talk or if he really wanted to know. Charlie was always half jumped-up, reacting to anything – especially female – that moved on the street, in the café or on the jukebox. He really didn't need coffee.

'I don't know. Okay, I guess,' I answered.

'Whaddaya mean, *okay*?' He looked at me this time.

I shook my head. 'I don't know.'

'You're missing New York, your friends … her.'

'Yes, and Tate's …'

'He's not making it easy.' Charlie finished my sentence.

I looked out the window. Pumpkins and other festive things had been painted on the glass to celebrate the upcoming holiday. I found myself looking out between the legs of an enormous turkey.

'I'm to blame for you being here. I'm sorry, but your dad wouldn't have survived if he had stayed in New York. You realise that, don't you?'

'I don't blame you, Charlie. But it doesn't matter if we're here or back east. He's just not … here. Do you know where he's at?'

Mabel brought our order. The banana split was beautiful – as good as any I could remember from back east. I was still admiring the textures and colour of the whipped cream, banana and cherries when Charlie answered, 'Your dad's had a rough time of it.'

'I know,' I said quickly.

'I didn't tell you this kid, but when I met him he was still in a bad way over your uncle's death. I think the rest of the war saved him. If he hadn't been distracted by all that shit I don't know what he would have done. Once it was over he would have cracked – you know – loony or worse, I'm sure. I introduced him to your mother just in time. She was like a doorway of light for him. Now that she's gone …' he shook his head and sliced into the Danish with a fork, 'he's lost again.'

I picked up my spoon but I couldn't use it. 'What about me? What about what I need? He's got you to talk to, what have I got? Nothing. No one. He's like a block wall. Why can't he talk to me?'

'I don't know. Give him time. You know you can talk to me too, kiddo. Uncle Charlie's here for you – I told you that already.'

A couple of girls walked by.

Charlie put down his fork and put on his hat. 'Hold that thought. I'll be right back.' I looked over my shoulder and could see him under the painting of a spilling cornucopia, stopping the two girls. I turned back to my banana split. The ice cream was melting, so I got stuck in. Charlie returned when I was about a third of the way through it. 'Sorry about that. Future secretaries, if you know what I mean.' He winked, lifted the coffee to his lips, winced and called Mabel over for a top-up. 'Where were we?'

'You had a proposition for me.' I kept eating.

'Right. Look, you got time on your hands and I'm short-handed over at the lot. I've already squared it with your dad. It's just washing cars, sweeping up and being a general gofer but I'll pay you a decent wage plus all the instant coffee you can handle, ay? What do you say, Jackie?'

I wiped my mouth. It wasn't my dream job, but I wasn't doing anything else. I could use the cash, and besides that it was working with Tate.

'Sure, but you know what? Can you please call me Jack or Jackson from now on?' I extended my hand.

On Thanksgiving, we pulled up to Maggie and Joe's garage on time.

'*Bienvenidos.* Welcome.' Maggie opened the screen door.

'I'm so glad you're here. Joe's feeding the pigs. He'll be back soon. Come on in.'

Charlie hugged and kissed her on the mouth. She kissed Tate and me on our cheeks. 'Thanks for inviting us, Maggie,' Tate said. 'That was very neighbourly.'

He handed her a distinctive square bottle of Manischewitz concord wine. Maggie burst out with the advertising slogan of the company: 'Man-O-Manischewitz! What a Wine!' Charlie and Tate laughed. I instantly took a liking to her.

'Sit down and relax. My, you all look nice.'

It was true. Tate and Charlie were wearing sports jackets and I wore my best slacks, a pressed shirt and tie. We went through to the living room, which was not much larger than ours, but very cosy and neat. The faded wallpaper had a large tropical flower design, probably from the '30s. Photos were set out on the mantelpiece, crocheted doilies were draped over the backs of the forest-green chairs, and the TV console and phonograph were against the far wall. A plaque on the wall celebrated the military service of Sergeant Joseph Dos Osos in Korea, 1950 to 1951.

Joe came in and apologised for his lateness.

'Wash up,' Maggie told him, 'you stink like a pig.' She covered her mouth. 'I'm so sorry. I completely forgot. I hope I didn't offend you.'

'Why – because we're Jewish?' Charlie asked. Maggie hunched her shoulders. Charlie looked at Tate. They both grinned. 'Don't worry about it. It would take a hell of a lot more than that to offend us.'

'We both eat Smoky Links occasionally,' Tate added.

'That's good,' Maggie said, 'because you being Hebrews slipped my mind. The turkey we're having tonight has bacon stuffing.'

We laughed. Joe came back in slacks and an ill-fitting tie, balancing a tray with crystal wine glasses, the bottle of Manischewitz and a small bottle of Dr Pepper for me. He filled the glasses. 'A toast – to new friends in a new land. Happy Thanksgiving.'

'*L'chaim*,' Charlie countered, 'to life.'

'*L'chaim*,' we chimed.

Tate lit a cigarette and everyone followed suit.

'Where's Maria?' Charlie asked between drags.

'She won't be eating with us. She isn't feeling well, but she did want to say hello.' Maggie stood up.

'Don't bother her, Maggie.'

'No, she was very definite about it.' Maggie returned with a girl around my age who had the same high cheekbones and full mouth as her mother, but her eyes were red and swollen. Maggie introduced us.

'Pleased to meet you.' Maria extended a limp hand to Tate and me. She attempted a smile.

'The pleasure is mine. I hope you feel better soon.'

She held a tissue to her nose briefly, she excused herself and melted back into her room.

'She's getting to be quite the young lady, very pretty,' Charlie said politely.

'Thank you. That she is,' Joe said. 'Takes after her mother, thank God.'

Maggie blushed. 'Oh, Joe.' They grinned at each other. I had seen the same thing between my parents before. I sighed. Tate smiled, but a shadow passed over his face.

The conversation drifted to the assassination and then to President Johnson's first speech in Congress, which became the famous 'Let us Continue' speech. With his Texas drawl, Johnson pronounced it 'let us con-tin-ya'.

'The most important thing in the speech was the president's commitment to the Civil Rights Bill,' Charlie declared. 'Everyone has the right to be treated equally and with respect.'

'I don't think the Civil Rights Bill will go far enough,' Maggie said as she passed a tray of hors d'oeuvres, cold cuts and cheese on crackers.

'Why?' Tate asked.

Maggie looked at Joe briefly and his eyebrows crinkled up for a second, 'You gentlemen are Jewish. We are Indians. Is this Bill going to extend to us? Legally it will, but do you think it will get you into an exclusive country club, Charlie? Do you expect to see a Jewish president soon? A woman? A Mexican?'

I was fascinated by what Maggie was saying. I never thought about the whole civil rights thing being about anyone else except the coloured people.

'You're a radical,' Charlie quipped. 'No offence.'

I chuckled at that.

'Come on, Charlie, you know what I'm talking about.' Maggie leaned forward. 'Do you know how many times I've been called "squaw"? How many times they've called Joe "chief"? What have they called you? What little words suddenly made you stop in your tracks or tense up?'

'Maggie, don't,' Joe pleaded.

Maggie held up her hand to silence him. 'Have you ever got angry about it? Ever said anything? Or, did you let it slide?' She had been inching forward in her seat as she spoke. She realised it and sat back, 'We've got to speak up no matter how it rocks the boat, or things will never change.'

'Please, Maggie, these are our guests and on this night we are supposed to be giving thanks for what we have.' Joe raised the bottle of Manischewitz and topped up everyone's glass.

'Don't get me started on Thanksgiving,' Maggie said, taking a gulp of wine. 'Those damned pilgrims ate what food they could get from the Wampanoag, slaughtered forty per cent of the tribe and took their land. Then they kept on giving thanks every fall. In the three hundred and forty years since then, white and Indian relations have been nothing but the same old thing over and over.'

'There is more than one way to get justice, Mag,' Joe said. He gestured at me, Tate and Charlie. 'Look at their culture. They were an old people – even in the time of Jesus. The Romans kicked them out of their land and spread them all over the world. They survived as a people because they held on to the old ways and didn't let their culture die. That's where we went wrong.'

'It's true. We lost our ways. We lost our centre,' Maggie conceded. 'No matter where we come from, we need to hold on to what makes us who we are.'

'And have more babies,' Charlie added.

'Of course, more babies.' Maggie slapped her leg.

'I can give thanks for that,' Joe said, 'or at least for trying.'

Tate offered a polite, but weak, smile.

I stuffed my face with hors d'oeuvres and tried to look like

I didn't know what they were talking about.

We ate a great feast, Maggie and Joe asked about New York, Joe told us about hiking, camping and rattlesnakes in the hills and Charlie talked about his plans for the car dealership. There were plenty of laughs and a great dessert of pumpkin pie and ice cream. We left early because Joe had to open the gas station in time to catch the morning commuters.

On the way home Tate and Charlie spoke quietly with the radio on low. I pretended to be asleep.

Charlie said, 'You know there's a lot to what Maggie says. Growing up in Nebraska and being Jewish, I learned who my friends were damned fast. Because I didn't look like a Landsman I heard all kinds of shit. You know what I mean? Guys I knew well, Hymie, who I played football with in school, praised Nazis and their warped idea of 'racial purity'. It was enough to make me vomit. But, you know what, buddy? You know what? I never said a damn thing. I even smiled once or twice to hint that I agreed. Can you believe that shit?'

Tate sighed. 'Yeah, self-loathing is an ugly thing, but you know what? It's more common than fly shit. Don't beat yourself up.'

'Yeah.'

They drove the rest of the way in silence. I wondered if Tate had ever felt like Charlie, if anyone had ever given him shit. Then I wondered what it was like for him and Mutti to be together – an American Jew soldier dating a young, blonde German woman? That must have riled some Munichers to the rotten core. I smiled to myself. How brave they must have both been. I would have liked to talk to Mutti about that. I wished I could talk to Tate about it now.

When we got home, I lay awake and thought about the

evening. The whole racial thing didn't mean much to me, really. Sure, I believed everyone should be equal, but it wasn't a big thing for me. In New York, in the Village, I never felt weird or anything. No one ever treated me different, as far as I could tell. Yet I did feel different. I always thought it was the art thing but maybe it was being Jewish too.

What really stuck out for me from the dinner was the look that Joe and Maggie shared. I kept going back to that. It was special. It made me hurt inside. But it was good. I wanted it for me, for Tate, even for Charlie. I wanted to own it.

Later, when I was sure Tate was asleep, I turned on my desk lamp and sat up. I had to do something or I wouldn't be able to sleep. I looked on my bookshelf – still more or less empty – and found a copy of *The Story of Hiawatha* that belonged to my dad when he was a kid. It had a coloured illustration of Hiawatha and Minnehaha done by some guy named ML Kirk. I found the picture of the Indian hero and his true love looking at each other. They looked like Joe and Maggie, except that the faces weren't right and it looked like they were dressed for a Halloween party. It made me squirm. I couldn't leave it at that. My desk was empty except for comics next to the lamp and the drawing pad from my suitcase. I pulled the pad out and grabbed the HB pencil. I sketched a variation on the Kirk illustration putting them in modern clothes and made the faces more like Joe and Maggie's. Instead of a forest I set them in front of the gas station with the red flying horse of the Magnolia Oil Company sign behind them. I tried my damnedest to capture that tender look. It wasn't very accurate, but it caught the most important thing about them.

I felt a jolt. This was a drawing. I had clearly made a drawing when I wasn't doing any art.

Suddenly my door opened. I covered the drawing pad lightning fast.

'What the hell is going on?'

'Nothing, Tate.'

'What are you doing?'

'Nothing. I couldn't sleep. I think I ate too much. I was just reading *Hiawatha*.'

He rubbed his eyes and stared at me.

'I swear, nothing's happening.'

He shook his head and looked at his wristwatch, 'Yeah, I think I ate too much too. Okay. Get to sleep. I need you to help me with the apartment tomorrow, you hear?' He paused, like somehow he was going to learn more from just standing there. 'G'night.'

It was a close call. I hid the pad in the bottom drawer and stuffed the obvious question to the back of my mind; why was I drawing at all?

6

BY THE NEXT DAY TATE AND I were settled into apartment number twelve. He didn't like the prints in the apartment any more than I did so he took them down. The walls looked really bare and you could see that the hooks had been moved a couple of times. It looked scarred and shabby. I saw our paintings stacked against the wall near the kitchen table, still wrapped.

'Do you mind if I put something up, some of our paintings, maybe,' I asked, 'to hide the marks on the wall?'

He walked over to the stack of paintings in the corner and paused. His fingers opened but he didn't reach out. He looked down. 'It's fine the way it is.'

'But Tate.'

'It's fine.'

'We've got all these paintings, though. Wouldn't it be better to use some of them?'

'It's fine, for Christ's sake. I'll get the apartment manager to fix the goddamn wall.'

I didn't ask again.

After breakfast some of our neighbours from the complex, Fred and Marion Barker and Kate Hickey, came over for coffee.

Mr and Mrs Barker brought leftover turkey and Mrs Hickey brought a bottle of Bushmills Single Malt Irish Whiskey.

I was on my best behaviour – for Tate's sake – and fascinated by this new set of people, who were unlike any I had ever encountered in New York. After introductions Tate invited them to sit down, but it was awkward. All we had were three bent-iron kitchen chairs and one sofa. Fred offered to stand. Tate busied himself in the kitchen frantically trying to figure out how to provide cups, saucers and coffee for so many guests and I helped him.

'Have you settled in yet?' Mrs Barker took a cup of Folgers from Tate.

'Not really. We've only just unpacked our stuff and until now we haven't met anyone.'

'Except for Maggie and Joe,' I interjected.

'People are giving you time,' Mrs Barker said, 'and there is the assassination.'

This started the inevitable recital of where everyone was when *it* happened. 'I am semi-retired. I substitute teach at the high school when I am needed. I wasn't called into work that day and was happy for it. It was so warm, in any case, we heard it on the car radio.'

'I heard it on the transistor,' Mrs Hickey said. She was young and had this kind of Sandra Dee thing going on with her hair. I thought Sandra Dee was swell. 'You're right, Marion, it was a beautiful day. I was at the beach with a friend.' She took a drag on her cigarette. Tate told everyone how we had found out about the president. Everyone nodded.

After a pause Mrs Barker turned to me. 'You will find, young man, that there are plenty of other young people about. You will make friends easily.'

I leaned on the sofa arm and forced a smiled, 'Yes ma'am.'

Mrs Barker took another demure sip and addressed Tate. 'Mr Salmond tells us that you are going into business together. That must be exciting.'

Tate poured the last coffee – his own – into a ceramic beer mug. 'To tell the truth, I'm apprehensive. I'm new to this.'

'My, how novel,' Mrs Hickey said. 'A man that admits fear.'

Mr Barker laughed.

Mrs Barker threw him 'a look', but kept talking to Tate. 'I'm sure you will do fine. Fred and I will recommend you to our friends.'

'I used to be in the finance business before I retired.' Mr Barker added, 'I know a few people I can send your way.'

'I'm looking to change cars,' Mrs Hickey interjected. 'I'll come see you.'

'Thank you,' Tate said, 'my first customer!'

He took a gulp from the mug.

Mrs Barker told a predictable story about the time she went to New York 'before the war' and made a few comments about how fast California was growing, before she said, 'We really must go.'

Mrs Hickey was the last to leave. As she walked out the door, she turned to Tate, 'I was sorry to hear about your wife. Charlie told me. I know what it's like to lose a spouse, so if you ever want to talk or have a drink …' She pointed to the Bushmills. 'I'm in apartment six, halfway around the pool.'

'Thanks.' Tate gave a tight-lipped smile. 'I'll do that.'

She gazed at him for a moment before she walked away. He closed the screen door.

'Damn it,' he said when she was out of earshot.

'What's wrong, Tate?'

‘Why in the hell is Charlie telling people personal things about us? I don’t like that, man.’

Charlie showed up later after work. I was in my room fiddling around on my transistor radio. There were three stations I could pick up that played good music – KHJ, KRLA and KFWB. At night there was another English language station that came out of Rosarito, Mexico, with the call letters XERB. It blasted out two hundred and fifty thousand watts, drowning out stations for hundreds of miles into the US. It was crazy.

Gene Weed’s show was ending and Bill Ballance’s was about to come on. I could hear Tate’s voice from the living room, the bass an insistent beat. I turned off the radio, opened my door and tip toed as close as I dared to the lounge. I could see them, but I was in the shadows.

‘I’m sorry, buddy,’ Charlie said plaintively from the sofa. ‘If you haven’t figured it out yet, she’s the hottest thing in the complex. I’ve been trying to make it with her for months but she’s a hard filly to break.’

‘So, you’re using my dead wife, who you knew and loved, as currency so you can shack up with some dame? You sick fucking bastard.’

‘What are you talking about?’

‘Oh, come on, Charlie, you didn’t think I knew?’

‘Knew what? I swear I don’t know what you’re talking about.’

Tate pointed at Charlie’s bowed head with two fingers, like he was blessing him or holding a pistol. His language didn’t shock me anymore. Charlie’s shoulders slumped. Tate shook his head. ‘Jeez, is there anything you won’t do? Any … depth you won’t sink to, and, with some girl in your own backyard, to boot? I would have thought that you had learned by now. What if it went bad? Are you going to live with that problem every day? Or move? Why take the chance?'

'You're right, man, of course. Plenty of other fish, right?'

We didn't see Charlie for a few days after that. I wasn't really sure what had happened. Why was Tate so pissed off? With Charlie out of the scene I thought Tate and I would spend more time together. We did, sort of. Except Tate was busy studying car manuals and I don't know what else. When he took a break he would listen to his records. Mrs Hickey came over a few times and she and Tate would talk over a drink or two. I stayed in my room, mostly reading and listening to the radio. After a while I got tired of hanging around and explored the town on foot, but there wasn't much to it. The pool was closed for the season. I had seen the movies at the Monte Vista already and they didn't change them for weeks. The San Sebastiano Municipal Library, next to the courthouse, was about the size of our lounge and had a pretty tired collection. I hung around at the Farmer's Basket a few times drinking a Dr. Pepper or munching on potato chips, candy bars or some other junk, but that got old. If there was anyone over twelve or under thirty that lived in town I never saw them. I walked around farther afield: down the railroad line, amongst the orange groves and even up the canyon a bit, but I still felt strange in the open. I liked being inside, between walls, secure.

Then, one day, unexpectedly, Tate got me up early and we caught the bus heading south down Beach Boulevard. 'Why are we doing this, Tate?' I asked him as we waited for the bus to go.

'It's what you want, isn't it?'

Somehow, his answer annoyed me. Yeah, it was exactly what I wanted, but, what bugged me was the way he said it.

Air drew into the pneumatic system closing the door. The air brakes released and we were on our way. I forgot about the why and just gazed out the window. The weather was overcast, sort of foggy, but warm by our standards. The scenery was so flat. There were few buildings more than two storeys tall. Every so often there was a gap between the shops and houses with a field of flowers or strawberries stretching back for acres.

Now that Thanksgiving was over, Christmas decorations were everywhere. Most of the houses had at least one string of lights around their rooftops. Street lamps were adorned with huge plastic candy canes, wreaths or Santa Claus faces. In the storefronts, people had set up aluminium Christmas trees with purple and pink snow floss. Strangest of all was the fake snow on the windows. It was bizarre. Here it was, approaching the dead of winter, and I was wearing nothing more than a sweatshirt.

After a half hour the bus turned off the highway onto Main Street in Huntington Beach. It drove past blocks of wooden and stucco bungalows, a large park and the town itself, which wasn't much to speak of. It dropped us off at the corner of Main and Pacific Coast Highway, opposite the pier.

The air was thick with a salty mist and there wasn't a hint of breeze. The sand on the sidewalk made a shuffling sound under our feet. I smiled. This was the closest to the East Coast I felt since we had been in LA. Me and the guys back home had mornings like this at Coney Island. The sound of everything was different by the sea, kind of muffled.

'What do you say we grab a bite before we look around?' Tate asked.

'That sounds good. I'm starving.'

We looked up and down the six lanes of the highway and then back towards the town. The place on the corner apparently did food, but it was closed.

'Golden Bear.' Tate read from the sign. 'I've heard of this place.'

'No kidding?'

'Yeah, some cats, musician friends of your mother, said that when they toured the West Coast they played here and it was one of the coolest gigs around. Man, I wish she was here to see it.'

He hadn't mentioned Mutti once since we left New York. When he mentioned her, it felt like she was alive – maybe around the corner on Walnut Avenue, maybe in the Rexall drugstore getting some cigarettes and lipstick. It felt good, real good. I realised everything I was doing to keep the hurt away. Tate sighed deeply, as if he was reading my mind. All he said was, 'Yeah', and shoved his hands in his pockets.

We found a place to eat up the street. I thought about Mutti but we didn't talk about her. The fog burned off by ten and it got up to the high sixties on the thermometer. We walked out to the end of the pier, marvelled at how broad the sand was, inspected every fisherman's bucket, and watched half a dozen diehard surfers ride the modest waves as we fed scraps of French fries to the seagulls. We took off our shoes and walked in the foam towards Bolsa Chica. It was chilly but bearable. We turned back at the channel that went inland to the wetland reserve and then caught the bus home.

That was the only time my dad and I went to the beach; just

the two of us. By the next summer I had friends, a licence and a car. Although nothing really happened – we didn't have any deep discussions or discover anything really incredible – it's the day I remember most; that grey, nippy day on the beach. I still see us standing at the corner of Main and Pacific Coast Highway.

That night I had a vivid dream. Mutti, President Kennedy, my dad's brother Nathan and I were at the beach and I wanted to swim in the warm, clear water. I tried to get everyone to come with me. The president and Uncle Nathan, who looked like Tate but was much shorter, didn't hear me – they were deep in conversation comparing their headaches. Mutti sunbathed with her eyes closed. The longer she was asleep, the paler she got. I tried to push her into swimming, but nothing came out of my throat but a guttural croak.

Then another dream – we were all in the same place, but this time it was like a sequence of animated charcoal drawings. The water rolled up and Mutti ran away, Uncle Nathan and the president were dark smudges in the far left corner of my paper and Mutti disappeared. I forgot about the swim and my stomach sank. I looked desperately for my mother but she was nowhere to be found. The grey sky darkened and so did the sea. The setting sun was a glowing bear, languidly swimming towards the horizon. Mutti splayed across his back. Her hand was trailing in the sea foam.

I woke up. I was seething with anger but I couldn't tell why. My pillow was soaked. I turned on the radio and heard a broad accent singing something about a platypus duck. It was funny and distracted me while my head cleared. Before long I heard

Sam Riddle say, 'That was the hit *Tie Me Kangaroo Down Sport* by Australian Rolf Harris …' I didn't hear the rest. Sam Riddle came on at twelve o'clock, so it must already be the afternoon. What happened to the morning?

I found my notepad and tried to get down what I could remember of the dreams. While I drew, a snappy guitar intro – something I had heard before but could only vaguely recall – came out of the speaker. I drew the broad sweep of the sandy shore. Voices started singing in harmony and then a little guitar riff like it was answering the singers. 'Uh-huh, go on,' it seemed to say. The voices continued: 'I wanna hold your hand … I kept drawing, but slower. The song softened and was more reflective. This was something different. I understood what they were singing because it could have been about me. I had heard this band before. Where was that? Who were these guys?

When it was over, Sam talked about how this British band called The Beatles had been on Walter Cronkite the night before. They were so new their records weren't even for sale in the US yet. He thought we would be hearing a lot more from them.

My bladder was about the size of a basketball. I had to get up. On the way to the bathroom I heard voices in the lounge; Tate and a woman. I took care of business and didn't flush so I could creep up to the living room and peek around the corner. I was in my pyjamas and not ready to see anybody. The two figures were backlit by a bright glow from outside. It was Mrs Hickey sitting there next to my dad, eating a sandwich and drinking lemonade. She was wearing a fine white blouse, with sleeves that reached halfway to her wrists, over orange pedal-pushers. She had her hair tied in pigtails – which made her look a hell of a lot younger – and she was barefoot. I could see her immaculately-painted crimson toenails. She rubbed them slowly together. Her laughter rose and fell like the feet of skipping schoolkids – not hearty and earthy, like Mutti's. I tried to tear my eyes away.

I couldn't go back to my room and sit around. I couldn't stay still. I went back to get dressed. The radio was playing the same Beatles song again. I had never heard any station do that before.

In the living room they had finished their food and were sipping on coffees.

'Good afternoon, son. Good sleep? You remember Mrs Hickey.'

'Call me Kate.'

'Okay, Kate.' I shoved my hands into the pockets of my slacks.

'Help yourself to a sandwich,' Tate said.

I slouched over to the kitchen and pulled out a plate from the cupboard.

'Kate and I are on our way to the car lot. She's going to see what kind of a deal we can give her on a new ride.'

'I'm sure it will be a good one,' I muttered.

'What?' Tate asked.

Kate didn't notice it but the menacing tone in his voice was unmistakable to me.

'I hear you had a good day at Huntington yesterday,' she said. 'I love the beach.'

My mouth was full of sandwich so I didn't answer. Tate darkened. I nodded at Kate.

'We'll have to take you grunion hunting when they're running. You'll love that.'

'What are grunion?' Tate asked.

'You don't know what grunion are? They're tiny fish that come up on shore to lay their eggs during the full moon. You aren't allowed to catch them with anything but your hands. They're squiggly and slippery and fast. It's so much fun.'

Fun for humans, not so fun for the fish, I thought.

'Sounds groovy,' Tate said.

Kate stifled a laugh with her hand. 'Hymie, you're going to have to tone down that beatnik lingo if you want to be a good salesman.'

Tate was taken aback. 'What's wrong with the way I talk?'

'The way you "twoak"?' She laughed. 'You want to relate to as many customers as you possibly can. The more generic you are in the way you dress and talk, the more people can relate to you and the more they'll be open to what you want to sell them. Trust me, I know; I used to work in advertising.' Tate looked confused. 'Lose that accent,' she stooped and grabbed him by the tie, 'or it will distract your clients.'

I cackled as I cleaned up my plate. Kate smiled, looked at me for a long time and then slowly wiped the corner of her mouth. 'Why don't you join us?' she asked.

Now it was my turn to be surprised. If she was flirting with my dad then why invite me? I couldn't answer that question. She seemed genuine, she made me laugh and of course there was the Sandra Dee thing.

'Sure, okay, why not?' I said.

'Swell.'

Tate's shoulders relaxed and he grinned. We left the apartment and hopped into Kate's black-and-white '59 Ford Fairlane. It was in good shape, inside and out – I couldn't figure out why she wanted to change it.

When we got to the car lot, Charlie greeted us. He acted like he had only seen us the day before. He called Kate 'honey' and me 'sport' and slapped Tate on the back more than once. He asked Kate questions about price range, look and colour. He was a smooth one, all right; a true professional. I could see that my dad could learn a lot about selling cars from him.

Kate stopped him in his tracks. 'Look Charlie, thanks. I appreciate your help, but Hymie is my salesman.'

'Sure.' Charlie smiled but it was plastic. He turned to Tate. 'Let me know if you need any help, buddy.'

He slapped Tate on the back and walked away.

This was my first time in the showroom. My eyes darted from one sleek surface to the next. A brand-new car is like a piece of candy. If you get a half dozen or more in one place it's like a Whitman sampler or a tray of Fabergé eggs. They shine bright and smell untouched … they're irresistible. But, one car stood out above the rest for me. It was displayed on a raised, circular platform under lights in the window facing the street. The lines were flowing and aerodynamic, which went against the trend for boxier-looking cars that year. This one was wide at the front and narrower behind, like a bull or an Olympic swimmer. The hood swept to a point and the trunk was flat across the back without any detailing. Every single form, every transition was perfect. To stand next to it was to hear music – rock 'n' roll music, no less. It was white and mysterious and I wanted it more than I had ever wanted any object in my life.

Kate walked up behind me and lightly put her hand on my shoulder. 'It's gorgeous, isn't it?'

There was very little that could have distracted me from the excitement of that car, but her touch did it. 'Yes, ma'am.'

'You don't have to be formal with me, Jack.' She didn't move her hand from my shoulder. I shuddered like her flesh was electrifying. 'I think I'll take it.'

'You mean you're going to buy this? Are you serious? '

'Yes, of course. I like it, I can afford it and life is short.' She signalled to Tate, who was by the office talking to Charlie. They walked over. Charlie had his hands tucked into the pockets of his sports slacks.

'This is the one I want, Hymie,' Kate said.

'The Stingray?' Charlie said. Without missing a beat he added, 'A fine choice.'

'Groov– I mean,' Tate caught himself. 'I agree. It's an excellent choice.'

'Only this is my – our – floor model and it has a standard transmission,' Charlie said. 'You know there are all kinds of extras you can order. If you give us a week or two we can get you ...'

She cut him off. 'I don't care. I want to drive it away today.'

'It has a stick shift. Wouldn't you prefer a Powerglide automatic?'

'No thank you. I'm perfectly comfortable with a stick. Butch, my husband, insisted that I learn to use one. Besides, Hymie is my salesman,' she said with arched eyebrows. Charlie kept smiling. His neck pushed harder against his starched collar, he kept his lips closed and the corners of his eyes didn't crinkle. I covered my mouth with my hand. I wasn't sure what might come out of it and I didn't want to embarrass Charlie.

After Kate and Tate were out the door Charlie grabbed me by my shirtsleeve. 'How was the beach?' He careened his neck around the corner to gape out the window at them.

'It was great.' I paused. 'Did you say anything to Tate?'

'About what, sport?' he was hardly listening.

'About spending time together.'

'Nah, Kate said something at drinks the other night, though.' He darted behind the door when Tate looked back.

The ride home wasn't very comfortable for me. I had to sit between Tate's legs. My knees were jammed up against the dashboard and Kate wasn't that hot at shifting gears, but I didn't care. She promised she would take me to the beach in the Stingray sometime and she was true to her word – I have to give her that. It was an important day. Tate had made his first sale, we had some cash and, most significantly, Kate and I became friends.

Christmas came up fast and the nights got cold. I swear to God, it never felt that cold back east. Nothing – the apartment, the clothes – nothing was designed for bad weather. It seeped in everywhere. In the morning I had to bundle up with a scarf and cap, but by ten I was down to a T-shirt. It was crazy. I learned never to wash the cars in the car lot first thing in the morning otherwise my fingers would be numb until noon.

We didn't celebrate Chanukah or Christmas but I had cash – thanks to my new job – and I wanted to buy Tate a present. One day at work, when Tate was gone, I asked Charlie for advice.

'I don't know, sport,' he seemed distracted. 'He seems to get everything he wants.'

'What do you mean?'

'Nothing. Forget it. Now, let me see …' he rubbed his hands together. 'I got it. Grant Green has a new LP record out called

Idle Moments. I heard some tracks from it down at Gothold's Music a couple of days ago and it swings. I'm sure he'll dig it.'

'Thanks, Charlie. Oh, man, that's perfect!' I was about to run out the door when Charlie stopped me.

'One thing, sport.' He slid his hands into his pockets and dropped his chin – which made him look more serious than he ever was. 'Has Mrs Hickey been coming around to your place lately?' 'She never seems to be in her apartment these days.' He tried to say it casually. I could see his forehead starting to fold together like corrugated iron – not much – but enough to expose how absorbed he was with what I might say. What he was feeling was as plain as Kansas. I almost laughed but it wouldn't have amused him. Nothing was going on with them anyway, so what did it matter?

'Kate? Yeah. She's around a lot.'

He nodded. 'I see. Okay, thanks. See you tomorrow.'

I headed towards Gothold's Record Emporium, next to the MonteVista movie theatre, but as soon as I left Charlie I started to wonder myself if something was sparking with Tate and Kate. I mean, he was with her more than he was with Charlie – supposedly his best friend – and she was over all the time. The way she lounged around, how relaxed Tate was around her – it was all adding up. I walked faster. By the time I got to Gothold's I was almost running.

7

TATE GAVE ME TICKETS to the opening Dodgers game at the new stadium in Chavez Ravine. We never made it – I was in hospital by then.

He also gave me a framed photograph of Mutti. It was the one where she was standing in front of Niagara Falls but it was blown up to a full eight-by-ten. It was none too clear, but it didn't matter.

I looked at him. I could hardly talk. 'This is my favourite photo of Mutti.'

'I figured. I noticed the way you looked at the snapshot in the family photo album after she …'

'Thanks,' I said and put it on my night stand.

He bent his head and grinned. 'You know, I wish we could have …' he screwed up his face and rubbed his chin. He had a bit of stubble and I could hear the rough scraping sound. 'I mean, if we'd had more time …' he slowly rocked his head like he was listening to a soft beat. He winced again. Finally he waved it away. 'Forget it.'

I sighed. 'What, Tate?'

'Never mind.'

'What – do you need a drink to say it?'

He flinched before his eyes came up to mine hot and hard.

'You little *drek*.'

I didn't know what he was saying so I just ignored it. 'Just tell me. Talk to me, for God's sake.'

'You don't make it easy, kid. I'm doing everything I can for you, you know. You should be grateful we –'

I cut him off. '*Grateful*? Grateful for what? Grateful you dragged me away from everything? Grateful I'm alone here, bored out of my gourd? Grateful you're out all the time, getting drunk, probably balling Kate?'

He slapped me. It wasn't hard, but it stung, and it shocked me and it felt like the first real thing between us since Mutti died.

Through blurred eyes I saw him raise his arm again. Black pits opened up where his pupils had been. I braced myself for the next blow. I waited but it never came. He put his arm down. He pointed at me. 'Don't you dare say that about Kate.' He put down his hand, blinked several times and rubbed the palm of his hand. 'It's not like that with Mrs Hickey. How could you think that? I couldn't … not now. We're just friends, good friends. She's a lady. Show some goddamned respect.'

I rubbed my cheek.

He wiped his hands on his pants and stood up.

'Happy holiday,' I mumbled, as he walked out the door. If he heard me he didn't show it.

Later that night I was reading a new book I found at the library called *Planet of the Apes* by a French guy named Pierre Boulle. Dave 'The Hullabalooer' Hull was beginning his show on KRLA. The first song up was *Runaway* by Dell Shannon. I gazed at the photo of Mutti. The lyrics drew me in … *what went wrong with a love that was so strong* … and something ripped open inside of me that I had tried to keep closed. My gut tightened and my breathing got shaky. Dell's falsetto distracted me slightly from the tears gathering in my eyes, but as soon as I heard the last line of the song I touched my cheek and sobbed.

The Barkers, especially Mrs Barker, were our friendliest neighbours outside of Charlie and Kate. She often brought us baking – cookies and stuff – and always knew where to go for the best bargains on anything under the sun.

She had to pick up her lesson plans from San Sebastiano High before the end of the semester. She offered to take me down to register. As we drove to school she asked me, 'How are you settling in? Have you acclimatised yet?'

'I beg your pardon?'

She smiled, 'Have you gotten used to the difference in weather?'

'I like that it's so warm, but I miss things, too, you know. We used to have snowball fights until the snow got too dirty or slushy, we went ice-skating at the Rockefeller Centre – things like that.'

'I can imagine.' We drove in silence, but it didn't feel uncomfortable. 'And your father? He seems to see a bit of Mrs Hickey, is that right?'

'Yes, ma'am.'

'Humph. Well, I'm sure that is good for both of them.' Her lips, which she held like pressed paper, relaxed. 'What about the dust? My father was originally from back east, Pennsylvania, and he complained that he couldn't believe how dusty California was.'

I laughed. 'Yes, ma'am, it sure is.' The colour of my snot was now brown, but I kept that to myself. 'I can't believe how big the sky is. In the city – especially in the winter – the sun would shine for about an hour at midday and then it would be hidden by buildings for the rest of the day.'

'The open air is good for you – or it should be – with all this air pollution I'm sure it's doing more harm than good.' She turned into the driveway of San Sebastiano Memorial High School.

'Wow. It's so modern.'

'The building is three years old. The old school was built in the '20s, but it was too small for all of the students coming from the new tract houses going up everywhere.' She parked the car. I got out and opened her door for her. 'Thank you, Jackson. A young man with good manners is a rare thing, I'm afraid. Be warned – you will be ridiculed by your peers.'

'Yes, ma'am.'

'I am sorry to say it would be wise to lose the "ma'am", also.'

'Yes, ma'am.'

She smiled and steered me towards the administration office.

One of the secretaries got to her feet when we walked in. She was a large woman – as tall as me – enveloped in a lively floral dress. She greeted Mrs Barker and threw me a smile so big I liked her instantly. The other two secretaries nodded and smiled, but didn't stop tapping on their typewriters.

'Jackson, dear, this is Mrs Brennan,' Mrs Barker said. 'She is the head secretary of the school.

'Pleased to meet you, Jackson. Welcome to San Sebastiano High, the best little school in California.'

Most of the paperwork was easy enough, until it came to choosing classes.

'Excuse me, Mrs Brennan, but do I have to take art?'

'It's a compulsory subject for all students in their first semester.'

'Can't I take music, or something else? I know a lot about art and I really don't want to do it, with all due respect.'

'I understand, young man. I didn't particularly like it when I was in school, either. I could never draw. Anyway, it's only for one semester and I'm sure you'll enjoy it. Your teacher is a nice young man named Mr Talbot. Mind you, he has some wild ideas.'

'My dad won't be pleased, but ... okay, I guess, if I have to.'

After so long I couldn't wait for school to start; anything to get away from the boredom and Tate. I had a certain idea about what was going to happen. I knew I was going to get an education – but as it turned out it wasn't the one I expected.

I got to school early the first day and hung around trying to look like I was relaxed. It was damn cold and I stood leaning against some railing at the edge of the quad, shifting from foot to foot and blowing into my hands. Everyone else looked confident and comfortable to me. The girls squealed and huddled together. The guys hardly looked at each other and spoke even less. Every so often you might hear a laugh or someone was shoved. One group had a football and they passed it back and forth lazily.

At eight-thirty we were directed to the gymnasium, which served as the school's assembly hall. I recognised a guy in a burgundy letterman jacket. It was Mr Lost Cause from the swimming pool. I barely recognised him in school clothes. I almost went over, but checked myself. He didn't know me from Adam.

I took a good look at the rest of his gang to see if the other two – the brother and sister – were with him. I spotted the brother eventually, standing halfway across the quad with three guys with black rimmed glasses, slide rulers attached to their belts and plastic pen guards in their shirt pockets. It had to be the science, math and audio-visual mob. The sister was nowhere to be seen.

The gym was the largest room I had ever been in. The ceiling was at least three-storeys high and the bleachers could seat all two thousand students. The sound inside was terrific. The school's marching band was playing as we entered, and the hard walls echoed mercilessly. The bleachers were sectioned off into four quadrants, each with a banner above reading 1964, 1965, 1966 or 1967. My group – the freshmen – was farthest from the podium and the band, for which I was grateful.

The feeling in the gym was electric. It reminded me of a Disney nature movie I had seen once of bees swarming in a hive. There was a movement at the front of the hall, next to the band. The cheerleaders and the school mascot flailed their arms to the rhythm of the trombone. I squinted hard and saw that one of the cheerleaders was the sister.

When we were seated and the band finished the USC Trojans fight song, a skinny middle-aged man with an enormous bald head and wire-rimmed glasses walked up to the microphone.

'On behalf of the Board of Trustees and the staff I want to welcome you …' he began.

I tuned out and scanned the mob. Everybody was quiet and attentive. In front of every section of the bleachers there were a couple of teachers sitting in folding chairs, facing the students.

'Spring term is when you need to keep focused and try your mightiest …'

'We expect the very best from you ...'

'I am sure that 1964 is going to be the best year ever for San Sebastiano ...'

'So I am going to ask you to bow your heads in remembrance of our slain president.'

Almost everyone did. Now, I loved the president as much as anyone, but it had been nearly two months. I didn't stop and silently remember Mutti every waking moment of the day, yet the president was being mentioned in almost every conversation. On that day, I sensed that something else was going on. All this reverence wasn't really about poor old Jack Kennedy, rotting away in his grave, but about something else.

The easiest way to chat to a total stranger without offending them or feeling awkward is to talk about the goddamn weather. It's not just small talk, it's a way of saying, 'I don't intend to hurt you.' This was the same thing. All this talk about the president had already started to lose its real meaning, but everyone was sincerely following along. I was clearly out of sync, but it felt okay.

Mr Madison, my new principal, finished his speech. The vice principal, Mr Cannon, stood and told us to line up in alphabetical order so we could collect our class schedules. I hadn't talked to anyone. Then I met Ray.

8

AFTER THE BULLSHIT ASSEMBLY, the freshmen signed up for classes. A cocky little bastard poked me hard from behind.

'Where you from, Jack?'

I half-turned towards him. He knit his brows and tilted his head back and to the side. I guessed his stance was supposed to intimidate but he was such a runt it just seemed funny. 'How did you know my name?' I stuck out my hand. 'I'm Jackson, Jackson Ryder, but my friends call me Jack. I just moved here from New York.'

'Nu Yawk? That's cool.' We shook hands. 'I'm Ray Rodriguez, your local *vato loco*.'

'Spanish?'

'*Chingado*, no, man. I'm Mexican. Can't you tell by how good-looking I am, *ese*?' Ray grinned. 'That's a good sign – a lot of the time gringos go stiff-necked when they hear *caló*, you know, Mexican street lingo. They start drawing their vowels out like they're John Wayne or some honky from the Bible belt.' He nodded, 'I like you, dude, you're all right.'

I grinned. It was good to be talking to someone my own age. I wasn't a chattermouth but it had been a long time. I told Ray where I lived, about my job and my dad. I was taller than him by almost a head. He made fun of my freckles and pale skin.

'*Ese*, man, you are white – even for a white dude. You're like a ghost – Ghost Ryder, yeah man, that's good.'

It stuck.

'Hey, *ese*, what classes you taking?' I told him. When I mentioned art he exclaimed, 'Suavé, *ese*, I can show you the ropes. That's my favourite class, man.'

The rest of the morning went fast – figuring out where my classes were, trying to carry a shitload of books, sorting out a locker and being introduced as the new student from New York at the start of every damn class. A few people approached me and introduced themselves, like Scotty Cisco in history, but Ray was the first friend I made … and my first rival.

By lunchtime it was about seventy degrees. I stuffed my jacket and sweater into my new locker and went to the quad. Someone called my name from a distance. Ray sat under a sycamore tree with a couple of guys.

'Sit down, *ese*, and meet my cousins.'

'Your cousins?'

'Yeah, man. I got *familia* everywhere. This is my *primo carnale*, my first cousin, Carlos – Carlos Quinto.'

'Hey.'

Carlos nodded as he chomped down on a burrito. He was darker than Ray with thick black hair and sideburns. He was wearing an immaculate white T-shirt that contrasted with his rich, dark skin.

'And this *chivo* is Unai Elizalde.' Unai is half Basque, all bastard,' Ray chortled. Unai hit him on the arm.

'Damn you, Unai, that was my good arm. You gave me a

Charley Horse!' Ray waved a fist in Unai's face and they lunged at each other, but lost momentum quickly.

'They been like that since we was kids,' Carlos said, wiping his mouth. 'Don't worry about it.'

'Hey, what you got to eat, Jackson?' Ray asked. 'You got any Oreos?'

'Nah, man. I've got a peanut butter and jelly sandwich, an apple and a banana.'

'*Qué lástima*,' Ray sighed. 'White-man food.'

Then the sister from the pool passed by with a couple of other cheerleaders. She was in uniform but wearing a powder-blue pea coat over her shoulders.

'Hey, Ray, who's that cheerleader in the blue coat?'

'*Híjole*. Aren't you setting your goals a little high, cowboy?'

'No, you don't understand. She swims in my pool.'

'You got a pool?' Unai asked.

'Well, it's not my pool. It's the pool at the apartments where I live.'

'I hear what you're saying, *hombre*, but she's not in your pool now.' He gave a low, scratchy chuckle and the other two joined in.

'Her name is Connie-Jean Templeton,' Carlos said. 'She's a junior and as off limits as they come.'

'I'll say,' Unai agreed. 'Joe Penderecki, *el pendejo*, is warning every sucker away. He's the junior varsity football co-captain, he and that pretty boy, Milt Bryson.'

'I think it's a state educational requirement that every cheerleader dates a football asshole, *ese*.' Ray said, peeking into my lunch bag.

'But she's not into him. Her brother Clovis told me,' Carlos said.

'Connie and Clovis?' I asked.

'They're twins, *guero*, if you couldn't tell.' Ray swiped my apple. 'I'll tell you somethin' though, she's not bad for a *gabacha*.'

'What's that?'

'I'm sorry, man,' Ray raised his hands like I was arresting him.

'It's nothin', Jackson. It used to mean Frenchman but we use it to mean anyone who isn't Mexican.'

'Except maybe *los negros*,' Carlos said.

'You should talk, *hombre*. You're so black I bet your mama was scared by some *mayate* when she was pregnant with you,' Ray said.

Carlos caught him in a stranglehold at the water fountain and dragged him back to the tree.

'Let him go, Carlos. He owes me money,' Unai said. '*No manches, carnale*. It's not worth it. El Cañón will suspend you.'

'*Chingado, carnale*, I almost choked on that apple.'

'Serves you right for stealing it from Jackson.' Unai kicked Ray in the thigh.

'See what I gotta put up with?' Ray looked at me pleadingly. I shook my head.

'So where you from, Jack. The Bronx? Brooklyn?' Unai asked.

'No way, Washington Square, man, Greenwich Village.'

'Any *Chicanos* there?' Ray asked. He went in for my banana but I pulled it away in time.

'*Chicanos*?'

'Mexicans, like us, *ese*.'

'Not that I know of, but there's a lot of different people in a small place. You never know.'

'Know any Mafia gangsters?'

'Don't be such a dumb shit, *carnale,*' Unai hit Ray again. 'What do think this is, the roaring twenties?'

'*Wáchale, primo*, I'm warning you.'

Ray rubbed his arm.

'*Puro pedo,*' Unai retorted.

I looked at my watch. 'It's been nice to meet you guys, but I gotta go find my next class.'

'*No te apures.* Don't worry. We got art. I'll take you there.' Ray got to his feet. 'We can cruise, you dig?'

'Sure. Great.'

'Solid, Jackson.' He bent over with laughter, then to Carlos and Unai he said, '*Luego, caras de fuegos.*'

'What's that mean, Ray?'

'It's Mexicano rhyming jive, *ese*. *Luego* means later. *Cara de fuego* means ... well, face of fire. It don't make no sense but it rhymes and it's funny.'

Ray swaggered in a way that few people could pull off. His chin was high and each step was deliberate and slow. Every few feet it was 'Ladies', '*Que tal, mescal*?' or 'Hey, what's happening?' He knew everyone.

When he wasn't greeting people, he gave me advice.

'Most of the teachers are okay, *ese*. Some are left over from dinosaur times but no one hits you anymore like the old days. Man, I used to hate that.' He turned to a passing brunette. 'Hey, *muchachita*, be my candy and I'll be your cane.'

He rocked his hips a couple of times. She scooted past and didn't look back. It cracked me up.

'You gotta watch out for El Cañón, Vice Principal Cannon, man. He's badass. He don't like me. It's because I'm Mexican.' He called to three passing girls: '*Mamacitas,* I must be dead 'cause I'm seeing angels.'

They giggled and he growled.

'He's a bigot?'

'Maybe, *ese,* I don't know. You got nothin' to worry about, *guero*, with a white-bread name like Ryder. What are you, a Mick? That's cool. Half my cousins are Irish.'

'You probably wouldn't believe me if I told you. What's a *guero*?'

'A white guy, you know, a paleface.'

'You got a lotta words for whites.'

'Well, there's a lot of you.'

No one was in the art room except for the teacher and a chubby kid helping him put out supplies. The teacher looked like he was fresh out of school himself. His hair was thick and brown, but he didn't have any Brylcreem or anything on it. He was wearing a tie, as all teachers did, but he was wearing it with a faded blue work shirt and his sleeves were rolled up.

Ray took me up to the two of them. 'Excuse me, Mr Talbot, may I introduce Jackson Ryder, a new student from the great state of Nu Yawk. We will both be in your class this term.'

'Ryder, yes. I knew you were starting today. Don't you know Kate Hickey?'

'Yes, sir. Kate – I mean, Mrs Hickey – lives in our apartment complex.'

'She said you were a good-looking kid.'

I could feel the blood rush to my face.

'You're beet red, *ese*,' Ray chortled.

I changed the subject. 'Look, sir, I'm not sure what I think about your subject. I'm just warning you. Nothing personal, but I wouldn't be here if I didn't have to be.'

'Ooh, that's harsh, *ese*.'

I fidgeted. 'Besides, I don't think my dad's too keen on it.'

'Why not?'

'I don't know. I used to draw a bit, but …' I shrugged, 'maybe he thought I did it too much.'

Talbot sat down and leaned back in his chair. 'Tell me, Jackson, who did you do your art for? Your dad, or you?' I didn't answer him. 'Okay, well whatever the problem is it doesn't have to come to school. I won't go against your father's feelings or wishes, of course, but I do have an obligation to do my job. I happen to think it's the greatest thing a human being can do.' His voice actually quivered a little. 'Just keep an open mind and draw. At least while you are here, at school and learning. This is your sanctuary.'

He grinned and patted me on the back, 'Take a seat wherever you want. And Rodriguez, I'm happy you're back. You've got a lot of potential, my friend. You could even be the best artist this school has ever produced, but you got to try to make it to every class this semester, okay? You're the only one who misses out, buddy.'

'I'm sure I won't be so sick this time, *jefe* – I mean, sir.'

'Right.'

'He's pretty cool,' I said under my breath as we walked to the back of the room.

'He's solid.'

'For a *gabacho*?'

'*Simón, guero, simón*, that's right. And, he doesn't bust your balls, you know what I mean?'

I did know.

'Why are we all the way back here?'

'This is where I sit, *ese*. The door is there, the heater is right behind me and if I get drowsy the Wolf Man won't notice.'

That suited me fine. The back of the class was where you sit if you wanted to be invisible.

'The Wolf Man?'

'Mr Talbot, *ese*. Lawrence Talbot, like the Wolf Man from the movie. Isn't that crazy?'

Two Asian girls came in. They sat quietly together at the front of the room and pulled out their workbooks. Ray didn't offer anything about them except their names, Ming Li and Sing Li – twins.

Three more girls came in, giggling, and went up to Mr Talbot. One of them was kind of cute. Their conversation sounded stupid: 'My new pedal-pushers … she was sooo … what did you get?' – that kind of business.

Mr Talbot was polite, but he kept looking up at the clock. The bell rang and the door spilled over with bodies and books. Everyone seemed to know where to sit except for two guys, who argued over who was going to sit next to this blonde girl. While they debated, a black-haired girl slipped into the seat and grinned up at them. She looked familiar. The boys shuffled away. The taller of the two settled down next to me. He had coarse blonde hair and tanned skin.

'Hey, whaddya know, daddy-o?' he greeted me.

Before I could answer there was a loud handclap.

'Here we go,' Mr Talbot said. 'Welcome to Art 102. If it doesn't say that on your schedule for Monday at one, you don't belong here.'

There was general tittering. The shorter guy who had missed out on sitting next to the cute girl got up and edged his way out the door. 'See ya later, dude,' the guy next to me yelled out. The rest of the class laughed. Mr Talbot crossed his arms.

'First thing, get out the notebook you're going to use as your art journal. It's right there, Simpson, on your stationery list. If you don't have a notebook, use a sheet of paper and glue it into your book when you get one. That means you, Rodriguez.' When he was convinced everyone was ready, he continued, 'I want you to answer the questions I'm going to write on the blackboard. Write them as headings. Put the date first. You'll have ten minutes to write and then we'll discuss them. Are there any questions?'

Ray put up his hand. 'Mr Talbot, sir, when are we going to draw?'

'Don't worry, Rodriguez, soon enough. This is important, trust me.' He turned around and wrote:

1) What is art?

2) What creative thing(s) did I do over the break?

The questions were so simple I was disappointed. Looking around the room, I wasn't the only one. But being the new guy, I wasn't going to *putz* out on the first task.

What is art? What is art? I had lived with it my whole life. I could tell it anywhere. I could practically *taste* it … but define it? I glanced at Ray. He sat with his arms crossed, stared at the ceiling, closing one eye and then the other.

I wrote down: *Art is the best that can humanly be done.* Then I added: *It is the visible soul of mankind.*

By the time I'd come up with my first answer, the ten minutes was up. I scribbled down that I'd done some drawings over the break.

'Now, we're going to use a technique called 'thinking up' or 'brainstorming', which was developed for advertising more than ten years ago. These are the rules. One – no criticism. Two – you are all to contribute at least one idea. Three – it doesn't matter how crazy it is.' A few people laughed. 'Also, I want you to yell them out. You don't have to raise your hand. I'll write down everything I hear.'

Mr Talbot turned to the board and hunched down like he was getting ready to run a race.

'Okay,' he said, holding his piece of chalk up to the blackboard. 'Anything.' The silence continued. 'Rodriguez, what do you have?'

'*Chingado.*' Ray muttered. Then, 'Art is cool, sir.'

Mr Talbot wrote it down. Ray relaxed his shoulders, cocked his eyebrows and nodded around the room.

'Pretty,' one of the pedal-pusher girls said.

'Creative,' a dark-haired guy in a plaid vest called out. The words started to come fast, and Mr Talbot wrote them all down.

I called out, 'The best that can be done.' Mr Talbot broke the chalk, but he didn't stop. The stray shard rolled away from the board and under the desk. When we finished, there were twenty-five words on the board. *Confusing, beautiful, important, hard, crazy, daring, holy, fake, craft, clever, scam, challenging …*

Mr Talbot brushed the chalk dust from his hands.

'You see?' He looked at the board. 'I don't have to teach you much at all. Everything you said is true.' He sat on a tall stool at the front of the room. 'Art is all these things and more. It's constantly changing. It's new and timeless at the same time. Like right now, I know a few artists that are trying to do something the LA area has never seen before. They're trying to shake things up. Art does that too. It invites people to look at the world in a different way.' There wasn't a word from the class. 'I'm going to show you a few slides that make the point. Billy – the lights, please.'

The kid who had been helping Mr Talbot set up earlier jumped up and hit the light switch. He walked over to the slide projector and activated it. The fan whirred and the pull-down screen at the end of the room lit up.

'*Ese*, this is what I was talking about,' Ray whispered. 'After lunch a *vato* needs a little *siesta*. You can't do this up front, man.'

He rolled his windbreaker into a ball, rested his arms on it and placed his chin on top. From further away it would look like he was staring intently at the screen, but I could see his eyes close.

Billy dropped the first slide into the breach and slid it into place. The screen went dark, and then nine cartoon eyes stared out from a jumble of angular shapes in yellow, orange and tan. There were sniggers from the class when people recognised naked figures. Steel-grey areas like shards of glass separated the forms into stiff, robot-like figures. At the bottom of the image was a recognisable bowl of fruit – grapes, pear, apple and a slice of melon. I drew in my breath.

'Compare this with what you said.' Mr Talbot pointed at the screen. 'Is it art?' No one answered, 'Does anyone know what this painting is?'

There was shifting in seats and a few whispers, but no one spoke up. I was lost in a memory. I was about seven years old. My hand cradled in the warmth of Mutti's.

I raised my hand. It took a while to catch Mr Talbot's eye, and then when I opened my mouth to speak, he cut me off.

'Hold on a second, Ryder. Rodriguez, are you awake?'

I jabbed Ray with my knee.

'Sure, Mr Talbot. Beautiful, really beautiful.'

Mr Talbot didn't say anything. That was cool.

'Okay, Mr Ryder. Shoot.'

'It's called *The Young Ladies of Avignon* and it's by Pablo Picasso.'

'Yes!' Mr Talbot yelled like I had won a prize on a TV game show. 'By the way, class, Mr Ryder is new to the school. Show him how friendly San Sebastiano High students can be. What else can you tell us, Jackson?'

I wanted to say that every time we went to the museum Mutti and I paused in front of it like it was an alter or a truly beautiful sunset. I always walked away with a sense of satisfaction, a secret shared.

'Nothing,' I said.

Mr Talbot looked briefly like a deflated balloon but then he recovered. 'How do you know this work?'

'I've seen it … a few times, at MoMA.'

'The Museum of Modern Art in New York?'

I nodded in the dark. 'That's good, Jackson. You've been fortunate.'

'Yes, sir.'

'*Les Demoiselles d'Avignon* is the name in French,' Mr Talbot told us. 'Picasso is Spanish but he has lived in France all his adult life. He painted this when he was the same age as I am right now, twenty-six years old. What you are looking at is the beginning of modern art. The very first painting that changed the way we look at the world. This is the artistic equivalent to Einstein's theory of relativity. It's the Wright brothers at Kitty Hawk. It's the atomic bomb of art.'

'It's a bomb all right,' the tall guy next to me said under his breath.

'I heard that, Hornsby.'

'Yes, sir, Wol – I mean, Mr Talbot.'

Mr Talbot ignored the disruption. 'My point is, people, keep an open mind. All of you. I want you to make a special effort when you see something you don't like. Stop and look without judging. And remember what's on the blackboard.' He pointed at the words we had brainstormed. 'See how they relate.'

He showed more slides, including Méret Oppenheim's fur cup and a Mark Rothko I recognised from MoMA too. But it was *Les Demoiselles* that stuck in my mind – the painting and my mother's warm touch. I breathed deeply.

'These are the images of our time. But if you had lived in medieval Europe, you might have thought that the radical realism of *this* image was disgusting.' Billy flicked the slide to Giotto's *The Betrayal of Christ*. 'The drama, the modelling of the form and that outrageous yellow cloak on Judas were as confusing to them as *Les Demoiselles* is to you.'

'Or consider this.' The slide changed, 'It's an Ancient Egyptian bas-relief from about 1365 BC. It shows the pharaoh Akhenaton and his queen on cushioned chairs playing with their three children. See the rays of the sun and the hieroglyphs. Looks innocent enough, doesn't it? But believe it or not, this style was considered so outrageous that it contributed to the downfall of the pharaoh, his religion and his capital city, and even led to his death.'

I could hardly see the slide, it was like looking through frosted glass.

'So, what's my point? That what seems crazy now will be commonplace in the future. Keep your eyes open and be the first on your block to see.'

The lights went up. I sniffed and wiped the moisture from my cheeks.

'What creative things did you do over the break? Let's start with Hornsby and go clockwise.'

This was the guy next to me; the first surfer I had ever seen up close.

'I made tikis for my surfing buddies,' Luke Hornsby said. He pulled out a wooden carving about the length of his thumb from inside his shirt. It looked like a miniature version of an Easter Island stone head. It was threaded onto a string and stained a deep red-brown with rhinestone eyes.

There were murmurs of praise and a few cries of, 'Can you make me one too?'

One by one, everyone told the class what they'd done during vacation. A few were learning the guitar, piano or violin. Most of us had done some drawing. One dark-haired girl across the room kept looking at me and smiling. Something was vaguely familiar about her but I couldn't pin it down. Had she come to the pool at some time? Maybe I saw her at the supermarket or the movies. Then, to my surprise, she gave a tiny wave. I looked at Ray. He was cleaning his fingernails. I looked at the guy on the other side, Luke. He was leaning back trying to balance on the two rear feet of his chair. His eyes were turned to the ceiling. I looked back at the girl and was convinced she was waving at me. No girl had paid attention to me since that skank at the pool in Blythe. My heartbeat raised and I felt lighter. But, who was she? She hadn't said what creative thing she had done yet. I looked at Ray, but decided to wait to hear her name. Finally it was her turn. Dos Osos – of course, Maggie and Joe's daughter, Maria. I didn't recognise her because she looked way different. Her eyes weren't swollen any more. She did look mostly like her mother, but when she smiled I could see Joe in the way her teeth flashed and in the dimples on both of her cheeks.

'My mother took me to the Pasadena Art Museum and Bowers Museum in Santa Ana.'

'Great. My friend Walter Hopps runs the Pasadena. What did you see?'

'There were some paintings by an artist named Ed Ru –'

'Ed Ruscha. Yes, I know him. We did a design class at Chouinard Art Institute together.' He turned to the class. 'Ed Ruscha is one of the new artists I was talking about. He's looking around and painting things from this world, from this time, now. Very good, Maria.'

When it was Ray's turn, he said, 'I watched TV.'

A few girls giggled.

'No, that's fine. Television is moving visual images – like movies. Most of it doesn't strive to be art, not yet, but it's a young medium. In the future it will be as artistically significant as good movies, maybe even painting. Anything else?'

Ray squirmed. 'I did some drawing.'

'Of course, and we all know how good they must be. Bring some in so you can share them with us.' Ray beamed. 'What about you, Ryder?'

'Me?' I looked around the room, but I could see most people had lost interest. It was a big class, about thirty, 'I did some drawing, sir.'

'Good,' was all he said.

After class, I tried to catch up with Maria. She went out the back door. I had to scramble around the whole class. Outside, the hallways were a sea of ponytails, bangs and pomaded short-back-and-sides haircuts, with the odd ducktail thrown in. I spotted Maria's raven cascade not far ahead of me moving towards the quad.

Almost at that exact moment I noticed three boys heading

in her direction. They may have had on fewer clothes than the bully toughs at my school in New York, but the swagger was the same. All three wore dirty white T-shirts, filthy jeans and scuffed cowboy boots. The leader, a plump sausage, had a flat-top haircut and a checked shirt on – completely unbuttoned – that flapped behind him like a flag in the wind. The crowd parted for them or were shoved to the side if they were too slow. The leader's pig-like eyes were scanning the crowd, not like he was looking for a friend, but for prey. He reminded me of the stray tomcats that stalked sparrows and pigeons in Washington Square at sunset.

His eyes fixed on Maria. She wasn't in his path, but he veered towards her with definite intent. He looked over his shoulders at his two goons and his thick lips twisted into a smirk. He looked her up and down. His face screwed up like he smelled three-day-old fish. He lowered his head, set his mouth and raised his elbows out like short wings.

I saw what was about to happen, I connected the dots, saw the arc. I didn't make a choice, nothing as cerebral as that. Maria was pretty much the only person I knew at that school before that day. I liked her parents. Strangely, Mutti came to mind. A geyser of hot effervescence bubbled up from deep inside of me, frothy and stinging on my skin. Everything went white and when I jolted back to reality I stood astride this asshole, who was bawling his eyes out. The entire hallway was laughing and cheering. I looked at the two other punks. They looked around. One started laughing, cautiously at first, then openly. I thought the other one was going to step up but he looked at me then melted back beyond the crowd. I could still feel my muscles tightening and relaxing. My breath was short. I wiped my forehead, blinked and grinned.

Maria was standing there, stunned.

'Remember me? Jackson, Jackson Ryder?' She kept her eyes on the ground. 'Are you alright?' she nodded, then she was engulfed by other girls from art class.

For a second I tried to figure out what had happened. Maria looked back and said, 'Thank you.'

I hadn't consciously done anything. It was like being thanked for breathing regularly or for growing your fingernails.

A clamp-like force came down on my shoulder. 'Come with me, young man.'

'Vice-principle Cannon,' Maria exclaimed.

'Are you alright, child?' he asked her.

'Yes. Jackson saved me.'

'Saved you from what?'

'Buster was going to hit me.'

'Did he touch you?'

'No.'

'So, if I understand correctly; Master Nicholls did not touch you nor did he touch this young man …'

'Jackson, sir, Jackson Ryder. I'm new.'

'Indeed. So you attacked Master Nicholls.'

'Who's Master Nicholls, sir?'

'Buster,' Maria explained.

He picked up Buster by the scruff. 'Come with me,' he told both of us.

Buster Nicholls. What a shithead *putz*. But, I'll tell you, I should thank him. I made my mark that day by knocking him down.

Don't get me wrong, I wasn't a hero. It happened in a blur. If

I had thought, I would have been too scared to move a muscle.

I didn't like fighting but a part of growing up is finding that place where you can stand tall. Buster gave me that. And it worked okay … for a while.

'Wait outside my office, Master Ryder, while I have a brief word with Master Nicholls.' Buster went a pale green tone under his freckles. I sat at the door of the vice-principal's office. I wrung my hands like it was freezing outside and tried to hear what was going on through the door but it was useless. Buster finally came out with his head bowed, shuffling like a convict in a chain gang. He threw me a pathetic glance, cocked his head towards the open maw of Cannon's office and headed silently along the corridor. My stomach headed somewhere between the floorboards and the water table. My knees felt like rusted hinges but I willed them to unfold.

The furniture in the office was all mismatched, although every piece was some shade of brown. There were three standard-issue institutional chairs, hard and solid as the day they were made, a big but simple oak desk and a leather desk chair with brass tacks. Mr Cannon was standing by the window looking out onto the quad, camouflaged by all the dreary tones. The light behind him caught the scattered fine hairs on his head and the dust in the air.

He turned around and fixed me with his milky-grey eyes. 'Please sit down, Master Ryder.' I eased into one of the straight-backed school chairs. He settled down into his chair and stretched his arms along the length of the desk. He looked down at an open manila file. I could see the liver spots through his thin, close-cropped hair. 'You are a transfer from PS 41 in Greenwich Village, New York City, is that correct?'

'Yes, sir.'

He looked up, brought his hands together and interweaved his thick fingers. 'So, is it the custom at …' he looked down at the file again, 'Public School 41 to attack unsuspecting, defenceless, fellow students that you do not even know?' He raised one eyebrow.

'Sir, he was going for Maria. I could see it in his eyes.'

'Come now, Master Ryder, why would he do that?'

'Because she's an … an Indian?'

He sat back in the chair. It creaked. He put two fingers to his thin lips and tapped a couple of times. 'And what business is that of yours?'

It sounded like Ray might be right. My breathing calmed. 'Because my dad and I know her parents. They're our friends, and it's not right.' I said this in as confident a voice as I could muster.

'Master Nicholls is not unknown to me. In fact, he has warmed the seat that you occupy right now more than once.' He considered me a long time before he opened his mouth again. 'I am inclined to accept the veracity of your explanation. It is in accord with Miss Dos Oso's account and fits, what they call in the pulp novels, Master Nicholls's MO. Because you are new to this institution I am going to let you off with a warning this time, young man.' He sat forward and pointed at me. 'However, be forewarned that I run a tight ship, and I mean water tight. If you have occasion to be my guest again, you will wish that corporal punishment was still sanctioned. Because, by God, I will make your life such a torment that even the worst of *Gehinnam* will seem like a tropical holiday by comparison. Do I make myself clear?'

'Yes, sir.' I shifted in my seat and bit my lip. 'Actually … no sir. What's *Gehinnam*, sir?'

He sat forward in his chair and opened the file in front of him again. Without tilting his head up, he looked over the top of his glasses at me and replied, 'I suggest you ask your tate, young man,' and dismissed me with a wave.

9

ON MY WAY INTO THE apartment complex that afternoon I saw Connie-Jean and Joe – the sister and Mr Lost Cause – sitting beside the pool. They were still in their school clothes. Joe wasn't any further along in his quest to win over the cheerleader, judging by the way she gripped the arms of her deckchair and avoided eye contact with him.

They looked up at me as I came into view. Connie-Jean's expression didn't change. Joe knitted his eyebrows, but relaxed and went back to talking to Connie-Jean in a low voice. I gave her a close-mouthed smile. I didn't know if either of them lived in the complex, or not. Now that I knew their names, I was curious to find out.

As I reached our apartment I realised how exhausted I was. Getting up early, the excitement and the sheer anger of the afternoon did me in. Tate wouldn't be home for a couple of hours, so I went to my room to take a nap. I lay there awake with the transistor radio playing low and my muscles twitching nervously for about twenty minutes. Finally I got up and stretched. I went out to the living room and peeked between the Venetian blinds. Connie-Jean and Joe were gone. I slumped onto the sofa.

I wasn't there thirty seconds when there was a sharp rap on

the door. I was in my boxers. I sprang up like a jackrabbit.

'Who is it?' I asked through the door, my voice an octave higher than usual.

'Jack, dear? It's me, Kate. Can I come in?'

By that time I was used to her showing up unannounced at any hour.

'Hold on a second.'

I rushed into my bedroom and threw on some slacks and a shirt, but I was in too much of a rush to do up the buttons. I opened the door halfway. She was in a sleeveless yellow dress, and held a full brown-paper grocery bag in each arm.

She didn't say anything at first. I noticed her eyes moved slowly from my face down to my bare chest then down towards my navel. My face went hot. I fumbled to do up the buttons on my shirt. She swallowed and said in an unnaturally chirpy voice, 'Hi, darling. How was your first day at school?'

'Hi Kate. Let me help you.' I unlocked the screen door and took one of the bags.

'I thought I'd make you and your dad dinner tonight. Is that all right?'

'Sure. Swell.'

'I'm not much of a cook, but I can open a can.'

'You gotta be an improvement on my dad; he even burns water.' She giggled.

I put the bag down on the kitchen counter and took the other one from her. She reached into her handbag and pulled out a packet of Benson & Hedges and a gold-plated lighter. I slid the heavy glass ashtray over to her.

'Thanks.' She flicked the lighter and it instantly erupted in a brilliant amber flame. She took a long drag and tilted her head back to direct the smoke above my head. 'So, how did it go?'

'It was good.' I looked into her eyes and decided to take a chance. 'I did this in class.' From between the pages of my math textbook I pulled out a scribble I made of Kate's Corvette while I was supposed to be practising algebra variables. Immediately I regretted showing her. In my excitement I hadn't thought about the implications.

'You made this in art class?'

'No, not quite.' I blinked involuntarily. 'I did it in math class from memory.'

'Oh, Jack, this is really good. Can I see?' She held out her perfect hand.

I handed it over, filled with the satisfaction of pleasing her but mixed with the dread that my father would find out.

'It's amazing. You captured everything, even the antenna in the back and the side-view mirror. I've got to have this. Can I buy it from you?' She reached for her handbag.

'No, no.' I held her hand down over the mouth of her purse. It was the first time I had touched her. I felt the molecules of my torso pop in all directions. 'I couldn't accept anything for this. I want you to have it. It will be a gift – please – but only on one condition.' Reluctantly, I pulled my hand away. 'Under no circumstances tell my dad that I did it.'

'Why not?' She sounded light and sure.

'It's too complicated to explain right now. He just doesn't get it, you know?'

'I'm sure he would be very proud …'

I cut her off. 'Kate, you have to promise me. Please.'

She searched my face.

'Never,' I added.

'Of course, Jack. I promise, I swear.' She smiled, 'Thank you so much for the drawing. I absolutely love it.'

I had dodged an arrow and there was also the unexpected excitement of sharing something intimate with Kate; something hers and mine now, a secret.

'By the way, my art teacher Mr Talbot said to say hello,'

I unpacked the grocery bags. Two cans of Chef Boyardee spaghetti and meatballs, two packets of pasta, cooking oil.

'Larry Talbot?' Kate said casually. 'Oh, that's good. I was hoping you would have him. He's a good guy; an unusual man – like your dad.'

'How do you know him?' I pulled a packet of Oreos out of the second grocery bag.

She hesitated. 'When I worked in advertising he did some freelance design for us. I really liked his work. It was different, you know? Fresh. But we couldn't use him. "Too edgy, not enough popular appeal," at least that's what the creative team said. They were all about a hundred years old.' She scanned the benchtop then peered into the two empty bags. 'Since then we've kept in touch – have drinks occasionally, you know, that kind of thing.'

I held up the cookies. 'You thought of everything.'

'No, darn it, I forgot to get Parmesan cheese.'

'That's okay. I'm not a great fan.'

'Oh. So, you don't like strong cheese, huh? Too stinky?' She chuckled, 'You should expand your horizons; be open to new sensations.'

I wrinkled my nose. 'Yeah, well. There are limits, aren't there.'

'Are there?' She drew on her cigarette. 'What if you had the chance to have an adventure, I mean, a *real* adventure … say, go to the south seas – maybe New Zealand – but you might never be able to come home again. What would you do?'

'That's not fair.'

'What do you mean?'

'It's not a fair question. Do you mean never see my dad again? Never see the US?'

'I don't know. It's a hypothetical question. Okay, how about this? What if you had to choose between being happy or … or losing your eyesight? Which would you choose?'

That was an impossible question to answer. Seeing is everything. How could one be exclusive of the other? 'I don't know.'

'Being safe or feeling real passion?'

'I don't know. Safe, I guess.'

'No!' She grabbed me by the hands, pulled me into the middle of the room and started to dance a mambo. 'Be bold and daring. Take chances if you want to live.'

She pulled me up against her. I could feel her warmth and the soft rise of her breasts on my chest. My nose filled with the rich musk of her being: Chanel Number Five – Mutti's favourite – cigarette smoke and something else; something moist and lush like the smell of cut grass after a spring shower. It was barely distinguishable, but definitely there.

She let me go me as effortlessly as she had captured me, laughing and unaffected.

To my horror I realised I was getting a boner. I had to immediately slouch onto the sofa.

'What's the matter? Are you out of breath? Are you gonna let an old lady tire you out?' Kate said.

My face was a coal furnace. 'No, ma'am. I'm feeling dizzy. Hungry, I guess.'

'Don't call me ma'am. I said I was old, but that makes me feel like I'm a hundred-and-eight. Call me Kate, okay?' She walked over to the counter, picked up the Oreos and sat down next to me, hip to hip. 'Here, eat these slowly. If you start to see sparkly lights, put your head between your knees.' She put her hand on my back, between my shoulder blades, and rubbed slowly. It really didn't help. 'Relax. Breathe deeply.' She rubbed some more then said, 'Oh, darn. My cigarette went out. I'll be right back.'

She went to the kitchen, rummaged around in her purse and finally tipped it upside down. No lighter came out. She stood there tapping her foot.

'I guess it doesn't matter. I was going to quit anyway.'

'Why?' I asked, my head in my hands.

'Didn't you hear the Surgeon General's announcement a couple of weeks ago?'

'Nah. Is he an army general?'

She laughed, but it didn't make me feel bad. 'No, silly, he's the top doctor in the country. He's on the president's cabinet – his chief health advisor.'

'Oh.' This was good. There's nothing like a dose of serious health news to settle a throbbing meatstick. 'What did he say?'

'Only that cigarettes – no, *all* smoking – is bad for you. It can cause emphysema, heart disease and even cancer.'

'Really?' This was very good. My trousers slackened considerably.

'Really.'

'Wow, I wonder if my dad knows that.'

'Yeah, he knows. He, Charlie and I talked about it the other night over drinks.'

'What did he say?'

She shrugged her shoulders. 'He said, "What a drag."' I laughed. 'Charlie said – right out – that it it didn't make any difference to him. He said he had to die of something; it might as well be something he enjoyed. How are you feeling?'

'Good, thanks.' I finished the Oreo and licked my fingers. 'Do you want some help with dinner?'

'No. Don't you worry, honey. Sit there and rest. It's only going to take a minute, anyway.' She studied the instructions on the packet of pasta. 'Make that seven.'

I lay out on the sofa so I could watch her as she worked. She talked the whole time about freedom, choice and making positive changes in her life, Ralph Waldo Emerson and George Eliot who apparently said, 'The strongest principle of growth lies in the human choice.' I made all the appropriate noises but mostly I was just looking at her.

She reminded me of Sandra Dee but that's not the whole story. The truth is, when the movie *Gidget* came out I fell desperately in twelve-year-old love with Sandra Dee. She was so cute with those oversized brown eyes. I wanted to learn to surf, to 'shoot the tube' and 'hang ten'. I wanted to be the Big Kahuna. My awesome performance and skill on a board would overwhelm her and lure her away from Moondoggy.

To my shock, Sandra Dee married Bobby Darin the next year and I was in deepest desolation for weeks.

Lying on the sofa that afternoon, Kate could have been Gidget in the flesh – and she was as unattainable as that adorable divinity in CinemaScope. I had only started high school and Kate was a full-grown woman, and a widow to boot. Besides that, I suspected that she was closer to Tate than a shave with a straight razor. What kind of a disgusting deviant did that make me?

'There's some Jack cheese in the fridge. Should I put that on top?' Kate was wearing my dad's red-and-white chequered barbecue apron, which only made her look cuter. I nodded.

'Did you get Monterey Jack cheese back in New York?' She asked over her shoulder. I shrugged. Her golden hair bobbed back and forth under the kitchen bulbs, like the flame from her lighter. She looked around the living room.

'Do you guys have TV trays?'

I shook my head. 'It's okay, I'll eat at the table.' The aroma of the spaghetti made me leap up.

'You must be feeling better.'

'It smells good.' I flung myself into the mound of sauce-covered pasta like it was sex itself. It wasn't as good as you would get in any restaurant on the East Side of New York; but it satisfied my need to devour something.

Kate sat opposite me with a tumbler of whiskey and water. She ran her forefinger around the rim of the glass slowly. 'Loss is a bitch, isn't it? Pardon my French. The best of us – the most sensitive – can go off the deep end and never make it back.'

That threw me for a loop. I didn't want to talk about Mutti – not with her – so I turned it on her. 'But you've made it back, haven't you?'

She raised her eyebrows and chuckled. I realised what I had done and tried to apologise but she held up her hand. 'Don't worry about it, Jack. You're right, actually.' She topped up the whiskey but didn't bother with the water. 'Butch and I met when I was at high school and he was learning to fly for the old Army Air Force. I was the queen at our school Christmas dance. He was there with a cheerleading friend of mine named Madge. She never talked to me again.' She grinned and took a sip. 'Six months after he got back from Korea we were married and he started testing experimental jets at Edwards Air Force Base in the Mojave Desert.'

'He never told me the expected lifespan of a test pilot was

about a week. One day he couldn't pull out of a controlled dive fast enough. He ejected himself, as per procedure, but the cockpit was upside down. He slammed to the ground with the power of a large-calibre bullet.'

'Kate, I don't need to …'

She held up her palm towards me. 'On the day he was killed, the Cuban Missile Crisis ended. Everybody in the western world was elated, ecstatic. The world wasn't going to end. We were saved. Woohoo! Ironic, isn't it?' She looked beyond me. She had this look when she was unguarded, like the central figure in George Tooker's *The Subway*. Kind of out of place, like a classic Greek sculpture in a laundromat. 'Butch was well insured, though, so I don't have to work again for the rest of my life.'

I wrinkled my forehead. 'I'm sorry.'

A sleepy, syrupy sound bubbled up out of her throat. It took a while for me to realise it was a laugh.

Tate came home just as I finished my dinner. As he said hello to Kate I got up, took my plate to the kitchen sink and made a beeline towards my bedroom.

'Hold on, buddy, aren't you forgetting something?'

'Thanks for the dinner, Kate. If you'll excuse me I've got some homework to do.'

Tate's brow went smooth and I could see the muscles of his jaw flexing. I knew I was being rude to him – not even saying hello – but I also knew he wouldn't call me up on it while Kate was there. 'How was school?' he said in a voice that sounded like a scalpel edge.

'Okay.'

Kate blinked and looked at Tate with the shadow of a smile on her lips, 'Don't worry, Hymie, I'll fill you in. Let the boy do his homework.' She turned to me. 'You're very welcome for the dinner, Jack.' She leaned back so Tate couldn't see and silently mouthed something to me while tracing a rectangle in the air with her fingers. I got her message clearly – *thank you for the drawing*. I smiled.

I lied about the homework but I knew that it would keep Tate off my back for hours. I sat at my desk within the glare of the lamplight. I could still smell Chanel Number Five – so like Mutti – and fresh grass. I played the best parts of the night in my head: touching, dancing and Kate caressing that glass. I went to my bottom drawer and pulled out my drawing pad. I tried to draw Kate with that *Subway* look she had.

In that painting, the woman and over a dozen other poor souls are in the prison-like maze of a subway station. Virtually every face is blank. The woman is walking towards us; her eyebrows knitted, her mouth partially open and the whites of her eyes flicker in the harsh, cold light. She is trapped, and filled with holy terror.

I certainly tried my hardest but I wasn't very successful. In fact, it was crap. I couldn't capture her. I felt guilty, too. Why was I drawing? What if Tate saw it?

I crushed the paper into a ball.

The next morning before school I went around to the dumpsters at the side of the complex and threw it in the trash. That was when I discovered where Connie-Jean and Clovis lived.

Although the El Caballero apartments were new, they were set in a neighbourhood that was built in the nineteenth century.

The house next door was a classic Victorian house. It looked like a decorated cake. It was a single family dwelling but was twice as big as anything being built in the new suburbs. It was well maintained and had an enormous backyard. A gigantic oak tree, about a hundred feet tall, shaded the garden in the afternoon. I could see it from my bedroom window and, on hot days, I imagined sitting on a swing bench in its cool shadows, sipping an ice-cold lemonade.

After I dumped the drawing, I followed the narrow path alongside the complex and came out onto the sidewalk on Western Avenue. A six-foot-high whitewashed wooden fence, not in the best repair, separated the backyard of the old house from the apartment complex.

The twins stepped out of the front door of the white cake house. We were headed towards the sidewalk at the same pace. A panic came over me. What should I do? If I kept walking, we would bang into each other. I would finally have an excuse to meet them. But, on the other hand, they would know that I knew they didn't live in the apartments, and that they'd been using the pool illegally.

The night before, at dinner, Kate had talked about being bold and taking chances. *What the hell*, I thought. With a firm a step I walked up to the street as they rounded the corner. I hadn't allowed for the width of their lawn – it was going to take them at least twenty paces before they got to me. I crouched down and pretended I was tying my shoelaces. When they were an arm's-length away, I stood up.

'Hi. I'm Jackson. I'm new here.'

'I'm Clovis.' He extended his hand. 'Glad to meet you.' His hand was narrow and clammy, but the grasp was firm. 'You live in the apartment complex?' I nodded to him, but I looked at Connie-Jean. She didn't introduce herself. She looked at me like she had the evening before when our eyes met at the pool – staring, like she was studying a fruit fly with a magnifying glass or an amoeba through a microscope. She had a blasé air, like she could observe me in detail but I couldn't possibly return her gaze. She was half right.

Finally Clovis broke the silence. 'This is my sister, Connie-Jean.'

She extended her hand, palm down. 'Charmed, I'm sure.'

Did she expect me to kiss it or shake it? I took the fingers from the second joint on and gave one shake. Her hand was cold, dry and soft. I could smell her perfume. It was fresh and light – lilacs, I thought. 'Likewise,' I mumbled.

The conversation was dull. What grade I was in and how did I happen to be in San Sebastiano. Clovis and I did all the talking until I mentioned New York.

'You lived in New York City?' Connie-Jean asked.

'Yeah, Greenwich Village.'

'Connie wants to be a stage actress, on Broadway,' Clovis explained.

'Did you go to the theatre? Did you see any plays?'

'I saw a few, but mostly I went to the movies.'

'Have you seen *It's a Mad, Mad, Mad, Mad World*?' Clovis asked.

Before I could answer, Connie-Jean interjected, 'Which plays have you seen?'

'Ever? Well …' I had to stretch a bit. 'Let me see. Oh, yeah, last year my mother took me to see *The Merchant of Venice* at the Delacorte Theatre in Central Park.'

'Love is blind, and lovers cannot see the pretty follies that themselves commit,' she recited in a convincing English accent.

'That's Jessica – when she's disguised as a boy, right?'

She arched an eyebrow and the corners of her lips curled upward, slightly. 'What Broadway plays have you seen?'

'I saw *Stop the World – I Want to Get Off* at the Shubert Theatre before it moved to the Ambassador. That was about a clown and a bunch of different girls.'

'Anthony Newley directed it.'

'That's right. He also played Littlechap, the main character.'

'What else?'

I struggled to remember. 'I saw *A Funny Thing Happened on the Way to the Forum* at the Alvin Theatre a couple of years ago. Now that was funny.'

'Stephen Sondheim.'

'Yeah, I think so.'

'Oh, she's right. You can bet on it.' Clovis declared enthusiastically. 'She knows them all.'

He proceeded to tell me the whole storyline of *It's a Mad, Mad, Mad, Mad World*, complete with dialogue and his opinion on which were the funniest bits. I had seen the movie already and he talked for the rest of the twenty-minute walk, but it didn't bother me. It was one of those great California mornings – clear and crisp with light dew over everything and the promise of a glorious warm day ahead. It gave me the chance to look at Connie-Jean at leisure, close-up. As she walked she played with a lock of her hair and the sun skipped over it shimmering in the pale-blue morning light.

We got to the front steps of the school. I slowed down to pull out my schedule. They kept walking but Clovis turned back to wave, and then Connie-Jean did the same and blew me a kiss.

'*Órale, vato*,' a voice called out. It was Ray, hanging out at the top of the steps with Carlos and Unai. 'You weren't shittin' us, *ese*.' He turned to the other two. 'Can you believe this *pendejo*?'

'Wow,' Unai exclaimed.

Carlos shook his head. 'Man, I hope you know what you've gotten yourself into.'

'Hi, guys.' I tried to sound nonchalant but I was quaking on the inside. 'Do you know where room C130 is?'

Even Ray was speechless. Finally he said, 'Man, you got *cojones* the size of my head, *ese*. You gotta tell me the whole story at lunch.'

'Yeah, we heard that you smashed Buster too, *ese*,' Unai said.

'It wasn't anything.'

'It's the talk of the school, *guero*, good job,' Carlos added. 'That redneck has been picking on anyone he can since we was in kindergarten.'

'I can show you 130,' Unai offered. 'It's on the way to my class.'

'Great,' I said. 'See you guys at lunch.'

'Not bad for the second day of class, Ghost Ryder,' Unai said when we were out of earshot. 'What you got up your sleeve for tomorrow, *ese*?'

Scotty Cisco ran up to us before I could respond. 'I hear you pulverised Buster, Jack. That really needed to happen. He's pretty dumb and takes it out on everyone else like it's our fault. Where you going?'

'History with Mr Brice in –'

'Yeah, C130, I know. Me too. So, tell me about the fight.'

'It was nothing.' I shrugged.

When we reached the 120s block Unai said, 'I'll catch you at lunch, man. Then you got to tell us what *that* …' he puckered his lips, ' … was all about.'

'What? You mean Connie-Jean? She's an actress. They always do exaggerated showy shit like that.'

'If you say so, lover boy. See you later, Cisco.' Unai pronounced it 'Sees-co'. I couldn't tell if he was joking or not but Scotty didn't seem to mind.

The history classroom didn't look much different from the art room. The walls were the same tired beige, but with maps and posters of historical figures like Washington and Napoleon. Scotty introduced me to Mr Brice, who smiled distractedly, gave me a book and a set of papers and told me where to sit.

As soon as the bell rang Mr Brice launched into the topic of the semester, the origins of World War II. I knew very little about what happened before the war. But I knew that if it hadn't been for that little mess Tate and Mutti would never have met and I wouldn't exist. Still, it wasn't long before I was distracted by the clouds outside the high windows.

At lunchtime I purposefully avoided the quad. Ray and the guys would grill me, and they were sure to be disappointed when they found out that nothing had really happened between me and Connie-Jean. I didn't want to talk about Buster either. Instead, I headed for the school library. I was never much of a scholar but I did read – slowly – and I probably learned more from hanging out at the library than I did in class.

Around the corner of the science block I ran straight into Maria and another girl from art class, one of the Li sisters.

'Way to go thumping Buster, new guy,' the Asian girl said.

'This is Ming Li,' Maria offered.

'That pig was always hassling my sister and me.'

I gave her a mechanical grin. 'Do you mind if I talk to Maria alone?' She said okay, but didn't move too far away.

I leaned in close to Maria and lowered my voice. 'I wanted to apologise for not recognising you in class yesterday. You looked different.'

She nodded. 'It's no wonder. When you came to Thanksgiving my eyes were all puffy.'

'You were sick.'

Ming laughed. 'That wasn't *sick* sick, that was lovesick over Ray's cousin.'

'Who, Unai?' I asked.

'I swear, Ming Li ...' Maria hissed, but instead of finishing the sentence she gestured for her to zip her mouth. Ming Li shrugged.

Maria moved us a few steps further away. 'I'm sorry I ran away from you yesterday after class.'

'So that's why you were moving so fast?'

'Yes, I ... I don't know, I just felt shy all of a sudden. But then, after you saved me I –' she bent her head, 'I felt embarrassed. Sorry.'

'It's okay. But, you're fine now, right?' She raised her head and smiled.

Those dimples. They slayed me. They only appeared when she was truly animated and they danced on her cheeks like sunlight on rippling water.

'I'm glad. Look, I did a drawing of your parents after Thanksgiving. I'd like to give it to them to thank them for being so nice to us. Could I give it to you some time?'

She raised her eyebrows in surprise. 'You did? That's sweet. Why don't you give it to them yourself? They would love that.'

I had already canned that scenario in my head. I couldn't walk to the gas station, it was too far. I couldn't ask Tate to take me – obviously. I could try Charlie but I couldn't take the chance he'd tell Tate I was drawing, 'I can't. It's complicated. Can you deliver it for me?'

'Sure. It would be a pleasure.'

'Great. I'll bring it tomorrow. Thanks.' I turned and waved at Ming Li, and continued on my way to the library.

I went to the card catalogue and searched for books on *Les Demoiselles d'Avignon*. I didn't know much about its background. All I really knew was what I saw and how it made me feel. Unfortunately, the school library's art section had little more than coffee-table drivel, so after school I walked down to the Municipal Library. There I found John Canaday's *Mainstreams of Modern Art: David to Picasso* as well as Anthony Blunt's *Picasso, the Formative Years: A Study of His Sources*.

Canaday was easy to understand, but Blunt was heavy going.

When I discovered that the title *Les Demoiselles d'Avignon* referred to a street in the red-light district of Barcelona called Carrer d'Avinyó, it really got me going. This painting, a holy icon of Modern Art, was actually about whores and venereal disease. When I told Ray later, he nearly split his skinny gut.

'No wonder it's so messed up, *ese*. *Chingado*. It's got the clap.'

Carlos sniggered, but Unai asked questions. 'Why did he want to paint a *casa de putas*, a whorehouse? It's not exactly pretty, *ese*.'

I had only gotten the books. 'Yeah, it isn't pretty, but … not all art has to be pretty.'

'Good art does,' Carlos declared.

'When I was a kid my mother and I would go to the Museum of Modern Art, in New York, where it's at. I used to see it all the time. This painting made perfect sense to me.'

'Hey, *ese*, it sounds like your mother was putting some *mota* in your cornflakes.' Ray put his hand up to his mouth like he was holding a reefer and pretended to take a long drag. He half-closed his eyes and wiggled his head slowly, muttering, '*Ay ay ay*,' and then he giggled.

'What do you mean?' Unai asked. 'It made perfect sense?'

I looked around the quad trying to see the right words. Finally, I opened Canaday's book and leafed through it until I found the black-and-white print of *Les Demoiselles*. Unai came in close and Ray looked over his shoulder. Carlos hardly moved, but he did peer down at the page.

'See, I told you guys, it's all *wango*,' Ray said.

'No, man, look at it. I mean, try to look at it like a kid would. You know how when they draw someone the head is sometimes bigger than the body and maybe there's one big eye and one small one?'

'Carlos draws like that,' Ray said with mock seriousness. Carlos shoved him into Unai. Unai pushed Ray back with his shoulder.

'Well, this painting is big. It's like eight feet by eight feet, so these women are bigger than real. When you're little they look huge and you just accept that they're as real as any picture of a person, right?' They were all listening. 'In fact, more real because they are so darn big. They've got eyes and bodies and you accept that they are all angular, made with straight lines, like you might draw yourself, you know, as a kid.'

'*Simón*, *ese*,' Unai said. 'I think I get it.'

'I don't buy it, *vato*. It looks messed up to me.' Ray looked away as some girls passed by.

'*Simón, carnale.* I'm with you,' Carlos said. 'We're not kids anymore.'

'At least you're not, *panzón* – you're the size of two kids,' Ray said, jabbing his finger into Carlos' pudgy stomach.

'I swear to God –'

'Look, Ray,' I interrupted, 'Accept that the painting is five people. Then you can see beyond how they look and start to dig what's going on. It's a party. There's food, and those two are wearing masks. When you stand in front of it your eyes can't stay still. They dart all around. It makes it seem like they're dancing or shaking. You can't tell that from looking at a little picture in a book.'

'Shaking their asses, all right,' Ray said. 'Hey, it's a line-up. They're posing for the clients, for the Johns. They're showing their stuff and saying, "Pick me."'

'Yeah, but where's the John? There is no John, *ese*,' Carlos countered.

'No, no, I get it,' Unai said. 'There's no John because, if you're looking at the painting, *you're* the John.'

I hadn't thought about it that way before – the fallen ladies in a bordello presenting themselves and hoping to be chosen. Suddenly I saw the women differently. There was sadness in their eyes. Maybe the masks they were wearing weren't actual masks but symbolic about hiding their true feelings. Most of all, I saw the glaring steaminess of the painting; four women standing up, jutting out their breasts and one sitting with her legs spread wide open. I couldn't believe I hadn't noticed it before. I could feel heat coming from my face and my breathing got shorter.

'You're right, Unai. The audience is the John.' I closed the book quickly.

The five girls in the cheerleading squad walked across the quad, heading towards the football field. Ray looked over at them and gave me a shove. 'Hey *guero*, *wáchale*, your girlfriend.'

I had to come clean. 'Look, she's not my girl. We walked to school together, and that's all.'

'*Chingado*. And I thought you were some kind of a stud or something, *ese*, *El Macho Gigante*.'

'Then why did she blow you a *beso*, man?' Carlos asked.

I was wondering the same thing. Was it because I'd been to a few plays in New York? Did she think I was cute, or was she putting on a show for the boys – making fun of me? 'Hell if I know,' I finally answered. '*Chingado* – as you say.'

They all cracked up.

'*Órale*, *vato*,' Ray said. '*Chingado*.'

That night I dreamt in violet. I'm not kidding. Everything was diffused in that one mysterious hue. There was a luscious female whose face kept changing. One minute she looked like Connie-Jean then I would look again and she was definitely Kate. She was sunning herself by the pool, blowing me a kiss, dancing close, touching me and rubbing my back. Then she moved to the patio table and sat, sipping coffee. I saw her from behind and her hair was still blonde but the style changed – it was older, and familiar, but I couldn't place it. Suddenly her head dropped down into her cup and she was stone still. I didn't want to look. Some small part of me knew I could change this scene – and I desperately tried – but it wouldn't budge. My heart pounded so hard I could hardly catch my breath. I knew that I had to see her, I had to know. Slowly and reluctantly, I lifted her head only to wake in a cold sweat. It was one in the morning.

My pyjamas were wet too – sticky wet.

I changed and lay in the dark with the radio on low. I let the violet dream slip from my consciousness. Sam Riddle was on and every other song was a Beatles tune. I couldn't wait until Sunday night. I knew they were going to be on *The Ed Sullivan Show*. Was Connie-Jean listening to them? And what was she thinking?

I felt an unexpectedly sharp pang of longing for the city; the traffic noise echoing off the walls of the high-rises, the feeling of being anonymous and free, the bite of the first cold snap in the fall and how good it felt to go inside into the warmth.

I could hear Mutti's full-bodied laughter as I dropped back to sleep and I shivered.

10

WITH NO INTRODUCTION ED SULLIVAN presented The Beatles live to seventy-three million Americans, including Tate, Kate, Charlie and me. As we lounged in the flickering blue-grey light of our TV, the girls in the audience screamed. I looked around at the adults in our living room from my position on the carpet. Kate was grinning and Tate was nodding to the beat, although he looked a little perplexed. Charlie could have been watching anything. He was already three scotches down.

'They're so cute,' Kate said, giggling.

'Yeah, you like them like that, don't you?' Charlie said.

'What's with you?' Kate glanced at him.

He ignored her. 'What the hell is that on their heads?'

'Cool it, cats, I'm trying to listen,' Tate said.

'They're younger than me,' Kate whispered.

After *All My Loving*, the camera zoomed in on the one with the baby face. He sang a conventional song, *Till There Was You*, but he did it well. Kate actually moaned. The name 'Paul' flashed up on the screen below his face. Then the camera cut to each member of the band close-up as their names were displayed. Under 'John' were the words 'Sorry, girls, he's married'.

'Aww!' Kate cried.

'I mean it, what the hell is on top of their heads?' Charlie partially suppressed a burp.

'Don't be a bore, Charlie. Give them a chance. I think they've really got something. What do you think, Hymie?'

'Yeah, they got somethin', man.' Tate was moving his head to the rhythm. 'They got somethin' and it's different.'

'Everybody knows about them at school,' I said. 'They're on the radio all the time.'

'Why is their 'air zo long?' Charlie slurred.

We all ignored him.

That night was a turning point – not just for rock 'n' roll. Before that Sunday night in February, the Beatles were only an English pop band. After *Ed Sullivan* they were fast on their way to becoming the biggest cultural legends of the '60s.

Seeing them for the first time, along with the rest of the country, I could feel it immediately. They jumped right out at me. They looked like they were having an impossibly good time. It didn't look like they were performing at all; just four guys playing, belting out really catchy tunes and smiling a lot. When George Harrison did his guitar solo in the first song, *All My Loving,* he really put his body into it. It was like he was saying, 'Look at me. This is what I can do.' I found out years later that George was sick during that performance, but you would have never known.

Tate was right about their music. What they were doing was different. I knew a bit about jazz because of my parents. I grew up with Elvis, the Everly Brothers and all of the early rock 'n' roll greats. Except for The Beach Boys and some of the Motown Records the stuff on the radio was commercial and predicable, boring. These guys kind of mixed harmonizing, like Phil and Don, some guitar that sounded like surfer music, rhythms like jazz and rock plus some strange stuff I had never heard in American music. I didn't know how they did it but I couldn't get enough of it.

The next day, in class, everyone talked about The Beatles. Anything seemed possible again, if you were open enough to embrace it.

'No way,' Luke Hornsby said, tucking his bleached locks behind his ears. 'Those Limey dudes are totally bogus, man.'

'What are you talking about?' Twinkie asked him. She was blonde with a pixie haircut and freckles. I never learned her real name. 'Are you cuckoo?'

Mr Talbot had split the art class into groups of four. We were preparing for our first watercolour paintings by drawing clumps of turf.

'Yeah, Luke, how can you say that?' said Sing Li. 'The Beatles are the greatest band in the world.'

Luke laughed. 'No way, The Beach Boys rule, babes.'

'Of course you would say that, you surfing fool.' Sing Li rolled her eyes. 'What do you think, Jackson?'

I was making every blade of grass and every weed show up crystal-clear, like Albrecht Dürer had in his *Great Piece of Turf* painting. I had no intention of getting so wrapped up in the project until I saw Ray start to draw. Everything, all of his bullshit and posing, his joking and constant talking stopped. He looked like a different person, a different being. He hardly blinked and his nose kept twitching. His line was sure, accurate and delicate. His eyes and his hands were one.

He was good but I was sure I could do as well; maybe even better. Before I knew it I wasn't hearing anything. I didn't see anything except the clump of grass and my drawing – not even Ray. I couldn't tell how much time had gone by. I didn't care.

'Who's better, Jackson?' Twinkie echoed. 'The Beatles or The Beach Boys?'

'Yeah, dude, who's the most bitchin' band?' Luke added.

I was so focused on my drawing that I didn't think about the possible consequences of what I was going to say. Without thinking, I answered. 'The Beatles, hands down, no question.'

'Bogus, dude, bogus.'

I didn't hear the rest of the conversation. Looking at my work, I realised I could make it stronger by going darker in the shaded places – increase the contrast to give it some punch.

As a result of my kneejerk answer, I never learned to surf. Instead I became part of a huge, but strangely select group – Beatles fans. The surfers were a tribe, a relatively small, tight-knit gang with their own group of wannabes – 'hodads', they were called – and beach bunnies. Luke would have been my ticket in. I probably would have learned to ride the waves that summer, and at least partially fulfil my *Gidget* fantasies. But in the winter of '64, you couldn't like both The Beatles and The Beach Boys, no sir. To the surfers, The Beach Boys were gods, and they would defend them to the death. It was war.

My first Beatles comrades were Twinkie and Sing Li. The other pedal-pusher girls, Jojo and Elizabeth, came with the deal. Ming Li (I always referred to the twins as Sing Li and Ming Li, not realising Li was their surname) was in neither camp. She was a serious violin student and more interested in Jascha Heifetz than John Lennon or Brian Wilson.

At the end of class I considered my drawing. I was pleased. Ray rolled out of his trance.

He looked at my drawing then at me. He shook his finger in

my face. 'Not bad, *guero*. You've been holding out on your old *amigo, ese*.' He nodded several times. 'Sharp.' He pronounced it 'charp'.

I should have been pleased by his praise but it didn't satisfy. There was something in the way he said it – I don't know; the way his shoulders relaxed, the lazy tone of his voice and the shine in his eyes. I thought about it at the end of class as I walked around to Maria's table to give her the drawing I made of her parents. By the time I was in front of her I had figured it out. It was his confidence, his comfort. I didn't threaten him. That annoyed me.

I passed the manila envelope to Maria. She looked up at me and cocked her head.

'It's the drawing I did of your folks, remember?'

'Oh, yes,' she exclaimed and unfolded the flap of the envelope.

'Don't … please.' I held my hand over the opening. 'I'd rather you didn't open it until you show them, if that's okay with you.'

At lunchtime in the quad, Ray was lukewarm when I asked him about The Beatles.

'I didn't see them, *guero*, I was at work, *ese*. I work every Sunday night.'

'Make that every night, *primo*,' Carlos said.

'No, no, I got Tuesday off this week, *carnale*.'

'You work six nights a week?' I asked incredulously.

'It's pretty shitty that you slave away in that *pinché* restaurant and they don't even feed you, *primo*,' Unai said. 'It's probably not even legal, *ese*. You should get another job, man.'

'Where am I going to get a job in this stinking fruit town? I'm underage. Besides, our *chingado Tio* pays me almost minimum wage.'

'He pays you less than a dollar twenty-four?' I asked.

Ray shrugged his shoulders. 'A dollar twenty but it's cash, under the table, *ese*. I don't pay no taxes.'

'You wouldn't pay taxes, *tonto*, that's what I've been telling you.' Unai was starting to raise his voice. 'You don't make enough.'

'He's right, Ray,' I said. 'The government takes it out but you claim it back at the end of the year.'

'I don't know. I'm okay. I'll stick with it till something better comes along,' He was quiet for a long time. Finally he said, 'Anyways, yeah, The Beatles are okay. I heard them on the transistor. But my favourite is Johnny Rivers.'

'And The Temptations,' Carlos said.

'Yeah, The Temptations.' That rallied Ray's spirits. He started singing *The Way You Do the Things You Do* and trying to dance a waltz with Carlos, who stood stubbornly in place.

'I swear to God,' Unai said to me under his breath, 'he's such a dumbass sometimes.'

'No wonder he's half asleep in class all the time. Why does he work so much? Is he saving up for a car or something?' I asked.

'If only. Nah, man, it's his folks. They need the cash, *ese*.' As we watched, Carlos finally gave in and started moving his shoulders a little. 'That's what you do when you're Mexican; every *pinché* thing goes to the family.'

'Wow.'

'Yeah, it's tough sometimes, but on the other hand you know everyone's got your back too. It's about *sangre*, *guero*, blood. You know? It's about *familia*.'

I felt a pang of … I don't know; envy, longing, regret? I changed the subject.

'So you and Maria Dos Osos?' I said to Unai.

He winced. 'No, man. She's cool and all, but, she looks like my little sister. It creeps me out, *ese*.'

'Really? So you're going to rule out any girl that has a passing resemblance to your sister?'

'Hey, you don't know, man. I know you don't have any.'

I sighed. I had wanted a sister. Now that was never going to happen. 'How different does she have to look?'

'You know, not have black hair and brown eyes, maybe?'

'You realise that's more than half the girls in the world? When you take out all the old ladies and babies that's about seven million chicks; too bad if one of them is your true love.' I sucked in my cheek and shook my head.

Unai stopped looking at the grotesque display of his cousins dancing and I thought he nodded slightly. 'That's a lot of chicks,' he murmured. When he looked back at Ray and Carlos he was completely focused on them.

'Unai, do you know why I hit Buster?'

'I don't know. He's an asshole. What other reason do you need?'

Finally Carlos had enough and pushed Ray away. Ray laughed, and then got distracted by a girl walking by with a well filled-out sweater. He whistled but she ignored him.

'So, how's your *novia*, Connie-Jean?' Unai asked me.

'I told you, man, she not my girl.' He laughed. 'Anyway, I haven't seen her lately.'

'I bet you *she* likes The Beatles.'

I couldn't tell if Unai was being sarcastic or not. 'Don't you?'

'*Simón*, bro, *simón*, anything but those white-ass Beach Boys.'

He stood up and called loudly to the others, '*Ándale locos*, we're going to be late for metal shop.'

After school I walked to work. I had plenty of time to think. My birthday was coming up in a month, and that was starting to overtake my thoughts about The Beatles, Connie-Jean and Kate.

I was going to turn sixteen. I would be able to get a licence. I wanted a car but I didn't think Tate would give me one. He didn't have a lot of extra cash.

Work was going well for him. He was picking it up and, with Kate's help, he was getting a steady stream of customers. I swear she sent him so much business he should have given her a cut of the action. But Charlie and Tate had a deal. Every time he made a commission, Tate would give Charlie some of the money so that he could slowly buy into the business.

My problem was that even a wreck would have cost close to a couple of hundred bucks and I had only managed to save twelve dollars and fifty-two cents from work so far, so chances were I would be old enough to join the army, vote, have a beard and maybe even grandkids before I could afford to buy a car myself.

Charlie was already consulting Tate about business decisions, which was a good thing. Charlie was an effective salesman but Tate had one beef with him – it was over the dames he would hire as secretaries. The last things Charlie looked for were first-class typing, organisational skills and good customer service. His first requirements were pointy boobs, a firm ass and pouty lips. The younger and dumber she was, the better. The girl after the one I met when we first got to San Sebastiano looked like Ava Gardner – right down to the dimple in her chin – but she couldn't type ten words a minute. The next one would come in an hour late, take two-hour lunch breaks (often with Charlie) and then would leave on the stroke of five no matter what. Tate lost a commission on a Corvair Monza because of that one.

When I got to the dealership Mrs Barker's Packard was parked in the staff parking area. I walked through the screen door into the office and there she was, sitting behind the desk holding some papers and talking to Charlie.

'Hi, Mrs Barker. Are you going to buy a new car?'

Charlie turned to me. He touched his forehead and squinted his eyes, 'Ouch, I'm a little tender from last night. I think it was that racket on *Ed Sullivan*.'

Mrs Barker and I looked at each other and exchanged ever-so-slight smiles. 'How are you, Jackson?' she asked. 'I'm just filling in until your father finds a permanent secretary.'

'Yeah, sport. Your dad has taken over the hiring of our secretarial staff. I can't seem to find ones that will stick.'

I stifled a smile and turned to Mrs Barker, 'I'm glad you're here, ma'am,' I said to her.

'Jackson, what did I tell you about calling me ma'am? Mrs Barker will do fine. After all, we are neighbours.'

'Sure, Mrs Barker.'

'If you'll excuse me, I've gotta get me a coffee,' Charlie said.

'I'll get that for you, sir,' Mrs Barker offered.

'No, no, I need some fresh air. I'm going to go down to the Bus Stop Café,' he put on his aviator sunglasses.

'Give my love to Mabel,' I called after him.

With a point of his finger and a wink, he walked out the door.

'I was going to make myself a cup of tea,' Mrs Barker said, 'Would you like a hot cocoa? I brought some with me.'

I was a little early to work so I said yes. As we sipped our hot drinks I told her about school and my new friends. Then I told her about my birthday coming up.

'Oh, how enchanting. Well, we must have a party.'

'I'm not sure. I really don't know that many people.'

'It doesn't have to be a big party, my boy, but it is such an important milestone in your life. You must celebrate it properly. I first met Freddie, Mr Barker, on his sixteenth birthday. It must have been, good lord, 1915.' She reached up and pushed the hair away from my eyes, 'You should do something to remember it.'

'I don't know what my dad will think of that.'

'Think of what?' Tate said as he walked up to Mrs Barker's desk.

'I was just telling Jackson that he needs to have a birthday party.'

Tate lowered the handful of papers he held and pursed his lips, 'I don't know.'

'Don't you worry – I'd arrange the whole thing.'

Great, I thought, *an old-lady party*: cakes on doilies, punch, large flower-print dresses, eccentric hats and *eau de mothballs* filling my nostrils.

'I was thinking of taking him out,' Tate said. I wasn't convinced he'd remembered my birthday was coming up at all.

I kept thinking of what Mrs Barker might inflict on me. 'Yeah. That would be better, I guess.'

'Okay, great. No party. It will be a father-and-son day,' he grinned. 'See Stretch before you start, son.'

'Yes, sir.' I remembered something. 'Tate, what does *gemmin, gahoman* or something, mean?'

'*Gehinnam*?'

'Yeah. What does it mean?'

Tate glanced at Mrs Barker before he answered, 'It means hell in Yiddish. Why?'

'Mr Cannon used it the other day.'

'Is that so? Crazy.'

Why would Cannon do that? I couldn't figure it out right away and I didn't really care. I forgot about it and sprinted the length of the corridor towards the workshop.

Stretch was lying under the chassis of a white '47 Mercury which had seen better days, with his legs protruding. I pounded on the hood.

'Hi ya, Stretch.'

'Howdy, professor,' came his muffled voice.

Buzz was working on a differential box. His big hands were covered in grease and, as always, a cigarette was hanging from his lip.

'Hi ya, Buzz.'

The old man grunted and nodded ever-so slightly. Stretch slowly slid out from under the car, the trolley wheels rumbling on the concrete floor.

'Charlie said I should see you before I started work. What's that Merc doing in our workshop, anyway? I thought we only serviced Chevys.'

Stretch looked over at Buzz and adjusted the shoulder straps on his blue overalls before he answered. 'It's a personal favour for management. It belongs to a friend of Charlie's.'

'That's weird.'

'Nah, not really. Charlie knows Buzz used to be a Ford mechanic before the war. A Merc is basically an upmarket Ford. Buzz can fix it good and learn us a thing or two in the bargain.'

'It's a bit of an old wreck, isn't it?'

'No, no, my friend. She might need some tender lovin' care, but she'll clean up good. The '47 Merc was the Corvette Stingray of its day, yeah. It was very smooth, very classy. Look at those lines and that chrome grille. They don't make them like that anymore, no sir.'

'So what do you want me to do?'

'Help me with the drivetrain to this ol' thing. Me and Buzz are going to start your education. Get you some overalls on.'

I walked over to the pegs by the doorway and found the cleanest pair of blue overalls. 'Say, did you see Ed Sullivan last night?' I asked.

'Yeah, yeah, those English guys are rockin'. They're going to be on next Sunday from Miami, too.'

'I know. I can't wait.'

'Say, you think I should grow me one of them "mop tops"?'

'Yeah, you'd look like a redheaded Ringo.'

'He's the pretty one, right? Okay, here we go. Hand me a left-handed wrench.'

The next day on my way to school I heard the smart click of high heels behind me.

'O villain, villain, smiling, damnèd villain!'

I turned around. 'What did you say?'

'One may smile, and smile, and be a villain.'

'What? I haven't done anything. What? Why?'

She trotted past me and I sped up to match her pace.

'Hamlet: Act 1, Scene 5. Don't tell me you don't know it?'

'No, not really. I know the "To be or not to be" part and "Alas, poor Yorick," but that's about it.' She kept walking. 'So why am I a villain? I didn't tell anyone …'

'You didn't tell anyone what?'

I realised I had trapped myself. 'Why am I a villain?'

'Where are you from, boy?' she asked condescendingly.

'Right next door, the apartment complex. El Caballero.'

She sniffed. 'Where were you born, you senseless youngster?'

'New York, in Greenwich Village.'

'So you're from the Village.'

'Yeah.'

'Well, the original meaning of "villain" is someone from a village, silly. Ergo, you, Master Jackson Ryder, are a villain.' She smiled.

'Ha. I guess I am.' I grinned. 'What a relief.'

'Hurry, I'm late for play practice.'

'What's the play?' She looked at me like I had forgotten my own name. 'Oh, I get it.'

'Oh, what a noble mind is here o'erthrown!' I couldn't answer that. 'I play Ophelia, Hamlet's crazy lover who kills herself.'

'I know Ophelia.'

'I thought you said you didn't know the play.'

'I don't, but I know the painting by Millais.'

'Millais?'

'Yeah, John Everett Millais, the Pre-Raphaelite painter?' She looked at me blankly, 'He did this painting of Ophelia. She's floating in a stream with her dress billowing out and her lips parted, looking straight up. It's like she's in a trance. Her eyes are grey and she has a necklace made out of violets. It's a beautiful painting.'

'Her clothes spread wide; And, mermaid-like, awhile they bore her up – That's how Gertrude, the queen, describes it.' Some of Connie-Jean's artifice seemed to drop away. 'I'd love to see that painting.'

'I've got it in a book, but, it's small … and it's in black and white.' She walked on in silence, the click of her heels on pavement the only sound. I realised there had been a gold-plated opportunity and I was losing it fast. I fumbled for the words. 'Say, I saw a real good print in a book at the municipal library. I can get it out and show you.'

'Really? That would be marvellous, but I don't want you to go to any trouble for me.'

I was too naïve to realise she really *did* want me to go to the trouble and she had every confidence – based on her experience – that I would. 'No, no. I was going to the library anyway,' I lied, 'I can bring it over to your house.'

She was quiet for a time. I was sure she was going to say no. 'I'm pretty busy this week with the play and all …' She glanced quickly at me. 'How about Sunday afternoon? You can help me rehearse my lines.'

'Yeah, yeah, okay. I don't think I have anything else on.' In my mind I cried, *yes, joy, rapture!*

We had reached the school steps.

'I've got to go to the auditorium,' Connie-Jean said.

Ray, Carlos and Unai were standing on the steps again. In a voice loud enough for them to hear, she said, 'See you later, you villain,' then she blew me another kiss. The boys whistled and howled like wolves. I tried to wave them down, but it only made them worse. Connie-Jean looked over her shoulder, smiled and winked at me.

At lunchtime, I scooted into the school library to check out if there was a better copy of the *Ophelia* painting there, but I didn't have any luck. As a result, I was a little late for art class and I had to sit next to Luke Hornsby instead of Ray. Mr Talbot had set up another still life. It was nothing fancy – a wine bottle, a wicker basket of wax fruit, a pathetic candle stump and a cracked wine glass on an old tablecloth.

'All right, students, this is like a test to see how well you take notice. I want you to use your eyes. Draw what you see, not what you think you see.'

He gave us each a fat stick of charcoal. Nearly all the girls cried out, 'Eww, it's dirty.' I laughed to myself and got stuck in. I had tried charcoal already, so I wasn't fazed like a lot of people in the class. I started to outline the shapes of the objects one by one. By break time, I had pretty much finished and was starting to deal with the details. Everyone walked around looking at the other drawings before going to lunch. I stayed in my seat expecting everyone to congregate around me and praise my work as they always had done. And a small coterie did form, but to my wonder it was around Ray.

'Hey Jack, you've laid down some groovy lines.' I looked up and was surprised to see Luke checking out my work. 'Ming just told me about Buster. Way to go, dude. He's a real turd.'

'Yeah, Thanks. He's a stand-out thug alright but you know, inside he's a scared little shit trying to climb his way to the top of his pile, like the rest of us. I can't blame him for that.'

'That's heavy, dude.'

I smiled automatically, but I couldn't take my eyes off Ray. I waited until everyone was out of the room, including Ray, and then had a peek at his drawing. When I saw it I couldn't help but laugh. As much as he put down *Les Demoiselles D'Avignon*, and appeared not to care, he had copied the style of Picasso's painting with a razor-sharp eye. What his drawing lacked in realism was made up for with the energy of his technique. Instead of using the charcoal like a pencil he had varied the line and pressure, rubbed the surface to make some of the lines softer and even used an eraser to let the paper show through as highlights. The *vato* really could draw. He was my buddy and all, but I was feeling unfriendly things towards him. The art heap was the only one that I had ever been on the top of. Of course, I didn't want it or need it. So, why was I feeling so annoyed?

When everyone was back Mr Talbot set us a challenge, 'This is our annual Freshman Art Competition sponsored by Vice-principal Cannon. It's co-ordinated with your next assignment. The assignment part is to choose an early twentieth-century artist, write a two-page biography with images you have copied from books, and finally produce an eighteen by twenty-four inch self-portrait in the style of the artist. The final portrait will go into the competition. The finalists will go on the wall and the grand prize is a certificate and a copy of Françoise Gilot's new book *Life with Picasso*.'

I knew Françoise Gilot had been Picasso's girlfriend during the war. I was dying to know what she wrote about him. I was fixed on winning the competition no matter what.

He gave us two weeks to work on it.

*

When Mr Talbot released us at three o'clock I ran to the public library. I checked out a book called *Paintings and Drawings of the Pre-Raphaelites and their Circle*, as well as a copy of *Hamlet*. The rest of the week seemed to drag on for about fourteen years. I read *Hamlet* and a good part of the notes, but it was a struggle. I didn't know much Shakespeare yet and it felt like slogging through mud, trying to feel the greatness I knew must be in there. The Pre-Raphaelite paintings were easier for me. There was something instantly attractive about them. Even if I didn't know the story behind them, the drama and the attention to detail really knocked me out, as did the crazy looking chicks.

My favourite painting from the book was one of the lesser-known ones, which didn't quite fit the spirit of the Pre-Raphaelite Brotherhood. It was *Ecce Ancilla Domini* by Dante Gabriel Rossetti. The story behind this painting had been covered so many times in Renaissance art that I knew it by heart. It was the Annunciation, the part of the New Testament where an angel comes down to earth and tells Mary that she'd better clear her schedule, because she's about to become the mother of God.

As far back as the Middle Ages, artists had shown Mary looking resigned to this mindboggling news.

By contrast, Rossetti's Mary is more real. She's barely a teenager; cowering against the wall, shrinking from her calm, majestic visitor. The archangel Gabriel has the formal air of a heavenly civil servant. 'Excuse me, Miss, I'm simply the messenger.'

Besides the change in Mary's attitude, the painting's design is so simple. There's a lot of long lines going up and down the painting with only a few horizontal lines to break up the space. The colour palette is mostly white, with a blue curtain behind Mary and a paler blue behind the angel's head. In the front is an odd, dark-red cloth draped over some kind of a thin towel rack. The cloth is patterned with lilies – Mary's symbolic flower. Gabriel also holds a lily in his hand and the bright halos make a bridge.

The painting is way ahead of its time – it's like something Ferdinand Hodler might have done forty years later. But Rossetti's radical vision earned him a lot of bad press. After that he stuck to the more easily digested Pre-Raphaelite style.

Okay, the real reason I liked the painting so much was because Mary reminded me of the woman in *The Subway* painting. She had the same expression that Kate did the night she told me about her husband, and that Connie-Jean had when she was with Joe Penderecki, Mr Lost Cause. That look really got to me.

Sunday finally arrived. I spent the whole morning wondering what exactly constituted 'the afternoon'. We hadn't made a definite time and, like an idiot, I hadn't gotten her phone number. When was too early, too eager? When was too late, too casual, too rude? I paced, bit my nails, took another shower … finally – in excruciating desperation – I asked Kate, who was lounging in the living room looking at magazines with Tate. What might a girl consider 'afternoon'?

'Oh,' she said. She gave me a long stare, a funny little smile and then glanced at Tate. I regretted asking her. 'It all depends, Jack. What are ya goin' to do?'

She said it in a very neutral way but suddenly I felt like my clothes didn't fit, and it became hotter in the room than the wall thermometer indicated. 'It's nothing,' I stammered.

'Homework. I'm going to help her with her lines for a play.'

Kate didn't say anything. Tate had his nose stuck in a copy of *Down Beat*.

'Go after lunch, man,' he said without looking up.

'No, Hymie,' Kate slapped him on his shoulder. 'These things have to be timed right.'

I shook my head, 'It's not … it's not like that, Kate. Honest.' They both stared at me. 'We – I know her from school, you know. She lives right next door.'

Tate nodded and offhandedly turned back to his magazine. Kate continued to stare and bite on her lower lip. 'Okay,' she said, 'I think three o'clock should be fine.'

I nodded a couple of times. 'Okay. Good. Thanks, Kate.'

'Don't mention it.' She smiled as she picked up her book.

I stayed in my room until three, listened to the radio and tried to copy the techniques I'd seen Ray use in his drawing, using a charcoal stick I brought from school. I wondered if Kate really believed this visit of mine was platonic. I convinced myself that she did.

'Is it okay if I stay for dinner if Connie-Jean invites me?' I asked Tate before I left.

He hadn't moved position, but he had switched to reading *LIFE* magazine. On the cover was a guy who looked like he was falling or floating above a medieval city at the foot of some snow-capped mountains. The caption on the left said *Winter Olympics.* Tate scanned the carpeted floor before he looked up. 'I would rather you ate with us, here.'

'Give him some room to move, Hymie. Besides, have you got anything planned?'

He shrugged his shoulders, 'It's Sunday,' he looked back at his magazine, 'Okay.' He waved me away.

'Great, thank you, sir.' Kate was hugging a paperback novel by Charles Webb. 'Bye, Kate. Thanks again.'

She looked up and blinked several times at me. She glanced at Tate before she looked back, smiled and waved in my direction. Her cheeks were flushed. As I headed to the side of the complex to jump the fence, Charlie was coming down the steps from his apartment. The dealership was only open until noon on Sundays so he was casually dressed in a pair of light slacks, a yellow polo shirt, brown sweater and loafers. He was whistling the theme to *Zorba the Greek* and had a brown paper bag tucked under his arm. He didn't see me until he got halfway to the bottom of the stairs. He saluted me with two fingers. When he got to the ground he turned towards Kate's apartment. I was in too much of a panic to tell him that she was at our place. I didn't know if I wanted to, anyway. He would figure it out – sooner or later.

The chill in the air was mixed with moisture and smog, but it was low-lying enough that it didn't block out the snow -covered San Gabriel Mountains in the distance. It looked like the place on the cover of Tate's *LIFE* magazine. What had that guy been doing?

I walked up to the large door of Connie-Jean's house and pushed the brass doorbell. There was the sound of fast foot-steps on tile. Clovis opened the door and grinned at me. We exchanged greetings. I explained that his sister was expecting me. His smile sagged.

'Come on in,' he said, closing the front door. 'Wait here.' He disappeared into the double doors opposite the front door.

I looked around. I had never been inside a Victorian house. My only reference points were old black-and-white Frank Capra movies from the '30s and '40s. This place had obviously been renovated – instead of patterned wallpaper and dark-stained wood, it was painted completely white. The light fixtures were gilt art deco sunbursts, slightly tarnished but still classy.

Connie-Jean burst into the foyer from the same room Clovis disappeared into. She looked more harried than happy to see me. I had anticipated this – as well as every other possible scenario – over the week, but it wrenched my gut all the same.

'I brought that book with the Ophelia painting for you to see.' I didn't mention the play practice; that would have been pushing it.

'Oh yes, hello Jack.' She reached out and touched the binding of the book gracefully. I peeked past her into the sitting room. A guy was sitting in an overstuffed leather chair to the left of the doors. I recognised him from school – he was the co-captain of the football team with Joe ('Mr Lost Cause') Penderecki and his name was Milt Bryson. He turned to look in my direction and stared fixedly at me. His big hands were spread over the ends of the stuffed arms like hawk's talons grasping prey. Connie-Jean glanced over her shoulder and closed the door behind her slowly. 'I'm so sorry, but I'm kind of busy right now,' she said. 'Can you come back later?'

I was crushed; but all was not lost. 'When?'

Connie-Jean looked at me properly for the first time. 'Later,' she said. 'What's your phone number? I'll call you.'

'Have you got a pencil and paper?'

'I'll remember.'

Maybe she would remember, but I was positive she wouldn't call. 'Okay, it's Olympic 45551.' She repeated the number and ushered me towards the door. 'What's your number?' I heard myself say.

'I beg your pardon?'

'What's your number? You've got mine. I'd like to have yours.' I kept my voice steady, 'Please.'

'Olympic 24002,' she answered. 'Okay? I'll call.'

'I'll be waiting.'

She steered me outside with a strained smile. The door slammed. I stood there and let the gloom of the afternoon slowly envelop me. I let out a deep sigh and turned back towards El Caballero. The weather had turned chilly and I shivered inside my synthetic V-neck sweater.

As I passed the corner window of the old mansion, there was a tapping on the glass. Clovis waved and pointed around the side of the house. The backyard was blocked by the ivy-covered fence, but the gate was halfway open. Clovis poked his head around the back door and beckoned me inside.

We were in a storage area – picnic baskets, table umbrellas and pieces of outdoor furniture were stacked up on both sides of a narrow room. We passed through into another room that hadn't been renovated since the turn of the century. It must have been the library at one time. Mahogany shelves lined every wall, but less than a quarter had books in them. Instead they held model airplanes, miniature wooden sailing ships, a globe and dozens of plastic monster figurines from movies. There was a window seat looking out onto the expansive backyard, a twin bed and a standing lamp with a spiral post, also mahogany.

Clovis told me to sit in the rocking chair near the window. He sat on the bed.

'Don't worry. No one can hear us in here.' He pounded on the wall of a shelf. 'Solid wood. Hey, I heard about Buster. It's sad. We used to play together when we were kids. He was okay until his mother got sick. He hasn't been the same since.'

'What's up, Clovis?'

He leaned forward and set his elbows on his knees, 'I wanted to say sorry about the mix-up.'

'It's not your fault.' I started to get up but he waved me back into my seat.

'Wait a minute. It is my fault, sort of. You see, I let this guy in not knowing that Connie-Jean had already invited you over. I should have asked her.'

'That's okay. I better go.' I got up again and this time Clovis didn't try to stop me. 'I can find my way out. Thanks for your apology.'

'She likes you, you know.'

I stopped in my tracks, 'Really?' I searched his face, but I couldn't tell if he was fooling with me. I sat down again. 'Then what's she doing with Milt Bryson?'

Clovis shook his head, 'It's not what you think. You see, Milt is a friend of Joey's, Joe Penderecki. Connie and Joe used to go together but something happened and … she doesn't like him anymore. Milt's trying to convince her to get back together with Joe before the prom.'

'What happened with Joe?' Clovis had my full attention now.

'I don't know,' he hung his head. 'Connie used to tell me everything, but …'

'She said she would call me later,' I said.

He seemed to brighten at that. 'She will then. She isn't always the easiest girl to get on with, but she keeps her word.'

'Okay. That's good,' I said. 'Hey, thanks, Clovis. You're a foursquare guy.'

*

I was nervous about going back to the apartment and explaining to Kate and Tate why I'd been gone for less than a half hour. To my surprise – and distress – the place was empty and dark. I turned on the kitchen light, put the Pre-Raphaelite book on the dining table and sat down; my foot tapping to no tune. They must have gone for a drink or something. I was relieved on the one hand but still uncomfortable when I didn't know where Tate was at. I got out some milk and poured myself a tall glass.

Clovis had said Connie-Jean liked me. What did that mean? Should I be renting my tux and ordering a corsage for the prom, or did he mean she didn't gag at the mention of my name? Was she toying with me all the time for her amusement? She was always so in control. Besides, what was I thinking? She was a junior and I was a freshman. There was a better chance of the US and Russia sending a man to the moon together than me jumping that divide.

I was hungry. In the end Tate probably hadn't been expecting me home for dinner. In the fridge I found some baloney, leftover Chinese food in a cardboard carton and three bottles of Pabst beer. I got out a midsized pot and dumped the Chinese food into it. Then I threw in four rings of baloney, torn in quarters, and topped it off with three generous shakes of ketchup. The stove was electric and took forever to heat up. I forgot to stir my 'stew' in time so the bottom was burnt, but at least it filled a hole.

Evening turned to night and I was sitting at the table, my mind darting around as fast as Cassius Clay's feet. When the telephone rang it made me jump.

'Hello?'

'Jackson, I am so sorry.'

'That's okay.'

'No, it was rude.' I said nothing. 'I know it's late ...' Connie-Jean continued.

On the starburst wall clock it was seven thirty-five. 'Yeah.'

'But I would like to see the picture. Can you come over now?'

The woman who answered the door was older than I expected. Her false eyelashes and heavy make-up didn't make her look any younger. She extended a skinny arm and several bangles slid down to her wrist.

'You must be Jackson.' Her voice was throaty and deep. 'Come in, dear, before you catch your death.'

I scooted into the foyer. 'Pleased to meet you, Mrs Templeton.'

'And I you, young man.' She took my coat and cap. 'I understand you have recently moved from New York.'

'That's right, ma'am.'

'Do you miss the East Coast? I do. I was born and raised in Buffalo.'

'Oh, really? It's nice up that way.'

'Yes, quite, and winters are really winters.' She guided me into the room where Milt Bryson had been sitting a few hours earlier. 'Over here every day is the same. It's such a bore.'

I nodded.

'The twins are in the TV room,' she said, pointing through an open door. 'It's been a delight.'

'Likewise, ma'am.'

'Not too late, children,' she called out. She blew a kiss to Clovis and Connie-Jean from the doorway.

'G'night, mother,' Clovis said mechanically.

Connie-Jean blew a kiss back to her, stood and walked over to me. She pouted, 'My poor, poor villain.'

Clovis stood up too and headed towards the door. I silently thanked him. He winked.

'I'll be back when *Ed Sullivan* starts,' he said.

Connie-Jean didn't react. Was it possible that they had arranged for the two of us to be left alone? As soon as the door closed, Connie-Jean took me by the arm and sat me down on the white leather sofa.

'I can't tell you how mortified I am about this afternoon.'

'Forget it.'

'If you only knew what I've been through.'

'Well, we've got a few minutes, if you want to talk about it,' I said hopefully.

She considered it, some of her old aloofness returning, 'No, I didn't invite you over to cry on your shoulder,' she said. 'Show me Ophelia.' I opened the book. She drank in the image. 'Look at all the different plants and flowers,' she whispered.

This was a part of the painting I hadn't really looked at. She stared at Ophelia's hands and mimicked the pose. She was doing it unconsciously, naturally, and not for my benefit at all. We were sitting close and I felt her warmth and devoured her aroma. It was a different perfume than her usual one. It hung in the air like wisteria on a warm, still night.

Clovis came in again and unceremoniously turned on the TV. It was a twenty-three-inch RCA Beauchamp, the first colour TV set I had ever seen. Unfortunately, there was only one station that transmitted in colour, NBC, and *The Ed Sullivan Show* was on Channel 2, CBS. Clovis sat beside me and turned off the table lamp we had been using to illuminate the painting in the book.

'Good evening, ladies and gentleman,' boomed the familiar voice of Ralph Renick, the newscaster. 'Tonight, live from Miami Beach, *The Ed Sullivan Show*.'

I closed the book on my lap and looked over at Connie-Jean. Her eyes were wide. Unai had been right – she was obviously a fan. Ed heaped praise on the band and told us they had attracted the largest TV audience ever. I had waited for this all week – this and seeing Connie-Jean – and now both were happening at the same time. It was coincidence of cosmic proportions.

'The Beatles!' Ed shouted.

The audience screamed, and Connie-Jean joined in. The curtains opened and the band launched into *She Loves You*. I had to strain to hear the lyrics over her hysterics. The words seemed to relate directly to us. Had she told Clovis to tell me that she liked me? He was bobbing his head and tapping his feet, grinning from ear to ear. The band finished on a great harmonic note and then quickly shifted positions, with John taking centre stage. This time they did a slow-dance song and Connie-Jean's thigh shifted next to mine. Again the music seemed to be about us, and about Milt Bryson and Joe Penderecki.

At the end of that song they switched positions and Paul said a few words. His accent was like nothing I had ever heard. It was English, but very different from the standard English accents of movies. When he started singing *All My Loving*, Connie-Jean sighed. Inexplicably, Kate came to my mind.

'They're so fab,' Connie-Jean breathed.

'Fab?' I asked.

'Fab, you know, fabulous,' Clovis said. 'It's what they say in England.'

Then it was over.

Ed introduced the next guest, the boxer Sonny Liston. The Beatles weren't going to be on again until the end of the show, which meant we'd have to sit through Allen & Rossi doing their comedy act and Mitzi Gaynor singing. I didn't think Allen & Rossi were very funny and – although Mitzi Gaynor was cute – her singing was pretty boring. I was also worried about overstaying so I decided to test the waters.

'I think I should go,' I said, waiting for them to protest.

'See ya, Jack,' Clovis said. Connie-Jean stood up and brought me my cap and coat, and before I knew it we were standing by the door.

'Thanks for coming over,' she said. Did she say the same thing to Milt? 'It was a shambles, but I promise I'll make it up to you.' The chill was seeping in from outside. I wanted to say more. I wanted to know where I stood. I forced a smile.

'One may smile, and smile, and be a villain,' I said.

Then she gave a little shiver and leaned over, closer and closer to my face.

This is it, I thought. My knees weakened, my lips felt tight and heated. I started to pucker up. The strong light on the landing diffused, casting a warm shadowless glow over us. Then she kissed me. On the cheek.

I stumbled down the path to El Caballero. In my head I tried to make the kiss more than what it was. I tried to convince myself that the cold touch of her skin was due to the chill in the air – that she wouldn't kiss her grandma, cousin or mother's friend in the same way – but I couldn't square it.

II

THE NEXT DAY BEFORE ART CLASS Luke was leafing through a copy of *Action Comics*. 'This is so bogus, man. President Kennedy disguised as Clark Kent? That's cold.'

'Yeah. I've seen that one,' I set out my pencils. 'It came out the week I moved here in November, but check out the date on the cover.'

'February? Whoa. *Totally* bogus.' Mr Talbot walked by and Luke stopped him. 'Look, Mr T.'

'Yes, I've seen it. A lot of people think it's in bad taste.'

'The drawing's radical, but the president as Superman? He was a skinny dude.'

Mr Talbot laughed and shook his head. 'Call it artistic licence.' He started to move away, but Luke carried on.

'It's not real art, just comics. Comics' licence.' Luke grinned.

Mr Talbot stopped. 'It's funny you should say that.' He turned to us and said, 'you'll be interested in this too, Jackson. I saw an exhibition last month at the Ferus Gallery called *A View of NY Painting*. It was quite a show. One of the artists was a guy named Roy Lichtenstein. He uses comics and the whole commercial printing process as the inspiration for his work.'

I smiled. 'I know Lichtenstein's work already, sir. My parents took me to the opening of his show at the Castelli Gallery two years ago.'

'Holy cow!' Mr Talbot stroked his chin. 'What was it like?'

'His work? It's like you said – bright and easy to look at; a lot like comics. The opening was crowded and loud and every painting had a red dot next to it. Lichtenstein was over the moon. He moved in this weird, angular way that made him look like a puppet.'

Mr Talbot nodded. 'Like I say; you got to be open. Art is everywhere, especially where we don't expect it.' He patted Luke on the back and carried on to the front of the room.

'Especially where we don't expect it? Dude, you think it could be in the toilet?' Luke cracked up.

'It's already been done,' I said. 'Check out an artist named Marcel Duchamp.'

'No shit?' Luke quipped.

Mr Talbot's lesson was about light and how important it was; how we see everything because of its radiance. Then he talked about the emotion of light. 'For example, light can set the mood and increase the drama of a scene.' He put a lamp under his chin and walked across the room stiff legged, like Frankenstein's monster. Everyone in the class hooted – everyone except me. I was brooding about Connie-Jean.

After leaving her house the night before, I had returned to our empty apartment. I didn't like it any better than I did before. In fact, it seemed even lonelier. I turned on the TV for distraction and caught The Beatles' last set on *Ed Sullivan* all by myself. The music brightened my mood a little, but any way I looked at it, the night had come up short – it was a dismal failure. I was no better off with Connie-Jean than I had been before.

'Forget about it, *guero*,' Ray said as if he were reading my mind. 'That bird was never going to fly, *ese*, it's fate.' He stretched over the table and whispered to Twinkie, who was sitting next to Luke, 'Hey, Twinkie.' He waited until he had everyone's attention and then said, 'I'm hungry for somethin' real sweet.'

'You're sick and disgusting, Ray,' she answered, but with a hint of a smile.

Ray laughed. I pushed his arm, but it didn't make a difference. 'Hey, Twinkie, you got a luscious cream-filled centre? Mmm ...' he ran his tongue over his upper lip. Twinkie threw her eraser at him.

'Knock it off, Ray. Can't you see you're just being a jerk?'

'What bee got up your butt, *ese*?'

I ignored him.

I was also tense because we were going to find out who won the Freshman Art Competition. While we were on morning break, Mr Talbot finished pinning up the finalists on the wall. I rushed in as soon as he opened the door. Most of the class chose Picasso as the artist model because they thought he would be easy – despite Mr Talbot's pleas for them to 'extend themselves'. In the end, most of it wasn't very good. Only a couple of portraits made it onto the wall. Luke had used Van Gogh, ignorant of the fact that Vincent died ten years before the turn of the century. Instead of the artist's intense, lost look, Luke blatantly copied the face of Beetle Bailey from the newspaper comics. He couldn't resist painting a trickle of blood dripping down from the bandaged ear. His painting didn't make it onto the wall, and neither did Twinkie's startlingly accurate Modigliani – bare boobs and all – which Mr Talbot appreciated, artistically, but thought might be offensive to Vice-Principal Cannon.

Maria did a fine work in the style of Marc Chagall. It wasn't one of the girly images like *La Mariée* or *Birthday 1915*, which I had seen in the Met with Mutti the year before. It was based on Chagall's *Self-Portrait with Seven Fingers*. The dreamy, cat-like eyes were the same – Maria only thickened the lips, broadened the cheekbones and changed the hair colour to match hers. It was an incredible likeness. She also replaced the Eiffel Tower in the window on the left with the Welcome to San Sebastiano sign over Main Street in town, and on the easel she reproduced the still life she had done in the first week of class.

'Wow,' I said, as Mr Talbot put the painting on the wall. 'That's really neat.'

'Thanks, Jack.' Maria was looking at me with a smile on her face. I couldn't deny it – she had really done well. 'I like yours, too. It was clever how you made the walkway into the Brooklyn Bridge.'

I had worked hard on mine. I really wanted that book. There was no way that Tate was ever going to buy it for me so it was a great chance to get it. My painting was in the style of Edvard Munch's *The Scream*.

Then Mr Talbot hung Ray's effort on the wall. Maria and I widened our eyes at each other.

'Who was his model, Mr T?' I asked.

'Paul Signac.' He pushed in the last pin. 'It's based on a painting called *Portrait of Felix Feneon, Opus 217* from 1890.'

'But you said twentieth century, sir.'

He turned to us, looking slightly uncomfortable.

'Yes, but I let it through because it looks so … *now*, don't you think?'

'Oh!' Twinkie exclaimed, before Maria or I could respond.

'You all have to see Ray's work.' The other girls began to 'ooh'and 'ahh'.

'Oh, brother,' Maria whispered to me.

'Tell me about it, sister.' We looked at each other and laughed.

At that moment, Mr Cannon came through the doorway. Everyone fell silent – even Ray. The vice-principal gestured for Mr Talbot to carry on. He didn't look at us. He peered at the artwork on the walls with his hands behind his back and then did a full circuit of the room, looking over all our shoulders. Since the class had recently started there wasn't much to see, except for the competition finalists. He was back at the doorway quickly. A sigh escaped from Ray's mouth. Then Mr Cannon turned and addressed us. 'I will be announcing the winner of this year's Freshman Art Competition before the La Cienega field trip. Very nice. Carry on.' He then turned to Mr Talbot. 'May I see Master Ryder in my office, please?'

Mr Talbot nodded and waved me over.

'*Mierda,*' Ray cursed under his breath. My stomach was filled with lead. None of our classmates made a sound, but their eyes followed me across the room.

Mr Cannon walked next to me, one hand behind his back.

This had to be about that goddamn Buster Nicholls again. And it might be the thing that would finally blow Tate's stack. My stomach dropped to the floorboards.

Once we were inside his office he walked to the window. 'Please take a seat, Master Ryder,' he said. 'How are you enjoying San Sebastiano?'

My mouth was dry. I had to clear my throat before I could squeeze out an answer. 'Fine, sir.'

He was silent, facing away from me. 'You know, there isn't much that escapes me in this school.'

'Yes, sir.'

He sat down, leaned back and his chair let out an almighty creak.

'Unfortunately, some of my responsibilities are, as you know, unpleasant. It gives me no great pleasure to remind students of their duties and responsibilities, day in and day out.' He glanced over his shoulder at the window, then turned back to me. 'Nevertheless, that's not why I invited you here.'

'It isn't?' I heard the heavenly trumpet of Handel's *Hallelujah* chorus. It was the marching band practising for the St Patrick's Day Parade out on the football field. My joy and relief were quickly dampened by suspicion. 'Then why did you call me here, sir?'

He leaned forward and wove his fingers together. 'Look around. What do you see?'

Countless possible answers flashed through my head. I couldn't mention his incredibly depressing interior-decorating skills. 'Nothing,' I finally said.

'Precisely.' He pounded the desktop and smiled, causing two small dimples to form on his cheeks. I was probably the first student in his forty-year career to see them. 'My walls are bare.' He looked around the room with the glare he usually reserved for misbehaving students. 'I need some relief – some visual relief – to lift my spirits. I want some … aesthetically pleasing pictures, paintings, drawings and the like, to grace my office.' He sat back. 'I saw that drawing you made of the clump of grass. It moved me very much. It reminded me of a wonderful trip that I took to Austria in my youth – before the war, of course. There was a painting I saw at the Albertina Museum …'

'*The Great Piece of Turf.*'

'Why, yes – that's right. You know it?'

'It was my inspiration for the drawing.'

'Yes, of course.' He stared beyond me, a faraway look in his eye.

'If you want it, sir, I'd be happy to give it to you.'

His look hardened. 'No,' he said firmly. 'You cannot gift it to me and I cannot buy it from you. It would be inappropriate, seeing as you are a student of this institution, and I am in a position of authority over you. However, you could *lend* it to me while you are at this school, and if you haven't sold it before you graduate, I would happily purchase it from you at that time.'

I smiled and held out my hand, 'You've got a deal, sir.' We shook firmly. 'Will that be all?'

'One more thing, Jackson.'

'Yes, sir?'

'A word of advice, young man – people will judge you by your actions. As tempting as it might be to act like a comic book hero, it can bring you to the attention of … the more formidable antagonists at this school. Be watchful, my boy. Not everyone is as understanding as I am.'

I nodded again and scooted out of his office as fast as I could.

That evening, as we ate Rice-A-Roni for dinner, I considered telling Tate about my session with Mr Cannon. Instead, I thought about Connie-Jean and what had happened the night before. 'Hey Tate, what happened last night? Where were you?'

'Kate and I went out for a drink. Charlie caught up with us at the Roadside Inn and we all went to the country club for dinner. I had a great T-bone steak. I swear it was two inches thick. Then we went to Kate's to watch a little TV. To tell you the truth, I thought I'd be home before you.'

That figured. I still felt deserted, but at least we were talking. 'Did you see Sonny Liston and Joe Lewis on *Ed Sullivan*?'

'Yeah, we just caught that.'

I wasn't interested in boxing, but I knew Tate was a fan. We chatted about the upcoming fight between the heavyweight champion and Cassius Clay – the young boxer with a mouth on him – who had won gold at the Olympics. It was the most relaxed chat we'd had since we left New York.

I got Tate to sign a permission slip for an art field trip that was coming up on Monday after school. I took a chance that he wouldn't ask what it was for, and he didn't. 'We'll get back late, but you don't have to wait up. My teacher can bring me home,' I added.

'That's fine. How is it going at work? Are you getting the hang of it?'

I told him about the Merc convertible that Buzz, Stretch and I were working on. He nodded, but didn't seem that interested. The conversation stalled. I wanted it to go on, so I told him the first thing that came to mind. 'When we were cleaning up I noticed a weird tattoo on Buzz's arm.'

'Oh, really? What was it?'

'It said *Vestal AR-4* and had a little symbol below it that looked like a cog wheel stuck on a sickle.'

'Uh-huh.' If he knew what it was, Tate wasn't letting on.

'Do you think … do you think he's been in jail or something?' I asked.

'What?' Tate put down his fork. I braced myself. I didn't know what I had done wrong, but I could tell from the tone of his voice that he wasn't happy. 'Is that what you think, son?

That we would put you in a job with a convict? Are you a *meshugener* or something?'

I felt awkward. 'Don't get me wrong, Daddy-o. You know I like Buzz. It's just that ...' I shrugged my shoulders. 'Who gets tattoos besides jailbirds?'

He raised an eyebrow, his fork half way to his lips. 'Daddy-o?' he queried. I shrugged, he chewed. 'Sailors, Jackson.' He picked up another forkful and softened his tone. 'It's been a naval tradition for three hundred years. The USS *Vestal* was a Navy repair ship during the war.'

'So Buzz was in the Navy?'

He paused. 'Yes, but it's not my story to tell. Ask Charlie – or Buzz – if you think you can get anything out of him.'

We ate quietly for a while.

'Do you think Mr Cannon could be Jewish?' I asked him.

'Why not?'

'Yeah, I guess. But he looks like such a *goy*.'

Tate laughed and pulled out a pack of cigarettes from his shirt pocket. 'You never know. Maybe his parents had high ambitions for him. What could be more respectable than a school administrator?' He got up, grabbed the glass ashtray off the kitchen bench and then sat down again. 'Have you thought about what you want to do when you get out of school?'

I was almost as thrown as when he slapped me. 'I don't know.'

He tapped the table with the butt-end of a cigarette, 'My *mamele* wanted me to be a doctor. Can you imagine?'

'What did *you* want to be?'

He looked at me quizzically. 'A musician; a horn player. My tate said, "Fine, *blozn shoyfer* after work, around the *piyane* like a normal person, why don't you?" He never got it. Nathan was okay with my parents' scheme, though. He was planning to go to med school – he could have done it too, he was that sharp – but I convinced him to join the Army with me instead. Can you beat that?'

'Oh, man.'

'Yeah.' He pulled the ashtray towards him slowly.

I didn't know what to say. 'I'll see you in the morning, Tate.'

Before I left the room, I glanced back at him. He was sitting with his head low between his shoulders, bathed in the harsh light of the low-hanging bulb over the table. He flicked his Zippo lighter and drew deeply on his cigarette. The hollows of his face were lit up bright-orange for a moment and I saw a tear gleaming on his cheek.

The next day after work I asked Charlie about Buzz. He got up and closed the office door. 'Have you asked him?'

'C'mon, Charlie, you know he won't say anything.'

He looked at me with his head cocked to the side for a minute. 'Shoot. You're right; he'll never tell you, so I guess I will. But remember, he's a private man. Don't go blabbing it around all over town, you dig?'

'Sure.'

Charlie reached into the bottom drawer of his desk, looked at me, then closed it again. 'Buzz was an experienced mechanic in Portland in the thirties. He joined the Navy before the war. Because of his training and experience, they rated him as a Machinist's Mate and then put him on the USS *Vestal* as a repairman. So instead of fixing Ford Model As, he was fixing battleship engines. It was a whole other ballgame.

The job of the *Vestal* was to go from naval port to naval port fixing up ships – San Diego, Newport News, Panama,

Manila … you name it, she went there. On 6 December 1941, she was docked off Ford Island on Oahu, Hawaii, right next to the USS *Arizona*.'

'One day before the Japanese bombed Pearl Harbor.'

'You got it, sport.'

'What happened?'

'When the raid began two bombs hit the *Vestal* right away. Right next to it the *Arizona* took a direct hit that ignited the forward magazine.'

'Where all the ammo was stored?'

'Yeah. The blast sent out a tremendous shockwave. Buzz was hurled into the water by the force of the explosion, along with everyone else on deck. He lost a good part of his hearing then – that's how he got his moniker.'

'His what?'

'You know, his nickname.' Charlie made a swirling gesture near his ear. 'That's part of the reason why he doesn't say much. Anyway, he saved a few sailors and made it back to the *Vestal* while the captain stopped the rest of the crew from abandoning ship. By this time, oil from the *Arizona* had started fires on the *Vestal*. Buzz untied her from the other ship by chopping at the mooring lines with a fire axe. The *Vestal* was listing badly, but a tugboat got them out of danger. The captain got a Medal of Honour and Buzz was recommended for a medal too. He turned it down. I don't know why.' Charlie flipped the lid of a red-and-white Marlboro box and pulled out a cigarette.

'That's mind-boggling. What happened next?'

'Except for his ears, Buzz was okay. It took the crew of the *Vestal* a week of pumping water and clearing debris before they could refloat the ship. In the meantime, her crew – including Buzz – were repairing other ships damaged in the attack.' He lit the cigarette with a chunky marble lighter that matched the ashtray on his desk. 'By attacking the ships and leaving the repair docks and oil tanks unharmed, the Japanese sealed their own fate. All the attack did was kill a couple of thousand helpless swabbies and piss off the US. Most of the naval ships were repaired, thanks to the *Vestal* and others like her. The aircraft carriers weren't in port that day, and we had enough gas and oil to last our Pacific fleet the better part of a year.' He took a long drag and coughed. 'At any other time Buzz would have been discharged on medical grounds but hey, it was war. Skills like his were rare. He didn't have to be able to hear to fix gigantic steam turbines, so he spent the next four years in the Pacific up to his elbows in grease and sweat. When the *Vestal* was decommissioned in '46, he was there. Jobs were scarce in Seattle, and after so long in the Pacific, he couldn't take the cold anymore. So eventually he made his way down here.'

'How did you find him?'

'There was a watering hole I used to drink at in Brea until I got too friendly with the owner's wife, if you know what I mean.' He straightened his tie and smirked. 'But before that, I tried to strike up a conversation with Buzz at the bar over the Floyd Patterson and Sonny Liston fight on TV. It took a bit, but after a few Bacardi's he opened up. I snapped him up as soon as I knew his story.'

That night in my room I lay in bed, in the dark. Finally, I turned on my bedside lamp, grabbed Walter Lord's *Day of Infamy* from my bookshelf and pulled out my drawing pad. I found the famous photo of the USS *Arizona* after the attack and looked at it hard. I wanted to draw the *Vestal* next to the

Arizona with Buzz in the water, but the *Vestal* must have been gone by the time the photo was taken. The only thing visible through the blanket of sooty grey smoke was an observation tower leaning at a forty-five-degree angle, with its two cranes like robot arms reaching up to the heavens.

I thought about the Lichtenstein opening. I liked all his work, but one painting in particular had me riveted. It was a close-up of a woman's face, shoulder and hand, surrounded by churning waves. There were pools of tears under her eyes and a speech bubble above her head that read: 'I don't care! I'd rather sink – than call Brad for help!'

As Charlie told Buzz's story, that painting, *Drowning Girl*, had been flashing through my mind. It was that scene that I wanted to sketch, but instead of the beautiful young girl, it would be Buzz. What would his speech bubble say? With the radio on low I attempted to reproduce Buzz's craggy, perpetually stubbly face. I added the *Arizona* in the background and some Hokusai-style waves swirling around the scene.

I didn't get very far before midnight, but as I fell asleep, I could see what I wanted, right down to the Ben-Day dots. The image tumbled into my dream, but now it had movement and sound. 'Boom!' went the deck of the battleship. I saw the word, complete with exclamation point, in a red, pointed speech bubble. Buzz raised his massive arm out of the brine, revealing his *Vestal* AR-4 tattoo as he powered through the water. A speech bubble appeared at his mouth with 'grunt' and 'mumble' and other symbols that indicated cursing. There were more booms and the black outlines of the waves grew thicker with oil.

*

By the end of the month, Buzz, Stretch and I had done everything we could to the Merc. 'She's off to the paint shop now, professor.' Stretch chirped. 'She's as good as new, at least under the hood.'

'She still *looks* like a wreck, though,' I said.

'Don't you worry, little buddy.' Stretch had been calling me that ever since he saw *Gilligan's Island* on TV. I guess it made him feel older, like he was my mentor or something. 'She'll be tip-top before you know it.'

'This must be one heck of a friend of Charlie's to deserve all the time we've put into it,' I said.

'Oh, yeah, yeah. I think Mr Salmond said it belonged to an Injun friend of his up in the canyon.'

'Joe? Did he say it was Joe who has the gas station?'

'Yeah, yeah, it could be. Say, if it was your car, what colour would you make it?'

My first thought was cherry red, but then I imagined the full lines of the car and realised it would look bulky and vaguely disastrous, like a fire truck. It needed something light – like yellow or white – something cool. I thought about Mutti's eyes in summer sunlight and the jacket Connie-Jean was wearing the first day I saw her at school. 'A kind of powder blue, like the sky,' I said.

'Yeah, yeah, I can see that.'

'What colour is it going to be?'

'I don't know, professor. That's up to the owner, I reckon.'

Vice-Principal Cannon came into art class Monday morning and announced the winner of the Freshman Art Competition. I was feeling pretty confident because I knew he liked my work. No one else seemed to be too excited except Maria – Ray didn't even stop working on the pastel drawing he was making.

'The winner is … Ramon Rodriguez.'

Ray looked up and grinned. He looked at me, raised his eyebrows and dusted his hands. Mr Talbot led the class in a round of applause. I cringed when Ray shook Mr Cannon's hand, held up the certificate – now smudged with lilac pastel – and grabbed the pristine book. Mr Cannon looked down at his hand and discreetly wiped it on his other hand. Ray came back to his seat, smirked at me, chucked the book in his desk, and got back to drawing.

I didn't talk to him the rest of the period. I didn't eat lunch with him and the guys that day either. Ray caught me, unexpectedly, as I was leaving the library. 'I thought you'd be hiding here. What's up, *guero*?'

I headed for the history room at speed. 'Nothing.'

'Bullshit. You said jack-all in art and didn't eat with us just now. That's not like you.' I didn't know if he expected an answer. I didn't care if he did. 'This isn't because of what I said about your cheerleader *princesa* is it? You know she's too old, up herself and the private property of fucking football Joe.'

'Just shut up, Ray. For Christ's sake, don't you ever shut up?'

He was carrying the *Life with Picasso* book – his prize – on top of his art gear. I wanted that book almost more than the prize itself. The cover was still smeared with polychrome pastel fingerprints. It disgusted me. Mutti's eyes flashed in my head. I grabbed the book as fast as I could and wiped it on the sleeve of my shirt.

'What the hell?' Ray blurted out. He tried to yank the book out of my grasp. I pulled it away.

'You don't deserve this book. You're treating it like shit. Are you goin' to take care of it?'

'Give it back, *pendejo*.' He reached for it again, but I just held it straight up. He was too short to reach it. 'Give it!' He jumped but I just moved it to the side. A hardness came into his eyes I had never seen before. He looked around. There were a few people about and they were taking notice. When he looked back at me his resistance was gone. 'You know what? You keep the *pinché* book. I don't want it. I was never going to read it, anyway.' Then he mumbled, 'I just wanted to show my mamá that I won somethin.' With that he veered away from our shared path and headed towards the gym.

I slowed down and then stopped. I looked at the book again. The paper cover was a kind of khaki green with orange, lime, brown and white letters. The chalky smear of bright pastel colours actually improved the uninspiring book cover. Underneath, the book was white linen with copper-embossed letters. Classy.

My stomach felt hard, solid. What the hell was I doing? Why was I so fucking mad?

I missed seeing the Merc off the following Monday because we had the field trip after school and I had to skip work. We were going to a place called La Cienega Boulevard. There were two big yellow school buses – one for seniors and teachers and one for the rest of us. 'Hey, Ryder,' I heard from the back of the bus. There, sitting on the back bench, were Ming Li and Maria. Billy Hughes – Mr Talbot's helper in class – was with them.

'Freshmen at the back of the bus, Jack-off,' Milt Bryson said loudly. Most of the kids in the front laughed. I tried to act like it didn't faze me, but it was intimidating being surrounded by the enemy. I headed towards my friends, not looking right or left.

'Jackson,' someone else called out. There was Connie-Jean, sitting with another cheerleader. Caught by surprise, I kept moving with a pathetic wave. 'I'll see you when we get there,' she called after me.

'Wow, you know Connie-Jean Templeton?' Billy said when I got to the back seat.

'She lives next door,' I replied. 'Say, where is everybody?'

'There wasn't enough room for all of the freshman art students, so Mr Talbot chose us,' Ming Li answered.

'Why us?'

'Can't you figure it out, Ryder?' Maria asked, 'It's because we're the pick of the bunch – the top bananas.'

'Except for Billy,' Ming Li added. 'He was chosen because he's the teacher's pet.'

It was the first joke I had heard from her. Billy blushed, but there was a grin on his chubby face.

'What about Ray? He won the award. He's the best artist in class,' I said flatly.

'He had to work, Jack,' Maria answered. 'Besides, he's good, but I think you're better.' She turned to Ming Li and Billy. 'You should see the drawing he made of my parents. It's so good.'

'They liked it?'

'They loved it, especially mother. She's going to call you this weekend.'

My stomach sank. 'No! That's nice, but tell her please not to call.'

'Why not? She wants to thank you.'

My mind was racing. I hadn't thought the situation out well enough.

'Tell her … tell her that I'll come by after school next week, okay?' This might buy me time.

Maria peered intently at my face. I had to look away. She said slowly, 'Okay, Ryder, I'll tell her.'

I changed the subject. 'Why are we going on this trip? What's La Cienega Boulevard?'

'Mr Talbot takes all the classes up to the Boulevard every year,' Billy said. 'That's where all the art galleries are. They're open late on Monday nights, I guess so people with jobs can go shopping. He knows a bunch of the gallery owners and sometimes the artists come down to talk to us. And we get to go to Tommy's for dinner first.'

I hadn't figured on paying for anything so I only had a few coins in my pocket. 'I've never heard of it. Is it good?'

'Yeah, it's the best,' Billy said. 'Their cheeseburger is like …' he rolled his eyes and slumped down in his seat like he had died. Then he sprang up and added, 'And they're fast.'

Food was one thing, but what I really hungered for was Connie-Jean. I caught glimpses of her now and then in the front of the bus between shifting heads. She was listening intently to the other blonde cheerleader.

'You got enough cash, Jack?' Maria asked bluntly. 'You look worried.'

'Uh … I got money; I just didn't bring it with me.'

'Don't worry about it. I can help you.'

'Me too,' Ming Li said. 'I have three dollars.'

I smiled and relaxed. 'Thanks.'

'You missed the field-trip instructions because you were in the vice principal's office,' Ming Li said.

‘Ooh,’ the other two murmured.

I rolled my eyes. ‘I wasn’t in trouble. Cannon wanted one of my paintings.’

‘Told you. You’re the best,’ Maria said. In the dim evening light I couldn’t tell if she was being serious, sarcastic, funny, or a mixture of all three.

By this time, we were approaching the on-ramp for the freeway, going north. Beyond the streetlights was the dark silhouette of the distant hills. Huge billboards lined the route – Marlboro, Dewar’s, TWA – they were hand-painted and thirty feet across. Kate used to work for one of the companies that made them. She told me that they were created by talented guys with little photographs and really big brushes. They looked perfect as we sped past.

Maria, Ming Li, Billy and I chatted, but my heart wasn’t in it. I was still sore about Ray and I wanted to talk to Connie-Jean. Dinner might have been my chance, but since I was short of cash I couldn’t exactly take money from the girls and then abandon them in favour of Connie-Jean. After Sunday’s fiasco, I wasn’t sure it was worth all the confusion and anxiety anyway.

Maria turned to me while Ming Li and Billy were talking about a comedy with Don Knott that was coming out next month. ‘What’s wrong, Jack. You’re acting weird.’

I liked Maria. We had a connection, but I couldn’t let her in. ‘Nothin’ really.’

Billy interrupted, ‘Hey, you want to go see *The Incredible Mr Limpett* with us?’ Maria and I both shook our heads.

The buses got off the freeway at Rampart. After three blocks of two and three-storey apartments dotted by incredibly tall palm trees, the buses parked beside a huge parking lot on the corner of Beverly Boulevard. On the corner of the parking lot was a tiny shack with a big red sign that said Tommy's. Around the perimeter of the asphalt lot was a single building with a row of counters with napkin dispensers every few feet covered by an awning. The lot was full of people standing in groups holding drinks and burgers.

My gang were the last off the bus. We were told to stay together and then marched across the four-laned boulevard towards a little red-and-white stand on the corner. Tommy's wasn't too impressive from the outside, and there were at least fifty of us. How was that little stand going to serve us all – and where we were supposed to sit?

'I can't wait,' Billy bubbled. 'I'm going to get two double cheeseburgers. Just stay out of my way.'

As we started to cross the street, a rolling steel door opened on the wall at the far side of the lot. Tommy's was actually the entire corner surrounding the parking lot and was three times larger than it looked. Miss O'Hare, the print teacher, split us into two groups. Billy and Ming Li were in the line going to the far side, while Maria and I went to the corner stand.

'Don't worry, Jack,' she reassured me. 'Tommy's is one of the cheapest places in town and I guarantee you'll feel full afterwards. Follow my lead and get what you want.'

'Thanks, Maria, you're a pal.' As we neared the counter, Maria leaned over and dug a bottle of root beer out of a large cooler, so I did the same. In less than a minute we had ordered, paid and collected our food. 'Wow, that *was* fast and cheap,' I said.

'I told you.' She scanned the edges of the parking lot. 'Help me find a counter with enough room for the four of us, okay?'

'Are we standing?'

'Sure. Where do you think we are, The Ritz?'

I laughed.

We headed towards an opening about halfway across the lot. I set our plastic baskets of food on the counter. Maria grabbed us half a dozen napkins each. 'You're going to need them,' she said, noticing my expression. 'Hold this place for us. I'll go find Ming and Billy.'

I scanned the crowd for Connie-Jean but couldn't find her. It was night-time now, but Tommy's was well lit. Beverly and Rampart boulevards were packed with bumper-to-bumper cars. For the first time, the West Coast felt as exciting as New York City.

'That's my spot, Jack-shit, get lost.' Milt Bryson was behind me, holding his red plastic basket. Two football goons in letterman jackets were at his side.

12

MILT HAD A SELF-SATISFIED SMIRK on his face. 'What you gonna do, hero? Push me over like I'm some sophomore punk?'

My stomach sank, but I was kind of surprised – and flattered – that Milt knew who I was. I got a feeling of twisted déjà vu, but this time I didn't see me on top. Trying to make a stand would be a stupid, pointless gesture. It was a no-win situation. Faster than a sneeze, options flashed in my head. I was ready to move, but instead I said, 'Whatever you're trying to prove, Milt, you've proved it. You three are strong and I'm weak. You can wop me and there isn't a damn thing I can do about it. I get it, I really do – I don't want any trouble but … I'm not moving from here.' My feet were frozen and my jaw was locked.

He blinked several times and shifted on his legs. 'Did you hear that, guys?' A charge built in the air, like the prelude to a thunderstorm, 'You *don't* get it or you would be moving your skinny little ass quick smart. When I'm done with you, your face is going to look like that chilli cheese oozing out of your hamburger. You get it *now*?' The two goons guffawed.

My stomach was halfway to China but I couldn't move my legs.

'You know what? I don't need any help from my team-mates either, you little shit. I can take care of you one handed.' Out of the side of his mouth he said to one of the thugs, 'Keep an eye out.'

I didn't see his hand curl into a fist. I didn't see his arm move. I just saw his shark-like eyes – black and still. His lower teeth wedged into his thin upper lip and oddly, beautifully, a dimple formed below his left cheek.

The wind was forced out of my lungs like air out of an exploding balloon; white, eye-popping pain seared in my gut. I sucked in. There were pins and needles on my scalp. Next thing I knew I was looking at my knees and I wanted to throw up. I looked up to see his chino-covered knees and tan loafers. 'Sweet Jesus,' I said to myself. The two gorillas hooted.

Stay down, logic told me. But I could smell the acrid parking lot asphalt; I could see the polychrome gum remnants – striking in their own way – staining the ground up close.

'Leave him alone, Milt,' Connie-Jean screamed from behind the defensive line-up. 'What has he done to you?'

'Stay out of this, Connie. It doesn't concern you.'

'Doesn't it?'

I got up, somewhat straightened, but was still hunched up with my arms wrapped across my torso. I panted. My head was light. I could feel beads of perspiration on my forehead. By then the ache was a throb, a bass note for my symphony of pain.

It wasn't over. I knew it wasn't over and that's what was scary. What was going to happen? What *could* happen? I couldn't think, and I didn't move an inch. 'I'm still here, Milt. I'm still here … and I'm not going to move.'

'Okay. It's your party, sucker. You make this so easy, you dumbshit.'

I braced for the next stab; tightened every muscle I could control. I squinted.

It would have been worse, but I was able to guard this one with my arms. I saw white for a second time but I didn't double over.

'Stop it!' Connie-Jean shrieked.

'How ya doin', kid?' a familiar, raspy voice came out of the darkness. A stocky figure wearing a Hawaiian shirt and a short-brimmed hat emerged from between two cars, carrying two double cheeseburgers in his basket and a bag of potato chips.

'Buzz? What are you doing here?' I dropped my arms.

'Same as you, kid; grabbing a bite before a big fight. 'Cept in my case, it's at the Valley Garden Arena.' Buzz looked over at Milt and his friends slowly. He looked them each in the eye, but didn't say a word. Milt leaned towards Buzz for a full ten seconds like he was going to punch him. Buzz was an old man, but he was beefy. Even more significant were his piercing blue eyes.

The goons backed away first. 'C'mon, Milt,' one of them muttered.

Finally Milt loosened his shoulders, breathed in through his nose, nodded at Buzz and said, 'sir.'

He grabbed at Connie-Jean's arm but she wriggled away. 'Don't you dare!'

He glanced at Buzz and me, sneered and disappeared into the crowd.

'Man, you saved my life.'

Buzz looked bemused. 'Maybe. I been standing over there for a while. I saw how you stood up to them. That was more interesting than any fight at the Olympic.' He plonked his food down on the counter. 'You didn't back down. That was stupid, but it took balls.'

'You saw them?'

'Sure.' He cracked a crooked smile. 'But you gotta fight your own fights, kid. Or in your case, get creamed. But enough is enough, and besides, I need you in the shop tomorrow.' He noticed Connie-Jean and tipped his hat. 'Beg your pardon, miss.'

'Jackson, I'm so sorry about that. Milt's usually not like that … he's completely the opposite. I don't know what got into him.'

'Don't worry about it.' I breathed deeply. I was shaky, but I couldn't believe it was over. It hurt – but I had no broken teeth, no blood splattered shirt. I was relatively okay. I put on my best face. 'Connie-Jean Templeton, meet Buzz … uh, Mr Burt Maddox. We work together.'

Buzz extended his meaty hand. 'I'm charmed to meet you, miss,' he said. At that moment, Maria returned with Ming Li and Billy in tow. I introduced them to Buzz and, although he was as polite with them, there was a change in his manner. He fumbled with his food, cocked his head and let his mouth drop open whenever anyone spoke. 'I'll shove off and leave you kids to it. Have a good time. It's nice to meet some of Jack's friends.'

I didn't want him to go. I was unnerved by the run-in with Milt. 'Say, what about that Cassius Clay?' I asked.

'Huh? Yeah, who would have thought the pretty boy would win? He's calling himself "Cassius X" now that he's the champ. Can you beat that?' I shook my head. Buzz grinned and mimed a couple of punches. 'Keep your guard up. See you at work, kid.'

He dissolved into the shadows between the streetlights on Rampart Boulevard.

Billy scrunched up the waxy wrapper paper into a ball as he gulped the last of his burger down. 'Hi, I'm William Fulton Hughes.' He thrust out his pudgy hand at Connie-Jean. It was dripping with Tommy's famous chilli sauce. She tried to smile.

'I saw you last year in *Romeo and Juliet* at the Sebastiano Community Theatre,' Maria said. 'You were really great.'

Connie-Jean lit up. 'You really think so? Thank you so much.'

'I wanted to go,' Billy said, 'but my parents wouldn't ... I mean, I had other pressing engagements.'

'Well, maybe next time,' Connie-Jean said. She looked at our uneaten burgers. 'We've finished dinner and I can see none of you – except William – has started, so I will withdraw and bid you all adieu.' She turned to me. 'Are you okay?'

I touched my side, 'Yeah. I'll be fine. Parting is such sweet sorrow.'

Connie-Jean gave me a sly grin and shook her finger. 'I'll find you on the walk, my villain.'

Between bites of his second burger Billy asked, 'What bad thing did you do?'

'It's not that kind of villainy.'

'Jackson's got a girlfriend,' Ming Li teased.

'C'mon,' I said, feigning annoyance. Inside, I revelled in the fantasy.

'Connie-Jean was good in that play,' Maria said, 'I wasn't just saying that.' She unwrapped her burger and took a bite. 'Eat up, Jack. It's probably cold by now.' I bit into the cheese-burger and cascades of chilli sauce oozed out of the sides, coating my fingers and dropping onto the asphalt. Everyone laughed, 'That's why there are paper-towel dispensers every-where,' Maria said.

I forgot the awkwardness and mess instantly. The chilli sauce wrapped around my tongue and coated my mouth with a warm, thick, mysterious sensation – spicy but also sweet. I don't know if my response to the taste was influenced by my lucky escape or the near brush with Connie-Jean, but I was hooked. I had never tasted anything like this – not even in New York. For the few minutes I ate the burger I was in ecstasy. Then I went cold thinking about Milt's threat – that was a lucky break. Next time I might not be so lucky.

We piled back onto the bus and headed west on Beverly for seventy or eighty blocks. The scenery was tedious. Under the cold streetlights, the buildings looked washed-out, and they were overshadowed by those impossible Dr Seuss-like palm trees. They hovered in the dark sky like tentacle-covered aliens, ready to pounce on their victims below.

I rubbed my side. It was still tender. It reminded me of a picture of San Sebastian by Giovanni Baglione that hung behind the counter in the municipal library. In the painting, the saint is sitting down in profile. A single arrow is lodged in his side and an angel is delicately pulling it out. Even with the graceful, light touch of the heavenly healer you can see the agony on the saint's face hardly held in check. His eyes are squeezed shut and his lips are parted. It struck me that the pain he is feeling is not some abstract religious sacrifice – he isn't taking this one for the Big Guy. It looks like he is totally feeling the pain – his pain – physical, real, immediate. Yeah, I could relate.

Finally we reached La Cienega Boulevard, made a right and drove for three more blocks before parking on the corner of Melrose Avenue. The driver wouldn't let us out until he had the go-ahead. Eventually Mr Talbot skipped onto the bus, his eyes bright.

'Okay, kids, this is the gallery district of Los Angeles. There are more galleries on this street than in the rest of the city put together. You'll see all kinds of artwork, from the very traditional to the most cutting-edge. I've contacted the galleries so they know you're coming, but remember they are businesses. They open late on Mondays so people can come and buy art. They don't have to see us. They're allowing us to come in and see what they do for *your* education. We are their guests, so be on your best behaviour. Do San Sebastiano High School proud.' He let this sink in before continuing, 'I've called a few artist friends to come down and talk about their work, so don't be afraid to ask questions. Take notes and remember names. Don't go down any side streets, and don't go any further than Santa Monica Boulevard. We don't have a lot of time. I need you all to be back on the bus by nine forty-five at the very latest. Do you understand? Good. Have a good time.'

We tumbled out of the bus and up the street. Billy, Maria, Ming Li and I stayed together towards the back of the group. The street was packed as if it was the middle of the day. There were people in suits and dresses, casual college types and scraggly people who didn't look too different from my parents' beatnik friends in New York. It was sensational to be out at night, in the city, with new friends. I was even able to ignore my injuries; but I still kept an eye out for Milt.

I don't remember all of the galleries we went into on that first trip, but a couple stood out. The Rolf Nelson Gallery was a converted storefront. It had an exhibition of local hard-edge abstract paintings on show. The abstract paintings I had seen in New York were splashed and dripped and expressive. These ones were crisp, bright and clean, with a lot of repeating motifs. They were two totally different things – like the cities themselves. I was pointing this out to Maria when a lean, bald-headed man in a brown suit walked up to us, smoking a cigarette.

'Can I do anything for you kids?'

'Sorry, sir, we'll move on,' I said.

'No, no, relax. You're not doing anything wrong. You're some of Larry's students, right? You look young.'

'We're freshmen, sir.'

'Well, you might be freshmen but you're the only kids from your school who have stopped and looked at the work. That's unusual – most adults don't look twice. That's why I came over.' He stuck out his hand. 'I'm Rolf Nelson. This is my gallery.' We all introduced ourselves. 'So?' he asked, gesturing at the painting in front of us.

'It's different,' Ming Li ventured.

'That's true, but what do you mean by that?'

'Jackson was saying it's not like the stuff he's seen in New York, sir,' Maria added.

He looked at me. 'I could tell by your accent you were from back east. So you're familiar with abstract paintings from the Big Apple, are you? Whose work have you seen?'

'Well, sir,' I began, 'Pollock, of course. Willem de Kooning, Mark Rothko …'

'I'm impressed. Somebody has raised you right. Well, LA's a whole different scene. Art has always been overshadowed by the movies here. Most of art that's been done up until now in this city has been pretty shallow stuff; trite, glorified decoration, really. Exciting things are just starting to happen. There's a whole new generation of artists that are going to give New York a run for its money. That's why I'm in the business. It's a thrilling time. So, what are you interested in? Do you want to be an artist?' I didn't want to have this conversation. Maria and Ming Li had disappeared and I used the opportunity to get away.

'Excuse me, Mr Nelson. Our friends have wandered off and we're supposed to stick together.' I turned to Billy. 'I'll go find Maria and Ming Li. I walked deeper into the gallery. The girls were talking to a slim woman with short, curly hair and a striped top.

'Oh, Jackson,' Maria said, 'I was just talking about you. This is Judy Gerowitz. She's an artist. This is Jackson Ryder.'

'Pleased to meet you, Mrs Gerowitz.'

'Call me Judy,' she said. 'And I'm not married anymore; I'm a widow. I don't belong to any man, not even Rolf over there. I hear you're named after Jackson Pollock?' My cheeks filled with blood. Ming Li and Maria giggled. 'Don't be embarrassed, Jackson. What a privilege.' Judy put her hand on my chest lightly. 'You've got a good artist's name. Wear it proudly.'

'Hey, Chicago,' Rolf Nelson called out.

'Come over, Rolf.' It was more a command than a request and Nelson complied, followed by Billy.

'I'm surprised to see you, all the way out from Pasadena.' He pecked her on the cheek, 'How you doing, Judy? How's the stomach?'

'Better thanks, Rolf. Maria and Ming here were asking me why almost every artist in this show is a man, and I wanted to know the same thing myself. I thought you'd be the best one to answer that question, since you curated it.'

Nelson fidgeted. 'The reality is, girls, that most artists – professional artists – are men.'

'That's bullshit and you know it,' Judy said.

'Judy,' Rolf pleaded, 'these are kids. Take it easy.'

'Pardon me, kids, but it's a lot more complicated than that. Rolf knows that most art students are women. But the majority of gallery owners, museum curators and critics are men and they don't respect women artists. In fact, the whole structure of the art business is biased towards males and has been for centuries. When women artists sell their work they get less than their male counterparts would for the same damn thing. It's outrageous. We're half the population, girls, but we are second-class citizens. We might as well be black for the kind of consideration we get.'

'Not this again.'

'You know it's true, Rolf.'

'I show your work, don't I? You're not being fair.'

Adults arguing in front of me creeped me out. I looked over at Maria and Ming Li. They were looking at each other with their mouths hanging open. 'We should move on. We've got a lot to see.'

'Yeah, you're right, Jack.' Billy added, 'I'm sorry, Mr Nelson, but we're on a tight schedule. It has been illuminating.'

'Best of luck to you, gentlemen, girls,' Nelson said. 'Enjoy the evening.'

Judy grinned and gave each of us boys a firm handshake. Then she pointed her finger at Maria and Ming Li. 'Girls, don't let them …' she cocked her head towards Billy and me ' … keep you down, you hear me?'

As we left the gallery Judy and Mr Nelson continued their vigorous debate. The cool, damp air smelled of the city with a hint of the sea underneath.

'She was amazing,' Maria exclaimed.

'She reminds me of your mother,' I said, without thinking.

'What do you mean?' There was an edge to her voice.

'Nothing. Your mother, you know, she thinks about what's wrong with the world.'

'What's bad about that, Ryder?'

'I didn't say it was bad. It's just that … people don't always want to hear it.'

'People *never* want to hear it,' Ming Li said. 'That's why somebody has to say it. Think about it, Jack.'

'Why did everyone get so serious? Come on, let's have a good time,' Billy pleaded. We walked half a block in silence before Maria declared, 'I liked Mrs Gerowitz.'

'Me too,' Ming Li added.

'I liked her artwork – that one done on the hood of a car,' I said.

'Painting on a sheet of metal instead of a canvas – that was crazy.' Billy exclaimed. 'I didn't expect that.'

We went into a gallery past Melrose Place, on the west side of the street with a huge sign over the door, *FERUS*. A poster in the window advertised a show called *The Studs*. The room was filled with cigarette smoke and there were people everywhere holding glasses of wine or beer. I didn't see Milt. I couldn't see the artwork through the throng, either. There was jazz on the stereo, *Monk's Dream* – my dad's newest album.

'I love Thelonious Monk,' Ming Li exclaimed.

'Let's see if we can get some beer,' Billy whispered.

Maria said, 'Hey, there's Mr Talbot.'

Our teacher was leaning in a corner with a paper cup in his hand. He was talking to a tall guy with a large hooked nose and an outrageously long moustache. Another man, short and stocky with thin hair, a goatee and a cigarette between his lips, listened.

The man with the moustache shifted back and I saw Connie-Jean standing behind him. She had a cup in her hand too and was talking to a lean, animated man in a slick suit.

He had very short hair and thick eyebrows. She waved me over. The suit looked over too. His expression was like Joe Penderecki's at the pool all those months ago – brief and dismissive. He grinned at Connie-Jean and spread his arms out in a grand gesture.

'Jackson,' Mr Talbot exclaimed. 'Come here, I want you to meet a couple of the best artists in the whole damn city.' His cheeks were red and shiny. 'Guys, this is Jackson Ryder. He's only a kid, but he could go places.' He pounded my chest to emphasise the last two words. 'He doesn't want to do anything different from anybody else – doesn't want to do art – but there isn't much he doesn't know about any kind of art, and that's a fact.'

He grinned and let that sink in. The two guys nodded.

'Jackson, this is John,' Mr Talbot pointed to the taller guy, 'John Altoon. He's the most talented, surprising joker in town. He draws like the devil and if I had half his talent I would stop teaching.'

'You could stop Wolf Man, if you ever got off your ass and did some work.' Mr Altoon stuck out his hand. 'Put it there, kid. Glad to meet you.'

'And this guy,' Mr Talbot continued, bowing towards the stocky man, 'he can take any pile of old junk you throw at him and make a moving and sublime artistic statement out of it – and make you laugh your guts out at the same time.'

'Ed Kienholz,' the man said. 'Larry's a character when he bends it a bit.'

I laughed nervously.

'So, what do you think of the show, kid?' Mr Altoon asked.

'To tell you the truth, there are so many people I haven't had a chance to see anything.'

'Yeah, is this shindig your doing, Wolf Man? Or did Bobby invite this gang?' Mr Kienholz asked.

'Did someone use my name in vain?' Mr Slick Suit strolled over.

'I'm wondering how this party happened, Bouquet,' Mr Kienholz said. 'Are you giving away art?'

'No, Ed, that's what happened when you and Walter owned the place. We're doing something novel – we're trying to *make* money.'

'Ooh,' Mr Altoon and Mr Talbot exclaimed together.

Kienholz's face went as stony as Mount Rushmore. Bobby Bouquet broke the tension.

'Say, Larry, you know the offer still stands – I like your vision. Make some work, and if it fits in with the guys, we'll exhibit it here in a group show, like this one.'

Mr Talbot sobered. 'Thanks, Bobby. I appreciate the offer. I'm pretty busy right now.'

'Hmm, yes, of course. In any case, are you coming to Barney's Beanery with us afterward? If you do come, bring this marvellous creature with you.' He waved at Connie-Jean. 'She's adorable.'

'Shame on you!' Mr Talbot snapped. 'She's one of my high-school students. She's off-limits.'

'Oh, well. Please excuse me, gentle maiden.' He kissed her hand. 'Gents, I *must* say hello to Mrs Arenson over there.' He slithered away.

Mr Talbot yelled into the crowd, 'Hey, Billy … Billy Al Bengston, Ed Ruscha, come 'ere.' Whoever he was talking to, the music was too loud for them to hear. He darted off, leaving me with the two other men.

'If Larry thinks you got it, that's saying a lot,' Mr Altoon told me. 'Is he as good a teacher as he is an artist?'

'I've never seen his work, sir. He says he wants us to learn to be us, not little versions of him.'

'Makes sense,' Ed Kienholz muttered into his cup.

'So, he's good?' I asked.

'Yeah, damn good – as good as any of us. But Larry's gotta decide if he's going to embrace this gift he's been given, or live a more genteel life – if you know what I mean,' Altoon said.

'Art's a jealous mistress, kid,' Kienholz added.

'I'm beginning to realise that. Tonight's been a real eye opener for me. I had no idea all of this was going on. I've been drawing, mostly alone, and not listening to anyone – even Mr Talbot. I want to do it but …'

'I don't know if it's saving me or driving me insane, but I got to do it. I bet you do too,' Altoon muttered.

'Yes, sir. But, I got a problem; it's my dad. He doesn't want me to be an artist.'

'That's a tough break, kid,'

'If you want to be an artist, don't let anything stop you,' Kienholz said. 'Trust me – your dad's not the only one who will get in the way.'

I heard what they were saying, but my mind was elsewhere. This was my opportunity to talk to Connie-Jean alone. Maria had a drink and was talking to a woman in pearls and a fur stole. Ming Li and Billy were nowhere to be seen. I said goodbye to the two artists and grabbed Connie-Jean by the arm. 'You wanna go outside?' I shouted in her ear.

We pushed our way towards the door. The air outside was cold. I felt goosebumps spring up on my arms.

'That was crazy in there,' I said, and let go of Connie-Jean's arm. 'What were you talking to that old man about?'

'Bobby? That was Bobby Bouquet, he owns the gallery.'

'What were you talking about?'

She looked at me. 'I don't see what business that is of yours, Jackson.'

I was taken aback. She was right, of course. Who in the hell did I think I was? This was a bad start. If we were going to get anywhere, I couldn't act like a jealous lover. 'I'm sorry. You're right – none of my business.'

She pulled at the scarf draped around her neck and sighed. 'We were talking about the theatre in New York. Bobby used to be involved. Then he got into selling modern furniture, and then art. It was interesting.'

'You don't have to tell me.'

'I know, but I want to.' She smiled. We walked a little way up the busy boulevard in silence. She shivered and I offered her my jacket, but she shook her head. We slipped into the Rex Evans Gallery, which was warm and empty. There were framed drawings and some sculptures, but I wasn't looking at them – I was looking at Connie-Jean. She leaned over a glass case to study a drawing.

'Connie-Jean, I like you a lot,' I said.

She looked at me and smiled, 'I like you too, my little villain.'

'No, I mean, I've been thinking and … can I take you to the prom? I know freshmen aren't supposed to go, but I'm sure if one of us is a senior it must be okay.'

She blinked. 'Oh, Jackson.' I knew I was sunk. 'I'm sorry, but I've been asked to the prom already and I've said yes.'

'By who?' I couldn't help asking.

'Whom,' she corrected. 'It's not important.'

'It is to me.'

'Joe Penderecki.'

'Mr Lost Cause?' I blurted out.

'What?'

'That's what I called him before I knew his name.'

She laughed. I was feeling light-headed.

'Why did you call him that?'

My side was throbbing. 'I've got to sit down.' We sat facing the wall. 'When I first saw you two together it looked like he was trying to be with you. But you didn't seem interested in him at all.'

'Was it that obvious?'

'So I was right?' My stomach churned. 'Why are you going to the prom with him?'

She started to rock backwards and forwards.

'Nobody knows this – not even Clovis – you can't tell anyone. Do you swear?' I wanted to agree, but if I became her confidant I may as well have been her brother. I hoped that it would bring us closer and she would realise I was the love of her life. I nodded. She spoke slowly at first. 'Before that day by the pool, Joe and I had been dating for a few months. He was nice and everything, but I didn't feel enough for him. Also, I had started seeing someone else, someone he knew. I didn't mean for it to happen. In fact, he's not my type at all. He's so infuriating and he doesn't care about the theatre one bit. But he was so handsome and we felt drawn to each other. The night before you saw me with Joe, this guy and I were together. It was a beautiful night and it felt so good and we … well, we went too far.'

I was shocked. What was 'too far'? Instead of asking, I crossed my legs. 'Why didn't you break up with Joe?'

'You don't understand. This guy is his best friend. They've

known each other since they were in kindergarten. If Joe found out that we had been together, it would break his heart.'

'Milt Bryson? You and that bully, Milt Bryson?'

Connie-Jean put her hand to her mouth. 'How did you know?'

'Are you kidding? Everybody knows they're best buddies. Besides, Milt was at your house that night I came over. I saw him and he saw me. He didn't look like he was there for his best friend.'

'No, he *was* there to talk me into going to the prom with Joe. I didn't want to, but Milt was insistent. He said Joe was so depressed that he was talking about …'

'What, killing himself?'

She looked up at me. 'He's tried it before; not long ago.' She grabbed my arm. 'You mustn't tell anyone.'

'Of course not. What happened the last time? Was that over you, too?'

'He never said anything about it to me. All I know is what Milt told me. He said Joe started the car in the garage with the door closed. His parents came home from the movies and found him unconscious. He was in the hospital for a long time.'

'What did the cops do?'

'One officer questioned him and his parents, but they all said it was an accident. So, you see, I can't upset him. It could send him over the top.'

This was too much to take in; too weird and complicated. I felt sorry for poor old Joe, but that was beside the point. The upshot was that I had drawn a bow with Connie-Jean and missed the mark completely. I didn't have a chance and she wasn't the girl I thought she was anyway, not if she was in love with that asshole, Milt. The consoling-little-brother act was pointless. 'That's too bad about Joe, but it's not really your problem.'

'What do you mean? I couldn't have Joe's death on my conscience.'

'No, that's not it. What good is it going to do in the end? Are you going to hide the truth from him forever? Will you be his girl all through college, get married, have kids? It's crazy. When does it stop?' She didn't look up. Was she disagreeing in silence, or blocking me out completely? 'When does it stop, Connie-Jean?'

'You think I don't know that?' Even in the dim gallery light her eyes looked red. 'You think I haven't thought about it every which way I can, you foolish child?'

Foolish child. That's all I was to her. 'Fine!' I shouted, making a wild gesture with my hands. 'You go to the stupid prom with your stupid boyfriend you don't even like. Sneak around behind his back with your stupid, bully, ass-jerk of a lover. What do I care? It's your fabulous life. Screw it up any way you like.' I walked away, then turned back and pointed at her. 'And you know what? I'm not your stupid, goddamn villain anymore – I never was.' I stomped out of the gallery and into the frosty night. I was perspiring. My breath was hot and sick tasting.

The rest of the night was a blur. I went into the David Stuart Gallery and saw Billy and Ming Li holding hands. It should have made me smile, but it didn't.

On the way home all the freshmen were in the back row again. Maria sat next to me and Billy and Ming Li were by the window. Connie-Jean was at the front of the bus, sitting with Milt. They didn't talk the whole trip. It was late and everyone was tired. Maria fell asleep on my shoulder. She was warm and soft and her black hair glistened in the passing lights. I breathed in her scent – beer, smoke, chilli sauce and, underneath that, Dove soap and something else elusive and comforting. As the bus sped down the freeway, I felt lonelier than I had in my life. My stomach was throbbing and I wanted to die.

Mr Talbot dropped all of us freshmen home. I was the last one.

'So, what did you think of tonight?'

'Some of the art was unbelievable. I especially liked talking with Mr Altoon and Mr Kienholz. They said you're a really good artist.'

'Yeah? Well, I don't have much time to paint these days.'

We both stopped talking. It got to the point where I didn't know how to start up again. Finally Mr Talbot said, 'Anything else about the night? You seem particularly quiet.'

'The rest you don't want to know.'

'Really? Girl troubles? It usually is.'

'Yeah, that *and* football hoodlums.'

He paused. 'What happened? Did they harass you?'

It was my turn to hesitate. I automatically touched my stomach but said, 'I'm okay, sir. It wasn't too bad.'

He looked at me. 'Who were these bullies?'

It would have been so easy to tell him. Connie-Jean might back me up – maybe. Those assholes would have got what was coming to them. But something didn't sit right. I could see that after Milt and his goons were punished it would just get worse. They would make my life ghastlier than the fires of Gehinnam.

You gotta fight your own fights, kid.

I shook my head. 'Sorry, sir.'

'I didn't think you'd tell me. It's a tough call. I understand – I used to have those kinds of problems myself. But you know what? I survived. I'm doing fine, and you'll be too. Just remember, the offer stands. If you need my help, let me know.'

I smiled. I didn't tell him I was bent-out about Ray getting the freshman prize, nor that the closer we got to El Caballero the more the thought of Mr Talbot meeting Tate was starting to freak me out. I was praying he was asleep.

Tate opened the door as we walked up. He was in slippers and he didn't have a tie on but he was still in his work clothes.

'Hello, I'm Larry Talbot, Jack's art teacher.' He offered his hand.

'Art teacher? I didn't even know Jackie was taking art.' He looked at me and frowned. They shook hands, 'Wait a minute, you know Kate Hickey, don't you? Sure, sure. I remember her talking about you. Come in. You want a drink?'

My stomach hurt. I was on overload. I couldn't believe this was happening on top of everything else. 'It's late. I'm going to bed. Thanks Mr T, g'night Dad.'

I left a crack open at my door. This could have been it; breaking Tate's heart and the end of any art in my life. Tate put on the record I gave him for a present. It wasn't loud but try as I might, I couldn't pick up what they were saying. I gave up and lay in bed, listening to the rumble of their voices and the music like distant shelling in a war zone. I rubbed my tender belly and waited until I heard the front door lock, the kitchen faucet, and finally Tate's kettledrum steps down to his bedroom.

I turned on the light and rummaged around in my pencil case for the charcoal stick I secreted from school. Nothing but the black agony of a charred living stem could voice the things I was feeling.

I thought about *The Race Course* by Albert Pinkham Ryder (no relation). To me it was one of the most terrifying paintings of all time. A skeleton rides a horse around a fenced race course in the dead of night. The trunk of a dead and branchless tree stands like a guard to the right. Raised in the skeleton's right hand is a scythe-like sword. In the front a cobra rears its head and the sky seems more solid than the scene below. It makes no sense. There is nothing for the skeleton, probably death himself, to kill. The landscape and race course are empty. He goes around and around eternally. I know he's coming for me. Connie-Jean's words are the sword.

But the image was too much somehow – too symbolic. I needed something less. I needed something from the gut.

One of Robert Motherwell's *Elegy to the Spanish Republic* paintings had the exact feel. As big as a gallery wall and made in nothing more than black and white, and the smallest amount of earth yellow. Three large pod shapes hang from a cross-like thing between two solid pillars of black. Like dead, charred bodies hanging on a tree – contained, powerless, spent. I didn't know what the hell it was about but I knew how it made me feel.

But I was angry too and this was too quiet. I wanted the energy of something like Franz Kline's *Black Sienna*. I wanted something that was sad and angry and lonely and black, black as night, black as hurt, and black as death.

I worked like the devil and didn't hold back. I drove it, pushed it, shoved it. It felt like being on the downward part of a rollercoaster without let up. I broke two pencils and ran out of paper. But something changed. I drew in a deep breath, let it out slowly and I could feel, quite unintentionally, my cheeks shaping into a smile. The clock radio said three a.m.

13

THE NEXT DAY I LOOKED FOR RAY at the front steps of the school before art class. I rubbed my stomach absent-mindedly. That morning after I showered I noticed that little red spots had showed up on my skin just below my ribcage. I could see vague red, blue and purple patches peeking out from deeper under my milky flesh. It was still tender.

The bell rang and I was forced to go to class. As I rounded the corner of the art block I saw him about to go into our room. 'Ray. Wait up,' I called. I ran to catch up with him. He stopped and looked over his shoulder. I was breathing hard by the time I reached him. 'Look man, about yesterday – I'm sorry. It's just …' I shrugged. 'I've got a hang-up about dirty books. I'm sorry.'

He looked at me like I was a TV and the sound was turned off. He looked down at the book I held out between us. He looked back at my face and I could see his dark eyes shift from one of my eyes to the other. 'It's not about the book, is it, *guero*?' I winced. '*No te apudes, Judes,* it's no big deal, Ghost Ryder.' He took the book.

Before we walked into the room I asked him, 'Can I borrow it sometime, I mean, when you're ready?'

*

All of us who went to La Cienega were dragging our feet, especially Mr Talbot. He hadn't shaved. He called Ming Li, Maria, Billy and me up to his desk and set an extra assignment for us. We had to put together a ten-minute presentation for the class about our gallery visits. His instructions were vague and loose – very unlike him.

'When, sir?' Ming Li asked.

'Uh, end of the week.'

'That's not enough time,' Maria protested. 'Can we do it next week?'

'Okay, sure, that's fine.'

He took a swig of coffee and dismissed us with a terse wave.

The others walked back to their seats. I stayed behind. 'Mr Talbot?'

'Yeah, Jack?'

'Did my dad say anything last night?'

'What do you mean?'

'You know, about me doing art or anything.'

'No. Mostly we talked about Mrs Hickey, jazz, the Warren Commission and the new cars coming out. Why?'

'Nothin'. Thanks.' I walked back to my seat, wondering why Tate hadn't got upset. Maybe he just liked the Wolf Man or he was too tired – maybe he wanted to talk to me.

Billy, Ming Li, Maria and I sat together at the far end of the class. Ray and Sing Li joined us.

I hoped Ming Li and Billy would get the ball rolling since they were the most academic of us. Sure enough, Ming Li spoke up right away. I was distracted by Maria. I had never really noticed her appearance before. Her face was round and her eyebrows and eyelashes were dark. She wore a lime-green shirt that complemented her eyes.

'Did you hear me, Jack?' Ming Li yanked on my shirtsleeve.

'Answer her, *pendejo*,' Ray said. 'I can't concentrate on my *pinché* drawing with Ming yapping.'

'Did you take any notes on the trip, like Mr Talbot asked us to do?'

'Uh, no. I didn't have a ballpoint with me.'

'Well, that's it then. None of us did. We're sunk.' Billy crossed his arms on the desktop and rested his head on them.

'Don't be so defeatist, Hughes,' Maria said. 'Let's just write down what we remember, to start.'

Billy slowly pulled out a lined notepad and a pencil. 'Okay, what do you remember, Jack?'

'Crap,' I said. Ray laughed. Billy tapped his pencil against the desk. I didn't want to remember anything about the night before – especially the look on Connie-Jean's face before I marched off. Yeah, she had lashed out at me, but I hadn't even thought about the anguish she must have been going through. All I cared about were my own feelings and my wounded dignity. Maybe I hadn't handled it so well.

'Jackson.' Ming Li said sharply.

'What?'

'What's wrong with you? What artworks do you remember seeing?'

'I remembered something,' Billy piped up. 'It was at the Ceeje Gallery, before we went back to the bus. Remember, Ming?'

'Yeah,' Ming Li said slowly. 'It was a family portrait by Charles … something like Garibaldi?'

'Garabedian,' Billy was excited. 'I liked it. It was of people.'

'The artist and his family,' Ming Li said.

'Yeah, three figures – a woman, a kid and the artist sawing wood. It was stylised in a weird way.'

‘He was building a house with a tile floor.’

‘It sounds like a holy family scene,’ I offered.

‘You’re right, Jack. The woman in the foreground is the Virgin Mary, the kid is Jesus and the artist is Joseph. Why didn’t I see that?’

I liked the idea. The artist is building a house, a home for his family. It’s what every father hopes to do.

Then it hit me – our tiny apartment at El Caballero had nothing hanging on the walls. It wasn’t a home, not really.

There were distractions during the day but whenever I was alone – especially first thing in the morning and last thing at night – there she was, Connie-Jean, right in front of me, taunting me and blowing me a kiss, making me ache. Everything reminded me of her. Everything hurt. I couldn’t watch *Ed Sullivan* or even look at the swimming pool without pretzelling up inside. I read, watched TV and even wrote letters to some of the gang in New York, but every time the memory of her rejection hit me, it was as vivid as rancid cheese.

‘I told you, *ese*,’ Ray said. We were washing a 1958 Brookwood station wagon at the dealership. I had asked Charlie and Tate if we could hire Ray when business picked up and they’d agreed to two afternoons a week plus Saturdays. Even though he was working shorter hours than he had at the restaurant, Ray was making more money.

‘And my nights are free, *chingado*!’ he screamed.

This Saturday I showed him the ropes and told him my sad story about Connie-Jean on the La Cienega trip.

‘Didn’t I tell you? Your little blondie is high-tone, man, a fuckin’ *princesa*; I could see it a mile away.’

'Shut up, Ray.'

'*Ay, guero*, don't be so touchy.'

'No, I mean it, man. You don't know her.'

'*Simón, ese*, but you don't know her either. What do you think all of that "Oh, villain, oh" bullshit was about? And that blowing kisses. Nobody does that. She had you by the *cojones*, man. She played with you like a *gato* does with a mouse. You're lucky to be out of it, man. You should give thanks to God.'

I didn't want to get into another fight with him. I regretted saying anything. 'Okay, you wrap it up here. I'm going to find Stretch and tell him we've finished,' I stopped and looked him straight in the eye. 'And you know where to shove the soap and hose when you're done.' I turned and walked away without waiting for a response. I could hear him muttering in Spanish.

I went into the workshop. Stretch was changing the head gaskets on a white Corvair.

'Howdy, professor,' he said. 'I'm cleaning up and then I'm free for the weekend.'

'You got anything for Ray to do before Monday?'

His expression shifted, 'I reckon not. Keep him away from the workshop, you hear?'

'Why?'

He dipped his hands in Goop cleaner and rubbed them together. 'To be on the safe side, little buddy.'

'You don't need to worry about Ray. He's foursquare and as straight as an arrow. The only thing he steals is my school lunch.'

He gave me a tight grin. 'You know, his kind is always up to somethin'.'

'His kind?'

'Yeah, you know.' He wiped his hands with a dirty cloth. 'Greasers, taco benders – I don't trust any of them.'

'Jesus, Stretch!' I said.

Up until then I'd had every reason to like Stretch. He had been good to me – I thought of him as a big brother. It would have been easy to ignore his comments but I remembered what Ming Li said on the art trip, and I choked.

People never want to hear it, that's why it's got to be said.

'Is it just Mexicans?'

He climbed out of his overalls, 'Whaddya mean?'

'Are you just prejudiced against Mexicans? How about blacks? What about Jews?'

'Now, hold on, little buddy.'

'No, I want to know.' I could feel my face getting hot. 'Ray is my best friend and I'm a Jew. So what the fuck am I supposed to think?' It was the first time I'd used that word in anger. Stretch was speechless. He raised his hands and shook his head but didn't say a word. I couldn't stop. 'He didn't choose who his parents were, any more than you chose to be born poor, white, ignorant trash.'

I saw a flash in Stretch's eyes – something I had never seen in him before. He always seemed so loose, but I had definitely wound him up. 'Wait one goddamn minute. Where do you get off talking to me like that? You think jus' because you're the boss's son you can bad-mouth me and my kin? Buzz and me has put up with you underfoot, puttin' things in the wrong place, not cleanin' up proper, slowin' us down. You don't think we got better things to do with our time than wipe your butt? Now you bring this wetback punk in here and 'spect us to treat him like he's worth somethin', like he's one of the family?'

I flinched, but I wasn't finished. 'Ray is the most talented, hard-working, funny and loyal guy I've ever met. I wouldn't trade him for ten white guys.'

Stretch had made the overalls into a ball and was rolling them around and around in his bony hands. 'Ten guys, aye?' His face was squeezed up tight. 'Is that the way it is? Ten of me? I thought we was friends.'

My face cooled and the muscles of my arms slackened. 'I thought you liked me.'

He kept rolling the bundle but shrugged his shoulders. 'I guess you ain't so bad. I'm kinda used to you now.' He grinned tightly.

'Look Stretch … I didn't mean what I said about, you know, the poor white trash stuff. I don't think that. It was wrong. I was angry.'

He stopped rolling the clothes and tossed them into the hamper, 'no hard feelings, little buddy.' He put on his old bomber jacket with the cracked leather on the shoulders. 'So, you're Jewish? Mr Ryder is Jewish?'

'Yeah, and Charlie Salmond too.'

'I'm sorry.'

'What, that we're Jewish?'

'No, no, I got a lot of respect for the Hebrew people. I saw the movie *Exodus*. Paul Newman's my favourite actor. I'm sorry I said that about Beaners. It's that I ain't had the best experience of them, that's all. I'm sure there's good ones and all, but damned if I've met one yet.'

Nothing had changed, but at least Stretch knew that it wasn't okay by me. 'Like I said, Ray's a good guy. He doesn't deserve this. Give him a break.'

He picked up his lunchbox. 'Okay, I get it, I do. I gotta go.'

He waved awkwardly and was out the back door before I could open my mouth.

14

I FOUND RAY IN FRONT OF MRS BARKER'S DESK. As soon as they saw me, they stopped talking. They couldn't have heard me yelling all the way from the workshop, but something was making them uncomfortable.

'Hello, Jackson,' Mrs Barker said with a smile. 'I checked with Stretch and there's nothing else for Ray to do for Monday.'

'You better check with Mr Salmond too.'

'Yes ma'am.' We headed to Charlie's office, but he wasn't there. I scanned the lot from his picture window. He was near the entrance, talking to a woman in a turquoise pillbox hat. 'Wait here, Ray. I'll go ask Charlie.'

'No problem, *ese*.'

As I got closer to Charlie and the woman, something struck me as not quite right. For one thing, the woman was writing in a small notebook. I had never seen that happen in a car sale before. Even stranger was the fact that Charlie stood a fair distance away from her. When we started at the dealership he said to me, 'sport, there's a lot of psychology in selling a car, a lot of psychology and theatre. You got a tiny opportunity to become someone's advisor, parent and best friend. You gotta read the client, you gotta figure out what it's going to take to make them listen to you. For some you gotta joke around, for others you just gotta tell them what to think. Most people want to trust you – and you just got to find what's goin' to let them do that. Physical closeness makes a big difference. There's an invisible line you don't cross or else you become a threat, but up to that point people tend to feel more comfortable the closer you are.' He took a couple of steps back. 'You see what I did? Doesn't it feel different now?' I had to admit he was right. 'I'll tell you what,' he added, 'it works for the ladies too. That's why I'm such a regular Casanova.' He did one of his corny mambo moves.

That was Charlie's philosophy, and he didn't stray from it. But this scene with the pillbox lady was different. It felt like he was giving her instructions, not selling her a car.

He saw me and stopped talking, 'Whaddya need, sport?' That was weird too. At work Charlie was totally focused on the client until they had signed the paperwork and walked out the door. He was a good salesman.

'Sorry to interrupt, Mr Salmond,' I never called him by his first name at work. 'Is there anything you need Ray to do for Monday?'

'Who's Ray?'

'You remember, you hired him to help out.'

'Yeah, yeah, your friend.'

The pillbox lady smiled. 'That's right.'

'No, it's okay, kiddo. You both take off for the day.'

'Thanks. See ya later.'

I nodded to the lady and she reciprocated. They didn't start talking again until I was out of earshot.

When I told Ray we could go he was ecstatic. 'Oh man, that's great. Tomorrow is my sister's *quinceñera*, her fifteenth birthday. It's a big *pinché* deal for Mexicans and we're having a special dinner tonight for the family. Mamá has been cooking for days – *enchiladas, posolé, cabeza,* the works. Hey, you know what, *guero*, why don't you come eat with us?'

'I didn't know you had a sister.'

'Yeah, she goes to San Gabriel Mission High.'

'Oh yeah, where is it?'

'At the mission, *tonto*. It's a girls' school.'

I was starting to learn about the history of California. I'd heard of Father Serra and the chain of missions the Franciscans had built at the end of the 1700s. 'The missions are still around?'

'Yeah, man. They're churches and museums now. There are bunches of them, twenty or twenty-one, from San Diego all the way up to San Francisco, *ese*. So what do you say?'

'Thanks, Ray, but I better not.'

'Why not, man? What's wrong?'

'I don't want to impose. Your mother doesn't know me, and …'

'Shit, man, it's not like that. I'll tell her you're from the Irish side of the family – she'll never know the difference.'

He laughed and gave me a push. Tate was at the freight terminal in LA for the afternoon dealing with paperwork on new stock. He would probably go out for drinks with Charlie and there was a good chance they wouldn't be back until late.

'I don't think so,' I said, without conviction.

'Listen, Mamá is happy I'm not working for my *pinché* uncle anymore. You're her new hero. It's not going to be a problem, *vato*, trust me. You'll be an honoured guest.'

'Okay, but I gotta go home and change my shirt and put on a tie.'

'*Chale, ese*, it's not a party. It's *cena*, that's all. Do you wear a tie for dinner at home? You're fine the way you are. Come on.'

I could have gone home and left Tate a note, but that would have doubled our walking time. I decided to go to Ray's and hope that I got home before he did.

We headed west on San Sebastiano Boulevard, down the valley to the railway station. Past the railroad line, a dirt track turned off the road. There were no signposts and the scrub chaparral grew thick along both sides of the track – high enough that anything could have been hiding in there.

'Are you sure we've gone the right way?' I asked Ray.

'Jesus, *guero*, I'm taking you home. Don't you think I know the way?'

I had heard about *La Olla* – it meant 'the cooking pot'. It was the Mexican *barrio* of San Sebastiano and a lot of white kids at school talked about it like it was the pit of hell. Even the police hardly dared to go there. But no matter what happened I figured I was safe with Ray.

We walked about a quarter of a mile. A light dusting of pale clay covered my slacks. I heard kids playing in the distance and accordion music coming from a radio. A woman yelled and a car backfired ... or was it a gunshot? I could smell wood-smoke and cooking. The bush opened up and revealed an unpaved street lined with modest wooden houses, painted like nothing I had ever seen before except in Juárez. These people didn't seem to care whether the colours clashed or not. I liked that. One house had corn planted in the front yard and chickens wandering around between the stalks. Another had two cars set up on blocks, without wheels or windows. The rows of houses stretched on for about eight hundred yards and then the chaparral started up again.

'Wow,' I said.

Ray looked at me, 'It's not Hearst Castle, *vato*, *pero es mi casa*, it's my home. I know everyone here and they know me.'

'No, I didn't mean anything by it. It's just so … colourful.'

'Yeah, that's Mexican taste for you.' He laughed. 'Come on.'

He pulled me into a driveway. The yellowing grass in the front yard was practically hidden by all the cars parked there. A gang of small kids ran around and on the porch were a half-dozen swarthy guys in sunglasses. They held longneck beer bottles and didn't smile as we approached.

'*Qué tal, carnales*?' Ray called out.

'*Ese, flaco*, what's up?' one guy answered. The others nodded. I stifled a laugh. I knew that 'flaco' meant skinny but I didn't know it was Ray's nickname.

'I got off work at my new job at Salmond Motors, Chato. It's pretty cool.'

'It's gotta beat washing dishes for Tío José, man. I did that *chingado* job when I was your age,' he answered.

'*Simón, ese*, me too,' another guy added, 'he worked me to the bone for peanuts, man.' They all nodded.

'Who's your *hormiga*?' Chato looked at me.

'*Hormiga?* Ant?' I looked at Ray then at Chato, 'I get it, *hormiga, amigo*. I'm Jackson Ryder, *mucho gusto*,' I said. Their heads were all cocked, satisfied grins on their lips.

Chato cracked a crooked smile and shook my hand. '*Flaco's* talked about you. I'm his brother. You want a brew?'

I sensed that saying no would be a bad idea. I nodded and an ice-cold longneck appeared in my hand with the cap already off. I took a swig and tried not to flinch at the bitter taste. Ray introduced me to the rest of his brothers and cousins and we sat out on the porch. Everyone relaxed. We talked about cars, girls and music. So this is what family was like.

The front door opened and a short woman with curly black hair and a floral apron poked her head outside. Someone grabbed the beer bottles out of our hands.

'Ramón. Is that you? Are you drinking beer again, *condenado*?' She started to take off her flat slipper.

'*Ay*, not the *chancla*,' Chato exclaimed.

'Mamá, I just got here. I'm not drinking, I swear.'

'*Mientas*, you little liar. I know you.' She came at us with the slipper held high.

The *vatos* closed in around Ray and Chato met her halfway. 'Easy, Mamita, easy. Don't worry. I'm taking care of him.'

'I should be hitting you too, Chato. You have no shame.'

'*Claro, claro*, Mamita, *pero* look – Ray brought home a friend.' She put down her slipper and smoothed her apron. The guys pushed me forward, '*Este es* Jackson Ryder, Mamita, Ray's friend from work.'

'And school,' Ray added from behind his brothers.

'*Mucho gusto*, Señora Rodriguez,' I said. 'I'm pleased to meet you.'

Ray sidled up to his mother and pecked her on the cheek. 'This is the guy I was telling you about, Mamita. He got me the job at the car lot and we sit next to each other in art.'

'*Mucho gusto*, Jackson. Thank you for what you've done for my baby.'

'Mamá,' Ray rolled his eyes.

'You, *cállate*, shut up. You will always be my baby.' She looked around and addressed the boys. '*Cuidado*, I don't want *la policia* around here again,' then to me she said, 'come inside, Jackson, you are welcome.'

Ray followed us in. There were people everywhere. Every wall and surface was covered with framed photos, prints, knick-knacks and plaster statues of saints. Coloured paper cut-outs hung from the ceiling and the aroma of meat cooking permeated the air. Carlos and Unai were talking to a girl next to an altar.

We followed Ray's mother into the kitchen, which was filled with women. Above their heads was a faded print of Leonardo da Vinci's *The Last Supper* and a photograph of President Kennedy with plastic roses stuck to the frame. Ray sprinted between the women, who all stopped to hug or kiss him. He reached down into a battered picnic cooler sitting in the corner and came back up with two cold Dr Peppers.

A girl about my age sat on the floor beside a portable phonograph, looking through a stack of 45s. The girl looked up as we entered and her eyes brightened.

'Finally,' she exclaimed.

'Qué tal, *chiquita*?' Ray hugged her.

'I was afraid you were going to be late.' She kissed Ray on the cheek.

I had never seen a brother and sister show affection like they did. It was cool.

Her hair was wavy, jet black and down to her waist. She wore a lime-green beret and had bangs that ended above her almond-shaped brown eyes. Her nose was short and turned up, and when she smiled two dimples appeared below her cheeks.

'Gracie, this is my friend, Jack. *Guero*, this is my sister Altagracia. It's her *quinceñera* tomorrow.' At the mention of her full name, she shoved Ray and rolled her eyes.

'Easy, *chica*.'

'Call me Grace,' she told me. 'Pleased to meet you.'

'The pleasure is all mine.'

'Ooh, "Call me Grace," how grown-up,' Ray jeered, making a limp-wristed gesture.

'Ray, I'm going to kill you. Anyway, look at you, *sucio*. Your face is covered in grease. Hurry, go clean up.'

'Okay, okay. I'll be right back. Take care of Jack, *Grace*,' he said, emphasising her name. He disappeared down the hallway.

'Ugh, he's so embarrassing,' she said. Then she smiled, 'Ray doesn't say much about school or friends, but he talks about you. I think you challenge him.'

'What?' I shook my head, 'You must be mistaken. Ray's never fazed by anything or anyone. He makes his own happy path.'

'Maybe. He was pretty upset when you went to the galleries and he didn't get to go, though. That, and you taking his prize.'

I was going to blush so I took a swig of Dr Pepper, hoping it would cool me down. To my relief, Unai and Carlos saw me from across the lounge and came over.

'*Ese, guero*,' Unai greeted me, 'So you've met the birthday girl.'

'*Simón, ese*,' I responded.

Grace burst out laughing.

'*Don't laugh, primita*, we're teaching him "the ways".' Unai put his arm around my shoulders. 'We'll make a *vato* out of his sorry Mick ass yet.'

I laughed. 'I don't know where you guys got the idea that I'm Irish. I don't have one drop of Irish blood in my body.'

'But Ray said …'

'What did I say, *carnale*?' Ray appeared next to Carlos, wearing a neat, black V-neck sweater over a crisp white T-shirt. I had never seen the combination before and it looked amazing to me – formal and casual at the same time, 'Whatever it was, it must have been good.'

Grace interrupted him, 'Quick, take him to meet Papá before dinner starts.'

Ray's dad and several other men were in the backyard, standing around the 'barbecue' – a fifty-five-gallon drum cut in half and standing on welded legs. Steaks, hamburger patties and frankfurters were cooking in a haze of delicious-smelling smoke. At least a dozen children were roaming around underfoot.

'*Con permiso*, Papá,' Ray said.

'*Qué quieres, mijo*?'

'I want you to meet my friend, Jackson Ryder.'

Mr Rodriguez put down his tongs, wiped his hands and looked me in the eye. 'I'm very pleased to meet you, Jackson Ryder. Juan Ramón Rodriguez, at your service.' We shook hands. His were thick and coarse, but smaller than my own.

'*Mucho gusto*, Señor Rodriguez,' I replied. The phrase rolled comfortably off my tongue now.

'Ramoncito says you're a big ladies man, is that true?' He grinned and patted me on the back. 'Well, you need great potency for lovemaking. Tell me, Jackson Ryder, how do you like your meat?' The question caught me by surprise.

'I don't know, sir. Done, I guess.'

'Well done?'

'I guess so.'

'No, no, no, no,' Mr Rodriguez said, shaking his head.

'You've done it now, *ese*,' Ray whispered in my ear, 'Papá grew up on a big *rancho* in Chihuahua and he knows his meat.'

'Jackson Ryder, *carne* is a living thing. It has character, personality. It has – *cómo se dice*? *Fuerza*, strength. If you cook it too long, you kill it.' He took a knife and cut a bite-sized wedge from one of the steaks. 'Taste this. Blow on it first, it is hot.'

The outside crust was burnt brown, but inside the flesh was crimson and juicy. It smelled as good as any steak I could remember. I touched it with my tongue, blew on it and snatched it with my teeth. The first thing I noticed was that the texture and taste were as variegated as the colour – the centre was soft and moist, the outside firm and dry. As I chewed the two mixed together, rearranging themselves into an explosion of flavour. I was transported. It was an epiphany.

'It works every time, *ese*,' Ray said with glee.

'*Simón, guero*,' Unai said. He and Carlos had followed us out to the yard. 'Everyone is powerless against the famous Rodriguez *barbacoa*.'

'You come see me when dinner is ready. I'm going to keep a special one for you,' Mr Rodriguez told me.

A short, fat man with curly black hair and a thick moustache came up behind us and put a solid paw on Ray's shoulder.

'Hey, Tío José.' Ray slipped out of his uncle's grip with an easy dance spin. 'How's it going?'

'I'm short of staff at the restaurant now, thanks to you. Are you sure you don't want to come back, *sobrino*?'

Ray looked uncomfortable for a moment, but finally he straightened up and said, 'I got a job, Tío, a good job with good pay and short hours.'

José didn't seem perturbed, 'I hope you don't get lazy.' He turned to Unai and Carlos. 'What about you, *jóvenes*?' They both mumbled something unintelligible. 'You young people don't know how lucky you are.'

'Can you believe that guy?' Unai asked when José had moved on.

'He's running out of nephews to enslave,' Carlos said. 'When are we going to eat? I'm starving.'

Ray pushed me towards the table. It was transformed into a buffet with a dozen different main dishes, everything from enchiladas to chicken mole. I picked up a paper plate and a plastic fork and moved down the line, sampling everything – except the roasted head of lamb – with the eyeballs intact.

'You should try the cabeza, *ese*. The cheeks are the best part,' Ray said.

'I think I'll pass.'

'Don't forget your steak,' Carlos reminded me, 'and *guero*, save a little bit for me to try, eh?

There was a huge platter of meat at the end of the table, but I went outside to the barbecue instead. Mr Rodriguez and his brother José were the only ones left in the backyard. As I approached I heard Ray's father say, 'That's bullshit, *hermanito*. Mind your own business. Besides, I'm a better cook than you'll ever be.' His words were drowned out by a mighty rumbling noise. I thought it was an earthquake, until I saw the freight train speed past along the back of the property. Neither man seemed to notice. Mr Rodriguez pointed at José's chest with his tongs. When the deafening noise died away he said, 'And if you weren't such a tight-assed Jew, you might be able to run your goddamned business without losing staff all the time, *cabrón*.'

I stopped, bolted to the ground. A chalky, sour taste rose in my mouth.

Ray's dad noticed me and grinned. 'Jackson Ryder, I did not forget you.' He put a T-bone steak on my plate, so big that it covered the rest of the food, 'you will need one of these too.' He handed me a steak knife. 'Put another plate underneath or it will get soggy. *Buen provecho*.'

I walked towards the house thinking about my confrontation with Stretch.

Inside, everyone was eating. All the sitting spots seemed to be taken – chairs, sofas, even the floor. Ray waved me over to a sofa covered with a beige terry-cloth bedcover. He slid over and there was Maria. I sat down between them, very conscious that my thigh was pressed against hers.

'Hi Maria, Ray didn't tell me you'd be here.'

'Maria is Gracie's best friend,' Ray said with a mouthful of food. 'She's always here, *guero*, she might as well be family.' Grace kicked him.

'I hear that your birthday is soon, too,' Maria said between bites.

'Yes, it's next week. How did you know?'

'Don't look at me, *pendejo*. It's news to me,' Ray said through a mouthful of refried beans.

'I have my sources.'

'So, we'll be the same age for a week,' Grace said. She was sitting in a dining-room chair on Maria's other side.

'You'll be able to get your driver's licence, *ese*,' Ray said.

'A fat lot of good it will do me. Maybe Charlie and Tate will let me move the cars around on the lot.'

Maria and Grace were both looking at me and their two faces, side by side, were a knock out combination – Grace had a twinkle in her eye and Maria had the warmest smile. For the first time since the gallery walk, Connie-Jean took a back seat in my thoughts.

Unai was sitting on a leather ottoman in front of me. He leaned over almost spilling his plate, '*Guero*, change places with me,' he mumbled and then looked at Maria almost like a pointer looking at a prize woodcock. I didn't want to move and I didn't respond. Unai leaned even closer and whispered, 'Look, *ese*, Gracie told me why you hit Buster. Why didn't you tell me you were protecting Maria? It made me angry.' I pulled back but he pulled me towards him. 'No, no, not at you. It made me angry at me, *vato*. That should have been *me* protecting her. You were right, it's crazy blocking her out. Come on, man, give me a break.'

His eyes were wide. I looked back at Maria. She was talking conspiratorially with Grace. She always seemed to be there for me. I remembered how good it felt when she slept against my arm on the bus from La Cienega. Then, I remembered what she looked like when I first met her; how her eyes were so swollen from crying over Unai. Unai was a good friend. He wouldn't even be trying this if I hadn't suggested it. *Yold. Estupido*. Idiot. I felt a possibility slipping away.

I said goodbye in my heart, half stood and changed places with Unai quickly. I took a slow, sad mouthful of *arroz con pollo* and looked up at Maria and Unai. They were already in their own world – shining eyes and smiles for no one else. Then I realised Grace was looking at me. When she knew she had my attention she glanced at the two of them, looked back at me and smiled. It wasn't just an *oh, look at them* kind of smile, it seemed like she was trying to share something with me, to communicate something specific. Did she know that I had encouraged Unai? Did she urge Maria to not give up? I grinned back and tried hard to interpret what her mysterious smile meant.

I caught Ray looking at me with that same weird, hard, look he gave me when I took his prize book. Ray murmured, '*Cuidado guero*, watch out. I see you.'

'What? What are you talking about, man?' I said weakly.

He shifted his weight and cocked his head. He looked like his older brother, Chato, just for a moment. 'Don't bullshit me.

You're my friend and all, but I don't like the way you're looking at my sister – that's what I'm talking about, *ese*. Back off.'

'No, you don't understand. I wasn't –'

'Oh, I understand plenty, *vato*. Just watch yourself.'

'No, really. I was just –'

'Look, *mi* papá sees how you're looking at Gracie too, man. If you want to leave here with your *cojones* intact you better cool it.'

It was no use trying to explain right then and there. I would tell him tomorrow. I looked back at Mr Rodriguez. Sure enough, his eyes were black and motionless, his face immobile. He nodded formally at me, 'Enjoying the meat I made for you, Jackson Ryder?'

'Yes, sir, *si*, *gracias*.'

'*De nada*,' he said, not smiling, '*De nada*.'

At Mrs Rodriguez's insistence, Ray's brother, Chato, gave me a lift home in his Buick Roadmaster. We didn't talk much. I was exhausted by the crowd, food and conversation. When he dropped me off he gave me a kind of upward nod, 'See you round, *guero*.' It would have seemed menacing, but I knew it was meant to be friendly.

15

AT HOME I FOUND CHARLIE, KATE AND TATE all asleep and sprawled out on the sofa. Charlie was curled over, his head on one arm rest. His mouth was wide open. Tate's head was resting on the back of the sofa, his eyes sunken, cadaver-like. Kate was between them, her head resting on Tate's shoulder. The two top buttons of her blouse were undone and I could see the lace edge of her bra. In the warm half-light of the living-room lamp, the three of them looked like a Mannerist sculpture carved in Carrara marble. The coffee table overflowed with longneck bottles, Chinese-food containers, chopsticks and cigarette butts. None of the butts had lipstick marks – Kate had taken the Surgeon General's warning to heart. The TV was playing *The Million Dollar Movie*. I turned it off.

I looked at Kate, her long neck, the gentle rise and fall of her breasts. I tried to calculate how I could get close enough to drink in her fragrance and still have a plausible explanation if she woke up. Then she stirred, murmuring something incomprehensible in her sleep, and it reminded me of a place far away, of another time when I was happy and wanted for nothing. A sigh rolled out of my chest.

'Screw it,' I mumbled. I grabbed a light blanket from the hallway cupboard, covered them with it and switched off the lights.

I lay in bed with a notepad in my hands, listening quietly to Dave Hull on the radio. I was tapping my pencil on the pad to the tune of *Bits and Pieces* by The Dave Clark Five. I flipped the pages over until I hit the cardboard backing. There were markings already there. Words I was working out how to spell, addition, long division and multiplication efforts, a phone number or two. I found an empty space and wrote 'Connie-Jean Templeton'. The band kept belting out its beat as Dave Clark sang. After another couple of verses, I scribbled 'Kate Hickey'. It was amazing how fast this group had adopted The Beatles' style. As the final chorus played I was poised to write another name to the list. I put the tip of the pencil down on the paper and started making the curve of the first letter but then the song ended and I stopped writing.

I dozed off and dreamed about the dinner at Ray's house. In my dream it resembled the painting *Last Supper* by Tintoretto, which was in a book I had inherited from Mutti. It was strange how that image came to mind rather than the Leonardo da Vinci version hanging over the Rodriguez's dinner table. The dinner had felt more like Tintoretto's swirling, rowdy scene.

In the Tintoretto, the table is at a sloping angle, although the line-up of disciples is the same as in Leonardo's painting. The frame is crowded with eight or nine servants going about their tasks, ignoring the extraordinary event taking place. Transparent angels dive and tumble in the air like moths drawn to the flame of the oil lamp hanging overhead.

Jesus sits smack-dab in the centre of the composition, back-lit by a Hollywood-sized keg light. The whole painting is in high contrast with weirdly cast shadows. The disciples' faces are in the dark while the features of the servants are lit up. To top it off, there's a ginger cat sitting in a basket in the foreground and a small dog under the table eyeing the cat. It is delicious chaos, like the dinner at Ray's. In my dream, Mr Rodriguez was sitting in Judas' place, eying me with threatening intent.

When I got up for school Charlie and Kate were gone, the coffee table was clean and Tate was sitting at the kitchen table in his new thin-lapelled suit and an even thinner black tie. Kate had helped him choose it the week before in preparation for the release of the new-season cars.

'Charcoal suits your dad's colouring and makes him look as smooth as James Bond,' she'd told me. That evening they had come home laden with bags from The May Company, The Broadway and Bullocks Wilshire.

'Good morning, son,' Tate put down his newspaper. 'Where were you last night?' There was an edge to his tone.

'I had dinner at Ray's house. I didn't know how to get in touch with you. I'm sorry, sir.'

'The new kid at the dealership?'

'Yes, sir.'

'How was it?'

'It was swell. There was lots of food and so many people. Man, that guy has a big family.'

'Spanish, right?'

'No, Mexican.' I reached for the Sugar Frosted Flakes. 'But he's got a cousin who's half Basque and other cousins that are Irish.'

'They sure like their families big.'

I put a spoonful of cereal into my mouth.

'I was a little uneasy.' Tate paused for the longest time and then smiled dryly. 'In the future, try to let me know where you are.'

I stopped chewing, 'How am I supposed to do that when you're not around?'

'It depends on where I'm at – leave a message with Mrs Barker or tell Charlie.'

'What about if you're out drinking? Or out with Kate? Or God knows where?'

'Now, wait a minute –'

'And you were "a little uneasy"? Most parents would have called the police or yelled their brains out. I'm surprised you noticed at all. I could have been anywhere, kidnapped or dead in some hole somewhere.'

'You're way out of line, Jackson. Most kids would be over the moon to have the kind of freedom I give you. Okay, maybe I'm not the strictest father in the world but I know you're sharp and you can take care of yourself. What's your problem?'

I was breathing hard. 'What's my problem? I saw something last night. It was fun and warm and whole. I saw people who wanted to be together because they loved each other and they showed affection and laughed, and it felt good, it felt like … like family.'

Tate drew back into his shirt. He took a deliberate sip of coffee. 'I want to be with you, Jackie. I'm trying hard to make a life for us. Look, once the new line is launched I'll get Charlie to cover me a few days. Maybe we can go down to Mexico or up to San Francisco, or something.'

He really didn't get it. 'I'm not talking about a vacation. I'm talking about all the time, Tate.'

'I understand, but we can start with a trip; get away from this place and everyone. You know, get a fresh start.'

How many fresh starts do we need? I sighed. 'What about school?'

'I don't know. Don't you have Easter break or something?' I picked up my spoon. He took a bite of dry toast. I didn't look at him, but I could feel his eyes on me. 'In fact – we can start Friday. Friday's the big day, right? What do you want to do?'

I had thought about my birthday a lot. I didn't know if Tate would remember. I shrugged my shoulders. 'I don't know.'

'C'mon,' he said. 'I'm here now; I'm listening. I'm going to take the day off, get you out of school and take you anywhere you want. It's your day.'

'Why not wait until Saturday? Then we won't have to take time off.'

'I really can't. With the new line coming out, Saturday will be our best day for sales – maybe of the year. I've gotta be at work then, buddy. Taking Friday is a real luxury as it is.'

Well, that's where I fit in, isn't it – squeezed in before the new line of cars, I thought. What was the use? I took another spoonful and chewed deliberately. 'Okay, what about we go to San Gabriel Mission in the morning, have lunch at Tommy's and then go to the County Museum of History and Science in the afternoon?'

'That sounds cool, as long as we can be away before the traffic starts at five.' He glanced at his watch. 'Gotta go. I gotta be early.' He stood up and straightened his jacket. 'How do I look?'

Kate was right; Tate looked good in grey and had more than a passing resemblance to Sean Connery. 'Dressed to kill, Tate.'

Mr Talbot was worked up that morning in class. He told us how important the Warren Commission – the official government report on the murder of the president – would be when it came out. 'You'll see,' he said. He loosened his tie and it wasn't even the afternoon yet. 'Lee Harvey Oswald didn't act alone. He couldn't have. To get off three shots so fast, and so accurately, on a moving target, there had to be more than one gunman. It had to be a conspiracy.'

'Whoa, that's heavy, Mr T,' Luke mumbled. He flicked his head back to keep the bleached locks out of his eyes. 'Yeah, my dad says he doesn't think that Oswald killed that cop either. He says the eyewitness statements are all over the place. Who do you think it was?'

Mr Talbot scratched his chin. He hadn't shaved since we went on the gallery trip and, although he wasn't the most hirsute man around, he had a beard now. 'The Russians, no doubt. Khrushchev has had it in for Kennedy since the Cuban Missile Crisis.'

'And Oswald used to live in the USSR,' Billy added. 'His wife's a Russkie. They must have hired him or brainwashed him or something.'

'If you ask me, none of it matters.' Maria crossed her arms. 'The president is dead and no matter who did it or why, nothing is going to bring him back.'

Mr Talbot tapped on the desk with his fingers. 'Someone has to pay, and so far nobody has.' No one in the class argued with that. 'Something has changed. It's like hope has died. If we have any chance of getting it back Bobby Kennedy has to take up his brother's place and lead us. Anyway, that's my opinion.' He cleared his throat and looked down at the papers on his desk.

'Is your group ready to report back to class, Billy?' Billy looked at Ming Li, who smiled and nodded. Mr Talbot hitched up his tie and addressed the class. 'Okay, first off Billy, Jackson, Ming and Maria are going to report back on the trip we took to La Cienega Boulevard and the exciting exhibitions we saw.'

Maria had been right – we actually remembered more than we realised, and after bouncing off one another we had put together something that resembled a report. Ming Li read from notes on cards that we had made up the week before. She gave an overview of the night and the significance of La Cienega in the art scene. When she mentioned the David Stuart Gallery, she gave Billy a coy look. He winked.

Billy talked about Ceeje Gallery and the Garabedian painting that had impressed him. Maria told the class about Judy Gerowitz and her talk about girls not getting the same chances as boys, and about *Car Hood.* Instead of painting on a rectangular canvas, Judy Gerowitz had taken the hood off a Chevrolet Corvair and spray-painted it with automotive lacquer. It was hard-edged and bright and unexpected. She also talked about *The Studs*, the show at the Ferus Gallery, and the four artists: Ed Moses, Billy Al Bengston, Robert Irwin and Ken Price.

Finally it was my turn. I had a dry mouth and I felt clammy everywhere else. I felt detached from what was happening. I looked at my notes. 'Hello. As you have already heard it was an amazing evening of art …' Ray was drawing, Luke was whispering to Elizabeth and the rest of the class looked blank. Maria was the only one watching me with any sympathy, 'There was something for everybody …' I looked over at Maria again. Her eyes were clean and clear and bright ' …but for me … for me, the thing that stood out the most was a painting at the Rolf Nelson gallery called *Roll Your Own (Zig-Zag)* by an artist named Ronald Davis.'

Luke laughed out loud. 'I know what Zig-Zags are for, man.' He put his thumb and forefinger up to his lips and made short sucking sounds. Ray and some of the other guys giggled. Mr Talbot glared at him and gestured for me to continue.

'It was part of a show called *Hard Edge*. They were all abstract paintings.' No one seemed to be listening. Even Mr Talbot was drawing in the margins of his notepad. It was futile talking about a painting without having a photograph or a slide to show the class. Then I remembered something Charlie said about selling cars: 'You sell a car in the first few seconds that you're with a customer. You need a hook – something that will grab them and pique their curiosity. You gotta make them want more. If you don't do that then it's a tough sell; not impossible, but a damn tough sell.'

My first few seconds with this audience were gone, but I had to try something, '*Hard Edge*. Think about what that means.' I raised my voice slightly. 'I mean it. Think about it.' Some kids looked up.

'The fin on my surfboard, dude. I got a gnarly cut on my arm from it when I …'

Then Ray cut in. 'The chrome tail fins on a 1957 Chevy, *ese*. Sharp.'

'The broken glass from a Coke bottle in the gutter,' Twinkie called out.

'Yeah. Remember when that glass cut your foot right through your flip-flops last summer?'

Mr Talbot growled at the class, 'This isn't a brain-storming session, students,' then to me, 'What does this have to do with the trip to La Cienega, Jackson?'

'Yes, sir, right.' I wiped the sweat from my upper lip with the back of my hand. 'My point is, our whole lives are hard edged.

Modern life – this thing that's going on right now – is so fast. It's glass and metal and plastic and rockets, crowded streets, atomic missiles and satellites in space … it's like the assassination of President Kennedy. We all knew about it in minutes, all over the country – all over the world. We even saw Jack Ruby murder Oswald live on TV.'

I scanned the room quickly but I wasn't looking for acceptance any more. I was inspiring myself, filling with the spirit, talking in tongues.

'These guys, these amazing artists in the *Hard Edge* show know that. They know that life is different now than it was before – even in the '50s. It's all about change; new ideas, new materials. They know that the art they make has to show that. They can't paint pretty landscapes or Jesus and Mary or splotches of paint that may or may not mean something. It has to be of this time and this place. New York. New York is the past. What I'm saying is it's like California, man; it's hip, it's hot and bright and razor-sharp and cool, it's loud colour and fun. It's rock 'n' roll and just … what it is, pure and simple. It's now, it's here, it's nothing else.' The room was silent. I took a deep breath. 'By the way, Judy Gerowitz gets it too. She's pretty cool.' I looked at Maria and she was beaming. 'Thank you,' I managed to say as I made my way back to my seat.

Ray looked up from his drawing, pulled down the corners of his lips and nodded. I knew what his expression meant, 'That was shitty, *ese*, pure *mierda*. What were you thinking? But it's over now so forget about it' – at least that's how I interpreted it.

I looked over at Maria but she was back sitting next to Elizabeth, getting out her supplies.

Mr Talbot thanked us and assured the rest of the class that they would all be invited to the art walk next year. Then he told us to continue with the projects we had started last week. Before he sat down at his desk, he called out, 'Ryder. Can you come up here, please?'

'Yes, sir.'

'You done it now, *pendejo*,' Ray said.

'Shut up, Ray,' I hadn't had a chance to explain about Grace and Maria and Unai yet and he was being an asshole. He might have still been pissed off about the book thing too; I didn't know. He never mentioned it – which was a good thing. If he had done that I would have hated him forever.

As I walked up to the front I couldn't help thinking of Mr Talbot transforming into the Wolf Man. It made me relax as I got closer to his desk. 'Yes, Mr Talbot?'

He stroked the fair hairs away from his mouth, 'That was a very interesting talk you gave.'

'Oh?'

His teeth seemed to be getting sharper and his nose twitched. 'Yes, very interesting. Where did you get that information from?'

'I'm sorry, sir? I don't understand.'

'Come on, Jack, you must have talked to someone or seen it written somewhere.' I shook my head.

'Are you trying to tell me you pulled all that stuff out of thin air? That it came from you? Really?'

I nodded. He sat back and played with his beard. 'I have never heard anyone – not even art critics – describe what those guys are trying to do so well. You really get it. That was something else, my friend.'

'I was desperate, sir, but thank you.'

He smiled, 'Okay. What are you working on?'

'The painting of –'

'It doesn't matter. I set those things for kids who can't think. What would you really like to be painting?'

'Truly, sir?'

'Yes,' he said, 'what pushes your buttons?'

A sigh escaped from my chest, 'I'm okay doing the project you assigned us, sir.'

He tapped his pencil against his open mouth. His face returned to its human form, like the Wolf Man's when he was mortally wounded by the silver cane. 'Okay, that's fine, but I'm going to give you a special homework assignment.'

'But Mr Talbot, I thought you liked what I said.'

'I did, Jackson. I do.'

'So why are you giving me more work?'

'It's not more work, it's different work. I want you to try oil paints.'

'Sir, I've never painted in oil. I don't know what to do.'

'Don't worry, I'll show you. I've got an old set of oils here that I used to use.' He reached into the bottom drawer of his desk and pulled out a battered, paint-splattered oak case the size of a shoebox. 'Pick these up after school. Take them home and mess around with them. Use the turpentine in the clear flask to thin the paint and to clean your brushes. Don't let water near them. I'll give you an old canvas to play with.'

'Can't I do this in class? My dad doesn't like me doing art.'

'If the other students see you have oils they'll want them too. Don't worry about your dad. He'll be fine. If he has a problem tell him to give me a call. Okay?'

When I got back to my desk Ray was looking at me expectantly. 'What was it, *guero*? Did Wolf Man tell you off?'

'Dude, have you seen that movie?' Luke interrupted, 'It's pretty gnarly, man.'

I had seen the *The Wolf Man* movie when I was about seven years old. It was on TV on a Saturday night when Mutti had gone out with Helen. It scared the shit out of me and I couldn't sleep without the light on. Mutti got mad at Tate for letting me watch it.

'He's looking the part now, *ese*, with his beard and all. Hairy Larry,' Ray said.

'It happens every year,' Billy said without looking up from his charcoal drawing. 'The whole Wolf Man thing. Somebody realises that his name is the same and then Mr T becomes "Wolf Man" for the rest of the year. Clovis Templeton told me.'

'What retards would name their kid after a friggin' monster, man?' Luke asked.

'Do the maths, Beach Boy,' Ming Li said, 'Mr Talbot is twenty-six years old. That means he was born in 1938.'

'That's like, old, man,' Billy laughed. Ray mouthed something at me – I couldn't tell if it was '*tonto*' or '*loco*'.

'You missed the train, Luke,' I said, 'Mr Talbot was three years old when the movie came out.'

'So they named the Wolf Man after baby Mr T?'

I snorted.

'Jeez, *pendejo*, that sun must have bleached your grey stuff as well as your hair, *ese*.' Ray said, 'The monster was named after Mr T's father, Larry Talbot Senior. Mr T is the Wolf Man *Junior*.'

I agreed with a straight face, and Billy and Maria backed us up.

True to his word, after school Wolf Man set me up with paints, jars of linseed oil, turpentine and three worn but usable brushes. 'Thanks, sir, but you only gave me five colours.'

'Actually, three colours and two tones. Black and white are not colours.'

I raised my eyebrows. 'That's worse, then – only three colours.'

'You know your colour wheel already, don't you?'

'Yes, sir.'

'I've given you the primary colours – red, blue and yellow. I want you to use them to make the rest of the colours. It's a great exercise.'

'Okay, sir, I'll give it a try.'

'Good man. Now, there are a few things you need to know.' Over the next hour he told me how the canvas has to be sealed first, or else the oil will draw away from the pigment into the canvas or paper. Then he explained how to care for the brushes. 'Any craftsman knows that tools are not inanimate objects, Jackson. They are extensions of your energy – of your will – as well as your hand. You can wield them like a sledgehammer or flourish them like a surgeon's scalpel. You can even tickle, like a feather.' He told me how long it can take for oils to dry and how frustrating this can be. 'However, it is that annoying quality that gives oil its strength as a medium, this ability to be manipulated extensively. You are going to hate it at first, but persevere. I know you can do it.'

He gave me a couple of cardboard panels that were prepared with a gesso ground. 'Do some sketches first,' he instructed. 'Don't go directly to the boards. That's the biggest mistake new painters make. It sounds like fun to attack the canvas, but you end up stuck in a compositional cul-de-sac that could have been avoided if you had solved some simple design problems on paper first. Trust me; painting in oil has enough problems of its own without creating more.'

*

My head was swimming by the time I got home. I grabbed a weenie from the refrigerator, dipped it in mustard, and poured myself a glass of milk. I didn't have any other homework and I needed something to distract me from thinking about Connie-Jean. I went into my room to paint. The light in the living room would have been better, but I never knew when Kate might show up. I wasn't ready to share my experiments with her – or Tate, for that matter.

I didn't have an easel so I used a trick my old art teacher in New York, Mr Fernando, had shown me – placing one chair upside down on top of another chair so the legs stuck up like four bull's horns. If your canvas is wide enough, you can angle it so it rests between the front and back legs. It takes a little manoeuvring, but you get used to it.

I squeezed a thumbnail-sized dab of each paint onto the stained palette, carefully placed the turpentine and oil next to it and sat back to survey the scene. The scent of pine forests wafted up from the turpentine jar. It reminded me of hiking around Lake Arrowhead, and of Christmas time. Something was missing. I mentally went through Mr Talbot's checklist. I needed a rag. I went to my underwear drawer and picked out the Y-fronts with the most perished waistband.

I thought about copying Millais's *Ophelia* for Connie-Jean, but, after La Cienega, what good would it do? Yeah, I was thinking about her – but I didn't want her to know that.

I leaned back in my chair and thought about all kinds of possibilities. I already knew that the hardest part about doing art is deciding what to do. When anything is possible, where do you start? I could go to my secret drawings, but already they seemed dated, from the past. Going to La Cienega changed how I saw, what I looked at. Everything before seemed … not irrelevant, but like a prelude. I pulled out my drawing pad from the bottom drawer and started to draw little quick design ideas.

It was dark by the time Tate got in. For once his absence hadn't made me nervous. I had roughed out the concept on the board with a 2B pencil by then. On the way to the bathroom I heard him talking to Charlie in the lounge.

'I'm going to the car show in Chicago, buddy, for a few days,' Charlie said.

'Are you fucking kidding? You can't go now. We have the new car release coming up,' Tate replied, then he dropped his voice, 'and there's the *simkhe*, you know?'

'I know, I know, but I've got to get away.'

'What's wrong, Chaz. I know something's bugging you. You have been acting weird for weeks.'

'It's not your fault, but Christ, I just feel like a third wheel around you and Kate.'

'It's not like that, you know that. She's … she's a neighbour. A friend.'

Silence. 'Be reasonable. I can't do this by myself.'

Another silence. 'Yes you can. You've worked hard and learned quickly. You already manage the place better than I do. You're not aggressive enough, but that seems to work in your favour – you're ready. You got Buzz, Marion, Jack and the Spanish kid to help you, too. I gotta fucking go.'

'Not like this, Charlie, come on, man.'

'I'll try to make it back in time. I'll call.' Charlie's voice was level.

'Wait, Charlie, let's talk about this.'

I heard the screen door shut. A long pause. Tate said, 'Shit,' and then the door closed.

I heard his footsteps coming down the hall. I raced out to meet Tate so he wouldn't see what I was doing in my room. He reeked of Marlboros and Johnny Walker Red. 'What's that smell?'

I couldn't come up with a convincing lie. 'Turpentine. Mr Talbot wants me to paint in oil.'

I braced for his response, but all he said was, 'Open your window, man. It stinks like a gas station in here.'

'Yes, sir.'

'You eaten yet?'

'No sir, just a weenie when I got home.'

He undid his tie. 'I think there are a couple of Swansons in the freezer. I'll heat up the oven. He walked away and then turned back. 'About Friday, son I'm sorry, but I gotta be on deck down at the dealership. Charlie's going to be in Chicago at a car show. Sorry, buddy.'

'That figures,' I mumbled.

'I can't help it. Charlie's just stormed off, the asshole.'

'This is the way it's always going to be, Tate. Don't you see that? Next time it will be something else, and the time after that – but you're always going to do the same thing; put whatever it is before me – before us.'

'I'll make it up to you, I swear.'

I didn't answer. What would be the point? I wasn't surprised he was going to *putz* out on me again. I dragged myself back to my bedroom. There was chattering in my head. I needed music. I reached over and flicked on the transistor. 'I Want to Hold Your Hand' was finishing, but it was enough to get my head moving.

I looked at my design on the board. Everything was there that I wanted. The base of it was going to be abstract, hard edged, clean and bright with vague California references – the sea, palm trees and even surfing. Then over the top of that I was going to layer expressive passages with the brush. I wanted this to suggest life, movement, energy.

I couldn't concentrate. Tate didn't even react; he didn't get angry or defensive.

I stared at my bare drawing. Something was missing.

Modern art is all about concept and surface. It's all head stuff – that's what Picasso gave us. When I did my secret drawings they were all about the way I felt, about emotional release. I wanted this painting to be about me; my world, my single knowledge and history and how that's mixed with this new scene. But where's my pain and loneliness? Where's Tate? My friends? Where is Mutti?

How could I juggle these totally opposed goals on an eighteen by twenty-four inch surface?

I had at least twenty minutes before the meals would be ready. I couldn't wait. I took a #6 flat brush, plunged it into the centre of the pool of blue paint and daubed it in a large flat area I had marked out. I had blocked in the whole background when Tate called me from the kitchen. I dropped the brush into the turpentine and stopped to consider what I'd done. It was good to start, but I shuddered too. What the hell was I going to do?

Tate was sitting in the living room with a TV tray in front of him and another one set up for me. *The Outer Limits* was on the box. I'd missed the beginning. 'Is it that late already?' I asked.

'Afraid so, buddy. I didn't catch everything, but I think all these people were on an amusement park ride, like the moon-rocket ride at Disneyland, then they found out it was really a spaceship. And the fellow in the alien suit is really an alien.'

I peeled back the aluminium-foil cover of my TV dinner. Steam billowed from the thin steak, mashed potatoes and peas. On screen a couple of guys were fighting. I wondered what colour to put down next on the painting. 'I'm going to eat in my room, okay?'

Tate looked up. 'With that *shtunk*?'

I shrugged. 'I opened the window and it's not too bad.'

'Sure, then. Knock yourself out. By the way, Kate called and I told her about Friday. She said she'd love to spend your birthday with you and be your chauffeur, that is, if you'd like.'

I blinked, repeatedly, in disbelief. 'Really? That sounds swell.' I practically danced back to my room. A day with Kate. I hadn't seen much of her lately, and the thought of her made my toes tingle.

A whole day with Kate.

I chewed a forkful of peas and mashed potato and looked at my efforts so far. The large geometric building shapes were the next least-scary part, so I mixed a bit of red with the white and a little yellow and was happy with the result.

I grabbed some paper towels from the kitchen. Tate was asleep in the living room, illuminated by the blue light of the TV. He had one hand on each armrest, like the statue of Abraham Lincoln in Washington DC. I rarely saw him like this anymore, unmoving and quiet. I studied his forehead. It looked like mine, but his hair had started to recede. His skin had taken to the West Coast sun. He was far darker than me now. I had the urge to touch his cheek like I used to when I was a kid, but I tapped his shoulder gently instead. 'Tate, go to bed.'

'*Liebchen*?' he muttered.

I knew he meant my mother. He never called me that. '*Keyn*, Tate, no. It's me. Come on.'

His eyes flew open and a weak smile crossed his face. '*Gelibt boytshikl*, sweet boy.'

I pulled the TV tray away from his lap and helped him up. 'Don't worry about cleaning up. I'll be up for a while.'

'I was having a dream.'

'I know.'

'Did I do the right thing, son?'

'What are you talking about, Tate?'

'You know. This. Moving us here, leaving New York, the whole business.'

I steered him towards the hallway. 'I don't know, Tate. I don't know if things would have been much different if we had stayed at home. All I know is that we're here. That's about it.'

He opened his mouth but nothing came out. He stumbled down the hallway, his feet wide apart like he was on an obstacle course. We stopped in front of his door. He shook his head. 'I don't know. Your mother always knew the right thing to do. She always made the right call.' He looked at me, his eyes half shut and raised one hand. 'Not too late, okay? G'night, son.'

'Goodnight, Tate. Sleep well.' I cleaned up the kitchen, turned off the TV and grabbed my paper towels. Back in my room, I cleared the mess off my palette. More than half of my dinner was still in the aluminium tray. I cut a bit of steak and heaped some peas onto my fork, but they were stone cold.

I ate the steak and left the rest. I picked up my eraser and flipped it over and over in my hand.

The contrast on the pink and blue was good.

What had Tate been dreaming about? Mutti, obviously, but what about her?

I wondered what mattered to him.

A whole day with Kate ... what was I going to say to her?

Had it really been right for us to move here from New York? I could have stopped it. If I had said no to Tate, we would have stayed.

If I woke up to the painting the way it was, I would be pissed all day tomorrow.

I tried a new technique, wiping away the paint from the areas I wanted to lighten, and that seemed to work. The building forms were starting to pop out. It was enough for tonight.

Dave Hull signed off on the radio, which meant it was midnight. The music news came on. 'The Beatles started filming on their first movie today, titled *A Hard Day's Night*. The Fab Four are filming in a train station in London.' I imagined my own movie, *A Hard Night's Design*. I was tired. I couldn't have lifted the brush again even if I'd wanted to.

The rest of the week dragged by. I had homework on Tuesday and Wednesday. I didn't do any more work on my painting, but I kept stealing glances at it.

Mr Talbot asked me how it was going. I told him how much I was struggling. 'The thing is, Mr T, I don't think I want to paint in oils. Why can't I do what everyone else is doing?'

'Don't be discouraged, Jack. It's a process and you are just starting. Of course there will be hiccups. That's part of it.' He brushed the hairs away from the corners of his mouth. 'Or, is it fear that your father will disapprove?' I didn't answer. He exhaled loudly through his nose. 'Okay, maybe it was too early. I was hoping I could excite you, inspire you to take art more seriously. You know, I don't usually let students even touch oils until they are seniors.'

I sighed too. 'I don't want to disappoint you, sir. I'm not ...'

'Like I said, Jackson, maybe I made a mistake.'

'I would like to finish this painting, at least.'

'That's fine. Bring the paints back when you're finished. Any time is okay.'

As I walked back to my desk I thought about the painting. I really didn't want to let the Wolf Man down. I knew he was treating me special and I appreciated it. I wanted to make the painting mine, to do something from now and here, like Mr Talbot was always talking about.

'You're spending a lot of time with the Wolf Man, *ese*. What gives?' Ray asked when I got back to my seat.

'Forget about it.'

'Hey, don't bite my head off, *guero*. Billy's going to think you're the Wolf Man's new pet puppy.' Twinkie laughed, but Ming Li didn't.

I looked at Mr Talbot. He was facing to the left and looking out the window. He reminded me of a leaner version of Titian's *Portrait of a Man* but without long hair. I wondered what Kate thought of his new look.

A whole day with Kate! I had to laugh out loud.

'What is it now, *ese*?'

'Don't worry,' I told Ray. 'Tomorrow everything's going to be just fine.'

He stopped drawing and looked up at me. His face was slack, but his eyes were wide and searching. 'You know, don't you? Who spilled the beans?'

'What are you talking about?'

'What are *you* talking about?' he countered in an aggressive tone.

'*Vato*, I got a date with a chick who has a Corvette,' I bragged.

His eyes relaxed and he grinned. '*Orale*. Ghost Ryder strikes again. Who's the chick? Does she go to this school? You been holding out on me, *cabrón*.'

My shirt felt sticky all of a sudden, 'No, she doesn't go to this school.'

Ray waited a minute then gestured with his fingers for more. I shrugged, 'What about you? Who spilled the beans about what?'

He sat back and looked down at the table before looking up, giving me a forced grin and saying, 'Oh, I got a date too, *ese*. Yeah, a hot date with a little *mamacita* from La Habra.' He leaned in close and hissed, 'But don't tell anybody. If Twinkie finds out she'll kill me.' He mimed stabbing like in the shower scene in *Psycho* and shrieked, 'hwee, hwee, hwee, hwee,' before doubling over with laughter.

16

AFTER SCHOOL I RAN into Mrs Barker outside the school office. She patted my arm with a kid-gloved hand, 'now, don't worry about your father reporting your absence tomorrow. He engaged me as his agent and I've arranged it all with the school office.'

'Thanks, Mrs Barker.'

'Not at all. And Jackson?' She cupped my face with her hands and kissed me forcefully on the cheek. 'Have a wonderful birthday, my boy.'

I looked around to see if anyone had been watching, but we were alone in the admin hallway. 'Uh, thanks.'

I woke up on Friday morning to Bob 'The Emperor' Hudson playing *Just One Look* by The Hollies. They were another British band that sounded a lot like The Beatles, but that was fine by me – they were good and no American band could come close.

I'd had another restless night but the first thing I did was look at my painting. So far I had only worked on it at night. It was different in the daylight. The blue was uneven and the pinks looked cooler and lighter. I had been stealing glances at it all week. By Friday the damn thing was screaming out to me, practically telling me what to do next. I wasn't sure whether I liked it or not, but, a realisation hit me. I wasn't going to give up on it. It wasn't a matter of wanting to – I had to conquer it. It was going to happen. I was going to do it.

I felt different – tingly, restless, powerful.

Only then did I remember it was my birthday and I was going to spend it with Kate. I jumped out of bed, showered and dressed in a new pair of khakis, a white dress-shirt and my best brown wingtip shoes. I buffed them with a shoe brush and some polish. Back in the bathroom, I slathered pomade onto my hair.

Tate poked his head through the doorway. 'Happy birthday, son.'

'Thanks, Tate.'

'Look at you. Your mother would be proud.'

'You really think I look okay?'

'If I didn't know better I'd say you were going out on a date, man. Listen, I gotta get to work. I'll give you your present this evening. Is that cool? Kate knows to have you back by five.'

I hadn't even thought about Tate getting me a present. 'Tate, that's great. I can't wait.'

'Look, about last night …'

I thought he was going to say that he realised that it was wrong to move to California, that he had decided that we would move back.

'Get rid of the oil paints, would you? The turpentine makes my head hurt and it's a fire hazard. Have a good time today.' Then he was gone.

He didn't even give me a chance to argue. Still, I had already made a decision about the paints and we would have to have that conversation soon. I wasn't going to let it ruin this day. As soon as Tate was out the door, I started daydreaming. By the time Kate knocked on the door I had the makings of a good-sized boner.

'Happy birthday, old man.' She skipped through the doorway, wrapped her arms around my neck and gave me a firm kiss on my lips. She smelled of soap and lilacs and her body was warm against mine. The embrace was fast, but I had to admit it didn't feel sexual. It wasn't much different than Mrs Barker's kiss on the cheek the day before.

Kate held me at arm's length and looked me up and down. 'Look at you. How handsome.'

My face flushed and I bowed my head.

'I hope you're ready for a fun day. Bring your bathing trunks, a towel and a jacket. It might get chilly. I've got the auxiliary hardtop off of the Vette.'

'Aren't we going to the Mission?'

'I know you had plans with your dad, but I'm changing them. I am taking you on a mystery tour.' She pulled a scarf out of her pocket and wrapped it around her head. 'You better be ready.'

Kate put on a pair of oversized sunglasses and unlocked the passenger door of her Corvette. I rushed over to the driver's side to open her door.

'Why thank you, sir.'

I bowed at the waist and closed her door.

Connie-Jean was standing on the sidewalk outside her house. She was wearing her blue coat and had a pile of books clasped in front of her. I froze. She saw me too, and didn't move a muscle.

'What's taking so long, Jack?' Kate asked. 'The day is going, let's move! Did you forget something?'

'No, no.' I gave Connie-Jean a smile and a nod. Then I climbed into the car.

'Geronimo!' Kate shouted as she jammed the gearstick into first. She had given it too much gas and the wheels screamed as they tore across the loose gravel. I grinned.

'I didn't mean to do that. It was fun, though, wasn't it?'

As we drove along the wind whipped through my hair. It was chilly, but I couldn't stop smiling. 'You took the removable hardtop off. I've never been in a convertible before,' I confessed.

'It's the best. It feels like flying.' Kate steered the Corvette onto San Sebastiano Boulevard. I hoped people would see us together and think we were dating. 'So, have you got a girlfriend yet?' she asked.

I stared at the passing hills, dotted with cows and oil wells. 'Maybe.'

'Come on, you can tell me. Is she pretty?'

'Yeah, she's very pretty. Beautiful.'

'Is she in your class? What's her name?'

I shifted in my seat, 'You know, Kate, I'm not too happy to be talking about this. I'd rather not discuss it.'

'I don't want to make you uncomfortable, especially on your birthday. But we're friends, and usually friends talk about these kinds of things.'

'Like I said, it's only maybe. It's very complicated.'

'These things usually are. "Affairs of the heart", Butch used to call them. Whenever I would try to talk to him about some love crisis one of my girlfriends was having he would say, 'Affairs of the heart, affairs of the heart.' It was his pat answer. He wasn't really listening.

'What about you?'

'What about me?'

'Have you got a boyfriend?'

Her face changed ever so slightly, 'I get it. Turnabout is fair play, right?' She gave me a grin.

'Well, do you?'

'Jackson, I do believe you are being impertinent, young man,' she shoved me and I laughed. We drove in comfortable silence until Fullerton, where we turned onto North Harbour Boulevard. 'You know, after Butch was killed I wasn't interested in having another boyfriend, let alone a husband,' she said. 'It's a hard thing to lose someone who … I mean, I didn't take a breath without considering what he might think about it.'

We drove past Hillcrest Park. I could see ducks wading in the creek. 'I'm so sorry. You must have loved him very much.'

She laughed, loud and long. I shifted in my seat again and stared at the dashboard. Finally she said, 'Jackson, I'm the one who should be sorry. Some friend I am. I've never told you – or anybody for that matter – but I absolutely loathed Butch. He was a certifiable, number-one son of a bitch. Pardon my French. He was domineering and sarcastic. I'm sure he was cheating on me. I depended on him and I did love him, once, but by the end I knew I wasn't important to him. He was single-minded, obsessive really, about pushing the odds. He loved the thrill of danger. That was what he lived for, not for me.'

'I had no idea.'

'Well, I don't blab about it. A lot of people thought he was a hero. America needs its heroes. He was shortlisted to become an astronaut. I wonder what they'd think if they knew he used to beat the hell out of me.'

'Really?'

'Oh, yeah. Nothing was ever good enough. Dinner had to be perfect otherwise I'd get a slap or two. And you know I'm not the withering type, either. My defiance got me black-and-blue souvenirs more than once.'

'Oh, wow. I'm so sorry.'

' … I've said too much. Oh, Christ, it's your birthday and here I am dumping all my garbage on you. *I'm* the sorry one.' She put her hand on my leg.

'That's okay.' The blood instantly rushed down below my belt again.

'Anyway,' she said, returning her hand to the wheel, 'there was a happy ending. He was killed and I was free. Does that sound callous?'

'What does "callous" mean?'

'Hmm …' she chewed her lower lip, 'cold blooded. Heartless.'

'No, no. I mean, you had reason. Who would blame you?'

'You're a doll,' she said. 'Are you sure you're only turning sixteen? You've got a wise head on your shoulders.'

Harbour Boulevard ended and we turned left onto Newport. The landscape hadn't changed for miles, but now the temperature dropped a couple of degrees and I started to smell fresh salt air.

Past Hospital Road we drove downhill. At the risk of being disappointed again I asked her, 'So, you don't want a boyfriend?'

'Well, Butch died two years ago. I'm not going to become a nun.' She looked at me, but I couldn't tell what was going on behind those giant sunglasses.

'I'm going to take you to one of my favourite places on earth – Balboa Island.'

There was a marina to our right and beach houses lining the highway, jammed up next to one another. I could see the water – two blocks back away on both sides. We made a left on Palm Street and rolled to a stop behind a line of other cars.

'We're going on a ferry?' I asked, unable to hide my excitement.

'Yes we are, but there's a bridge on the other side of the island and we'll go that way when we leave.'

I could see the ferry in the distance, only halfway to the other side. It would have to dock, load up, return and unload before we could get on, so we had plenty of time, 'So, what kind of guy do you like? Tall, dark and handsome?'

Kate giggled. 'My, you don't let up, do you?' She tilted her head, trying to see beyond the car in front of us. 'I've dated a few times since I've been a widow and, really, I don't have one type of guy that I like. It's little things, individual things that seem right.'

'Like?'

'Oh, a sparkle in his eyes, confidence, a creative outlook, someone who laughs often, someone who wears good shoes ...'

'What? Are you kidding?'

'Not at all. You can tell a lot about a man by his shoes – whether he cares about himself, how well off he is, his tastes. It's even better if his shoes are off.'

'What do you mean?'

'Think about it. If his feet are tanned it means he gets out. He probably likes doing sporty things. You can see if he has athlete's foot or corns or calloused heels. And, most of all, you *have* to get a good look at the toenails.'

'Toenails?' I guffawed.

She hit me on the arm. 'I mean it. I won't date anyone who has horny, long toenails. A guy can look great on the outside and not give a damn inside. He thinks people won't see his feet so he doesn't care for them. That kind of man is cunning, a fraud, and a sham.' I instinctively curled my toes inside my shoes. 'Butch's fingernails were always well manicured, but his toenails were shocking. No sir, that's my bottom line.' She slid her sunglasses down her nose and peered over top of them. 'Now, your shoes,' she said. 'Florsheim Imperials, right? Very nice and well shined. I'm sure you will impress your lady love.'

I looked down at my shoes. They were the last thing Mutti bought me before she died. They were a good price, but the store had run out of my size. She had wanted to get the larger size and we argued about it.

'They are good shoes,' she had insisted. 'You will grow into them and you can wear an inner sole until you do.'

'But Mutti, I'll look like a clown until then.'

'You will thank me one day; you will see.'

Thanks, Mutti.

The ferry docked and the two vehicles in front of us started their engines. Kate revved up the Corvette and we moved slowly towards the dock. There was a slight bump as we hit the deck and we inched forward. Kate braked and turned off the engine.

'Come on, we can get out. It's a great view.'

The overcast morning was burning off and everything was coming into bright focus. A couple of hundred yards ahead was the island, completely covered in little two-storey beach houses. Boats were docked all the way along the waterline.

We drove off the ferry and onto Agate Avenue. The whole place was intimate and village-like, very clean. A block down we turned right on Park Avenue and the road widened out, making room for a traffic island dotted with palm trees. I tilted my head back and looked at the pristine sky. I felt myself drift. We slowed down and I opened my eyes. There was a white fire station on the corner. Kate turned left and parked in front of Hershey's Market.

'Come on, let's take a walk.' I got out and faced south, expecting to stroll along the eucalypt-lined shopping street. 'No, this way,' Kate said. 'I want to show you something.'

She took my hand and pulled me around the corner of the market, past a narrow alley and along a sidewalk. In front of us was a canal, about twenty yards wide with a walkway running alongside it. That's where we were heading.

As we walked, I tried to feel every inch of her skin that touched mine. Her hand was cool and slight and I marvelled at its softness. Perspiration oozed out of my pores. I wiped my other hand on my slacks.

'Isn't it beautiful?' she asked.

'Uh-huh.'

Eventually we stopped walking. She dropped my hand. She took me by the shoulders and spun me around. 'What do you think?'

In front of us was a two-storey weatherboard house, painted blue-grey with white trim. There were two large picture-windows on the ground floor. Above them a small balcony jutted out, with two chairs and a small, round table on it. Attached to the white picket fence was a 'For Sale' sign with the words Martha Anwiler, Realtor on it.

'What am I looking for?'

'At,' she corrected me. 'What am I looking *at*?'

'Okay, what am I looking at?'

'Isn't it cute?'

'The house?'

'Yes, the house, silly. What do you think?'

'Are you going to buy this house?'

'I'm thinking about it, but I want to know what you think.'

'But if you buy this house, you'll have to move out of the complex.'

'I've always wanted to live on Balboa Island. And look, I would have my own boat ramp.'

I leaned against the cement wall barrier that separated the canal from the walkway. 'I don't know what to say.'

'There's only one thing.'

'What's that?'

'They want ninety-five thousand dollars for it.'

'Really?' I laughed. 'Tate scans the newspaper every week looking for a house. You can get a house twice this size in the best part of San Sebastiano for a sixth of that price.'

'I know, I know.'

'You could live in a mansion and have enough left over to rent this place every summer.'

'I know, but it's so cute, and it would be mine.'

'You would leave me – I mean – our town?'

'You could come stay with me, you and your dad. It has three bedrooms. It would be fun.'

I looked down at my shoes, my last gift from Mutti. They

were filling with cement. I had read everything wrong about Kate. How could I have been such an idiot?

'I can afford it, but I would probably have to go to back to work … or get married, I guess. I don't know.'

The sun and breeze played with her hair, making it dance and flash. It was glorious, but my mood deepened. 'Well, that would make sense.'

'Don't be like that, Jack. I thought you would be happy for me.' She wrapped her arm around my waist but I went limp. 'You're the first one I've told about this, not your dad or Charlie or … I brought you here because you're my friend and I wanted your help.'

My insides were churning and I was feeling dizzy. I pulled away from her. 'I don't get it. You say we're such good friends but then you want to leave me. Aren't good friends supposed to stick together? Aren't they supposed to go through thick and thin?'

'It's not like I'm dying,' she said. Her hand flew to her mouth. 'Oh, Jackson, I'm so sorry.' I stood there and blinked. My stomach rumbled. She looked at her watch, 'Oh dear, I haven't fed you a thing and it's almost eleven o'clock. Are you hungry?' She grabbed me gently by the elbow. 'Come on. I know what you need.'

We walked along the canal for a block, then turned up Balboa to Marine Avenue. Halfway down the street was a little brick-and-glass ice-cream shack called Sugar 'n' Spice, with a blue awning and a sign above showing a six-foot-long, half-peeled banana. The sign said The Original Since 1945.

'Have you ever had a frozen banana before?' She asked. I shook my head. 'You're in for a treat. It's a peeled banana on a stick that's dipped in chocolate, sprinkled with nuts and put in the freezer. I used to have these all the time when I was a kid. I love 'em.'

We went inside. An elderly man was behind the counter. Katie said, 'Hello, Mr Phillips.'

'Why, Katie. Little Katie Amaté. How are you? We haven't seen you for a while.'

'I'm fine, sir, just fine.'

'I'm glad to hear it. What can I do you for?'

She ordered a medium for herself and a large for me, both with nuts. We headed up the road past St John Vianney Chapel. I took a bite of the chocolate-covered banana. It was delicious.

'Katie Amaté?' I asked.

'My maiden name – Katarina Maria Amaté.'

'Are you Italian?'

'Swiss-Italian. I was born in Locarno on Lake Maggiore, across the border from Italy. We moved here during the war but I don't remember Switzerland at all. So, what do you think about the frozen banana? Great, isn't it? Let's get some doughnuts for later.'

We wandered into Dad's Doughnuts, which was virtually a carbon copy of Sugar 'n' Spice, right down to the frozen banana on the roof. She ordered two cream puffs, two jelly-filled doughnuts and two glazed doughnuts. I offered to pay, but she wouldn't let me.

'There isn't much more up here,' she said as we left the shop. 'We should head back to the car.'

My stomach wasn't rumbling anymore, but it was still in knots. By the time we got to the Corvette we had finished our bananas, so we threw the sticks and napkins in the gutter. We had driven less than two blocks when the bridge to the mainland rose up in front of us. I looked at the boats along the canal and wished I was on one, going out to sea.

'Look, Jack, don't worry too much about the house.' Kate had read my mind. 'It's one possibility amongst many. I don't know what I'm going to do. You never know, I could even go back to Locarno.'

'*Buon viaggio*.'

'*Lei parla Italiano*?'

'No. Tate spent some time in Italy during the war. I picked up a word or two from him.'

'How about that? Your dad is full of surprises.' We drove in silence for a while.

'Anyway, whatever I do we'll be friends. You know that.' We turned right onto Bayside Drive.

'Where are we going now?'

'To my favourite beach in all of Southern California.'

We drove along a cliffside. A few hundred yards along the ridge, Kate turned down a steep street. The sign at the top said Corona del Mar.

'You feel like a swim?'

The parking lot along the beach was vast but only had a scattering of cars, despite the improved weather. Kate drove all the way down to the other end then she turned around and drove back towards the entrance. I raised my eyebrows.

She looked at me. 'Larry – Mr Talbot – has the afternoon off work. I thought he might be down here.'

The thought of seeing the Wolf Man, and of sharing Kate, did not thrill me. I looked around again and didn't see him.

We parked between the shop and the dressing rooms. The male one was clean, but I folded my clothes extra carefully, trying to keep sand off my good slacks. Outside, Kate was standing in a white bikini, an unbuttoned white blouse and a wide-brimmed straw hat with a pink band. I felt giddy and breathless and hardly dared to look at her for fear of what might crop up in my stupid palm tree-patterned trunks.

'What a cute swimsuit.' she said. She noticed Uncle Leo's mezuzah around my neck. 'Jack, that's beautiful.'

'Thanks. It used to belong to my great-grandfather.'

'A family heirloom.'

'I guess so.'

We went back to the Vette to put our clothes in the trunk and then walked towards the north end of the beach, where limestone rocks towered over us.

'This is a great place to watch the sun go down,' she said. 'Maybe we can do that another day.'

'Maybe when the grunion run.'

'Yeah, you remembered. We'll do that.' There was a path of sorts, leading to the crest of the rocks. 'That's Pirate's Cove down there. It's more private, but only good at low tide. And that's Balboa Peninsula, where we caught the ferry. That western point there is called The Wedge. Only the craziest surfers ride there. It's a killer.'

'I'd like to learn to surf.'

'After that *Gidget* movie Butch tried it. He probably would have kept doing it, too, if we hadn't moved to the desert.'

'Were you a beach bunny back then?'

'I'm a beach bunny now, aren't I?' She struck an exaggerated pin-up pose with her ass jutting out one way and her boobs the other. We laughed and walked along the seawall towards the jetty. Pelicans and seagulls circled overhead. 'You can walk out to the end of the breakwater, but it's rough jumping from rock to rock and there's bird crap everywhere.'

I was hardly listening. She was trying to distract me from the one thing that was shattering my perfect day. 'So you're going to move away, then.'

'Oh, Jackson, I don't know. I don't know what I want to do. I've got this, you know, itchy feeling that something's gotta change.'

'Maybe the change you need isn't a move. Maybe you need a guy, a boyfriend.'

She didn't say anything for the longest time. 'You got anyone in mind, tiger?'

Now it was my turn to clam up. Should I make my play? The signs weren't that good. If I blew it I couldn't try again, not ever. I had to play it cool. 'I know a guy who would like to be your boyfriend.'

'Oh, really?' She slowed down her walk and looked at me expectantly.

'Yeah, he's creative and has good shoes. There is a serious age difference, though. Does that bother you?'

'How serious is serious?'

'About ten years.'

'Ha, that's not bad. I've dated older men before. Now, twenty years would be serious. How is he set up? Is he a good guy? Who is it?'

'I can't tell you.'

'You teaser. Is it Charlie? No, he doesn't have a creative bone in his body. And he wears cheap shoes.'

'I told you, I can't say. I'm sworn to secrecy.'

She hit me on the arm, 'Well, he better hurry before I make other plans.'

She took off running across the sand towards the water. It took me a moment to realise she was going to swim. I followed her, squinting in the sunlight. Kate dropped her hat, glasses and blouse in one motion and ran into the surf. I tried to take off my T-shirt while I was running and ended up tumbling into a pile. Sand got in my eyes, nose and mouth. I wrestled my shirt off and plunged into the water. It was colder than I expected, but it felt good. Kate was standing about thirty yards away and I swam out to her.

'Careful when you put your feet down, Jack. There are a lot of stingrays here, especially by the breakwater, and if they get startled they'll lash out at you.'

'I've never seen a stingray.'

'They aren't aggressive, but they have a nasty barb on their tail that's poisonous and very painful. I had a boyfriend who got wounded here once and he screamed like he was being murdered. It was a bloody mess.' No sooner did she say that than she screamed, wrapped her arms around my neck and clasped my torso with her legs. 'One brushed by me.'

In any other circumstance I would have been as hard as a rock, with so much of her naked skin next to mine. I would have looked her in the eyes and told her I was the one, and then I would have kissed her passionately until she kissed me back. I could see us falling onto the sand, like Burt Lancaster and Deborah Kerr in *From Here to Eternity,* kissing as the surf lapped around us.

But the fact was that a stingray was right next to me and probably startled by Kate's flaying legs. My balls were in my abdomen. Without saying a word, I turned towards the shore and inched forward, shuffling my feet through the sand. Soon my waist was at water level and I was bearing Kate's full weight. She wasn't big by any standard, but a hundred pounds of dead weight to a sixteen-year-old is heavy enough and I was struggling.

‘I think we’re safe now,’ she breathed. Her arms were around my neck, and other feelings started to override the animal fear in me. She smiled and gave me a peck on the cheek before I put her down. ‘I’m sorry I panicked,’ she said.

‘That’s okay. I did too, but we’re safe.’

‘That was really brave of you, Jack. My hero.’

‘It was nothin’.’

We lay down next to our clothes and she shut her eyes. ‘If I ever meet this mysterious gal of yours I’ll tell her the whole story. That should at least get you to first base.’

I agonised over that thought. I could sense the heat of her body, the rise and fall of her breath, even the pulse of blood running through her veins and arteries. I peeked at her breasts, the supple contour of her belly and the curve of her thigh. Suddenly she stirred.

‘I’ve got to make a phone call. There’s a payphone at the shop. What do you say I grab us some food while I’m at it?’

I watched her as she walked away. Her top half was hidden by her billowing blouse, but I could study her bare legs from heel to thigh. They were perfect – lean and straight with strong calves. She moved lightly across the sand. I lay back and closed my eyes.

The encounter with the stingray had really thrown me, but maybe it had been for the best. Maybe my chances had just got better. She said I was her hero, that she liked my shoes and we laughed a lot. Best of all, she said ten years’ difference wasn’t bad. I know she meant older guy, younger gal – but why should it be any different the other way around?

She returned holding a cardboard box. It contained two

chilli cheese dogs, fries and a Coke for me, plus a plain hot dog with mustard and a 7Up for her.

'We don't have long,' she said. 'By three o'clock the wind comes in from the sea. It's like being in a sandstorm if you're on the beach.'

'There's not much surf.' I sat up and jammed food into my mouth. It wasn't anywhere near as good as Papaya King, but I didn't care.

'There never is. The beach faces south and the breakwater shelters the shore, too. It's always very gentle. That's why I like it here.'

We finished eating and lay down again in the sun. I closed my eyes. I was under the water but I wasn't drowning. I smiled and bubbles escaped out of my mouth and floated up past my eyes. I watched them rise slowly to the surface, where I could make out clouds and the shimmering sun. I looked around and saw fishes and crabs, starfish and urchins. The sandy ocean bed sloped down, rolling into a darker indigo.

There was movement on the ocean floor. It was a gigantic white stingray, as big as a human. I panicked and thrashed my hands and legs. The stingray moved towards me and I tried to swim in the other direction, but I couldn't move. Then it called out to me, 'Don't move. Relax. It's okay. It's only a dream, Jackson.'

The creature was upon me. It rose up from the sand and covered me, blocking out the light from the sun. Its wings wrapped around my arms. Its mouth was on mine and it was soft and moist and warm. I wasn't afraid anymore. I woke up. I could feel the stingray's lips on mine.

When I opened my eyes, I was looking straight into Kate's.

17

MY EYELIDS FLUTTERED, trying to adjust to the light. My lips were tingling. Kate had her fingertips to her lips too.

'What happened?'

'You fell asleep and you were dreaming. You got a fright. Forget it. We really should go.'

I looked out at the ocean. A fine spray of sand dusted my face, forcing me to squint, 'Okay.'

Kate helped me up and we gathered our things. My bathing trunks were already dry so I put on my T-shirt, shirt and jacket and bundled my slacks under my arm. Kate wrapped around a skirt. The clouds had rolled in with the wind and the temperature had dropped. I had goosebumps on my arms.

'How long was I out?' I asked as I climbed into the car.

'Maybe twenty minutes. I don't know.'

By the time we reached the Pacific Coast Highway I was wide awake. 'In my dream,' I began, 'I could have sworn …'

She cut me off by putting her forefinger to my lips. 'Shh. Whatever you dreamed was a dream, Jackson. It was a fantasy, nothing more. You're awake now and we are going home. I've got to go home.'

It was an odd thing to say and I didn't know how to interpret it. Could it be possible that Kate really did kiss me? Why would she do that? Did I have a chance with her? The more I thought about it the more preposterous it seemed – and the more delicious.

We headed up the 55 freeway. I felt around behind my seat for the box of doughnuts and offered Kate a jelly-filled one, but she shook her head. It seemed like she was mad at me or something. I couldn't figure it out. I dug into a glazed doughnut and its greasy, sticky sweetness. It was so good that I polished off four more, until there was just one jelly-filled left.

'C'mon, Kate,' I said, holding it out to her. 'It's the last one.'

'No thank you.'

I leaned over and kissed her on the cheek, as close to her lips as I could manage.

'What the hell?'

She swerved across two lanes, cutting off a black-and-white Ford Falcon, and came to a rest on the curb. The Falcon blasted its horn. 'What are you doing?'

Words started pouring out of my mouth. 'I know you kissed me back there on the beach. You must have. It wasn't a dream. I know it, Kate. It wasn't a dream.' Her face was stony behind her sunglasses, but I kept gabbling 'And it's okay, it really is. I like you, Kate. I've always liked you. When I'm with you nothing else matters. I'm not unhappy or scared. I'm not afraid or alone. I feel whole. I feel like I can do anything and I'm strong, I'm really strong. I love you. I want to be your boyfriend.'

Oh, shit, there it was. The entire thing was out there. I trembled.

'I know you're a grown woman and I'm just, just …'

'A kid.'

I tried to ignore the flatness in her voice. 'Yeah, yeah, I'm young. So what? You said ten years wasn't too big of an age gap, remember? You said that you had been with older men and it didn't matter. So what's wrong with the other way around? Why can't it be the same, you know? You're not any different from me. We laugh, we have a good time and I feel older when I'm with you, I do.' Even as I spoke I knew it was all wrong. She and I together could never be right. Something else was in the way, something else I sensed I couldn't fight. A big hole had opened up in front of me and I was losing my footing. In my desperation I blurted out, 'Don't leave me, Kate, please, don't leave me. I don't know what I'd do without you.'

She bowed her head for a long time. Cars passed us with rhythmic regularity. Nothing in her demeanour gave away what she was thinking. She took off her glasses. Her eyes were damp. 'Oh, Jackson, I'm so, so, sorry.' She wiped at her cheek. 'It wasn't fair of me to take advantage of you. I can't. We can't. Don't you see that?' The sounds of the cars were lulling, like a chant. 'It's not you. It truly isn't. You're a great guy. Any gal would be lucky to have you. I'm so sorry if I led you on, but …' she leaned forward as if she were telling me a secret, 'I don't know what I'm doing right now. I'm so confused. I need, I want … I don't know what.'

I didn't want her to look at me. I would have gotten out of the car right there and made my way home, but I was half naked and I didn't know where the hell we were. My mouth was dry and disgusting from eating too much sugar. 'I guess that means we're not …'

'No. I'm sorry.' She went to reach for my arm but then pulled back.

Kate, Connie-Jean, Mutti … in my head they all turned their backs on me. They had ripped out my insides and left me to die. My stomach contracted and my breathing was shallow.

I crossed my arms. I was determined not to cry in front of Kate. Men don't do that, right? That would have been the last straw, the worst indignity. I needed something to replace that sadness, something stronger. My mind went dark. In my heart I started to hate her.

'I'll take you to your dad,' she said.

'I want to go home.'

'Your dad wants me to take you to the dealership.'

In my head I yelled at her until the blood vessels in my neck exploded and my eyeballs popped. She looked at me and then put her sunglasses on, started up the Stingray and slid back into the flow of traffic.

We didn't talk for the rest of the trip. For half an hour I loathed and detested, questioned, laughed ironically, felt sorry for myself, hit, tore, ripped, stabbed, questioned again, screamed, pleaded and fell. Finally, a quiet came into my heart and mind. The evening dampness settled, making everything hazy. Kate checked her watch like she couldn't wait to get rid of me.

She didn't break the silence until just before five o'clock, when we pulled into the dealership.

'Jackson, I don't want to leave it this way. I know you're upset and disappointed in me …' I looked down at my knees. ' … and you have every right to be. I'm the adult here and I shouldn't have … I *should* have been more responsible. Listen. Please listen. You've got a lot of living to do – a lot of fantastic things to experience. You're just starting out. The kind of things you have to do I can't help you with. I can't be a part of them. My time for that kind of involvement is over, long past. I can't do it again. I know it's hard and lonely and so painful, but someday you're going to thank me for this.'

I laughed bitterly. 'Well, unfortunately it isn't "someday" – it's today – and I got the crap torn out of me and I feel like shit.' She opened the trunk of the car. I pulled out my sandy, wrinkled slacks. 'So thank you for the most memorable birthday I've ever had, ma'am.'

I blew her a kiss, turned my back and walked towards the office door. There was a long silence before the Vette started up and drove off. It sped up the boulevard. I looked back at it, but only after I was sure she wouldn't see me.

Ray and I had covered the display windows with newsprint paper so passers-by couldn't see the new models. Tate was going to take them down tomorrow in an unveiling ceremony, complete with balloons, hot dogs and door prizes – the works. Light was shining through the paper. Someone was inside. Tate probably wanted me to help him prepare for the launch, which was the last fucking thing I wanted to do.

The office door was locked. I pushed the service button and leaned against the doorpost, rubbing my forehead. I wanted to go home, bury myself in my bed and die.

Tennis shoes squeaked on polished linoleum. The lock released and the door swung open, revealing Ray's grinning face.

'*Ese, vato. Felicidades.* Happy birthday, *guero*.'

He leaned over, gave me a hug and slapped my back. It was the first time he'd ever given me an *abrazo* and it took me by surprise.

'Thanks, *amigo*, thanks.' I slapped his back too. Only then did I notice what he was wearing – a white shirt, black tie, dress trousers and a two-tone grey button-down sweater.

'Hey, why are you all duded up? Why aren't you wearing your work clothes?'

'Oh, I finished in there, *ese*. I changed in the bathroom. I gotta date, remember? A hot date with a little chilli *mamacita*?' He made an hourglass gesture with his hands. 'You know what I mean?'

'Yeah, I remember. That sounds boss, man. Hey, where's my dad?'

'Oh, he's inside, *ese*, in the showroom.'

Ray stayed blocking the doorway. Something wasn't right. 'Can you excuse me, man?'

'Why? I don't smell anything.' He doubled over, cackling. I rolled my eyes and pushed him away from the door. 'Hey, wait a minute!' he called, running after me.

'What for?'

'He's not ready for you yet.'

'What? C'mon Ray, I'm really tired, man. I haven't had a good day. Cut the bull. What's this all about?' He squirmed and for once in his life, he was speechless, 'Oh, wait a minute, I get it. This is about my birthday present, isn't it?'

'Oh, yeah, *Simón*, *ese*, you guessed it.'

'Okay, okay. So what do I have to do?'

He glanced towards the showroom. 'Ah, I want to tell you something.' He looked down at his Keds, 'I don't talk good, I know that, but, I just wanted to say, ah, I'm glad I met you, I'm glad you're here.'

'Thanks, Ray.' I tried to get past him again but he stopped me.

He looked over his shoulder then down again, 'No, let me finish. You can be a real asshole sometimes, but, you've made me see things different, you know, man? You showed me stuff about art I never would have thought about, and you work hard. Sometimes that's a good thing. And you know what? You're a good friend. I overheard what you said to Stretch, *ese*, that was solid. You're about the brownest white dude I've ever met.' He grinned.

I grinned back at him, 'Thanks … *hormiga*.'

'Okay, it's probably cool by now, *ese*. Go ahead, go in.' He stood aside with a grand gesture as I walked through into the showroom. It was all done up for the opening. There were three long folding tables set up along the interior wall with dessert plates, cups, an enormous crystal punchbowl and – curiously – our family's silver samovar. Folding chairs were placed around in groups of three or four and there were balloons everywhere. Tate had even thought of music – there was a big hi-fi setup near the door to the garage.

He was standing under a banner, wearing a white dinner jacket, with his hands folded in front of him like he was Rick from *Casablanca*. He was smiling widely. Next to him was a gleaming aquamarine car – obviously the *pièce de résistance* of the new models, but there was something odd about it.

'Tate?'

He raised his hand towards the banner and I looked up at the words emblazoned across the four-yard-long canvas: HAPPY SIXTEENTH BIRTHDAY, JACKSON!

18

DOZENS OF PEOPLE SPRANG OUT from behind the cars.

'Surprise!'

'Oh, shit,' I whispered.

'Happy birthday! Are you surprised?'

'Tate, oh man, yes, very surprised!'

'Where's Kate? Isn't she with you?'

'Did she know about this?'

'Of course. She knew about it from the start. But look at you. What happened? Where are your pants?'

By this time more people had gathered around me. Everyone was there from school: Maria, Unai, Carlos, Billy, Ming Li and Sing Li, Luke, Elizabeth, Jojo, Scotty and Clovis.

'Tate, how did you find all my friends?' I asked. 'Did Ray tell you?'

'Don't blame me, *vato*, it was Mrs Barker.'

'That's right. Marion set up the whole thing, along with Ray and Maria. I had no idea you had so many friends.'

I looked around and saw Mr Barker standing by the punch-bowl with Joe and Maggie. They waved.

'He doesn't have any friends, Mr Ryder,' Ray said. 'These are *my* friends. They're taking pity on the poor little Noo Yawker.'

'Not true, Mr Ryder,' Unai interjected. He put Ray's head in a half-nelson. 'In fact, I'm surprised you even invited this knucklehead.'

'*Chingado.*'

'Hey, take it easy, boys,' Tate said. Unai unhanded Ray and they both apologised.

Connie-Jean sat near the stereo with Grace and Maria.

What the hell was she doing here?

She was wearing a red velvet mini-dress, the first I had ever seen. Her long legs were as toned and as tanned as her shoulders, and her knees were pressed tightly together. Connie-Jean looked stunning, but she wore that same mournful expression as that morning on the sidewalk.

Maria thrust a paper cup of pink punch into my hand, 'You better get dressed, Jack,' she said. 'The night is just beginning.'

I looked down at my swimming trunks, suddenly self-conscious. 'We were at the beach.'

'I hope so, because otherwise you would look pretty silly.' I headed for the bathroom to change. 'I'll put on some music,' Maria called after me.

I stopped to say hello to Mr and Mrs Dos Osos and Mr Barker.

'We haven't thanked you for the fine-looking drawing you gave us,' Maggie said. Then she looked almost worried. She took me aside. 'It is an exceptional gift you have, Jackson. Your spirit is free and large but I also see that it is … bound up. If you can do work like this, you already have the means to untangle your fetters. Blessed fortune, my boy.'

Joe joined us. 'Maria just told us what you did to that punk.' He made a fist. 'If I ever catch him …' Maggie gently lowered his hand and his fingers relaxed. 'Thank you, my son, thank you.'

I wanted to talk more to them but I was feeling self-conscious with my naked legs. I promised to come by the gas station to see them and pulled myself away.

Past the restrooms was a small waiting room for customers who were having repair work done on their cars. There was a stack of out-of-date car magazines and a ten-inch black-and-white TV with awful reception in there. The lights were on and I could hear voices. I passed the men's bathroom and peered around the corner.

Buzz was sitting on the sofa with a can of Brew 102 watching what appeared to be a fight on TV. 'Cassius X has changed his name to Muhammad Ali,' he said, to no one. 'What next, Ali Baba?'

In the corner, Mrs Barker and Stretch were putting candles into a three-tiered cake, and next to them was the pillbox lady from the car lot. She wore an apron with *Sadie's Catering* stitched across the front. They didn't see me and I figured I wasn't meant to see the cake yet.

In the bathroom I was glad of the breathing space – it was the first time I had been alone since morning. I felt shy around almost everyone.

Damned Kate.

I had never had a surprise party before. Tate must have made a huge effort to get this done and keep it from me, and everybody had shown up. I had no choice but to go back out there and try to enjoy it.

I looked in the bathroom mirror. I expected to see an old man with dark circles under his eyes, but it was just my face – not much different than it had been that morning, except maybe a shade pinker. I tried a big smile.

There was a single shower stall for staff in the bathroom. My hair was gritty with salt and sand. The pressure in the shower wasn't the best, but it was hot. The warmer and cleaner I got, the more the frustration of the day eased. I dried myself off and got dressed. My clothes weren't too wrinkled. They didn't look bad. I didn't have a tie, but I was sure everyone would understand.

'What's taking so long, son? The natives are restless,' Tate said through the half-open door.

'I'm tying my shoelaces.'

'Great, 'cause I've got a surprise that will blow your mind, man.'

'I can't wait,' I said, trying not to sound tired.

Can't Buy Me Love by The Beatles echoed down the hallway. It was number one on the Billboard chart that week. There was no way Mrs Barker had chosen that music.

In the showroom everyone was dancing. That is, my friends were. The adults stood around, but Tate was snapping his fingers. Luke talked and gestured wildly at Connie-Jean, Maria and Grace. Maria was looking at Unai, and Grace seemed to be looking in my direction. Connie-Jean stared off in the direction of the hi-fi. Ray danced with Twinkie, Sing Li danced with Scotty, and Billy and Ming Li tried to dance, but it looked like they were trying to find their sea legs in a storm. Elizabeth and Jojo pulled at Unai and Carlos's shirts, trying to drag them onto the dance floor.

Tate strolled over to me. 'Look who just got in, Jackie.'

He signalled towards the office and Charlie came out in a new blue sharkskin jacket. He had grown a pencil-thin moustache while he was in Chicago. He did a double-take at Connie-Jean – that I didn't like – but I thought, that's just Charlie being Charlie.

'This is the best birthday present ever,' I said. 'Thanks, Charlie.'

'Don't mention it, kid.' Charlie looked at Tate. 'So, you haven't?'

'Not yet.' It was quick, but Tate waved his hand in front of his face in the old army signal for 'cease fire'. 'Excuse us for a second, sport.' Charlie took Tate down the hallway.

On the makeshift dance floor, Grace had taken over the record player and put on *Bits and Pieces*. Luke and Maria were dancing. Connie-Jean and Grace huddled in conversation, their knees pointing in towards each other. Jojo and Elizabeth had given up on Unai and Carlos and danced with each other. The boys were at the food table and Carlos was seriously engaged with the mini hot dogs.

Tate, Charlie and Mrs Barker came out of the hallway followed by Stretch pushing the food trolley with the enormous cake. Grace cut the music and Tate started to sing *Happy Birthday*. Everyone joined in. Stretch wheeled the trolley right up to me and everyone in the room gathered around.

Tate asked me to make a wish. I scanned the room. Connie-Jean wore her sad face. Grace's eyes sparkled. Maria's eyes shone with tears. Beyond the cake, Kate walked through the office doorway. She had changed into neat cream slacks and a maroon cashmere sweater, but she didn't look comfortable. Where did she get the nerve to come here? I tried to ignore her and hold onto the moment, but it wasn't easy.

What *did* I want? Blowing out candles and making a wish is a stupid tradition, but it does make you think. I wished Mutti was here to see this, but that was never going to happen. I wished I had someone – someone who cared about how I felt, someone I could touch – someone to kiss me and caress me and explore deep mysteries with.

Tate looked the happiest I had seen him since before Mutti died. As much as we saw each other and shared an apartment together, we were both walking around in a fog. We couldn't grasp each other. He didn't understand what was going on with me and I couldn't explain it. Like the art thing. It bugged me that I didn't know why Tate hated art. I wanted to please him and I wanted him to be proud of me, but drawing gave me something that nothing else did – a world where I could take control. I wanted to be an artist. I knew that clearly now. Maggie understood, so did Mr Talbot. That was the one thing that was going to make me happy and whole. It was the only way to go forward. To deny it was wrong.

I stared at the sixteen candles. They didn't have the answer.

What did I really want? I wanted to be as close to Tate as I could be. I wanted to be an artist too. I wanted both of those things. I *did* know the answer. The answer was me. It was up to me. It was going to hurt, but it was going to make me as free as if I had wings on my shoes. I thought about my unfinished oil painting. I knew what it needed. I smiled to myself and sighed. The flames flickered. I took a deep lungful of air and blew every candle out. Everyone clapped.

Tate spoke. 'I want to thank you all for coming tonight. We haven't been here in San Sebastiano that long and it's been rough for us since my wife died. You all have taken us in and given us a new life and new friendships, and I thank you with all my heart.' There was more applause from the crowd. 'I want to especially thank my partner, Charlie, and the lovely Kate Hickey for all of their help in setting this up. Mrs Barker, Ray, Maria, Buzz and Stretch – you have been incredible too. We'll get to the cake in a minute but, without further delay, I want to give Jackson his present.' I looked at him, confused – he was empty-handed. 'You're standing in front of it.' He reached into his pocket and handed me a set of car keys.

'Are you serious?' I asked, '*This* car? The Mercury?'

Tate nodded. 'It's not just from me – Charlie and I bought the body off Joe. You, Buzz and Stretch did the engine work and I had our body people remove the rust, take the dents out and paint it. Stretch said you wanted "powder blue", but the closest I could get was medium-aqua metallic. I hope that's okay.'

Stretch gave me the a-okay sign. Buzz stayed by the hallway door and gave me a casual salute. I hugged Tate.

'This is unbelievable, Tate! Thanks! Thanks, Charlie.' I ran my hand over the hood and then opened the driver's door. The mechanism was smooth, just like new.

'Dude, we can cruise San Sab Boulevard on Saturday night,' Luke called out. It was the first time he'd suggested doing anything with me outside of class.

'We can take it to Whittier Boulevard, *ese*, where the real cruising is done,' Ray said. '*Órale*.'

'Or go to the beach,' Twinkie added.

Joe yelled, 'I'm giving you three full tanks.' Maggie tugged on his coat. 'Make that four tanks of gas, Jackson. Happy birthday.' I waved at them.

I could go anywhere. I could go on real dates. I would be free like I had never been before.

'Cake, everyone,' Mrs Barker called out. This got the attention of Ray, Carlos, and Luke. Grace put another record on: *Hello Muddah, Hello Faddah* by Allan Sherman. I rolled my eyes, but sang along to it anyway. Mrs Barker brought me a piece of cake on a paper plate and I thanked her.

‘It’s a pleasure, dear young man. May I suggest that you mingle a bit? Some of your friends are a little shy.’

She was right. Connie-Jean was sitting alone and Joe and Maggie hadn’t moved an inch.

I didn’t want to talk to Connie-Jean. I didn’t even know what she was doing here. I had been so rude to her on La Cienega Boulevard. Shouldn’t she have avoided the party? Charlie walked up to her. I could read him like a guidebook. I took a sip of punch and when I looked up, they had both disappeared. I scanned the room and saw Kate. I didn’t want to talk to her either. We had both said way too much already. She stood by the office with Fred and none other than Mr Talbot himself. I hadn’t even noticed him arrive. The two men talked but Kate stood there, smoking a cigarette and staring at me. She hadn’t smoked for weeks. Then she reached for Mr Talbot’s hand.

19

THERE WAS NO MISTAKING IT. She wanted me to see her holding hands with the Wolf Man. Tate walked over to greet them. As soon as Kate saw him she dropped Mr Talbot's hand, but it was too late. Tate froze in his tracks. The smile evaporated on his lips. He recovered and shook hands with Mr Talbot and they talked. Kate was taut. She kept her hands behind her back and didn't say a word. He looked at Kate with a tight smile and turned away.

All the pain that had washed away in the shower flooded back into my consciousness. I was nauseous. I forced the contents of my stomach down with a swig of punch, but the feelings didn't go away.

Then Connie-Jean stumbled out of the office followed by Charlie. Her lipstick was smeared onto her cheek.

Tate saw them too and walked over, 'Are you alright?' he asked her.

She nodded. 'I'm fine. I just want to go home.'

He turned to Charlie. 'What the hell?' Charlie shook his head. 'Jesus,' Tate muttered. He dragged Charlie back into the office. It didn't occur to me that something could have happened between Charlie and Connie-Jean. It was ludicrous. I told myself I didn't care anyway.

'Open your presents, Jack,' Twinkie said.

'Yeah, they're in the back seat,' Clovis added.

'Jack.' The Wolf Man grinned at me.

'Mr Talbot.'

'Happy birthday. I just talked with your dad and …'

I cut him off. I couldn't stand to think of him and Kate together. 'Thanks Mr T' I looked around for Connie-Jean. 'Look, I've changed my mind about the paints. Can I keep them longer? I think I'm going to dig oil painting.'

He beamed. 'You can keep them. That can be my gift to you and I'll throw in a full range of colours – new ones.'

We shook hands, 'Thanks! And … thanks for everything.'

'Sure. Look, It's not my business, but, Kate told me you two had words today. Give her a break, would you? She really likes you and she's pretty upset. No matter what it is I'm sure she meant the best by it. Okay?'

I was stunned but I didn't get the chance to answer.

'Hi, Jackson.' Grace interrupted. The Wolf Man slapped me on the back and walked off. 'I haven't had a chance to tell you happy birthday. I hope you don't mind me being here.'

'No, no, I don't mind. I'm very happy you're here.'

She smiled, 'Ray didn't want me to come. He got all staunch and everything, but who cares?'

I made a superhuman effort to focus on her. 'How did your *Quinceñera* go?'

'Good accent,' she said, 'it was more fun than I thought it was going to be. I wish you had been there.'

Maria was back at the stereo. She played 'I Saw Her Standing There', the first song on the album *Introducing … The Beatles*. Grace looked at me with those sparkling eyes.

'I wish I had been there, too,' I couldn't decide if I should go to Connie-Jean or not. 'Say, do you want to dance?' Grace nodded and smiled. I took her hand, which was slim and soft. 'Your dad isn't around, is he? I'm just kidding.'

Her smile faltered slightly. She leaned forward and whispered, 'he doesn't know I'm here,' and covered her mouth.

I lost my smile then and instinctively looked for Ray. Over Grace's shoulder I saw Connie-Jean straighten her dress and walked towards the door. 'Grace, can you please excuse me for a minute?' I tried to get to Connie-Jean but my friends kept stopping me. Connie-Jean paused to say something to Maria, who had been chatting to Unai. He was standing close to Maria – very close. I caught up with Connie-Jean near the office door. Her eyes were red.

'I've got to go, Jackson,' she said. 'Happy birthday.'

I couldn't help myself. 'Where's your boyfriend, Joe? Oh sorry – I mean Milt. Why didn't you bring him, or the other one, or both? I don't know, I can't keep up with you.'

'Leave me alone,' she whimpered. 'I do repent. But heaven hath pleased it so, to punish me with this and this with me.'

'Shakespeare, no doubt,' I spat out.

'Why are you being so cruel?' She didn't wait for an answer, but turned and walked towards the door. I followed her. 'You know,' she said without turning around, 'from the first time I saw you at the pool I knew you were different. You were from New York City. Right away I thought of Broadway. I knew you were going to live right next door and I was curious. I talked Joe and Clovis into going over to the pool with me, even though it was too cold to swim. We went back there three days in a row before you showed up.' She finally faced me. 'Then when you did turn up, Joe was in the middle of telling me … that terrible thing. I hardly got a chance to look at you, but even then, I saw something in your eyes that was unusual. You looked like you were devouring everything – you were so intense. I wanted to know more about you. I wished I could go up to you and say hello, but I was shy and I only knew how to act like the popular, confident girl. So when we met I teased you and acted conceited. When it suited the scene I smiled and flirted with you. You were younger than me and unsure but that didn't matter. I liked your enthusiasm for art and you had actually been to Broadway productions. I wasn't just a cheer-leader to you. I could relate to you better than anyone except Clovis. I wanted you to be my friend.'

'I didn't know,' I said. Then I remembered that Clovis had tried to tell me. I hadn't listened. Things were changing, though – all kinds of things – including me. 'It doesn't matter. It doesn't have to be this way, Connie-Jean. Look, we can start over. Forget about those guys and come to the prom with me. Please.'

She looked at me for a long time then shook her head. 'You want something I can't give you – I'll never be able to give you, Jack. I just can't do that. I can't play that part. I made a promise.' She walked out the door without looking back.

Fuck it, I thought. *Fuck it, fuck it, fuck it.* Should I follow her? I could work on her. It wouldn't be impossible to get her to break her promise to Joe or Milt – whoever it was. She liked me. But she always kept her word – Clovis told me. What did that mean to me? If I could get her to change I would truly be her villain – the bad kind.

Someone yelled from the showroom, 'Where's the Ghost Ryder?'

'Where's the birthday *vato*?' I heard Ray call. I went back into the showroom, but as I passed the office I could hear voices – Tate and Charlie. There was an edge in Tate's voice like the night he had yelled at Charlie for telling Kate our private business.

'Jesus, Charlie, what the hell happened? Did you try to jump her?'

'I swear, Hymie, we were just having a friendly drink. I wasn't doing anything she didn't want, you know what I mean?'

'What the fuck is wrong with you? That's a *kid*, you idiot, not a woman, a kid. She's not one of your pathetic bimbos. She lives right next door, for Christ's sake. You were being a fucking asshole again, you *nudnik putz*.'

I realised Tate was talking about Connie-Jean. I stepped into the office.

'Buddy,' Charlie said straightening his tie, 'your old man and me were just having a friendly drink.'

I was shaking all over and my stomach was halfway up my throat. I stepped towards Charlie but Tate grabbed me by the arm.

'I heard everything, Charlie, I heard every shitty thing. How could you?'

'It's not what you think, kid.' Charlie paused. 'I couldn't help it. Man, did you see those legs? You know what it's like. I was drinking and … you know.'

Tate stepped in. 'Oh, you were *drinking*. That's your explanation? You use booze as a goddamn excuse to shit on everyone and everything. It's like what you did in Rome, Florence and Munich all over again. Why do you think Kate won't be alone with you anymore? Jesus, how could you, man?' Another silence followed.

'You know, Charlie, I used to look up to you. You came and helped Tate when Mutti died. You talked to me. I thought you were the coolest.' I shook my head. 'I know you chase any girl you can – but Connie-Jean? You know I like her.'

'I didn't know that, buddy, I swear.'

'It wouldn't make a difference if you did,' Tate hissed, 'I know you tried to hit on Birgit at our wedding, you shithead. Why do you think we never attempted to see you all those years?'

'You and Mutti?' I muttered at Charlie.

'Kid, no offence, but you don't know the whole story.' Then Charlie said to Tate, 'Tell him, Hymie. He has a right to know.'

'Shut up, Charlie. You don't know jack. You're always opening your big, fat mouth.'

'No, I'm the one that did the dirty work and you got the reward. She owed me. You owed me.'

'What is he talking about, Tate?'

'Tell him, Hymie, or by God, I will.'

Tate put down his drink slowly, 'Your mother had made some … bad decisions during the war.'

'She worked for goddamned Walter Hofer, Herman Göring's art curator, for Christ's sake.'

'Jesus,' I whispered. 'She worked for the Nazis?'

'She had to, son, she didn't have a choice.'

'Come on, Hymie, everybody has a choice,' Charlie scoffed.

'Why did she owe you, Charlie?' I could feel cold sweat on my forehead.

'That's enough, Jackie. Now's not the time or place.' Tate tried to grab my shoulder but I shoved his hand away.

Charlie looked up at me, his eyes grey and oblong like a drawing by Pontormo. 'Okay, yeah, I loved your mother, kid, she was the only woman I've ever truly loved. I would have done anything for her and she knew it. She took my gifts, man, she took everything.' He stopped and looked at Tate.

'Go on, Charlie,' I urged him.

'I met her when her VW broke down on the Ludwigsbrücke near the bridge into Munich.' He turned to Tate. 'The rotor connections on the distributor were dirty. You taught me to clean them.' Tate didn't react and Charlie turned back to me. 'She was grateful and chatted non-stop. She was desperate. There was no way she could get a job. Her boss was interred at Hersbruck and the French had sentenced him to ten years in jail. She was scared. I saw a chance. If I could get her off – clean her slate with the military – maybe she'd play ball with me. So I pulled some strings, called in a few debts, and she ended up with the identity of a girl who had died during a bombing raid.'

'She wasn't even who she said she was?'

Charlie shook his head. 'Her boss, Hofer, wasn't Nazi either but her father – your grandfather – was SS, and an officer to boot. She wouldn't have had a chance of getting work with the Monuments Men or of getting permission to marry your father or to immigrate to the US with that kind of pedigree.'

I turned to Tate. 'And you knew this?'

He blinked a few times. 'She was the best thing that ever happened to me *benyokhed*. She made everything better. I wouldn't have cared if she was *yetzer hara*, evil incarnate. I loved her.'

I couldn't speak. I couldn't think. Everything had piled up, everything – one big, steaming, stinking shit-pile. 'Excuse me.' I stepped out of the office.

Mutti worked for Göring, stealing artwork. My grandfather was SS, Schutzstaffel. I had just learned about them in Mr Brice's history class. They were the bastards that were guards at the concentration camps, they were the exterminators; the ones that shot my relatives at Babi Yar. I rushed into the bathroom and threw up. When I came back I was floating, dizzy, but I tried not to let on.

Charlie was in the middle of asking Tate a question. 'Why did you come out here to California with me? Why did you become my partner and work with me, day after day, if you thought I was such a shit?'

Tate stood still. He looked like he was going to fall asleep. 'When I saw you at the funeral I wanted to slug you. I didn't want you anywhere near me or Jackie. But then I remembered that you knew Birgit in the old days, back when we three shared something that was glorious. I hated you, but I felt in my gut that through you – and Jackson – I could keep her alive. Everything else – New York, all our things – all of it reminded me that she was dead. But, she lives in our memories.' There was another long pause. 'Besides, you're the only friend I've got, you sorry son of a bitch. I've lost too many people I love to turn anyone away, even a deadbeat *schmuck* like you.'

'So you love me?'

'Don't flatter yourself.'

'What about Connie-Jean, Charlie?' I said.

'Honest, kid. I just tried to kiss her. I didn't even use my tongue or anything. I'm not attracted to that poor girl – not really. I don't know why I did it. I don't know why I *do* it. But look, I'll make it up to her, I swear to God, I'll apologise.'

'One thing's for sure, this is the last straw,' Tate said. 'You can't do this kind of shit anymore. I'm not going to stand for it, man. I'm serious. It's sick. I'll leave, I swear to God. I'll leave and you'll never see me or Jackie again. Do you get it?' He pointed at Charlie with those gun fingers.

Charlie looked up at Tate and then at me. His face was drawn and the tiny moustache looked like a twisted piece of discarded insulation wire. I knew Charlie pretty well by then but I had never seen that look in his eyes. I could see his deep loneliness like it was a ruptured pustule – exposed and raw-veined.

Tate turned me around. 'Okay, you need to get out there with your guests.'

'But, Tate …'

'I'll take care of this. Go.'

'Kid, I'm sorry I let you down.'

I couldn't answer Charlie. I just shook my head and walked out.

Charlie hit on Connie-Jean. He had done some low stuff, but I had to admit I had been a shit to her too. I couldn't follow her now, not with the party and all, but when all this was over I'd find a way to square things. I wasn't looking where I was going and I bumped into Maria in the showroom. She stumbled over but picked herself up quickly.

'Hey Ryder, if you're going to goose me at least look at my caboose while you're doing it.'

'Sorry, Maria, I was distracted.'

'That figures. Gee, you really know how to sweet-talk a girl, don't you?'

'Tell me about it.' Grace must have got tired of waiting – she was over at the food table eating cake and talking to Stretch.

'Anyway, happy birthday.' She looked at me like she was taking aim. 'Are you sure you're okay, Ryder?'

'You know, I've been awake for more than twelve hours today, it's my birthday, and this is the first time anyone has asked me that. Why?'

'I see you smiling, but under that it looks like you've been used for target practice from a couple of different directions.'

'How about that? Just like Saint Sebastian, eh? I guess I kinda have.'

Clovis grabbed me from behind, 'happy birthday, Jack. Great party. Have you seen Connie-Jean? I lost her. She was here a minute ago.'

I hesitated. 'Yeah. She's gone out the door and I don't think she's coming back.'

'I was afraid of that.' He squirmed. 'Look, Jack. I know CJ better than anyone and I don't know what's going on with her, but I'll tell you, something is weird with Joe.'

'Mr Lost Cause?' I blurted. Clovis laughed.

'Yes. He's … I don't like the way he looks at me.'

'What, you think he's a … a pansy?' I laughed but Clovis didn't. 'Really?'

'He tries hard with Connie-Jean but it looks like a chore. I can't figure it out.'

Every time I had seen them together I had concentrated on CJ so much I hardly noticed him. 'I'm sure you're wrong, partner. Besides, if he was going to go for anyone I bet it would be Milt.' We both laughed.

'I'm going to go find Connie-Jean. I'll see you. Great party.'

'Tell her,' I called after him, 'tell her I'm sorry,' Clovis frowned. 'It's a long story. I'll tell you later.'

'Hey there, little buddy,' Stretch slapped me on the back. 'Guess what, I knowed Gracie when she was a little girl.'

'Really? You do know that she's Ray's sister?'

'I found that out now. Ain't that somethin'?'

'Stretch used to be sweet on my big sister, Amelia, when they were in high school together,' Grace explained. 'He used to give me Tootsie Rolls and candy necklaces so I wouldn't tell on them when they were romping around in the bushes together.'

Now that really surprised me. 'Stretch, didn't you say the other day …'

'Now, now, little buddy,' he cut me off. He gave Grace a big smile. 'I was talkin' about them *hombres*, you know, fellas. I ain't got nothin' against the Mexican people per se, 'specially when they's as sweet and pretty as Grace here, and her big sister.'

'So you don't like Mexican men, huh?' Grace asked. 'Does that have anything to do with the fact that my brother, Chato, beat the bejesus out of you when he found you and Amelia under the bleachers at the football stadium? He broke the side mirror of your car and had the dogcatcher take your mutt away too, didn't he?'

'Yep.' 'It wasn't the best of times for me, Gracie. I liked Milly, I really did. And we weren't doin' nothin' that anybody else wasn't doin'.'

Grace stifled a giggle and took his arm. 'Poor Stretch. You never understood that family is everything to us. You threaten the honour of the *familia* and the whole lot of us step in. That's the way it is. What you should have done was come to my dad first, like a *macho*, with respect. You might have had a chance then. That is, if he didn't run you off with a baseball bat first.'

'What's ol' Milly up to, anyway?'

'She's okay. She met a Marine, Emilio, at a dance down in Oceanside when she was eighteen.' Grace hesitated. 'She got in the family way and she had to get married. They have three kids now. They live on the base at El Toro.'

'Well, I'll be damned. Three kids, like me. So what was the difference? The family honour was still broke.'

'He was a Marine and a Mexican. His family was from Jalisco, like my mother. He was practically family before they found out she was pregnant.'

'That's it? Because I wasn't Mexican?'

'That's right,' another voice interrupted. 'You skinny-ass, white-trash son of a bitch.'

'Chato!' Grace cried. I wheeled around to see Ray's brother standing behind me. His legs were apart, his hands were formed into fists and his face was red. He looked at me and gave me one of those chin-up nods.

'*Ese, guero*, What's this chicken-shit asshole doing here?'

I stepped in front of Stretch. 'What are you doing here, Chato? How did you get in?'

The colour faded from his cheeks. 'Some *ruco*, an old guy with tattoos, let me in. My old man blew a gasket when he heard that Ma let Gracie come to your party. I said I'd come to get her so I could get out of his way.'

'It's not even ten o'clock yet,' Grace said.

Chato was staring at Stretch. 'What are you doing touching my sister, *pendejo*? Did you forget what happened to you last time?'

'He wasn't touching me, Chato. I took his arm.'

'*Puta*,' Chato swore, sneering at his sister. He made a fist and jerked his arm like he was going to hit her. 'Come on, I'm taking you home.'

She flinched and then set her feet and stared at him. 'Don't touch me.'

Stretch moved towards Chato. His eyes were narrowed and his lips were turned down at the corners. His skin was tight against his skull. I could see a blue blood vessel pulsing at his temple. I put my hand on his shoulder.

'Look, Chato, Stretch works here and he's my friend. This is my party, man, and I don't want any trouble.'

Ray ran up and grabbed Chato's arm. '*Ese, carnale*, you come for Gracie? I thought Papá would have a fit.' He gave an icy stare to Stretch then turned to his sister. 'You're in trouble now, *chiquita*.' He looked around at the four of us and whispered to Chato, 'Hey, buy us some beer? I got money.'

'Get off, *Flaco*. You're lucky I don't take you home too.'

'Come on, man, it's Ghost Ryder's birthday. We can celebrate. I'll buy you some too.'

Stretch interrupted, pushing past me, 'Let's take this outside, Chato. I been waitin' a long time for this.'

'No!' I shouted. I tried to grab Stretch but he was already gone. Chato didn't hesitate either. He followed Stretch outside.

'Fight!' Ray yelled. He ran after them, quickly followed by Carlos, Unai and Luke. Grace grabbed my arm. 'Stop them, Jack. I think Chato carries a switchblade and he's not scared to use it.'

'Oh, shit.' I looked around for Tate. He, Mr Talbot and Kate were nowhere to be seen. Mrs Barker was the only adult around, so I rushed up to her.

'Where is everyone going, Jackson?'

'I need Mr Barker, ma'am, or Joe, or Buzz. Where are they?'

'Mr Maddox took Mr Dos Osos and Fred to look at the workshop. What's happening?'

If I went to get the men it might be too late. Stretch was strong for a skinny guy. I had seen him lift a hundred-pound transmission for an Impala once like it was nothing. But if Chato pulled a knife that wouldn't matter. Stretch wouldn't have a chance.

'Please get them, Mrs Barker. There's going to be a fight. It might get bad. Please hurry.'

I burst into the office. Charlie and Tate sat at their desks smoking as Tate tipped the last of a bottle of Red Label into his tumbler. 'Stretch is going to fight Ray's brother and he has a knife. Better call the police.'

I ran down the corridor and out the door. The damp and the cold hit me right away. The dealership lights showed mustard-colours that fell away to black shadows. The mob was gathered in a circle under the closest light. All I could see were heads and backs. I pushed through until I got to the clearing.

'Stop it, Stretch,' Grace was yelling. Ray had her by the arms.

'Get up, asshole. What's wrong with you?' Stretch roared.

Chato was on the ground, his lip bloodied. I looked over at Stretch. I knew enough from watching fights on TV with Tate to see that he had adopted a classic boxing stance – his left toe forward aligned with the heel of his right foot. His elbows were in, his head was low and his left arm was guarding everything from his belly to his chin. He even had his back heel slightly lifted – it was textbook. Chato had probably gone in too confident, thinking it was going to be easy, but Stretch must have had some training somewhere along the way. I didn't see a knife.

Chato got up, 'You surprised me.'

'I don't see how. You swung first.'

Chato moved slowly, darting every so often to see how Stretch would react. Stretch was moving to and fro, too. 'Dance like a butterfly, like Muhammad Ali,' Billy yelled.

Suddenly Chato threw a hard right hook. It would have floored Stretch, but he anticipated the move and ducked in time. Chato brought down his guard long enough for Stretch to get a one-two combo to his jaw and he went down with a heavy thump.

'Get up, you brown bastard,' Stretch shouted.

Ray let go of Grace. He, Unai and Carlos moved towards Stretch. 'Wait!' I said.

'What's it to you, *guero*?' Ray hissed.

'It won't be fair.'

'That's my brother, man. Blood sticks together.'

'It's between them.' I didn't want the fight to turn into an all-out brawl.

'It's because he's a Paddy, like you, huh, *vato*? You all stick together.'

'Jesus fucking Christ.' I pulled Ray by his collar and grabbed Uncle Leo's mezuzah from under my shirt. 'Do you know what this is, *estúpido*? I'm Jewish, goddamn it, not Irish or English or anything else.' The mob was looking at me now. I let Ray go and straightened his shirt. 'I'm Jewish and my mother was German.'

'No shit, *ese*? A Heb? You don't eat bacon or *jamón*?' Carlos asked.

I shook my head, but then thought better of it, 'Eh, sometimes.'

'You wear those funny little hats and don't believe in Jesus?' Ray asked.

'But you swore,' Unai pointed out. 'You said Jesus.'

'Yeah, well, sometimes it feels like the right thing to say.'

Suddenly Maria shrieked, 'He's got a knife!'

I reeled around. Chato was up again but he was unsteady on his feet. He had both hands on his face like he was trying to put his jaw back in place. Stretch was anything but scared. His face was pale but there was a grin on his lips. In his right hand was a three-inch silver blade, gleaming in the lamplight. Chato looked up and saw the blade too. His face changed and he groped desperately in his pockets. 'Oh, shit,' I muttered. I saw Stretch's knuckles go white as he tightened his grip on the blade.

'Stretch, don't!' I threw myself between them.

Buzz grabbed Stretch from behind and wrestled him to the ground. 'Calm down, boy, calm down,' he muttered. Mr Talbot and Charlie helped hold him down. Charlie pried Stretch's fingers open and took the knife away. At the same time I saw Joe, Tate and Mr Barker get Chato. Maria, Kate and Mrs Barker rushed over to me. I felt like I had been punched in the ribs. I looked down and saw that the knife had torn through my shirt and into my torso.

'Huh. I've been stabbed?'

20

THERE WAS NO BLOOD FOR A FEW SECONDS. Then it started to ooze out, brown in the yellow street lights. I tried to sit up.

'Lie down,' Mrs Barker ordered.

'I'm okay.'

'I didn't ask you, young man. Lie down.'

'Yes, ma'am,' I didn't even realise it, but I was clutching my side.

Kate pried my hand away from the wound and inspected it. 'The skin is sliced clean,' she told Mrs Barker in a level voice, 'I can't see how deep. It will need stitches for sure, but I don't think it's hit anything.'

'I pray you're right.'

'It doesn't hurt much,' I said hopefully.

'Be quiet, foolish boy,' Kate whispered.

'He's not foolish, he's brave,' Maria said, through tears. She was sitting behind me, cradling my head in her lap.

'Of course,' Kate took off her cashmere sweater and laid it over my torso. 'He'll go into shock soon. He needs to keep warm.'

Tate hurried over to me. 'Jack!' he yelled, kneeling down on one knee.

'I don't think it's bad, Hymie,' Kate said. 'I don't think it's bad.'

Tate's eyes were larger than normal. He pulled Kate's sweater aside to look at the wound and then stared at me. I could tell he wasn't so sure. 'Jesus, son, what were you thinking?'

'I'm sorry, Tate.'

'Okay. I'm going to put more pressure on it, *benyokhed*. It's going to hurt but it's going to be alright,' he whispered and put his hand over mine. I wondered how many times he said that in battle to a fellow soldier – and how many times he was just trying to make them feel good before they died.

I heard sirens approaching, louder and louder, until they were deafening. A police car pulled into the lot. 'Thank God,' Mrs Barker exclaimed.

Charlie talked to one of the officers and pointed towards me. He handed over the knife. The other policeman lifted Stretch to his feet. His mouth dropped open. 'I'm plum sorry, little buddy. I didn't mean for no one to get hurt, 'specially you.'

I tried to raise my hand but it felt too heavy. The policeman yanked him away to the patrol car.

'I'm Sargent Hornsby,' the other officer said to me. I had to grin. It was as if Luke had aged twenty years, cut his sun bleached hair and had grown a neatly cropped moustache. 'How are you doing, young man?' I tried to reply but nothing came out. 'Don't try to talk. We radioed for an ambulance and it should be here soon.'

There were more sirens, and then a red-and-white ambulance and another police car pulled into the lot. The officers from the new car pulled Chato away. Grace was crying. Ray yelled at the officers, 'why are you taking my brother? He didn't do nothin! It's because he's Mexican, isn't it, you *pinché, cabrõnes …*'

Mr Talbot stepped in. 'Ray, take it easy. Don't worry. We'll get to the bottom of it.' This seemed to calm him. He nodded and hugged Grace. Then she looked over at me and dragged Ray in my direction.

'*Que tal, vato*? You okay?' Ray asked me.

'*Simón, ese, simón*,' I said drowsily. I smiled at Grace. Her head blocked out one of the car lot lights. It seemed like a halo on a 16th century Spanish painting of a saint.

The ambulance attendants lifted me into the ambulance without saying a word. They hooked me up to a hanging bottle and gave me an injection. Tate hopped in the front and it sped off. I thought I heard Tate say, 'Hang on, Jackie.' I was more tired than I had ever been in my life. *Blue Velvet* by Bobby Vinton played over and over in my head as I wove in and out of consciousness.

My last thought was, *at least I have a car.*

Arrows – sharp as scalpels – shoot into my torso from all directions. Pale, transparent *Hakenkreuz*, in thousands, march rough-shod over millions of ungilted, twisted frames. Bloody drums beat in the temples of my head. Pink-and-grey watermelons crack – explode – seeds and juice everywhere. Purple, oozing dreams slapping me this way and that. Then – at some point, removed from context – blue fog, cool, light, calm covers me and creeps slowly into every crease and orifice. My muscles drowse, my chest rises and falls in silky calm.

I woke in an unfamiliar place. It was bare and half-lit by a reading lamp next to the bed. The room smelled of disinfectant and sterile linen. The insistent percussion became distant and was replaced by whispering and the rumble of rubber trolley wheels rolling on bare linoleum. A portable twelve-inch TV, turned off, sat on a shelf directly in front of me. I turned my head and saw a grey, crumpled mass at my side.

'Tate?' I croaked.

'Hey, man,' he said groggily. 'How you feeling?'

I felt exhausted and there was a dull ache in my side. 'I don't know. Kind of stiff, I guess. Where am I?'

'St Jude Hospital in Fullerton. You're okay now. You were transferred here from San Sebastiano Community when the doctor saw how bad your wound was.' His voice was trembling. 'I'm so sorry. If I had only been a second sooner I could have stopped Stretch.'

'Don't do that. It was a freak thing. No one would have figured that Stretch had a blade, or that he would try to use it – even me,' I grunted. The wound didn't really start to hurt until then. It was like my nerves had been napping and suddenly woke up. My side throbbed. I tried to ignore it. 'It was like when Mutti died. We couldn't have saved her, no matter what.'

'I beat myself up about that for months. I told myself I should have been home. I shouldn't have let her eat so much fatty food, I should have been a doctor, like my *mamele* wanted …' he laughed but there was no humour in it. 'The truth is, we don't control anything. Some things we have to accept and move on.' He broke off into a coughing fit. 'Oh man, maybe Kate's right. I should give up these damn smokes.'

With the mention of Kate, Balboa Island came back, the kiss at Corona del Mar and her rejection. And the party – her and the Wolf Man? 'Is Kate dating Mr Talbot?'

He stubbed out his cigarette in the ashtray beside my bed. 'I don't know. I don't think so. I thought she said he had some Paraguayan artist girlfriend, or something exotic like that. She hasn't mentioned anything since you got stabbed.'

'You've seen her?'

'Sure. She's been here the whole time – calling people to keep them up to date, making me dinner and making sure I change my clothes. I started to hit the bottle hard when you went into surgery. Kate was mad. "What's wrong with you, Hymie, why are you hiding in the bottle? Jack needs you." She was right, of course. I stopped right there, cold turkey. I haven't had a drop since. I tell you, she and Charlie have been solid friends, man. Charlie's given me all the time I need to be here and he insisted on paying for this private room.'

'What do you mean "the whole time"? How long have I been here?'

'It's been almost two weeks. The wound was worse than it looked, and then after your surgery there was an infection. You had a fever. You were delirious. I thought I was going to lose you there, *boytshikl.*'

On top of a bank of drawers sat several bouquets of flowers and a fruit basket wrapped in red cellophane, like the kind they sell at Christmas time. The flowers reminded me of Mutti's funeral and I shuddered.

'Who's the gift basket from?'

'Uncle Leo.' He fetched the card. The cover was probably ten years out of date – purple flowers with thin petals on a pastel-blue background. The words '*Get well soon!*' were printed across the top.

'Those flowers are asters,' Tate said. 'People used to believe they could heal. In France, in the old days, they put them on soldiers' graves to symbolise the wish that things might have had turned out differently.'

'How do you know that?'

He shrugged. 'You drive a cab a few years in the city, man, you find out all kinds of weird crap.'

I opened the card. The message was in shaky fountain-point pen. It read:

Benyokhed,

I'm thanking God every day that you are strong and getting well. What is life for if not for living? You have been given another gift, make the very best of it.

Live and love life.

L'chaim.

Fetter Leo

As I put down the card, I caught a strained and empty look in Tate's eyes. 'What is it?'

He shook his head, 'I didn't want to tell you until you were better.'

'What is it?'

'Uncle Leo passed away. It must have been the day after he wrote your card. I'm sorry.'

'Oh, Tate. I am so sorry for you.'

'It's fine, *benyokhed.* It wasn't a surprise. He knew he was sick the last time we saw him, at your mother's funeral. He told me then. He was ready, resolved, but he was also determined to live to the full until he died. He did. I could see it in his eyes.

I couldn't go to his funeral but I sent flowers and a note.' His voice quivered and his eyes welled up. 'I got a call a couple of days later from my *mamele.*' He pulled out his handkerchief and wiped his face. 'I hadn't heard her voice for ...' he cried aloud and shook his head. I patted his hand. 'I'm going to take you back home to meet her when you get better.'

He took a couple of deep breaths, smiled and looked at his watch, then grabbed his jacket. 'You're still weak and visiting hours are almost over. I'm surprised they haven't kicked me out already. They won't let me stay past the regular time now that you're out of danger.'

'How long do I have to stay in here?'

'The doctor will tell us tomorrow, I think.'

I nodded. He patted my arm, 'Pleasant dreams, my son. *Ikh hob dikh lib.*'

'Good night, Tate. I love you too.'

There was a light knock on the door. Tate opened it.

'Is this Jackson Ryder's room?' It was Mr Rodriguez, hat in hand.

'*Si, señor,*' Tate answered to my surprise. 'I'm his father, Hymie.' They shook hands.

'The nurse said we could see him for a minute, with your permission. It is almost the end of visiting hours.'

'Yes, of course, if Jack is up to it?'

I nodded.

He waved Mr Rodriguez, Grace and Chato into the room. 'See you tomorrow before I go into work, son.'

'Oh, Jackson,' Grace sighed. She was holding a bouquet of flowers. I shuddered again but smiled weakly.

'*Ese*, home boy,' Chato said as he gave me the nod.

'They said that you are better, *mijo*.'

Mijo – my son – Mr Rodriguez called me. I couldn't hold back a bemused grin but then it fell away. I blurted out, 'I'm Jewish.'

'I don't understand.'

'Don't you remember what you said to your brother, just before you gave me the steak at Grace's *quinceñera* party?'

His eyes moved everywhere then he looked up and shifted in his seat.

'What did you say, Papá?' Grace asked.

He shushed her with a gesture. 'I told your uncle José not to be as tight as a Jew,' he whispered. He straightened and gave a dry chuckle. 'It's only a saying, *joven*, it doesn't mean anything.'

'Oh, only a saying, like "dirty, lazy Mexican?"' I shot back.

His eyes flashed. Chato leaned towards me but Grace checked him with a hand on his chest. Mr Rodriguez spun his hat in his hand just like Tate did, and nodded slowly, 'I understand …' He held up a finger. 'You have not said it in a respectful way, but I understand that too. My deepest apologies.'

'Thank you, *señor*. It means a lot coming from you.'

He smiled, a bursting, healthy mouthful and my heart opened to him. 'Altagracia, Chato and Ramón were coming to see you but I wanted to come and thank you personally – deeply – from my wife and from me, for saving the life of my son, Chato …'

'Sir, you don't have to …'

'No, let me finish – he is a good boy: loyal, hardworking, devoted to his mother, but he got in with a bad crowd when he was in school with all that drinking and *mota* and hoochie coochie.'

Grace tittered.

'Pop,' Chato moaned.

'*Cállate*, shut up, before I give you a *cato*.' The old man made a fist the size of a cauliflower. Chato did what he was told. Mr Rodriguez smiled beneficently at me. 'He is trying hard to be a good man. I got him a job – a good job – in Orange County, in construction, but it isn't union work. If he had been stabbed and couldn't have come to work. He would have lost his job.

Do you understand? You saved him, *mijo,* you saved him and I will be forever in your debt.' He took my hand and kissed it. I could see tears forming at the corners of his eyes. '*Dios te bendega*, God bless you.'

'It's okay, *señor*.'

'Hey, *guero*, you took one for me. I won't forget.' Chato touched my arm with his fist. It was as close as a thank you I was likely to get from him. 'C'mon, Pop.' He lifted his father from the seat and took him towards the door.

'Give me a minute,' Grace said before they both disappeared into the hallway. She turned to me, took my hand, and gently wiped it with her own. 'Don't worry about Papá's tears. There is no shame for a real man, a *macho*, to cry. He really means it.'

'So he won't drive me off with a baseball bat if I come to see you?'

She visibly jumped in her seat but then a little smile – like the Mona Lisa's – brushed past her lips. 'If that's what you want,' she looked at me in the eye, 'I'd like that too.'

It was grand news, but my body started to feel like a pair of wet Levi's.

A voice came over the loudspeaker in the corner of the room. 'Visiting hours are over, visitors please make your way …'

Grace leaned over. I felt her warm breath, sensed her soft flesh and I was electrified. I looked at her and all the pain disappeared – it rushed out of me like a busted dam. She tilted her head slightly and leaned towards me, then pulled back again, a gentle dance. All of creation, the stars and galaxies aligned and I leaned towards her as much as I could. The air between us was alive. With each incremental fraction she drew towards me, this intensity compressed further. It was an external combustion engine, nitro-glycerine, it was a fifty megaton bomb about to go off, and, it did – a brush, a kiss – but a real one, full of promise, full of hope – finally right.

Then she was gone.

There was a Salvador Dalí feel to the empty room. My skin tingled, but it soon settled to a nervy exhaustion. I turned off the lamp and tried to get more comfortable. A pain like a heated wire shot up my side. 'Oh, shit.' I winced and tried to adjust the bed. Sitting upright seemed to help.

In the dim light two yellow-brown butt cheeks pressed against the glass.

21

'ÓRALE, VATO.'

'Ray!'

The butt cheeks disappeared and were replaced by Ray, Carlos, Maria and Unai's faces.

'*Ese, guero, qué tal*? What's up, Ghost Ryder?'

'Oh, man.' I clutched my side. 'Don't make me laugh. It hurts.'

Ray stopped giggling and looked genuinely concerned. 'It's cool, *vato*, it's cool. Don't hurt yourself. I'd hate to see you split a gut.' He burst into laughter again and looked to the others for a reaction, but they only rolled their eyes. 'Sorry, *vato*. Thought you might need a laugh after being in the *pinché* hospital for so long.'

'Thanks, man. It's good to see you guys. What are you doing outside?'

'This *cabrón gordo*,' Unai shoved Carlos, 'kept moaning about how hungry he was so we stopped to get him a hamburger at A&W and missed the damn visiting hours.'

'But it takes more than *pinché* visiting hours to keep us down,' Ray boasted.

'Your dad, Chato and Grace were just here, Ray. They didn't tell me what happened to Chato? Why did the police take him away?'

'The cops didn't know who started the fight or nothin'. Since Chato wasn't packing a knife or any weapon they had nothing to hold him on. I thought they would at least beat him up, because he's *Chicano*, but Wolf Man talked to Luke Hornsby's dad and I think he watched out for him.'

'So, Officer Hornsby is Luke's father.'

'*Simón, ese*. How many Hornsby's do you think there are in sleepy ol' San Sab?'

'Your dad didn't press any charges on that skinny, white dude either,' Carlos added. 'He said it was an accident.'

'Oh, wow. He didn't tell me that.'

'Gracie's tried to get them together,' Maria said. I noticed Unai had his arm around her shoulder. 'Chato and Stretch.'

'No luck yet,' Unai said, 'but that ain't stopping her from trying.'

I tried to absorb it all. It was okay, except for my guts being patched. 'Well, *hormigas*, at least I'm not dead,' I said.

'And you got a car,' Carlos added.

'Hey, well take your time getting better, *ese*. While you're away I'm top dog in the art room, man. All the little *mamacitas* are all over me with *besos*, man, you wouldn't believe it.' Ray groaned and kissed his own arm a few times.

Maria pushed him. 'You wish, Ray.'

'Enjoy it while you can, *cabrón*. When I get back I'm going all the way, man. I'm not holding back. I'm goin' to make you work your skinny ass if you want to stay top dog.' My words were bold but I started to feel tired again.

The door opened and light pierced the room. '*Mierda*,' Ray hissed.

'We'll see you tomorrow, *hormiga*,' Unai said. They disappeared.

The bushes rustled against the window. I watched the silhouette of a slim nurse tiptoe towards the window and peer outside. I pretended to close my eyes, leaving two razor-thin openings to peek through. She gently picked up my arm and placed three fingers on the inside of my wrist. Her hand was cool and soft. She smelled of medical soap and fresh clothing. I thought of Grace and my blood stirred. She lowered my arm and lifted my hospital smock to inspect my bandages. Everything must have looked okay, because she replaced the smock, tucked me in and retreated from the room, closing the door behind her.

I was alone in the dark. It was the first time I had been alone since my birthday – at least that I could remember. Sleep wasn't far off. Tate said I'd almost died. I listened to my own breath, wriggled my toes and opened my eyes wide, trying to will light around me. It didn't work, but I was alive, and I was going to live it, really live it. Even if it meant Tate wasn't going to like it. I wasn't going to live for someone else or wait until I was as old as Uncle Leo. I laughed quietly in the dark. I thought of Grace's lips, then of something important I had to ask Tate as soon as possible. I dropped off into a deep sleep.

As I was finishing up breakfast the next morning, Tate came in with a big paper grocery bag. Just the sight of it reminded me of home.

'Tate, I've got to ask you something this minute. Was Mutti a Nazi?'

'No, no. How could you think that? No.'

Even Charlie doesn't know that back in the '30s your mother worked for a guy in the Netherlands name Bachstitz. When another employee of the art dealership she worked for, Walter Hofer, decided to start his own business in Germany he talked your mother into going to work for him. Hofer was ambitious and he did end up being Göring's curator, but he wasn't a Nazi. In fact, your mother helped him to get a visa for Bachstitz so he could get out of German-occupied territory. Kurt Bachstitz was Walter's brother-in-law and a Jew.

She hated what her father was doing, but because he was SS she was well trusted amongst the Nazi elite. She kept good records of what Göring stole and it helped the allies to find the artworks after the war.'

'I knew it.' A great slab disappeared from my shoulders, but then it fell on my stomach, 'But, my grandfather. Why didn't she tell me? Why didn't you?'

Tate looked down at his hat. When he looked up his eyes were far away, 'How do you tell a five year old, a ten year old – even a fifteen year old – that their grandfather was a sadistic, psychopathic monster? We would have told you, together, in time, but … there was no time.'

'Jesus, Tate, what am I supposed to do with that? My grandfather murdered millions of your people – our people.'

Tate shook his head. 'Your mother scarcely knew how to deal with it either. But, she was wise, very wise. You have to accept it and move on. Your mother would have said that. She lived it. With every action, with every decision, she tried to be the most human she could be. Art, marrying me, even having you was the way that she fought the ugliness that produced her.' He shifted in his chair, 'When my brother was killed I blamed myself.' He pulled out a cigarette, lit it with his Zippo and took a deep drag, blowing smoke out of his nostrils. 'I don't talk with my family because I can't face them. I know they blame me. I should have protected my brother and I didn't. Your mother understood the way I felt. She told me … that if I kept on feeling guilty and didn't live my life with all of the love, hope and joy that Nate should have had, then it may as well have been me who was killed on that road to Casablanca. Nate wouldn't have wanted that and it did him a dishonour to go on that way.' He picked up his hat and spun it a few times in his hand. 'I feel pretty stupid. I forgot about that when she died.' He looked at me again and smiled. 'It's time for me to do that for her.'

I returned his smile. 'We both can.'

He bowed his head and nodded. The smile didn't leave his face when his eyes fell on my breakfast tray. 'It looks like your appetite is okay,' he said, taking my empty tray off me.

'I've never been so hungry. What's in the bag?'

'I brought you some things to kill time while you're cooped up in here.'

He reached into the bag and pulled out a book by Ray Bradbury, *The Machineries of Joy*.

'I haven't heard of this.'

'The lady at the bookstore in Whittier said it was just published.'

'Thanks. I like Bradbury.'

'I know.'

That kind of surprised me. He rustled around in the bag again and then handed me a clothbound book with no title.

'What's this?' I asked. I opened it up and leafed through the pages. 'It's blank.'

He pulled out a set of coloured pencils and a long tin pencil case. Inside the tin were a dozen drawing pencils of different grades, a sharpener and an eraser. 'I haven't seen you drawing since well, since before we left New York. I miss seeing your artwork, man. I thought you might want to get a groove on while you were here.'

I studied him, looking for any sign of sarcasm, jesting or testing. 'But Tate, I thought you didn't like art.' I could feel my eyes welling up. 'I thought you hated it.'

'What? No, no, no, my son. Nothing could be further from the truth.' He took my hands. I saw nothing but pain in his eyes. 'This is heavy, man. How could you think that?'

I sniffed and wiped my nose. 'You took down all the paintings and got rid of Mutti's art books. You stopped me tracing in the car, you never talk about art, or go to galleries or anything.'

He sighed heavily and patted my hand. 'Yeah, that's all true, but it's not because I hate art. How could I hate something that gave so much joy to your mother? She taught me so much about beauty and truth. She opened the world for me through art. No, you got it wrong, man, you got it very wrong.' He spread his fingers out over his knees. 'Why didn't you ask me? I was always here. We could have talked about it, couldn't we?'

'Always here? Yeah, but you haven't been talking much to me – not about anything important, at least. If I didn't overhear you talking with Charlie once in a while I wouldn't know how you felt about anything.'

He leaned back in the chair and pulled out a cigarette, tapped it a couple of times on the back of his hand and paused. Then he took the whole packet out of his pocket and dumped it into the ashtray along with the unlit cigarette.

'Shit,' he said. He sat up and laced his fingers together. 'You're right, man. I thought it would be different. I thought running away from New York – coming to California – would make it better too, but it didn't work.' He held up his hands. 'I was still me. I worried about you, plenty, but I slipped into what I always did when your mother was alive, except now she wasn't there to pick up the slack.'

He hadn't talk to me like that since we were in Juárez and he told me about Uncle Nathan. And he was sober now. I felt encouraged, 'Why did you get rid of the paintings and books?'

'The books I packed away to give to you when you're older. Your mother loved those books. God, she loved them. We would lie in bed and she would tell me which ones she would give you on which birthdays. I made a list from what I could remember after she died. There were two she wanted you to have on your sixteenth birthday, so I wrapped them up and put them in the back seat of your car before the party. They're on your bed now back at home, with the rest of your presents.'

'Really? From Mutti?' A tear rolled down my cheek. I sniffed and wiped it away. Tate pulled out his handkerchief from his coat pocket and handed it to me. I blew my nose and handed the handkerchief back to him.

'Naw, you keep it. I got another one in my pocket.'

'Why did you take down the paintings?'

Tate looked out the window and his eyes glazed over. 'You know, when your mother and I met we didn't have two *Reichspfennigs* to rub together. I mean, we were flat broke. But no matter how bleak things got, somehow your mother always found a way to stash some cash away – not much, but something. She was a great manager. We started buying little pieces of art. It wasn't much at first, just drawings by artists who were starting out, or prints by better-known artists. It was a long time before we bought our first real painting. Every one we bought, we chose together. We went to galleries and openings, we talked to artists, dealers and curators, we read reviews, we discussed, we argued and sometimes we disagreed.' He hesitated. 'After we argued, we usually ended up making love and having a laugh. Then we would agree on what to do.' He looked at me. I smiled, but I really didn't need to hear that. 'The point is, every time I looked at those paintings, I wasn't only looking at great art, man. I was looking at my life with your mother. Everything we had together – all of the love and struggle, the agonies and the joy. After she died, it was so raw, so constantly there, and I couldn't turn it off. I couldn't make it not mean anything. It was right there on the wall in front of me, man. It never let up. I couldn't bear it. So I packed them away so that I could forget – just to get through.' He pulled out his fresh handkerchief, wiped his eyes and blew his nose. 'Those paintings are the most precious things I own, those, and the drawings I have from you.'

'You kept my drawings?'

'I have every single one you ever gave me. I dated them and stored them all in a portfolio with the books. But you know what?' He sat up straight and stretched his back. 'The portfolio isn't full and I need some more. I need some new ones, man.'

I smiled. He stood up, came over to me and put his forehead on mine.

The door opened unceremoniously and a bald-headed man in a lab coat swept in. He picked up my chart and flashed a professional smile.

'Good morning, Hymie. You're here early.'

'Good morning, Dr D'Angelo. Jackson is finally awake.'

The doctor looked at me, back at the chart and at me again.

'So he is. How are you feeling?'

'A bit tired, sir, but okay.'

He nodded, 'Well, let's take a look, shall we?' He took my pulse and temperature and listened to my heart and lungs. 'So far, so good. But I will need to take a look at your injury, Jack.'

Without waiting for an answer, he lifted my smock and peeled the tape away. It was the first time I had seen the wound since the night it happened, and I was sobered. It was about eight inches long and inflamed. I couldn't count the stitches, there were so many. It looked like Dr Frankenstein had been on the job that night.

'The swelling has gone down and the redness is subsiding,' Dr D'Angelo said. 'You are a very lucky young man.'

'When can I go home?'

'If it looks better tomorrow you can go the next day. The stitches will have to be removed in ten days, but your doctor can do that in his office.'

'Thanks for everything, Doc,' Tate said. 'And I meant what I said about the best deal on a new Chevy – whenever you want.'

The doctor laughed, 'I have a few more miles left on the old Cadillac but I'll keep it in mind, Hymie.'

He saluted me and disappeared as quickly as he'd come in.

'I've got to go too, buddy,' Tate said. 'By the way, Larry Talbot and I went to see your vice-principal, Mr Cannon. Larry said you needed special tutoring to catch up. Mr Cannon was right behind it – had great things to say about your artwork – and offered to arrange for Mr. Talbot to have a free period every week that he can dedicate just to you until you're on track.

'I can't believe it. That's great.'

'Yeah.' He chuckled and shook his head.

'What is it?'

'Oh, it struck me that your wound is in the same place where I got shot during the war. Our scars are going to look very similar.'

'Whaddya know?' I touched my side. 'Hey, thanks for the sketchbook and pencils. You don't know what this means to me.'

'I'm getting the idea. Your mother would be very proud and happy. So am I.' He patted my foot through the bedcovers, 'Oh, and Kate sends her love. She and I had a long talk last night after she helped me put up some paintings. And you know what? She's not dating Larry, that's for sure.' He winked at me.

Out the window was the corner of Harbour Boulevard and Bastanchury Road. There wasn't much around but scrubby chaparral flats, but I could see the San Sebastiano Hills in the distance.

That evening I watched the sun go down, red and quiet in an amber haze. I looked over at the framed print of Pollard Willows at Sunset askew on the wall. Van Gogh painted it when he was exhausted and lonely. The twisted blue trees reach desperately for the last rays of light. I wondered what ol' Vincent would have made of a California sunset. One thing's for sure, he would have made it his own. He wasn't getting this one, though. This one was mine.

I opened the sketchbook and ran my hand over its pristine surface. It was good-quality paper and had a bit of a tooth to it – classy stuff. For a fraction of a second I hesitated. The paper was perfect. Anything I did would destroy that perfection. With art, the risk of failure isn't just high. It's damn near guaranteed. But that wasn't going to stop me. Maybe I was a *luftmensch*, like my dad.

I pulled out an HB pencil and then changed it for a 9B, and without another thought, I drew a single, delicate line.

ACKNOWLEDGEMENTS

Writing is a solitary pursuit but, indeed, it takes a village to make a book.

I would like to thank:

India Victoria López – muse, first reader, editor, copy writer and cheerleader.

Adrienne Jansen, Mary-Jane Duffy and Jane Parkin for their thorough and thoughtful editing.

Readers John McIntyre, Renee, and Norman Bilbourgh; also Thomas Brian Rice, David Groves, Logan Smith, Kirstie Cleary, Alison Linney, Hannah Schenker, Tony Burton, Adele Chapman, Jan Jordan, Penny Geddis, Clare Arnot, Alison Bell, Evan Cody, Trish Harris and Lucy McCahon.

Kaye Jujnovich and the Faculty of Arts, Whitireia Community Polytechnic for research support

The Whitireia Creative Writing Programme – with particular gratitude to Mandy Hager and Philip Mann.

Rachel Lawson and my team at Whitireia Publishing:

Jd Nodder, Emma Wolff, Amanda Booth, Pippa Maessen, Courtney Mann, Francesca Dutt-Maharaj, Natalie Lyon, Emma Adams and Emma Bryson.

The team at Esculator Press.

A special thanks to Ms Judy Chicago for letting me put words in her mouth.

Jan López and Ben López for unending support, time and love.

In 1986 Mexican-American artist, Rudy, and his Kiwi wife, Janice, walked 5000 km across the USA in support of global nuclear disarmament. Afterward, with a pregnant wife and $250, he immigrated to New Zealand and worked in art education for the next two decades.

He wrote his first novel, *The Song of Laughing Bird* (National Pacific Press), for daughter, India, in 2005. His project for his Graduate Diploma in Creative Writing at Whitireia in 2013 was the first draft of *Open Your Eyes, Jackson Ryder*. He was also given the Honour Award in the New Zealand Writing School Short Story Competition that year. In 2014 he started writing full-time.

He lives on the banks of the Pauatahanui Inlet, with Jan, India, his son Ben, mother-in-law, Patricia, three cats and several fish.

Other Escalator Press titles

A Line of Sight is a compelling whodunnit woven through a story of community, family and an extraordinary eight-year-old boy.

'Jansen's style is seamless without being slick; it's detailed but uncluttered. She knows when to pare back, what to include.' – *New Zealand Listener*

A grand piano falls off a crane and by bad luck ends up the responsibility of Stefan – piano restorer and illegal immigrant. His neighbours, a bunch of migrants and misfits themselves, weigh in to help him rebuild it.

'Jansen paints on a small canvas with skill and insight into the tough task of rebuilding a life with few resources past your own fortitude.'
– Catherine Robertson, *New Zealand Listener*